The Complete Psychotechnic League

Volume 2

T0097840

The Complete Psychotechnic League

Volume 2

POUL ANDERSON

Interstitial Material by Sandra Miesel

BAEN

The Complete Psychotechnic League: Volume 2

Forward copyright © 1982 by Sandra Miesel. Reprinted by permission of the author.

"Quixote and the Windmill" originally appeared in *Astounding*, 1950. Reprinted by permission of the Poul Anderson estate.

"Holmgang" originally appeared as "Out of the Iron Womb" in *Planet Stories*, 1957. Reprinted by permission of the Poul Anderson estate.

"Cold Victory" originally appeared in *Venture Science Fiction*, 1957. Reprinted by permission of the Poul Anderson estate.

"What Shall It Profit" originally appeared in *Galaxy*, 1955. Reprinted by permission of the Poul Anderson estate.

"The Troublemakers" originally appeared in *Cosmos Science Fiction and Fantasy*, September 1953. Reprinted by permission of the Poul Anderson estate.

"The Snows of Ganymede" originally appeared in *Startling Stories*, Winter 1955. Reprinted by permission of the Poul Anderson estate.

"Brake" originally appeared in *Astounding*, 1957. Reprinted by permission of the Poul Anderson estate.

"Gypsy" originally appeared in *Astounding*, 1950. Reprinted by permission of the Poul Anderson estate.

"Star Ship" originally appeared in *Planet Stories*, 1950. Reprinted by permission of the Poul Anderson estate.

Baen Publishing Enterprises
P.O. Box 1403
Riverdale, NY 10471
www.baen.com

ISBN: 978-1-4814-8306-3

Cover art by Kurt Miller

First Baen printing, February 2018

Distributed by Simon & Schuster
1230 Avenue of the Americas
New York, NY 10020

Printed in the United States of America

10 9 8 7 6 5 4 3 2 1

Contents

The Complete Psychotechnic League

Volume 2

Forward

by Sandra Miesel

The critical decades following World War III were years of chaos and stubborn courage. Looking back across the millennia at the colossal challenge our twentieth-century ancestors faced, we must salute the sacrifices they made to restore their shattered world. While mourning the follies of violent ages gone by, we humans can take pride in this: after each disaster, our species keeps on striving, like a trampled plant once more struggling towards the sun.

Of course in this case as in all cases timing as well as determination influenced the outcome of events. If World War III had erupted much later than 1958, perhaps no amount of heroism could have saved civilization from extinction. As it was, the East-West exchange of "nuclear Christmas presents" left key areas of both sides in radioactive ashes. Local wars followed global war; plagues succeeded famine. Civilization spun down toward darkness.

The first spark of hope kindled in Europe when Valti's theories of sociosymbolic logic proved themselves in practice. We who take psychodynamics as much for granted as hyperlight physics may find it difficult to appreciate what those first crude equations meant. No longer would we stumble through each day as it came; the future could be adjusted to fit the common good. To insure this happy outcome, the Psychotechnic Institute was founded. It became the self-appointed torchbearer for our race.

The United Nations, revived by the First Conference of Rio in 1965, was an effective instrument for putting the Institute's discoveries into action. This intimate and largely fruitful collaboration continued for more than a century. Together the Institute and the world organization presided over the rehabilitation of Earth.

Their first task was to preserve the hard-won peace. Our initial volume, The Psychotechnic League, recounts four significant episodes in the process. Guided by the new social science, men with "dirty hands and clean weapons" destroyed potential dictators before irreparable harm was done. Sacrificing the few today on behalf of the many tomorrow was the ethic that shaped an era.

With the return of peace came plenty. Once people could safely grow food and produce goods again, output surpassed all expectation. Automated equipment compensated for population loss. Pent up demand following decades of want sent the postwar economy soaring. The need for alternative energy sources to replace those ruined by the war was met by solar power and synthetic fuels with superdielectrics for storage. Once power-beaming satellites went into orbit, Earth's energy worries seemed over.

Earth grew green again. There was a keen, well-nigh universal desire to preserve whatever beauty the war had spared and restore what it had ravished. Acute ecological awareness would soon inspire foundation of the Pancosmic religion, a faith that continues to attract many adherents, human and nonhuman alike.

Zeal for reclamation plus the practical experience gained from building undersea settlements prepared Earthlings to colonize the Solar System. Soon domed cities rose on Luna, the asteroids, and even distant Ganymede. Bold terraforming schemes made Venus and Mars habitable after nearly a century of heartbreaking toil. The independent Order of Planetary Engineers (originally the UN's Planetary Engineering Corps) distinguished itself in all these projects but the "enterprise beyond the sky" was truly a species-wide concern. Mere survival did not suffice: Mankind was out to leave its mark on the universe.

But the Psychotechnic Institute foresaw that this burst of energy would fade. Remolding worlds was simpler than remodeling humanity. While continuing to chart and influence the behavior of whole societies, the Institute also experimented with individuals. For a time, an elaborate holistic conditioning system known as Tighe Synthesis seemed an excellent way to maximize human potential. Although a few receptive subjects benefited from the training, this promising discovery was never widely applied. Not only was it impractical to condition the entire population adequately, the process put too much power in the hands of the conditioners.

Yet despite its shortcomings, the science of psychodynamics was our margin of survival. Institute-trained personnel were indispensable in that first critical century following World War II. Foremost among these heroes were the UN-Men cloned from a maquis named Stefan Rostomily. (Humble, gifted, and steadfast, the Rostomily Brotherhood was destined to outlast the Institute that had created it.) United Nations agents were everywhere in those days but perhaps their most admirable feat—one which redounded to the Institute's credit—was the liberation of Venus from a bleak Stalinist tyranny in 2065. With the collective state gone, the colonists speedily developed a fiercely parochial clan-based society whose romantic folkways were celebrated in popular entertainment for generations afterwards. Political historians still analyze Venus as an experiment in local autonomy.

By the opening of the twenty-second century, the Psychotechnic Institute's power and prestige reached their zenith. The bright future it had planned for humanity seemed inevitable. High technology was triumphant. The blessings of the Second Industrial Revolution were available to all. No one went hungry or homeless anymore. Work had become a privilege instead of an obligation. From sophisticated Earthlings to roughneck colonial, mankind shared a common, semantically rigorous language called Basic. The space navy of the newly formed Solar Union stood guard from Venus to the Belt. The New Enlightenment bathed Sol's children in the cool radiance of reason.

But there were shadows . . .

Quixote and the Windmill

THE FIRST ROBOT in the world came walking over green hills with sunlight aflash off his polished metal hide. He walked with a rippling grace that was almost feline, and his tread fell noiselessly—but you could feel the ground vibrate ever so faintly under the impact of that terrific mass, and the air held a subliminal quiver from the great engine that pulsed within him.

Him. You could not think of the robot as neuter. He had the brutal maleness of a naval rifle or a blast furnace. All the smooth silent elegance of perfect design and construction did not hide the weight and strength of a two and a half-meter height. His eyes glowed, as if with inner fires of smoldering atoms; they could see in any frequency range he selected, he could turn an X-ray beam on you and look you through and through with those terrible eyes. They had built him humanoid, but had had the good taste not to give him a face; there were the eyes, with their sockets for extra lenses when he needed microscopic or telescopic vision, and there were a few other small sensory and vocal orifices, but otherwise his head was a mask of shining metal. Humanoid, but not human—man's creation, but more than man—the first independent, volitional, nonspecialized machine—but they had dreamed of him, long ago, he had once been the jinni in the bottle or the Golem, Bacon's brazen head of Frankenstein's monster, the man-transcending creature who could serve or destroy with equal contemptuous ease.

He walked under a bright summer sky, over sunlit fields and

7

through little groves that danced and whispered in the wind. The houses of men were scattered here and there, the houses which practically took care of themselves; over beyond the horizon was one of the giant, almost automatic food factories; a few self-piloting carplanes went quietly overhead. Humans were in sight, sun-browned men and their women and children going about their various errands with loose bright garments floating in the breeze. A few seemed to be at work, there was a colorist experimenting with a new chromatic harmony, a composer sitting on his verandah striking notes out of an omniplayer, a group of engineers in a transparent-walled laboratory testing some mechanisms. But with the standard work period what it was these days, most were engaged in recreation. A picnic, a dance under trees, a concert, a pair of lovers, a group of children in one of the immemorially ancient games of their age-group, an old man happily enhammocked with a book and a bottle of beer—the human race was taking it easy.

They saw the robot go by, and often a silence fell as his tremendous shadow slipped past. His electronic detectors sensed the eddying pulses that meant nervousness, a faint unease—oh, they trusted the cybernetics men, they didn't look for a devouring monster, but they wondered. They felt man's old unsureness of the alien and unknown, deep in their minds they wondered what the robot was about and what his new and invincible race might mean to Earth's dwellers—then, perhaps, as his gleaming height receded over the hills, they laughed and forgot him.

The robot went on.

There were not many customers in the Casanova at this hour. After sunset the tavern would fill up and the autodispensers would be kept busy, for it had a good live-talent show and television was becoming unfashionable. But at the moment only those who enjoyed a mid-afternoon glass, together with some serious drinkers were present.

The building stood alone on a high wooded ridge, surrounded by its gardens and a good-sized parking lot. Its colonnaded exterior was long and low and gracious; inside it was cool and dim and fairly quiet; and the general air of decorum, due entirely to lack of patronage, would probably last till evening. The manager had gone off on his own business and the girls didn't find it worthwhile to be around till later, so the Casanova was wholly in the charge of its machines.

Two men were giving their autodispenser a good workout. It could hardly deliver one drink before a coin was given it for another. The smaller man was drinking whiskey and soda, the larger one stuck to the most potent available ale, and both were already thoroughly soused.

They sat in a corner booth from which they could look out the open door, but their attention was directed to the drinks. It was one of those curious barroom acquaintances which spring up between utterly diverse types. They would hardly remember each other the next day. But currently they were exchanging their troubles.

The little dark-haired fellow, Roger Brady, finished his drink and dialed for another. "Beatcha!" he said triumphantly.

"Gimme time," said the big redhead, Pete Borklin. "This stuff goes down slower."

Brady got out a cigarette. His fingers shook as he brought it to his mouth and puffed it into lighting. "Why can't that drink come right away?" he mumbled. "I resent a ten-second delay. Ten dry eternities! I demand instantaneously mixed drinks, delivered faster than light."

The glass arrived, and he raised it to his lips. "I am afraid," he said, with the careful precision of a very drunk man, "that I am going on a weeping jag. I would much prefer a fighting jag. But unfortunately there is nobody to fight."

"I'll fight you," offered Borklin. His huge fists closed.

"Nah—why? Wouldn't be a fight, anyway. You'd just mop me up. And why should we fight? We're both in the same boat."

"Yeah," Borklin looked at his fists. "Not much use, anyway," he said. "Somebody'd do a lot better job o' killing with an autogun than I could with—these." He unclenched them, slowly, as if with an effort, and took another drag at his glass.

"What we want to do," said Brady, "is to fight a world. We want to blow up all Earth and scatter the pieces from here to Pluto. Only it wouldn't do any good, Pete. Some machine'd come along and put it back together again."

"I just wanna get drunk," said Borklin. "My wife left me. D'I tell you that? My wife left me."

"Yeah, you told me."

Borklin shook his heavy head, puzzled. "She said I was a drunk. I went to a doctor like she said, but it didn't help none. He said . . . I forget what he said. But I had to keep on drinking anyway. Wasn't anything else to do."

"I know. Psychiatry helps people solve problems. It's not being able to solve a problem that drives a man insane. But when the problem is inherently insoluble—what then? One can only drink, and try to forget."

"My wife wanted me to amount to something," said Borklin. "She wanted me to get a job. But what could I do? I tried. Honest, I tried. I tried for . . . well, I've been trying all my life, really. There just wasn't any work around. Not any I could do."

"Fortunately, the basic citizen's allowance is enough to get drunk on," said Brady. "Only the drinks don't arrive fast enough. I demand an instantaneous autodispenser."

Borklin dialed for another ale. He looked at his hands in a bewildered way. "I've always been strong," he said. "I know I'm not bright, but I'm strong, and I'm good at working with machines and all. But nobody would hire me." He spread his thick workman's fingers. "I was handy at home. We had a little place in Alaska, my dad didn't hold with too many gadgets, so I was handy around there. But he's dead now, the place is sold, what good are my hands?"

"The worker's paradise." Brady's thin lips twisted. "Since the end of the Transition, Earth has been Utopia. Machines do all the routine work, *all* of it, they produce so much that the basic necessities of life are free."

"The hell. They want money for everything."

"Not much. And you get your citizen's allowance, which is just a convenient way of making your needs free. When you want more money, for the luxuries, you work, as an engineer or scientist or musician or painter or tavern keeper or spaceman or . . . anything there's a demand for. You don't work too hard. Paradise!" Brady's shaking fingers spilled cigarette ash on the table. A little tube dipped down from the wall and sucked it up.

"I can't find work. They don't want me. Nowhere."

"Of course not. What earthly good is manual labor these days? Machines do it all. Oh, there are technicians to be sure, quite a lot of them—but they're all highly skilled men, years of training. The man who has nothing to offer but his strength and a little rule-of-thumb ingenuity doesn't get work. There *is* no place for him!" Brady took another swallow from his glass. "Human genius has eliminated the need for the workman. Now it only remains to eliminate the workman himself."

Borklin's fists closed again, dangerously. "Whattayuh mean?" he asked harshly. "Whattayuh mean, anyway?"

"Nothing personal. But you know it yourself. Your type no longer fits into human society. So the geneticists are gradually working it out of the race. The population is kept static, relatively small, and is slowly evolving toward a type which can adapt to the present en . . . environment. And that's not your type, Pete."

The big man's anger collapsed into futility. He stared emptily at his glass. "What to do?" he whispered. "What can I do?"

"Not a thing, Pete. Just drink, and try to forget your wife. Just drink."

"Mebbe they'll get out to the stars."

"Not in our lifetimes. And even then, they'll want to take their machines along. We still won't be any more useful. Drink up, old fellow. Be glad! You're living in Utopia!" There was silence then, for a while. The day was bright outside. Brady was grateful for the obscurity of the tavern.

Borklin said at last: "What I can't figure is you. You look smart. You can fit in . . . can't you?"

Brady grinned humorlessly. "No, Pete. I had a job, yes. I was a mediocre servo-technician. The other day I couldn't take any more. I told the boss what to do with his servos, and I've been drinking ever since. I don't think I ever want to stop."

"But how come?"

"Dreary, routine—I hated it. I'd rather stay tight. I had psychiatric help too, of course, and it didn't do me any good. The same insoluble problem as yours, really."

"I don't get it."

"I'm a bright boy, Pete. Why hide it? My I.Q. puts me in the genius class. But—not quite bright enough." Brady fumbled for another coin. He could only find a bill, but the machine gave him change. "I want inshantaneous auto . . . or did I say that before? Never mind. It doesn't matter." He buried his face in his hands.

"How do you mean, not quite bright enough?" Borklin was insistent. He had a vague notion that a new slant on his own problem might conceivably help him see a solution. "That's what they told me, only politer. But you—"

"I'm too bright to be an ordinary technician. Not for long. And I have none of the artistic or literary talent which counts so highly nowadays. What I wanted was to be a mathematician. All my life I wanted to be a mathematician. And I worked at it. I studied. I learned all any human head could hold, and I know where to look up the rest." Brady grinned wearily. "So what's the upshot? The mathematical machines have taken over. Not only all routine computation—that's old—but even independent research. At a higher level than the human brain can operate.

"They still have humans working at it. Sure. They have men who outline the problems, control and check the machines, follow through all the steps—men who are the . . . the soul of the science, even today.

"*But*—only the top-flight geniuses. The really brilliant original minds, with flashes of sheer inspiration. *They* are still needed. But the machines do all the rest."

Brady shrugged. "I'm not a first-rank genius, Pete. I can't do anything that an electronic brain can't do quicker and better. So I didn't get my job, either."

They sat quiet again. Then Borklin said, slowly: "At least you can get some fun. I don't like all these concerts and pictures and all that fancy stuff. I don't have more than drinking and women and maybe some stereofilm."

"I suppose you're right," said Brady indifferently. "But I'm not cut out to be a hedonist. Neither are you. We both *want* to work. We want to feel we have some importance and value—we want to amount to something. Our friends . . . your wife . . . I had a girl once, Pete . . . we're expected to amount to something."

"Only there's nothing for us to do—"

A hard and dazzling sun-flash caught his eye. He looked out through the door, and jerked with a violence that upset his drink.

"Great universe!" he breathed. "Pete . . . Pete . . . look, it's the robot! *It's the robot!*"

"Huh?" Borklin twisted around, trying to focus his eyes out the door. "Whazzat?"

"The robot—you've heard of it, man." Brady's soddenness was gone in a sudden shivering intensity. His voice was like metal. "They built him three years ago at Cybernetics Lab. Manlike, with a volitional, non-specialized brain—manlike, but more than man!"

"Yeah . . . yeah, I heard." Borklin looked out and saw the great shining form striding across the gardens, bound on some unknown journey that took him past the tavern. "They were testing him. But he's been running around loose for a year or so now— Wonder where he's going?"

"I don't know." As if hypnotized, Brady looked after the mighty thing. "I don't know—" His voice trailed off, then suddenly he stood up and then lashed out: "But we'll find out! Come on, Pete!"

"Where . . . huh . . . why—" Borklin rose slowly, fumbling through his own bewilderment. "What do you mean?"

"Don't you see, don't you see? It's *the robot*—the man after man— all that man is, and how much more we don't even imagine. Pete, the machines have been replacing men, here, there, everywhere. This is the machine that will replace *man!*"

Borklin said nothing, but trailed out after Brady. The smaller man kept on talking, rapidly, bitterly: "Sure—why not? Man is simply flesh and blood. Humans are only human. They're not efficient enough for our shiny new world. Why not scrap the whole human race? How long till we have nothing but men of metal in a meaningless metal ant-heap?

"Come on, Pete. Man is going down into darkness. But we can go down fighting!"

Something of it penetrated Borklin's mind. He saw the towering machine ahead of him, and suddenly it was as if it embodied all which had broken him. The ultimate machine, the final arrogance of efficiency, remote and godlike and indifferent as it smashed him— suddenly he hated it with a violence that seemed to split his skull apart. He lumbered clumsily beside Brady and they caught up with the robot together.

"Turn around!" called Brady. "Turn around and fight!"

The robot paused. Brady picked up a stone and threw it. The rock bounced off the armor with a dull clang.

The robot faced about. Borklin ran at him, cursing. His heavy shoes kicked at the robot's ankle joints, his fists battered at the front. They left no trace.

"Stop that," said the robot. His voice had little tonal variation, but there was the resonance of a great bell in it. "Stop that. You will injure yourself."

Borklin retreated, gasping with the pain of bruised flesh and smothering impotence. Brady reeled about to stand before the robot. The alcohol was singing and buzzing in his head, but his voice came oddly clear.

"We can't hurt you," he said. "We're Don Quixote, tilting at windmills. But you wouldn't know about that. You wouldn't know about any of man's old dreams."

"I am unable to account for your present actions," said the robot. His eyes blazed with their deep fires, searching the men. Unconsciously, they shrank away a little.

"You are unhappy," decided the robot. "You have been drinking to escape your own unhappiness, and in your present intoxication you identify me with the causes of your misery."

"Why not?" flared Brady. "Aren't you? The machines are taking over all Earth with their smug efficiency, making man a parasite—and now you come, the ultimate machine, you're the one who's going to replace man himself."

"I have no belligerent intentions," said the robot. "You should know I was conditioned against any such tendencies, even while my brain was in process of construction." Something like a chuckle vibrated in the deep metal voice. "What reason do I have to fight anyone?"

"None," said Brady thinly. "None at all. You'll just take over, as more and more of you are made, as your emotionless power begins to—"

"Begins to what?" asked the robot. "And how do you know I am emotionless? Any psychologist will tell you that emotion, though not necessarily of the human type, is a basic of thought. What logical reason does a being have to think, to work, even to exist? It cannot rationalize its so doing, it simply does, because of its endocrine system, its power plant, whatever runs it . . . its emotions! And any mentality capable of self-consciousness will feel as wide a range of emotion as you—it will be as happy or as interested—or as miserable —as you!"

It was weird, even in a world used to machines that were all but alive, thus to stand and argue with a living mass of metal and plastic, vacuum and energy. The strangeness of it struck Brady, he realized just how drunk he was. But still he had to snarl his hatred and despair out, mouth any phrases at all just so they relieved some of the bursting tension within him.

"I don't care how you feel or don't feel," he said, stuttering a little now. "It's that you're the future, the meaningless future when all men are as useless as I am now, and I hate you for it and the worst of it is I can't kill you."

The robot stood like a burnished statue of some old and non-anthropomorphic god, motionless, but his voice shivered the quiet air: "Your case is fairly common. You have been relegated to obscurity by advanced technology. But do not identify yourself with all mankind. There will always be men who think and dream and sing and carry on all the race has ever loved. The future belongs to them, not to you—or to me.

"I am surprised that a man of your apparent intelligence does not realize my position. But—what earthly good is a robot? By the time science had advanced to the point where I could be built, there was no longer any reason for it. Think—you have a specialized machine to perform or help man perform every conceivable task. What possible use is there for a nonspecialized machine to do them all? Man himself fulfills that function, and the machines are no more than his tools. Does a housewife want a robot servant when she need only control the dozen machines which already do all the work? Why should a scientist want a robot that could, say, go into dangerous radioactive rooms when he has already installed automatic and remote-controlled apparatus which does everything there? And surely the artists and thinkers and policy-makers don't need robots, they are performing specifically human tasks, it will always be *man* who sets man's goals and dreams his dreams. The all-purpose machine is and forever will be—man himself.

"Man, I was made for purely scientific study. After a couple of years they had learned all there was to learn about me—and I had no other purpose! They let me become a harmless, aimless, meaningless wanderer, just so I could be doing something—and my life is estimated at five hundred years!

"I have no purpose. I have no real reason for existence. I have no companion, no place in human society, no use for my strength and my brain. Man, man, do you think *I* am happy?"

The robot turned to go. Brady was sitting on the grass, holding his head to keep it from whirling off into space, so he didn't see the giant metal god depart. But he caught the last words flung back, and somehow there was such a choking bitterness in the toneless brazen voice that he could never afterward forget them.

"Man, you are the lucky one. *You* can get drunk!"

Perhaps the self-aware robot really was as much a victim as the displaced workers, but humans wasted no pity on its kind. Outbreaks of anti-robot rioting signaled growing public disenchantment with the New Enlightenment's automated Eden. Mankind does not live by bread—or citizen's credit—alone. Abundance may be harder to endure than scarcity.

Neither colonization of the Solar system nor the launching of the first "slow boat to Centauri" starship in 2126 relieved these pressures because they affected too few people.

The Humanist Manifesto shone like a beacon through the prevailing gloom. It promised personal fulfillment by restoring the simplicities of an imaginary past. "What if there had been no Third World War?" was a popular premise for fiction at this time. But the Humanists' anti-tech slogans inevitably spurred dreams of revolution.

Holmgang

THE MOST DANGEROUS is not the outlawed murderer, who only slays men, but the rebellious philosopher; for he destroys worlds.

Darkness and the chill glitter of stars. Bo Jonsson crouched on a whirling speck of stone and waited for the man who was coming to kill him.

There was no horizon. The flying mountain on which he stood was too small. At his back rose a cliff of jagged rock, losing its own blackness in the loom of shadows; its teeth ate raggedly across the Milky Way. Before him, a tumbled igneous wilderness slanted crazily off, with one long thin crag sticking into the sky like a grotesque bowsprit.

There was no sound except the thudding of his own heart, the harsh rasp of his own breath, locked inside the stinking metal skin of his suit. Otherwise . . . no air, no heat, no water or life or work of man, only a granite nakedness spinning through space out beyond Mars.

Stooping, awkward in the clumsy armor, he put the transparent plastic of his helmet to the ground. Its cold bit at him even through the insulating material. He might be able to hear the footsteps of his murderer conducted through the ground.

Stillness answered him. He gulped a heavy lungful of tainted air and rose. The other might be miles away yet, or perhaps very close,

19

catfooting too softly to set up vibrations. A man could do that when gravity was feeble enough.

The stars blazed with a cruel wintry brilliance, over him, around him, light-years to fall through emptiness before he reached one. He had been alone among them before; he had almost thought them friends. Sometimes, on a long watch, a man found himself talking to Vega or Spica or dear old Beetle Juice, murmuring what was in him as if the remote sun could understand. But they didn't care, he saw that now. To them, he did not exist, and they would shine carelessly long after he was gone into night.

He had never felt so alone as now, when another man was on the asteroid with him, hunting him down.

Bo Jonsson looked at the wrench in his hand. It was long and massive, it would have been heavy on Earth, but it was hardly enough to unscrew the stars and reset the machinery of a universe gone awry. He smiled stiffly at the thought. He wanted to laugh too, but checked himself for fear he wouldn't be able to stop.

Let's face it, he told himself. *You're scared. You're scared sweatless.* He wondered if he had spoken it aloud.

There was plenty of room on the asteroid. At least two hundred square miles, probably more if you allowed for the rough surface. He could skulk around, hide . . . and suffocate when his tanked air gave out. He had to be a hunter, too, and track down the other man, before he died. And if he found his enemy, he would probably die anyway.

He looked about him. Nothing. No sound, no movement, nothing but the streaming of the constellations as the asteroid spun. Nothing had ever moved here, since the beginning of time when moltenness congealed into death. Not till men came and hunted each other.

Slowly he forced himself to move. The thrust of his foot sent him up, looping over the cliff to drift down like a dead leaf in Earth's October. Suit, equipment, and his own body, all together, weighed only a couple of pounds here. It was ghostly, this soundless progress over fields which had never known life. It was like being dead already.

Bo Jonsson's tongue was dry and thick in his mouth. He wanted to find his enemy and give up, buy existence at whatever price it would command. But he couldn't do that. Even if the other man let him do it, which was doubtful, he couldn't. Johnny Malone was dead.

Maybe that was what had started it all—the death of Johnny
Malone.

There are numerous reasons for basing on the Trojan asteroids, but
the main one can be given in a single word: stability. They stay put in
Jupiter's orbit, about sixty degrees ahead and behind, with only
minor oscillations; spaceships need not waste fuel coming up to a
body which has been perturbed a goodly distance from where it was
supposed to be. The trailing group is the jumping-off place for trans-
Jovian planets, the leading group for the inner worlds—that way,
their own revolution about the sun gives the departing ship a welcome
boost, while minimizing the effects of Jupiter's drag.

Moreover, being dense clusters, they have attracted swarms of
miners, so that Achilles among the leaders and Patroclus in the trailers
have a permanent boomtown atmosphere. Even though a spaceship
and equipment represent a large investment, this is one of the last
strongholds of genuinely private enterprise; the prospector, the mine
owner, the rockhound dreaming of the day when his stake is big
enough for him to start out on his own—a race of individualists, rough
and noisy and jealous, but living under iron rules of hospitality and
rescue.

The Last Chance on Achilles has another name, which simply sticks
an "r" in the official one; even for that planetoid, it is a rowdy bar
where Guardsmen come in trios. But Johnny Malone liked it, and
talked Bo Jonsson into going there for a final spree before checkoff
and departure. "Nothing to compare," he insisted. "Every place else is
getting too fantangling civilized, except Venus, and I don't enjoy
Venus."

Johnny was from Luna City himself: a small, dark man with the
quick nervous movements and clipped accent of that roaring
commercial metropolis. He affected the latest styles, brilliant colors in
the flowing tunic and slacks, a beret cocked on his sleek head. But
somehow he didn't grate on Bo, they had been partners for several
years now.

They pushed through a milling crowd at the bar, rockhounds who
watched one of Archilles' three live ecdysiasts with hungry eyes, and
by some miracle found an empty booth. Bo squeezed his bulk into
one side of the cubicle while Johnny, squinting through a reeking

smoke-haze, dialed drinks. Bo was larger and heavier than most spacemen—he'd never have gotten his certificate before the ion drive came in—and was usually content to let others talk while he listened. A placid blond giant, with amiable blue eyes in a battered brown face, he did not consider himself bright, and always wanted to learn.

Johnny gulped his drink and winced. "Whiskey, they call it yet! Water, synthetic alcohol, and a dash of caramel they have the gall to label whiskey and charge for!"

"Everything's expensive here," said Bo mildly. "That's why so few rockhounds get rich. They make a lot of money, but they have to spend it just as fast to stay alive."

"Yeh . . . yeh . . . wish they'd spend some of it on us." Johnny grinned and fed the dispenser another coin. It muttered to itself and slid forth a tray with a glass. "C'mon, drink up, man. It's a long way home, and we've got to fortify ourselves for the trip. A bottle, a battle, and a wench is what I need. Most especially the wench, because I don't think the eminent Dr. McKittrick is gonna be interested in sociability, and it's close quarters aboard the Dog."

Bo kept on sipping slowly. "Johnny," he said, raising his voice to cut through the din, "you're an educated man, I never could figure out why you want to talk like a jumper."

"Because I am one at heart. Look, Bo, why don't you get over that inferiority complex of yours? A man can't run a spaceship without knowing more math and physical science than the average professor on Earth. So you had to work your way through the Academy and never had a chance to fan yourself with a lily-white hand while somebody tootled Mozart through a horn. So what?" Johnny's head darted around, birdlike. "If we want some women we'd better make our reservations now."

"I don't, Johnny," said Bo. "I'll just nurse a beer." It wasn't morals so much as fastidiousness; he'd wait till they hit Luna.

"Suit yourself. If you don't want to uphold the honor of the Sirius Transportation Company—"

Bo chuckled. The Company consisted of (a) *the Sirius;* (b) her crew, himself and Johnny; (c) a warehouse, berth, and three other part owners back in Luna City. Not exactly a tramp ship, because you can't normally stop in the middle of an interplanetary voyage and head for somewhere else; but she went wherever there was cargo or people to be moved. Her margin of profit was not great in spite of the charges, for a space trip is expensive; but in a few more years they'd be able to buy another ship or two, and eventually Fireball and Triplanetary would be getting some competition. Even the public lines might have to worry a little.

Johnny put away another couple of shots and rose. Alcohol cost plenty, but it was also more effective in low-gee. " 'Scuse me," he said. "I see a target. Sure you don't want me to ask if she has a friend?"

Bo shook his head and watched his partner move off, swift in the puny gravity—the Last Chance didn't centrifuge like some of the tommicker places downtown. It was hard to push through the crowd without weight to help, but Johnny faded along and edged up to the girl with his highest-powered smile. There were several other men standing around her, but Johnny had The Touch. He'd be bringing her back here in a few minutes.

Bo sighed, feeling a bit lonesome. If he wasn't going to make a night of it, there was no point in drinking heavily. He had to make the final inspection of the ship tomorrow, and grudged the cost of anti-hangover tablets. Besides what he was putting back into the business, he was trying to build a private hoard; some day, he'd retire and get married and build a house. He already had the site picked out, on Kullen overlooking the Sound, back on Earth. Man, but it was a long time since he'd been on Earth!

A sharp noise slashed through the haze of talk and music. Bo looked up. There was a tall black-haired man, Venusian to judge by his kilts, arguing with Johnny. His face was ugly with anger.

Johnny made some reply. Bo heaved up his form and strode toward the discussion, casually picking up anyone in the way and setting him aside. Johnny liked a fight, but this Venusian was big.

As he neared, he caught words: "—my girl, dammit."

"Like hell I am!" said the girl. "I never saw you before—"

"Run along and play, son," said Johnny. "Or do you want me to change that diaper of yours?"

That was when it happened. Bo saw the little needler spit from the Venusian's fingers. Johnny stood there a moment, looking foolishly at the dart in his stomach. Then his knees buckled and he fell with a nightmare slowness.

The Venusian was already on the move. He sprang straight up, slammed a kick at the wall, and arced out the door into the dome corridor beyond. *A spaceman, that. Knows how to handle himself in low-gee.* It was the only clear thought which ran in the sudden storm of Bo's head.

The girl screamed. A man cursed and tried to follow the Venusian. He tangled with another. "Get outta my way!" A roar lifted, someone slugged, someone else coolly smashed a bottle against the bar and lifted the jagged end. There was the noise of a fist meeting flesh.

Bo had seen death before. That needle wasn't anesthetic, it was poison. He knelt in the riot with Johnny's body in his arms.

❂ **II** ❂

SUDDENLY the world came to an end.

There was a sheer drop-off onto the next face of the rough cube which was the asteroid. Bo lay on his belly and peered down the cliff, it ran for a couple of miles and beyond it were the deeps of space and the cold stars. He could dimly see the tortured swirl of crystallization patterns in the smooth bareness. No place to hide; his enemy was not there.

He turned the thought over in a mind which seemed stiff and slow. By crossing that little plain he was exposing himself to a shot from one of its edges. On the other hand, he could just as well be bushwhacked from a ravine as he jumped over. And this route was the fastest for completing his search scheme.

The Great Bear slid into sight, down under the world as it turned. He had often stood on winter nights, back in Sweden, and seen its immense sprawl across the weird flicker of aurora; but even then he wanted the spaceman's experience of seeing it from above. Well, now he had his wish, and much good it had done him.

He went over the edge of the cliff, cautiously, for it wouldn't take much of an impetus to throw him off this rock entirely. Then his helpless and soon frozen body would be just another meteor for the next million years. The vague downward sensation of gravity shifted insanely as he moved; he had the feeling that the world was tilting around him. Now it was the precipice which was a scarred black plain underfoot, reaching to a saw-toothed bluff at its farther edge.

He moved with flat low-gee bounds. Besides the danger of springing off the asteroid entirely, there was its low acceleration to keep a man near the ground; jump up a few feet and it would take you a while to fall back. It was utterly silent around him. He had never thought there could be so much stillness.

He was halfway across when the bullet came. He saw no flash, heard no crack, but suddenly the fissured land before him exploded in a soundless shower of chips. The bullet ricocheted flatly, heading off for outer space. No meteor gravel, that!

Bo stood unmoving an instant, fighting the impulse to leap away. He was a spaceman, not a rockhound; he wasn't used to this environment, and if he jumped high he could be riddled as he fell slowly down again. Sweat was cold on his body. He squinted, trying to see where the shot had come from.

Suddenly he was zigzagging off across the plain toward the nearest edge. Another bullet pocked the ground near him. The sun rose, a tiny heatless dazzle blinding in his eyes.

Fire crashed at his back. Thunder and darkness exploded before him. He lurched forward, driven by the impact. Something was roaring, echoes clamorous in his helmet. He grew dimly aware that it was himself. Then he was falling, whirling down into the black between the stars.

There was a knife in his back, it was white-hot and twisting between the ribs. He stumbled over the edge of the plain and fell, waking when his armor bounced a little against stone.

Breath rattled in his throat as he turned his head. There was a white plume standing over his shoulder, air streaming out through the hole and freezing its moisture. The knife in him was not hot, it was cold with an ultimate cold.

Around him, world and stars rippled as if seen through heat, through fever. He hung on the edge of creation by his fingertips, while chaos shouted beneath.

Theoretically, one man can run a spaceship, but in practice two or three are required for non-military craft. This is not only an emergency reserve, but a preventive of emergencies, for one man alone might get too tired at the critical moments. Bo knew he wouldn't be allowed to leave Achilles without a certified partner, and unemployed spacemen available for immediate hiring are found once in a Venusian snowfall.

Bo didn't care the first day. He had taken Johnny out to Helmet Hill and laid him in the barren ground to wait, unchanging now, till Judgment Day. He felt empty then, drained of grief and hope alike, his main thought a dull dread of having to tell Johnny's father when he reached Luna. He was too slow and clumsy with words; his comforting hand would only break the old man's back. Old Malone had given six sons to space, Johnny was the last; from Saturn to the sun, his blood was strewn for nothing.

It hardly seemed to matter that the Guards office reported itself unable to find the murderer. A single Venusian should have been easy to trace on Achilles, but he seemed to have vanished completely.

Bo returned to the transient quarters and dialed Valeria McKittrick. She looked impatiently at him out of the screen. "Well," she said, "what's the matter? I thought we were blasting today."

"Hadn't you heard?" asked Bo. He found it hard to believe she could be ignorant, here where everybody's life was known to everybody else. "Johnny's dead. We can't leave."

"Oh . . . I'm sorry. He was such a nice little man—I've been in the lab all the time, packing my things, and didn't know." A frown crossed her clear brow. "But you've got to get me back. I've engaged passage to Luna with you."

"Your ticket will be refunded, of course," said Bo heavily. "But you aren't certified, and the *Sirius* is licensed for no less than two operators."

"Well . . . damn! There won't be another berth for weeks, and I've *got* to get home. Can't you find somebody?"

Bo shrugged, not caring much, "I'll circulate an ad if you want, but—"

"Do so, please. Let me know." She switched off.

Bo sat for a moment thinking about her. Valeria McKittrick was worth considering. She wasn't beautiful in any conventional sense but she was tall and well built; there were good lines in the strong high boned face, and her hair was a cataract of spectacular red. And brains, too . . . you didn't get to be a physicist with the Union's radiation labs for nothing. He knew she was still young, and that she had been on Achilles for about a year working on some special project and was now ready to go home.

She was human enough, had been to most of the officers' parties and danced and laughed and flirted mildly, but even the dullest rockhound gossip knew she was too lost in her work to do more. Out here a woman was rare, and a virtuous woman unheard-of; as a result, unknown to herself, Dr. McKittrick's fame had spread through more thousands of people and millions of miles than her professional achievements were ever likely to reach.

Since coming here, on commission from the Lunar lab, to bring her home, Bo Jonsson had given her an occasional wistful thought. He liked intelligent women, and he was getting tired of rootlessness. But of course it would be a catastrophe if he fell in love with her because she wouldn't look twice at a big dumb slob like him. He had sweated out a couple of similar affairs in the past and didn't want to go through another.

He placed his ad on the radinews circuit and then went out to get drunk. It was all he could do for Johnny now, drink him a final wassail. Already his friend was cold under the stars. In the course of the evening he found himself weeping.

He woke up many hours later. Achilles ran on Earth time but did not rotate on it; officially, it was late at night, actually the shrunken sun was high over the domes. The man in the upper bunk said there was a message for him; he was to call one Einar Lundgard at the Comet Hotel soonest.

The Comet! Anyone who could afford a room to himself here, rather than a kip in the public barracks, was well fueled. Bo swallowed a tablet and made his way to the visi and dialed. The robo-clerk summoned Lundgard down to the desk.

It was a lean, muscular face under close cropped brown hair which appeared in the screen. Lundgard was a tall and supple man, somehow neat even without clothes. "Jonsson," said Bo. "Sorry to get you up, but I understood—"

"Oh, yes. Are you looking for a spaceman? I heard your ad and I'm available."

Bo felt his mouth gape open. "Huh? I never thought—"

"We're both lucky, I guess." Lundgard chuckled. His English had only the slightest trace of accent, less than Bo's. "I thought I was stashed here too for the next several months."

"How does a qualified spaceman happen to be marooned?"

"I'm with Fireball, was on the *Drake*—heard of what happened to her?"

Bo nodded, for every spaceman knows exactly what every spaceship is doing at any given time. The *Drake* had come to Achilles to pick up a cargo of refined thorium for Earth; while she lay in orbit, she had somehow lost a few hundred pounds of reaction-mass water from a cracked gasket. Why the accident should have occurred, nobody knew . . . spacemen were not careless about inspections, and what reason would anyone have for sabotage? The event had taken place about a month ago, when the *Sirius* was already enroute here; Bo had heard of it in the course of shop talk.

"I thougth she went back anyway," he said.

Lundgard nodded. "She did. It was the usual question of economics. You know what refined fuel water costs in the Belt; also, the delay while we got it would have carried Earth and Achilles past optimum position, which'd make the trip home that much more expensive. Since we had one more man aboard than really required, it was cheaper to leave him behind; the difference in mass would make up for the fuel loss. I volunteered, even suggested the idea, because . . . well, it happened during my watch, and even if nobody blamed me I couldn't help feeling guilty."

Bo understood that kind of loyalty. You couldn't travel space without men who had it.

"The Company beamed a message: I'd stay here till their schedule permitted an undermanned ship to come by, but that wouldn't be for maybe months," went on Lundgard. "I can't see sitting on this lump that long without so much as a chance at planetfall bonus. If you'll take me on, I'm sure the Company will agree; I'll get a message to them on the beam right away."

"Take us a while to get back," warned Bo. "We're going to stop off at another asteroid to pick up some automatic equipment, and won't go into hyperbolic orbit till after that. About six weeks from here to Earth, all told."

"Against six months here?" Lundgard laughed; it emphasized the bright charm of his manner. "Sunblaze, I'll work for free."

"No need to. Bring your papers over tomorrow, huh?"

The certificate and record were perfectly in order, showing Einar Lundgard to be a Space-tech 1/cl with eight years' experience, qualified as engineer, astronaut, pilot, and any other of the thousand professions which have run into one. They registered articles and shook hands on it. "Call me Bo. It really is my name . . . Swedish."

"Another squarehead, eh?" grinned Lundgard. "I'm from South America myself."

"Notice a year's gap here," said Bo, pointing to the service record. "On Venus."

"Oh, yes. I had some fool idea about settling but soon learned better. I tried to farm, but when you have to carve your own land out of howling desert— Well, let's start some math, shall we?"

They were lucky, not having to wait their turn at the station computer; no other ship was leaving immediately. They fed it the data and requirements, and got back columns of numbers: fuel requirements, acceleration times, orbital elements. The figures always had to be modified, no trip ever turned out just as predicted, but that could be done when needed with a slipstick and the little ship's calculator.

Bo went at his share of the job doggedly, checking and re-checking before giving the problem to the machine; Lundgard breezed through it and spent his time while waiting for Bo in swapping dirty limericks with the tech. He had some good ones.

The *Sirius* was loaded, inspected, and cleared. A "scooter" brought her three passengers up to her orbit, they embarked, settled down, and waited. At the proper time, acceleration jammed them back in a thunder of rockets.

Bo relaxed against the thrust, thinking of Achilles falling away behind them. "So long," he whispered. "So long, Johnny."

◈ III ◈

IN ANOTHER MINUTE, he would be knotted and screaming from the bends, and a couple of minutes later he would be dead.

Bo clamped his teeth together, as if he would grip consciousness in his jaws. His hands felt cold and heavy, the hands of a stranger, as he fumbled for the supply pouch. It seemed to recede from him, down a hollow infinite corridor where echoes talked in a language he did not know.

"Damn," he gasped. "Damn, damn, damn, damn, damn."

He got the pouch open somehow. The stars wheeled around him. There were stars buzzing in his head, like cold white fireflies, buzzing and buzzing in the enormous ringing emptiness of his skull. Pain jagged through him, he felt his eardrums popping as pressure dropped.

The plastic patch stuck to his metal gauntlet. He peeled it off, trying not to howl with the fury ripping in his nerves. His body was slow, inert, a thing to fight. There was no more feeling in his back, was he dead already?

Redness flamed before his eyes, red like Valeria's hair blowing across the stars. It was sheer reflex which brought his arms around to slap the patch over the hole in his suit. The adhesive gripped, drying fast in the sucking vacuum. The patch bellied out from internal air pressure, straining to break loose and kill him.

Bo's mind wavered back toward life. He opened the valves wide on his tanks, and his thermostatic capacitors pumped heat back into him. For a long time he lay there, only lungs and heart had motion. His throat felt withered and flayed, but the rasp of air through it was like being born again.

Born, spewed out of an iron womb into a hollowness of stars and cold, to lie on naked rock while the enemy hunted him. Bo shuddered and wanted to scream again.

Slowly he groped back toward awareness. His frostbitten back tingled as it warmed up again, soon it would be afire. He could feel a hot trickling of blood, but it was along his right side. The bullet must have spent most of its force punching through the armor, caromed off the inside, scratched his ribs, and fallen dead. Next time he probably wouldn't be so lucky. A magnetic-driven .30 slug would go right through a helmet, splashing brains as it passed.

He turned his head, feeling a great weariness, and looked at the gauges. This had cost him a lot of air. There was only about three hours worth left. Lundgard could kill him simply by waiting.

It would be easy to die. He lay on his back, staring up at the stars and the spilling cloudy glory of the Milky Way. A warmth was creeping back into numbed hands and feet; soon he would be warm all over, and sleepy. His eyelids felt heavy, strange that they should be so heavy on an asteroid.

He wanted terribly to sleep.

❧   ❧   ❧

There wasn't much room in the *Sirius,* the only privacy was gained
by drawing curtains across your bunk. Men without psych training
could get to hate each other on a voyage. Bo wondered if he would
reach Luna hating Einar Lundgard.

The man was competent, a willing worker, tempering his
cheerfulness with tact, always immaculate in the heat blue and white
of the Fireball Line which made Bo feel doubly sloppy in his own old
gray coverall. He was a fine conversationalist with an enormous stock
of reminiscence and ideas, witty above a certain passion of belief. It
seemed as if he and Valeria were always talking, animated voices like
a sound of life over the mechanical ship-murmurs, while Bo sat
dumbly in a corner wishing he could think of something to say.

The trouble was, in spite of all his efforts, he was doing a cometary
dive into another bad case of one-sided love. When she spoke in that
husky voice of hers, gray gleam of eyes under hair that floated flaming
in null-gee, the beauty he saw in her was like pain. And she was always
around. It couldn't be helped. Once they had gone into free fall he
could only polish so much metal and tinker with so many appliances;
after that they were crowded together in a long waiting.

"—And why were you all alone in the Belt?" asked Lundgard. "In
spite of all the romantic stories about the wild free life of the rockhound, it's the dullest place in the System."

"Not to me," she smiled. "I was working. There were experiments
to be done, factors to be measured, away from solar radiation. There
are always ions around inside the orbit of Mars to jumble up a delicate
apparatus." Bo sat quiet, trying to keep his eyes off her. She looked
good in shorts and half-cape. Too good.

"It's something to do with power beaming, isn't it?" Lundgard's
handsome face creased in a frown. "Afraid I don't quite understand.
They've been beaming power on the planets for a long time now."

"So they have," she nodded. "What we're after is an interplanetary
power beam. And we've got it." She gestured to the baggage rack and
a thick trunk full of papers she had put there. "That's it. The basic
circuits, factors and constants. Any competent engineer could draw
up a design from them."

"Hmmm . . . precision work, eh?"

"Obviously! It was hard enough to do on, say, Earth—you need a *really* tight beam in just the right frequencies, a feedback signal to direct each beam at the desired outlet, relay stations—oh, yes, it was a ten-year research project before they could even think about building. An interplanetary beam has all those problems plus a number of its own. You have to get the dispersion down to a figure so low it hardly seems possible. You can't use feedback because of the time lag, so the beams have to be aimed *exactly* right—and the planets are always moving, at miles per second. An error of one degree would throw your beam almost two million miles off in crossing one A. U. And besides being so precise, the beam has to carry a begawatt at least to be worth the trouble. The problem looked insoluble till someone in the Order of Planetary Engineers came up with an idea for a trick control circuit hooked into a special computer. My lab's been working together with the Order on it, and I was making certain final determinations for them. It's finished now . . . twelve years of work and we're done." She laughed. "Except for building the stations and getting the bugs out!"

Lundgard cocked an oddly sardonic brow. "And what do you hope for from it?" he asked. "What have the psychotechs decided to do with this thing?"

"Isn't it obvious?" she cried. "Power! Nuclear fuel is getting scarcer every day, and civilization is finished if we can't find another energy source. The sun is pouring out more than we'll ever need, but sheer distance dilutes it below a useful level by the time it gets to Venus.

"We'll build stations on the hot side of Mercury. Orbital stations can relay. We can get the beams as far out as Mars without too much dispersion. It'll bring down the rising price of atomic energy, which is making all other prices rise, and stretch our supply of fissionables for centuries more. No more fuel worries, no more Martians freezing to death because a converter fails, no more clan feuds on Venus starting over uranium beds—" The excited flush on her cheeks was lovely to look at.

Lundgard shook his head. There was a sadness in his smile. "You're a true child of the New Enlightenment," he said. "Reason will solve everything. Science will find a cure for all our ills. Give man a cheap energy source and leave him forever happy. It won't work, you know."

Something like anger crossed her eyes. "What are you?" she asked. "A Humanist?"

"Yes," said Lundgard quietly.

Bo started. He'd known about the antipsychotechnic movement which was growing on Earth, seen a few of its adherents, but—

"I never thought a spaceman would be a Humanist," he stammered.

Lundgard shrugged wryly. "Don't be afraid, I don't eat babies. I don't even get hysterics in an argument. All I've done is use the scientific method, observing the world without preconceptions, and learned by it that the scientific method doesn't have all the answers."

"Instead," said Valeria scornfully, "we should all go back to church and pray for what we want rather than working for it."

"Not at all," said Lundgard mildly. "The New Enlightenment is—or was, because it's dying—a very natural state of mind. Here Earth had come out of the World Wars, racked and ruined, starving and chaotic, and all because of unbridled ideology. So the physical scientists produced goods and machines and conquered the planets; the biologists found new food sources and new cures for disease; the psychotechs built up their knowledge to a point where the socioeconomic unity could really be planned and the plan worked. Man was unified, war had sunken to an occasional small 'police action,' people were eating and had comfort and security—all through applied, working science. Naturally they came to believe reason would solve their remaining problems. But this faith in reason was itself an emotional reaction from the preceding age of unreason.

"Well, we've had a century of enlightenment now, and it has created its own troubles which it cannot solve. No age can handle the difficulties it raises for itself; that's left to the next era. There are practical problems arising, and no matter how desperately the psychotechs work they aren't succeeding with them."

"What problems?" asked Bo, feeling a little bewildered.

"Man, don't you ever see a newscast?" challenged Lundgard. The Second Industrial Revolution, millions of people thrown out of work by the new automata. They aren't going hungry, but they are displaced and bitter. The economic center of Earth is shifting to Asia, the political power with it, and hundreds of millions of Asians are skeptical aboard this antiseptic New Order the West has been bringing them: cultural resistance, and not all the psychotechnic propaganda in the System can shake it off. The men of Mars, Venus, the Belt, the Jovian moons are developing their own civilizations—inevitably, in alien environments; their own ways of living and thinking, which just don't fit into the neat scheme of an Earth-dominated Solar Union. The psychotechs themselves are being driven to oligarchic, unconstitutional acts; they have no choice, but it's making them enemies.

"And then there's the normal human energy and drive. Man can only be safe and sane and secure for so long, then he reacts. This New Enlightenment is really a decadent age, a period where an exhausted civilization has been resting under a holy status quo. It can't last. Man always wants something new."

"You Humanists talk a lot about 'man's right to variability,'" said Valeria. "If you really carry off that revolution your writings advocate you'll just trade one power group for another—and more fanatic, less lawful, than the present one."

"Not necessarily," said Lundgard. "After all, the Union will probably break up. It can't last forever. All we want to do is hasten the day because we feel that it's outlived its usefulness."

Bo shook his head. "I can't see it," he said heavily. "I just can't see it. All those people—the Lunarites, the violent clansmen on Venus, the stiff correct Martians, the asteroid rockhounds, even those mysterious Jovians—they all came from Earth. It was Earth's help that made their planets habitable. We're all men, all one race."

"A fiction," said Lundgard. "The human race is a fiction. There are only small groups with their own conflicting interests."

"And if those conflicts are allowed to break into war—" said Valeria. "Do you know what a lithium bomb can do?"

There was a reckless gleam in Lundgard's eyes. "If a period of interplanetary wars is necessary, let's get it over with," he answered. "Enough men will survive to build something better. This age has gotten stale. It's petrifying. There have been plenty of shake-ups in history—the fall of Rome, the Reformation, the Napoleonic Wars, the World Wars. It's been man's way of progressing."

"I don't know about all those," said Bo slowly. "I just know I wouldn't want to live through such a time."

"You're soft," said Lundgard. "Down underneath you're soft." He laughed disarmingly. "Pardon me. I didn't mean anything personal. I'll never convince you and you'll never convince me, so let's keep it friendly. I hope you'll have some free time on Luna, Valeria. I know a little grill where they serve the best synthosteaks in the System."

"All right," she smiled. "It's a date."

Bo mumbled some excuse and went aft. He was still calling her Dr. McKittrick.

❀ IV ❀

YOU CAN'T JUST LIE HERE and let him come kill you.

There was a picture behind his eyes; he didn't know if it was a dream or a long buried memory. He stood under an aspen which quivered and rustled as if it laughed to itself softly, softly, when the wind embraced it. And the wind was blowing up a red granite slope, wild and salt from the Sound, and there were towering clouds lifting over Denmark to the west. The sunlight rained and streamed through aspen leaves, broken, shaken, falling in spatters against the earth, and he, Bo Jonsson, laughed with the wind and the tree and the far watery glitter of the Sound.

He opened his eyes, wearily, like an old man. Orion was marching past, and there was a blaze on crags five miles off which told of the rising sun. The asteroid spun swiftly; he had been here for many of its days now, and each day burdened him like a year.

Got to get out of here, he knew.

He sat up, pain tearing along his furrowed breast. Somehow he had kept the wrench with him, he stared at it in a dull wonder.

Where to go, where to hide, what to do?

Thirst nagged him. Slowly he uncoiled the tube which led from the electrically heated canteen welded to his suit, screwed its end into the helmet nipple, thumbed down the clamp which closed it, and sucked hard. It helped a little.

He dragged himself to his feet and stood swaying, only the near-weightlessness kept him erect. Turning his head in its transparent cage, he saw the sun rise, and bright spots danced before him when he looked away.

His vision cleared, but for a moment he thought the shadow lifting over a nearby ridge was a wisp of unconsciousness. Then he made out the bulky black-painted edge of it, gigantic against the Milky Way, and it was Lundgard, moving unhurriedly up to kill him.

A dark laughter was in his radio earphones. "Take it easy, Bo. I'll be there in a minute."

He backed away, his heart a sudden thunder, looking for a place to hide. Down! Get down and don't stand where he can see you! He crouched as much as the armor would allow and broke into a bounding run.

A slug spat broken stone near his feet. The powdery dust hung for minutes before settling. Breath rattled in his throat. He saw the lip of a meteoric crater and dove.

Crouching there, he heard Lundgard's voice again: "You're somewhere near. Why not come out and finish it now?"

The radio was non-directional, so he snapped back: "A gun against a monkey wrench?"

Lundgard's coolness broke a little; there was almost a puzzled note: "I hate to do this. Why can't you be reasonable? I don't want to kill you."

"The trouble," said Bo harshly, "is that I want to kill you."

"Behold the man of the New Enlightenment!" Bo could imagine Lundgard's grin. It would be tight, and there would be sweat on the lean face, but the amusement was genuine. "Didn't you believe sweet reasonableness could solve everything? This is only the beginning, Bo, just a small preliminary hint that the age of reason is dying. I've already converted you to my way of thinking, by the very fact you're fighting me. Why not admit it?"

Bo shook his head—futile gesture, looked in darkness where he lay. There was a frosty blaze of stars when he looked up.

It was more than himself and Johnny Malone, more even than the principle of the thing and the catastrophe to all men which Lundgard's victory meant. There was something deep and primitive which would not let him surrender, even in the teeth of annihilation. Valeria's image swayed before him.

Lundgard was moving around, peering over the shadowy tumble of blackened rock in search of any trace. There was a magnetic rifle in his hands. Bo strained his helmet to the crater floor, trying to hear ground vibrations, but there was nothing. He didn't know where Lundgard was, only that he was very near.

Blindly, he bunched his legs and sprang out of the pit.

They found the asteroid where Valeria had left her recording instruments. It was a tiny drifting fragment of a world which had never been born, turning endlessly between the constellations; the *Sirius* moored fast with grapples, and Valeria donned a spacesuit and went out to get her apparatus. Lundgard accompanied her. As there was only work for two, Bo stayed behind.

He slumped for a while in the pilot chair, letting his mind pace through a circle of futility. Valeria, Valeria—strong and fair and never to be forgotten, would he ever see her again after they made Luna?

This won't do, he told himself dully. *I should at least keep busy. Thank God for work.*

He wasn't much of a thinker, he knew that, but he had cleverness in his hands. It was satisfying to watch a machine come right under his tools. Working, he could see the falseness of Lundgard's philosophy. The man could quote history all he wanted; weave a glittering circle of logic around Bo's awkward brain, but it didn't change facts. Maybe this century was headed for trouble; maybe psychotechnic government was only another human self-limitation and should be changed for something else; nevertheless, the truth remained that most men were workers who wished no more than peace in which to create as best they could. All the high ideals in the universe weren't worth breaking the Union for and smashing the work of human hands in a single burst of annihilating flame.

I can feel it, down inside me. But why can't I say it?

He got up and went over to the baggage rack, remembering that Lundgard had dozens of book-reels along and that reading would help him not to think about what he could never have.

On a planet Bo would not have dreamed of helping himself without asking first. But custom is different in space, where there is no privacy and men must be a unit if they are to survive. He was faintly surprised to see that Lundgard's personal suitcase was locked; but it would be hours, probably, before the owner got back: dismantling a recorder setup took time. A long time, in which to talk and laugh with Valeria. In the chill spatial radiance, her hair would be like frosty fire.

Casually, Bo stooped across to Lundgard's sack-hammock and took his key ring off the hook. He opened the suitcase and lifted out some of the reels in search of a promising title.

Underneath them were neatly folded clothes, Fireball uniforms and fancy dress pajamas. A tartan edge stuck out from below, and Bo lifted a coat to see what clan that was. Probably a souvenir of Lundgard's Venusian stay—

Next to the kilt was a box which he recognized. L-masks came in such boxes.

How the idea came to him, he did not know. He stood there for minutes, looking at the box without seeing it. The ship was very quiet around him. He had a sudden feeling that the walls were closing in.

When he opened the box, his hands shook, and there was sweat trickling along his ribs.

The mask was of the latest type, meant to fit over the head, snug around the cheeks and mouth and jaws. It was like a second skin, reflecting expression, not to be told from a real face. Bo saw the craggy nose and the shock of dark hair, limp now, but—

Suddenly he was back on Achilles, with riot roaring around him and Johnny Malone's body in his arms.

No wonder they never found that Venusian. There never was any.

Bo felt a dim shock when he looked at the chronometer. Only five minutes had gone by while he stood there. Only five minutes to turn the cosmos inside out.

Very slowly and carefully he repacked the suitcase and put it in the rack and sat down to think.

What to do?

Accuse Lundgard to his face—no, the man undoubtedly carried that needler. And there was Valeria to think of. A ricocheting dart, a scratch on her, no! It took Bo a long time to decide; his brain seemed viscous. When he looked out of a port to the indifferent stars, he shuddered.

They came back, shedding their spacesuits in the airlock; frost whitened the armor as moisture condensed on chilled surfaces. The metal seemed to breathe cold. Valeria went efficiently to work, stowing the boxed instruments as carefully as if they were her children. There was a laughter on her lips which turned Bo's heart around inside him.

Lundgard leaned over the tiny desk where he sat. "What y' doing?" he asked.

"Recalculating our orbit to Luna," said Bo. "I want to go slow to hyperbolic speed."

Why? It'll add days to the trip, and the fuel—"

"I . . . I'm afraid we might barge into Swarm 770. It's supposed to be near here now and, uh, the positions of those things are never known for sure . . . perturbations . . ." Bo's mouth felt dry.

"You've got a megamile of safety margin or your orbit would never have been approved," argued Lundgard.

"Hell damn it, I'm the captain!" yelled Bo.

"All right, all right . . . take it easy, skipper," Lundgard shot a humorous glance at Valeria. "I certainly don't mind a few extra days in . . . the present company."

She smiled at him. Bo felt ill.

His excuse was thin; if Lundgard thought to check the ephemeris, it would fall to ruin. But he couldn't tell the real reason.

An iron-drive ship does not need to drift along the economical Hohmann "A" orbit of the big freighters; it can build up such furious speed that the sun will sweep along a hyperbola rather than an ellipse and can still brake that speed near its destination. But the critical stage of acceleration has to be just right, or there will not be enough fuel to stop completely; the ship will be pulled into a cometary orbit and run helpless, the crew probably starving before a rescue vessel can locate them. Bo dared not risk the trouble exploding at full drive; he would drift along, capture and bind Lundgard at the first chance, and then head for Earth. He could handle the *Sirius* alone even if it was illegal; he could not handle her if he had to fight simultaneously.

His knuckles were white on the controls as he loosed the grapples and nudged away from the asteroid with a whisper of power. After a few minutes of low acceleration, he cut the rockets, checked position and velocity, and nodded. "On orbit," he said mechanically. "It's your turn to cook, Ei . . . Einar."

Lundgard swooped easily through the air into the cubbyhole which served for a galley. Cooking in free fall is an art which not all spacemen master, but he could—his meals were even good. Bo felt a helpless kind of rage at his own clumsy efforts.

He crouched in midair, dark of mind, a leg hooked around a stanchion to keep from drifting.

When someone touched him, his heart jumped and he whirled around.

"What's the matter, Bo?" asked Valeria. "You look like doomsday."

"I . . . I . . ." He gulped noisily and twisted his mouth into a smile. "Just feeling a little off."

"It's more than that, I think." Her eyes were grave. "You've seemed so unhappy the whole trip. Is there anything I can do to help?"

"Thanks . . . Dr. McKittrick . . . but—"

"Don't be so formal," she said, almost wistfully. "I don't bite. Too many men think I do. Can't we be friends?"

"With a thick-headed clinker like me?" His whisper was raw.

"Don't be silly. It takes brains to be a spaceman. I like a man who knows when to be quiet." She lowered her eyes, the lashes were long and sooty black. "There's something solid about you, something so few people seem to have these days. I wish you wouldn't go feeling so inferior."

At any other time it would have been a sunburst in him. Now he thought of death, and mumbled something and looked away. A hurt expression crossed her face. "I won't bother you," she said gently, and moved off.

The thing was to fall on Lundgard while he slept—

The radar alarm buzzed during a dinner in which Lundgard's flow of talk had battered vainly against silence and finally given up. Bo vaulted over to the control panel and checked. No red light glowed, and the autopilot wasn't whipping them out of danger, so they weren't on a collision course. But the object was getting close. Bo calculated it was an asteroid on an orbit almost parallel to their own, relative speed only a few feet per second; it would come within ten miles or so. In the magnifying periscope, it showed as a jagged dark cube, turning around itself and flashing hard glints of sunlight off mica beds—perhaps six miles square, all crags and cracks and fracture faces, heatless and lifeless and kindless.

Lundgard yawned elaborately after dinner. "Excuse," he said. "Unless somebody's for chess?" His hopeful glance met the grimness of Bo and the odd sadness of Valeria, and he shrugged. "All right, then. Pleasant dreams."

After ten minutes—*now!*

Bo uncoiled himself. "Valeria," he whispered, as if the name were holy.

"Yes?" She arched her brows expectantly.

"I can't stop to explain now. I've got to do something dangerous. Get back aft of the gyro housing."

"What?"

"Get back!" Command blazed frantically in him. "And stay there, whatever happens."

Something like fear flickered in her eyes. It was a very long way to human help. Then she nodded, puzzled but with an obedience which held gallantry, and slipped out of sight behind the steel pillar.

Bo launched himself across the room in a single null-gee bound. One hand ripped aside Lundgard's curtain, the other got him by the throat.

"What the hell—"

Lundgard exploded into life. His fist crashed against Bo's cheek. Bo held on with one hand and slugged with the other. Knuckles bounced on rubbery muscle. Lundgard's arm snaked for the tunic stretched on his bunk wall; his body came lithely out of the sack. Bo snatched for that wrist. Lundgard's free hand came around, edged out to slam him in the larynx.

Pain ripped through Bo. He let go and sailed across the room. Lundgard was pulling out his needler.

Bo hit the opposite wall and rebounded—not for the armed man, but for the control panel. Lundgard spat a dart at him. It burst on to the viewport over his shoulder, and Bo caught the acrid whiff of poison. Then the converter was roaring to life and whining gyros spun the ship around.

Lundgard was hurled across the room. He collected himself, catlike, grabbed a stanchion, and raised the gun again. "I've got the drop," he said. "Get away from there or you're a dead man."

It was as if someone else had seized Bo's body. Decision was like lightning through him. He had tried to capture Lundgard, and failed, and venom crouched at his back. But the ship was pointed for the asteroid now, where it hung gloomily a dozen miles off, and the rockets were ready to spew.

"If you shoot me," said Bo, "I'll live just long enough to pour on the juice. We'll hit that rock and scatter from hell to breakfast."

Valeria emerged. Lundgard swung the needler to cover her. "Stay where you are!" he rapped.

"What's happening?" she said fearfully.

"I don't know," said Lundgard, "Bo's gone crazy—attacked me—"

Wrath boiled back in the pilot. He snarled, "You killed my partner. You must'a been fixing to kill us too."

"What do you mean?" whispered Valeria.

"How should I know?" said Lundgard. "He's jumped his orbit, that's all. Look, Bo, be reasonable. Get away from that panel—"

"Look in his suitcase, Valeria." Bo forced the words out of a tautened throat. "A Venusian shot my partner. You'll find his face and his clothes in Lundgard's things. I'd know that face in the middle of the sun."

She hung for a long while, not moving. Bo couldn't see her. His eyes were nailed to the asteroid, keeping the ship's nose pointed at it.

"Is that true, Einar?" she asked finally.

"No," Lundgard said. "Of course not. I do have Venusian clothes and a mask, but—"

"Then why are you keeping me covered too?"

Lundgard didn't answer at once. The only noise was the murmur of machinery and the dense breathing of three pairs of lungs. Then his laugh jarred forth.

"All right," he said. "I hadn't meant it to come yet, or to come this way, but all right."

"Why did you kill Johnny?" Tears stung Bo's eyes. "He never hurt you."

"It was necessary." Lundgard's mouth twitched. "But you see, we knew you were going to Achilles to pick up Valeria and her data. We needed to get a man aboard your ship, to take over when her orbit brought her close to our asteroid base. You've forced my hand—I wasn't going to capture you for days yet. I sabotaged the *Drake's* fuel tanks to get myself stranded there, and shot your friend to get his berth. I'm sorry."

"Why?" Horror rode Valeria's voice.

"I'm a Humanist. I've never made a secret of that. What our secret is, is that some of us aren't content just to talk revolution. We want to give this rotten, over-mechanized society the shove that will bring on its end. We've built up a small force, not much as yet, not enough to accomplish anything lasting. But if we had a solar power beam it would make a big difference. It could be adapted to direct military uses, as well as supplying energy to our machines. A lens effect, a concentration of solar radiation strong enough to burn. Well, it seems worth trying."

"And what do you intend for us?"

"You'll have to be kept prisoners for a while, of course," said Lundgard. "It won't be onerous. We aren't beasts."

"No," said Bo. "Just murderers."

"Save the dramatics," snapped Lundgard. "I have the gun. Get away from those controls."

Bo shook his head. There was a wild hammering in his breast, but his voice surprised him with steadiness: "No. I've got the upper hand. I can kill you if you move. Yell if he tries anything, Valeria."

Lundgard's eyes challenged her. "Do you want to die?" he asked.

Her head lifted. "No," she said, "but I'm not afraid to. Go ahead if you must, Bo. It's all right."

Bo felt cold. He knew he wouldn't. He was bluffing. In the final showdown he could not crash her. He had seen too many withered space drained mummies in his time. But maybe Lundgard didn't realize that.

"Give up," he said. "You can't gain a damn thing. I'm not going to see a billion people burned alive just to save our necks. Make a bargain for your life."

"No," said Lundgard with a curious gentleness. "I have my own brand of honor. I'm not going to surrender to you. You can't sit there forever."

Impasse. The ship floated through eternal silence while they waited.

"All right," said Bo. "I'll fight you for the power beam."

"How's that?"

"I can throw this ship into orbit around the asteroid. We can go down there and settle the thing between us. The winner can jump up here again with the help of a jet of tanked air. The lump hasn't got much gravity."

Lundgard hesitated. "And how do I know you'll keep your end of the bargain?" he asked. "You could let me go through the airlock, then close it and blast off."

Bo had had some such thought, but he might have known it wouldn't work. "What do you suggest?" he countered, never taking his eyes off the planetoid. "Remember, I don't trust you either."

Lundgard laughed suddenly, a hard yelping bark. "I know! Valeria, go aft and remove all the control-rod links and spares. Bring them back here, I'll go out first, taking half of them with me, and Bo can follow with the other half. He'll have to."

"I—no! I won't," she whispered. "I can't let you—"

"Go ahead and do it," said Bo. He felt a sudden vast weariness. "It's the only way we can break this deadlock."

She wept as she went toward the engine room.

Lundgard's thought was good. Without linked control-rods, the converter couldn't operate five minutes, it would flare up and melt itself and kill everyone aboard in a flood of radiation. Whoever won the duel could quickly re-install the necessary parts.

There was a waiting silence. At last Lundgard said, almost abstractedly: "Holmgang. Do you know what that means, Bo?"

"No."

"You ought to. It was a custom of our ancestors back in the early Middle Ages—the Viking time. Two men would go off to a little island, a holm, to settle their differences; one would come back. I never thought it could happen out here." He chuckled bleakly. "Valkyries in spacesuits?"

The girl came back with the links tied in two bundles. Lundgard counted them and nodded. "All right." He seemed strangely calm, an easy assurance lay over him like armor. Bo's fear was cold in his belly, and Valeria wept still with a helpless horror.

The pilot used a safe two minutes of low blast to edge up to the asteroid, "I'll go into the airlock and put on my spacesuit," said Lundgard. "Then I'll jump down and you can put the ship in orbit. Don't try anything while I'm changing, because I'll keep this needler handy."

"It won't work against a spacesuit," said Bo.

Lundgard laughed. "I know," he said. He kissed his hand to Valeria and backed into the lock chamber. The outer valve closed behind him.

"Bo!" Valeria grabbed the pilot by the shoulders, and he looked around into her face. "You can't go out there, I won't let you, I—"

"If I don't," he said tonelessly, "we'll orbit around here till we starve."

"But you could be killed!"

"I hope not. For your sake, mostly, I hope not," he said awkwardly. "But he won't have any more weapon than me, just a monkey wrench." There was a metal tube welded to the leg of each suit for holding tools; wrenches, the most commonly used, were simply left there as a rule. "I'm bigger than he is."

"But—" She laid her head on his breast and shuddered with crying. He tried to comfort her.

"All right," he said at last. "All right. Lundgard must be through. I'd better get started."

"Leave him!" she blazed. "His air won't last many hours. We can wait."

"And when he sees he's been tricked, you think he won't wreck those links? No. There's no way out."

It was as if all his life he had walked on a road which had no turnings, which led inevitably to this moment.

He made some careful calculations from the instrument readings, physical constants of the asteroid, and used another minute's maneuvering to assume orbital velocity. Alarm lights blinked angry eyes at him, the converter was heating up. No more traveling till the links were restored.

Bo floated from his chair toward the lock. Goodbye, Valeria," he said, feeling the bloodless weakness of words. "I hope it won't be for long."

She threw her arms about him and kissed him. The taste of tears was still on his lips when he had dogged down his helmet.

Opening the outer valve he moved forth, magnetic boots clamping to the hull. A gulf of stars yawned around him, a cloudy halo about his head. The stillness was smothering.

When he was "over" the asteroid he gauged his position with a practiced eye and jumped free. Falling, he thought mostly of Valeria.

As he landed he looked around. No sign of Lundgard. The man could be anywhere in these square miles of cosmic wreckage. He spoke tentatively into his radio, in case Lundgard should be within the horizon: "Hello, are you there?"

"Yes, I'm coming." There was a sharp cruel note of laughter. "Sorry to play this dirty, but there are bigger issues at stake than you or me. I've kept a rifle in my tooltube all the time . . . just in case. Good-bye, Bo."

A slug smashed into the pinnacle behind him. Bo turned and ran.

V

AS HE ROSE over the lip of the crater, his head swung, seeking his enemy. There! It was almost a reflex which brought his arm back and sent the wrench hurtling across the few yards between. Before it had struck, Bo's feet lashed against the pit edge, and the kick arced him toward Lundgard.

Spacemen have to be good at throwing things. The wrench hit the lifted rifle in a soundless shiver of metal, tore it loose from an insecure gauntleted grasp and sent it spinning into shadow. Lundgard yelled, spun on his heel, and dove after it. Then the flying body of Bo Jonsson struck him.

Even in low-gee, matter has all its inertia. The impact rang and boomed within their armor, they swayed and fell to the ground, locking arms and hammering futilely at helmets. Rolling over, Bo got on top, his hands closed on Lundgard's throat—where the throat should have been, but plastic and alloy held fast; instinct had betrayed him.

Lundgard snarled, doubled his legs and kicked. Bo was sent staggering back. Lundgard crawled erect and turned to look for the rifle. Bo couldn't see it either in the near-solid blackness where no light fell, but his wrench lay as a dark gleam. He sprang for that, closed a hand on it, bounced up, and rushed at Lundgard. A swing shocked his own muscles with its force, and Lundgard lurched.

Bo moved in on him. Lundgard reached into his tool-tube and drew out his own wrench. He circled, his panting hoarse in Bo's earphones.

"This . . . is the way . . . it was supposed to be," said Bo.

He jumped in, his weapon whirling down to shiver again on the other helmet. Lundgard shook a dazed head and countered. The impact roared and echoed in Bo's helmet, on into his skull. He smashed heavily. Lundgard's lifted wrench parried the blow, it slid off. Like a fencer, Lundgard snaked his shaft in and the reverberations were deafening.

Bo braced himself and smote with all his power. The hit sang back through iron and alloy, into his own bones. Lundgard staggered a little, hunched himself and struck in return.

They stood with feet braced apart, trading fury, a metal rain on shivering plastic. The stuff was almost unbreakable, but not quite, not for long when such violence dinned on it. Bo felt a lifting wild glee, something savage he had never known before leaped up in him and he bellowed. He was stronger, he could hit harder. Lundgard's helmet would break first!

The Humanist retreated, using his wrench like a sword, stopping the force of blows without trying to deal more of his own. His left hand fumbled at his side. Bo hardly noticed. He was pushing in, hewing, hewing. Again the shrunken sun rose, to flash hard light off his club.

Lundgard grinned, his face barely visible as highlight and shadow behind the plastic. His raised tool turned one hit, it slipped along his arm to rap his flank. Bo twisted his arm around, beat the other wrench aside for a moment, and landed a crack like a thunderbolt.

Then Lundgard had his drinking hose free, pointing in his left hand. He thumbed down the clamp, exposing water at fifty degrees to naked space.

It rushed forth, driven by its own vapor pressure, a stream like a lance in the wan sunshine. When it hit Bo's helmet, most of it boiled off . . . cooling the rest, which froze instantly.

Blindness clamped down on Bo. He leaped away, cursing, the front of his helmet so frosted he could not see before him. Lundgard bounced around, playing the hose on him. Through the rime-coat, Bo could make out only a grayness.

He pawed at it, trying to wipe it off, knowing that Lundgard was using this captured minute to look for the rifle. As he got some of the ice loose, he heard a sharp yell of victory—found!

Turning, he ran again.

Over that ridge! Down on your belly! A slug pocked the stone above him. Rolling over, he got to his feet and bounded off toward a steep rise, still wiping blindness off his helmet. But he could not wipe the bitter vomit taste of defeat out of his mouth.

His breathing was a file that raked in his throat. Heart and lungs were ready to tear loose, and there was a cold knot in his guts. Fleeing up the high, ragged slope, he sobbed out his rage at himself and his own stupidity.

At the top of the hill he threw himself to the ground and looked down again over a low wall of basalt. It was hard to see if anything moved down in that valley of night. Then the sun threw a broken gleam off polished metal, the rifle barrel, and he saw Einar Lundgard walking around, looking for him.

The voice came dim in his earphones. "Why don't you give up, Bo? I tell you, I don't want to kill you."

"Yeh." Bo panted wearily. "I'm sure."

"Well, you can never tell," said Lundgard mildly. "It would be rather a nuisance to have to keep not only the fair Valeria, but you, tied up all the way to base. Still, if you'll surrender by the time I've counted ten—"

"Look here," said Bo desperately. "I've got half the links. If you don't give up I'll hammer 'em all flat, and let you starve."

"And Valeria?" The voice jeered at him. He knew his secret was read. "I shouldn't have let you bluff me in the first place. It won't happen a second time. All right: one, two, three—"

Bo could get off this asteroid with no more than the power of his own legs; a few jets from the emergency blow valve at the bottom of an air tank would correct his flight as needed to bring him back to the *Sirius*. He wanted to get up there, and inside warm walls, and take Valeria in his hands and never let her go again. He wanted to live.

"—six, seven, eight—"

He looked at his gauges. A lot of oxyhelium mixture was gone from the tanks, but they were big and there was still several atmospheres' pressure in each. A couple of hours life. If he didn't exert himself too much. They screwed directly into valves in the back of his armor, and—

"—ten. All right, Bo." Lundgard started moving up the slope, light and graceful as a bird. It was wide and open, no place to hide and sneak up behind him.

Figures reeled through Bo's mind, senselessly. Mass of the asteroid, effective radius, escape velocity only a few feet per second, and he was already on one of the highest points. Brains! he thought with a shattering sorrow. A lot of good mine have done me!

He prepared to back down the other side of the hill, run as well as he could, as long as he could, until a bullet splashed his blood or suffocation thickened it. But I want to fight! he thought through a gulp of tears. I want to stand up and fight!

Orbital velocity equals escape velocity divided by the square root of two.

For a moment he lay there, rigid, and his eyes stared at death walking up the slope but did not see it.

Then, in a crazy blur of motion, he brought his wrench around, closed it on a nut at one side, and turned.

The right hand air tank unscrewed easily. He held it in his hands, a three-foot cylinder, blind while calculation raced through his head. What would the centrifugal and Coriolis forces be? It was the roughest sort of estimate. He had neither time nor data, but—

Lundgard was taking it easy, stopping to examine each patch of shadow thrown by some gaunt crag, each meteor scar where a man might hide. It would take him several minutes to reach the hilltop.

Bo clutched the loosened tank in his arms, throwing one leg around it to make sure, and faced away from Lundgard. He hefted himself, as if his body were a machine he must use. Then, carefully, he jumped off the top of the hill.

It was birdlike, dreamlike, thus to soar noiseless over iron desolation. Then sun fell behind him. A spearhead pinnacle clawed after his feet. The Southern Cross flamed in his eyes.

Downward—get rid of that downward component of velocity. He twisted the tank, pointing it toward the surface, and cautiously opened the blow valve with his free hand. Only a moment's exhaust, everything gauged by eye. Did he have an orbit now?

The ground dropped sharply off to infinity, and he saw stars under the keel of the world. He was still going out, away. Maybe he had miscalculated his jump, exceeded escape velocity after all, and was headed for a long cold spin toward Jupiter. It would take all his compressed air to correct such a mistake.

Sweat prickled in his armpits. He locked his teeth and refused to open the valve again.

It was like endless falling, but he couldn't yet be sure if the fall was toward the asteroid or the stars. The rock spun past him. Another face came into view. Yes, by all idiot gods, its gravity was pulling him around!

He skimmed low over the bleakness of it, seeing darkness and starlit death sliding beneath him. Another crag loomed suddenly in his path, and he wondered in a harsh clutch of fear if he was going to crash. Then it ghosted by, a foot from his flying body. He thought he could almost sense the chill of it.

He was a moon now, a satellite skimming low above the airless surface of his own midget world. The fracture plain where Lundgard had shot at him went by, and he braced himself. Up around the tiny planet, and there was the hill he had left, stark against Sagittarius. He saw Lundgard, standing on its heights and looking the way he had gone. Carefully, he aimed the tank and gave himself another small blast to correct his path. There was no noise to betray him, the asteroid was a grave where all sound was long buried and frozen.

He flattened, holding his body parallel to the tank in his arms. One hand still gripped the wrench, the other reached to open the blow valve wide.

The surge almost tore him loose. He had a careening lunatic moment of flight in which the roar of escaping gas boiled through his armor and he clung like a troll to a runaway witch's broom. The sun was blinding on one side of him.

He struck Lundgard with an impact of velocity and inertia which sent him spinning down the hill. Bo hit the ground, recoiled, and sprang after his enemy. Lundgard was still rolling. As Bo approached, he came to a halt, lifted his rifle dazedly, and had it knocked loose with a single blow of the wrench.

Lundgard crawled to his feet while Bo picked up the rifle and threw it off the asteroid. "Why did you do that?"

"I don't know," said Bo. "I should just shoot you down, but I want you to surrender."

Lundgard drew his wrench. "No," he said.

"All right," said Bo. "It won't take long."

When he got up to the *Sirius,* using a tank Lundgard would never need, Valeria had armed herself with a kitchen knife. "It wouldn't have done much good," he said when he came through the airlock. She fell into his arms, sobbing, and he tried to comfort her. "It's all over. All taken care of. We can go home now."

He himself was badly in need of consolation. The inquiry on Earth would clear him, of course, but he would always have to live with the memory of a man stretched dead under a wintery sky. He went aft and replaced the links. When he came back, Valeria had recovered herself, but as she watched his methodical preparations and listened to what he had to tell, there was that in her eyes which he hardly dared believe.

Not him. Not a big dumb slob like him.

Although one plot had been foiled, the struggle continued for another generation. The values of the New Enlightenment fostered by the Psychotechnic Institute met increasing cultural and emotional resistance. No amount of psychodynamic manipulation could make pure rationality congenial to the average person. Despair deepened as opportunities shrank. The rage of Earth's superfluous masses finally exploded against the gifted elite in the Humanist Revolt of 2170. The Psychotechnic Institute was abolished and its surviving members fled into exile. "Hubris, nemesis, ate," wrote one observer. "The tragic flaw in the character of Institute personnel was only that they were human."

Like many conquerors before them, the Humanists soon learned that it is harder to wield power than to win it. Keeping it is another question entirely.

Cold Victory

IT WAS THE OLD ARGUMENT, Historical Necessity versus the Man of Destiny. When I heard them talking, three together, my heart twisted within me and I knew that once more I must lay down the burden of which I can never be rid.

This was in the Battle Rock House, which is a quiet tavern on the edge of Syrtis Town. I come there whenever I am on Mars. It is friendly and unpretentious: shabby, comfortable loungers scattered about under the massive sandwood rafters, honest liquor and competent chess and the talk of one's peers.

As I entered, a final shaft of thin hard sunlight stabbed in through the window, dazzling me, and then night fell like a thunderclap over the ocherous land and the fluoros snapped on. I got a mug of porter and strolled across to the table about which the three people sat.

The stiff little bald man was obviously from the college; he wore his academics even here, but Martians are like that. "No, no," he was saying. "These movements are too great for any one man to change them appreciably. Humanism, for example, was not the political engine of Carnarvon; rather, he was the puppet of Humanism, and danced as the blind brainless puppeteer made him."

"I'm not so sure," answered the man in gray, undress uniform of the Order of Planetary Engineers. "If he and his cohorts had been doctrinaire, the government of Earth might still be Humanist!"

"But being born of a time of trouble, Humanism was inevitably fanatical," said the professor.

53

The big, kilted Venusian woman shifted impatiently. She was packing a gun and her helmet was on the floor beside her. Lucifer Clan, I saw from the tartan. "If there are folk around at a crisis time with enough force, they'll shape the way things turn out," she declared. "Otherwise things will drift."

I rolled up a lounger and set my mug on the table. Conversational kibitzing is accepted in the Battle Rock. "Pardon me, gentles," I said. "Maybe I can contribute."

"By all means, Captain," said the Martian, his eyes flickering over my Solar Guard uniform and insignia. "Permit me: I am Professor Freylinghausen—Engineer Buwono; Freelady Neilsen-Singh."

"Captain Crane." I lifted my mug in a formal toast. "Mars, Luna, Venus, and Earth in my case . . . highly representative, are we not? Between us, we should be able to reach a conclusion."

"To a discussion in a vacuum!" snorted the amazon.

"Not quite," said the engineer. "What did you wish to suggest, Captain?"

I got out my pipe and began stuffing it. "There's a case from recent history—the anti-Humanist counterrevolution, in fact—in which I had a part myself. Offhand, at least, it seems a perfect example of sheer accident determining the whole future of the human race. It makes me think we must be more the pawns of chance than of law."

"Well, Captain," said Freylinghausen testily, "let us hear your story and then pass judgment."

"I'll have to fill you in on some background." I lit my pipe and took a comforting drag. I needed comfort just then. It was not to settle an argument that I was telling this, but to reopen an old hurt which would never let itself be forgotten. "This happened during the final attack on the Humanists—"

"A perfect case of inevitability, sir," interrupted Freylinghausen. "May I explain? Thank you. Forgive me if I repeat obvious facts. Their arrangements and interpretation are perhaps not so obvious.

"Psychotechnic government had failed to solve the problems of Earth's adjustment to living on a high technological level. Conditions worsened until all too many people were ready to try desperate measures. The Humanist revolution was the desperate measure that succeeded in being tried. A typical reaction movement, offering a return to a less intellectualized existence; the savior with the time machine, as Toynbee once phrased it. So naturally its leader, Carnarvon, got to be dictator of the planet.

"But with equal force it was true that Earth could no longer *afford* to cut back her technology. Too many people, too few resources. In the several years of their rule, the Humanists failed to keep their promises; their attempts led only to famine, social disruption, breakdown. Losing popular support, they had to become increasingly arbitrary, thus alienating the people still more.

"At last the oppression of Earth became so brutal that the democratic governments of Mars and Venus brought pressure to bear. But the Humanists had gone too far to back down. Their only possible reaction was to pull Earth-Luna out of the Solar Union.

"We could not see that happen, sir. The lesson of history is too plain. Without a Union council to arbitrate between planets and a Solar Guard to enforce its decisions—there will be war until man is extinct. Earth could not be allowed to secede. Therefore, Mars and Venus aided the counterrevolutionary, anti-Humanist cabal that wanted to restore liberty and Union membership to the mother planet. Therefore, too, a space fleet was raised to support the uprising when it came.

"Don't you see? Every step was an unavoidable consequence, by the logic of survival, of all that had gone before."

"Correct so far, Professor," I nodded. "But the success of the counterrevolution and the Mars-Venus intervention was by no means guaranteed. Mars and Venus were still frontiers, thinly populated, only recently made habitable. They didn't have the military potential of Earth.

"The cabal was well organized. Its well-timed mutinies swept Earth's newly created pro-Humanist ground and air forces before it. The countryside, the oceans, even the cities were soon cleared of Humanist troops.

"But Dictator Carnarvon and the men still loyal to him were holed up in a score of fortresses. Oh, it would have been easy enough to dig them out or blast them out—except that the navy of sovereign Earth, organized from seized units of the Solar Guard, had also remained loyal to Humanism. Its Cinc, Admiral K'ung, had acted promptly when the revolt began, jailing all personnel he wasn't sure of . . . or shooting them. Only a few got away.

"So there the pro-Union revolutionaries were, in possession of Earth but with a good five hundred enemy warships orbiting above them. K'ung's strategy was simple. He broadcast that unless the rebels surrendered inside one week—or if meanwhile they made any attempt on Carnarvon's remaining strongholds—he'd start bombarding with nuclear weapons. That, of course, would kill perhaps a hundred million civilians, flatten the factories, poison the sea ranches . . . he'd turn the planet into a butcher shop.

"Under such a threat, the general population was no longer backing the Union cause. They clamored for surrender; they began raising armies. Suddenly the victorious rebels had enemies not merely in front and above them, but behind . . . everywhere!

"Meanwhile, as you all know, the Unionist fleet under Dushanovitch-Alvarez had rendezvoused off Luna; as mixed a bunch of Martians, Venusians, and freedom-minded Earthmen as history ever saw. They were much inferior both in strength and organization; it was impossible for them to charge in and give battle with any hope of winning . . . but Dushanovitch-Alvarez had a plan. It depended on luring the Humanist fleet out to engage him.

"Only Admiral K'ung wasn't having any. The Unionist command knew, from deserters, that most of his captains wanted to go out and annihilate the invaders first, returning to deal with Earth at their leisure. It was a costly nuisance, the Unionists sneaking in, firing and retreating, blowing up ship after ship of the Humanist forces. But K'ung had the final word, and he would not accept the challenge until the rebels on the ground had capitulated. He was negotiating with them now, and it looked very much as if they would give in.

"So there it was, the entire outcome of the war—the whole history of man, for if you will pardon my saying so, gentles, Earth is still the key planet—everything hanging on this one officer, Grand Admiral K'ung Li-Po, a grim man who had given his oath and had a damnably good grasp of the military facts of life."

I took a long draught from my mug and began the story, using the third-person form which is customary on Mars.

The speedster blasted at four gees till she was a bare five hundred kilometers from the closest enemy vessels. Her radar screens jittered with their nearness and in the thunder of abused hearts her crew sat waiting for the doomsday of a homing missile. Then she was at the calculated point, she spat her cargo out the main lock and leaped ahead still more furiously. In moments the thin glare of her jets was lost among crowding stars.

The cargo was three spacesuited men, linked to a giant air tank and burdened with a variety of tools. The orbit into which they had been flung was aligned with that of the Humanist fleet, so that relative velocity was low.

In cosmic terms, that is. It still amounted to nearly a thousand kilometers per hour and was enough, unchecked, to spatter the men against an armored hull.

Lieutenant Robert Crane pulled himself along the light cable that bound him, up to the tank. His hands groped in the pitchy gloom of shadowside. Then all at once rotation had brought him into the moonlight and he could see. He found the rungs and went hand over hand along the curve of the barrel, centrifugal force streaming his body outward. Damn the clumsiness of space armor! Awkwardly, he got one foot into a stirrup-like arrangement and scrambled around until he was in the "saddle" with both boots firmly locked; then he unclipped the line from his waist.

The stars turned about him in a cold majestic wheel. Luna was nearly at the full, ashen pale, scored and pocked and filling his helmet with icy luminescence. Earth was an enormous grayness in the sky, a half ring of blinding light from the hidden sun along one side.

Twisting a head made giddy by the spinning, he saw the other two mounted behind him. García was in the middle—you could always tell a Venusian; he painted his clan markings on his suit—and the Martian Wolf at the end. "Okay," he said, incongruously aware that the throat mike pinched his Adam's apple, "let's stop this merry-go-round."

His hands moved across a simple control panel. A tangentially mounted nozzle opened, emitting an invisible stream of air. The stars slowed their lunatic dance, steadied . . . hell and sunfire, now he'd overcompensated, give it a blast from the other side . . . the tank was no longer in rotation. He was not hanging head downward, but falling, a long weightless tumble through a sterile infinity.

Three men rode a barrel of compressed air toward the massed fleet of Earth.

"Any radar reading?" García's voice was tinny in the earphones.

"A moment, if you please, till I have it set up." Wolf extended a telescoping mast, switched on the portable 'scope, and began sweeping the sky. "Nearest indication . . . um . . . one o'clock, five degrees low, four hundred twenty-two kilometers distant." He added radial and linear velocity, and García worked an astrogator's slide rule, swearing at the tricky light.

The baseline was not the tank, but its velocity, which could be assumed straight-line for so short a distance. Actually, the weird horse had its nose pointed a full thirty degrees off the direction of movement. "High" and "low," in weightlessness, were simply determined by the plane bisecting the tank, with the men's heads arbitrarily designated as "aimed up."

The airbarrel had jets aligned in three planes, as well as the rotation-controlling tangential nozzles. With Wolf and García to correct him, Crane blended vectors until they were on a course that would nearly intercept the ship. Gas was released from the forward jet at a rate calculated to match velocity.

Crane had nothing but the gauges to tell him that he was braking. Carefully dehydrated air emerges quite invisibly, and its ionization is negligible; there was no converter to radiate, and all equipment was painted a dead nonreflecting black.

Soundless and invisible—too small and fast for a chance eye to see in the uncertain moonlight, for a chance radar beam to register as anything worth buzzing an alarm about. Not enough infrared for detection, not enough mass, no trail of ions—the machinists on the *Thor* had wrought well, the astrogators had figured as closely as men and computers are able. But in the end it was only a tank of compressed air, a bomb, a few tools, and three men frightened and lonely.

"How long will it take us to get there?" asked Crane. His throat was dry and he swallowed hard.

"About forty-five minutes to that ship we're zeroed in on," García told him. "After that, *quien sabe?* We'll have to locate the *Monitor.*"

"Be most economical with the air, if you please," said Wolf. "We also have to get back."

"Tell me more," snorted Crane.

"If this works," remarked García, "we'll have added a new weapon to the System's arsenals. That's why I volunteered. If Antonio García of Hesperus gets his name in the history books, my whole clan will contribute to give me the biggest ranch on Venus."

They were an anachronism, thought Crane, a resurrection from old days when war was a wilder business. The psychotechs had not picked a team for compatibility, nor welded them into an unbreakable brotherhood. They had merely grabbed the first three willing to try an untested scheme. There wasn't time for anything else. In another forty hours, the pro-Union armies on Earth would either have surrendered or the bombardment would begin.

"Why are you lads here?" went on the Venusian. "We might as well get acquainted."

"I took an oath," said Wolf. There was nothing priggish about it; Martians thought that way.

"What of you, Crane?"

"I . . . it looked like fun," said the Earthman lamely. "And it might end this damned war."

He lied and he knew so, but how do you explain? Do you admit it was an escape from your shipmates' eyes?

Not that his going over to the rebels had shamed him. Everyone aboard the *Marduk* had done so, except for a couple of CPOs who were now under guard in Aphrodite. The cruiser had been on patrol off Venus when word of Earth's secession had flashed. Her captain had declared for the Union and the Guard to which he belonged, and the crew cheered him for it.

For two years, while Dushanovitch-Alvarez, half idealist and half buccaneer, was assembling the Unionist fleet, intelligence reports trickled in from Earth. Mutiny was being organized, and men escaped from those Guard vessels—the bulk of the old space service—that had been at the mother planet and were seized to make a navy. Just before the Unionists accelerated for rendezvous, a list of the new captains appointed by K'ung had been received. And the skipper of the *Huitzilopochli* was named Benjamin Crane.

Ben . . . what did you do when your brother was on the enemy side? Dushanovitch-Alvarez had let the System know that a bombardment of Earth would be regarded as genocide and all officers partaking in it would be punished under Union law. It seemed unlikely that there would be any Union to try the case, but Lieutenant Robert Crane of the *Marduk* had protested: this was not a normal police operation, it was war, and executing men who merely obeyed the government they had pledged to uphold was opening the gates to a darker barbarism than the fighting itself. The Unionist force was too shorthanded, it could not give Lieutenant Crane more than a public reproof for insubordination, but his messmates had tended to grow silent when he entered the wardroom.

If the superdreadnaught *Monitor* could be destroyed, and K'ung with it, Earth might not be bombarded. Then if the Unionists won, Ben would go free, or he would die cleanly in battle—reason enough to ride this thing into the Humanist fleet!

Silence was cold in their helmets.

"I've been thinking," said García. "Suppose we do carry this off, but they decide to blast Earth anyway before dealing with our boats. What then?"

"Then they blast Earth," said Wolf. "Though most likely they won't have to. Last I heard, the threat alone was making folk rise against our friends on the ground there." Moonlight shimmered along his arm as he pointed at the darkened planet-shield before them. "So the Humanists will be back in power, and even if we chop up their navy, we won't win unless we do some bombarding of our own."

"*Madre de Dios!*" García crossed himself, a barely visible gesture in the unreal flood of undiffused light. "I'll mutiny before I give my name to such a thing."

"And I," said Wolf shortly. "And most of us, I think."

It was not that the Union fleet was crewed by saints, thought Crane. Most of its personnel had signed on for booty; the System knew how much treasure was locked in the vaults of Earth's dictators. But the horror of nuclear war had been too deeply graven for anyone but a fanatic at the point of desperation to think of using it.

Even in K'ung's command, there must be talk of revolt. Since his ultimatum, deserters in lifeboats had brought Dushanovitch-Alvarez a mountain of precise information. But the Humanists had had ten years in which to build a hard cadre of hard young officers to keep the men obedient.

Strange to know that Ben was with them—*why?*

I haven't seen you in more than two years now, Ben—nor my own wife and children, but tonight it is you who dwell in me, and I have not felt such pain for many years. Not since that time we were boys together, and you were sick one day, and I went alone down the steep bluffs above the Mississippi. There I found the old man denned up under the trees, a tramp, one of many millions for whom there was no place in this new world of shining machines—but he was not embittered, he drew his citizen's allowance and tramped the planet and he had stories to tell me which our world of bright hard metal had forgotten. He told me about Br'er Rabbit and the briar patch; never had I heard such a story, it was the first time I knew the rich dark humor of the earth itself. And you got well, Ben, and I took you down to his camp, but he was gone and you never heard the story of Br'er Rabbit. On that day, Ben, I was as close to weeping as I am right this night of murder.

The minutes dragged past. Only numbers went between the three men on the tank, astrogational corrections. They sat, each in his own skull with his own thoughts.

The vessel on which they had zeroed came into plain view, a long black shark swimming against the Milky Way. They passed within two kilometers of her. Wolf was busy now, flicking his radar around the sky, telling off ships. It was mostly seat-of-the-pants piloting, low relative velocities and small distances, edging into the mass of Earth's fleet. That was not a very dense mass; kilometers gaped between each unit. The *Monitor* was in the inner ring; a deserter had given them the approximate orbit.

"You're pretty good at this, boy," said García.

"I rode a scooter in the asteroids for a couple of years," answered Crane. "Patrol and rescue duty."

That was when there had still been only the Guard, one fleet and one flag. Crane had never liked the revolutionary government of Earth, but while the Union remained and the only navy was the Guard and its only task to help any and all men, he had been reasonably content. Please God, that day would come again.

Slowly, over the minutes, the *Monitor* grew before him, a giant spheroid never meant to land on a planet. He could see gun turrets scrawled black across remote star-clouds. There was more reason for destroying her than basic strategy—luring the Humanists out to do battle; more than good tactics—built only last year, she was the most formidable engine of war in the Solar System. It would be the annihilation of a symbol. The *Monitor,* alone among ships that rode the sky, was designed with no other purpose than killing.

Slow, now, easy, gauge the speeds by eye, remember how much inertia you've got . . . Edge up, brake, throw out a magnetic anchor and grapple fast. Crane turned a small winch, the cable tautened and he bumped against the hull.

Nobody spoke. They had work to do, and their short-range radio might have been detected. García unshipped the bomb. Crane held it while the Venusian scrambled from the saddle and got a firm boot-grip on the dreadnaught. The bomb didn't have a large mass. Crane handed it over, and García slapped it onto the hull, gripped by a magnetic plate. Stooping, he wound a spring and jerked a lever. Then, with a spaceman's finicking care, he returned to the saddle. Crane paid out the cable till it ran off the drum; they were free of their grapple.

In twenty minutes, the clockwork was to set off the bomb. It was a little one, plutonium fission, and most of its energy would be wasted on vacuum. Enough would remain to smash the *Monitor* into a hundred fragments.

Crane worked the airjets, forcing himself to be calm and deliberate. The barrel swung about to point at Luna, and he opened the rear throttle wide. Acceleration tugged at him, he braced his feet in the stirrups and hung on with both hands. Behind them, the *Monitor* receded, borne on her own orbit around a planet where terror walked.

When they were a good fifteen kilometers away, he asked for a course. His voice felt remote, as if it came from outside his prickling skin. Most of him wondered just how many men were aboard the dreadnought and how many wives and children they had to weep for them. Wolf squinted through a sextant and gave his readings to García. Corrections made, they rode toward the point of rendezvous: a point so tricky to compute, in this Solar System where the planets were never still, that they would doubtless not come within a hundred kilometers of the speedster that was to pick them up. But they had a hand-cranked radio that would broadcast a signal for the boat to get a fix on them.

How many minutes had they been going? Ten . . . ? Crane looked at the clock in the control panel. Yes, ten. Another five or so, at this acceleration, ought to see them beyond the outermost orbit of the Humanist ships—

He did not hear the explosion. A swift and terrible glare opened inside his helmet, enough light reflected off the inner surface for his eyes to swim in white-hot blindness. He clung to his seat, nerves and muscles tensed against the hammer blow that never came. The haze parted raggedly, and he turned his head back toward Earth. A wan nimbus of incandescent gas hung there. A few tattered stars glowed blue as they fled from it.

Wolf's voice whispered in his ears: "She's gone already. The bomb went off ahead of schedule. Something in the clockwork—"

"But she's gone!" García let out a rattling whoop. "No more flagship. We got her, lads, we got the stinking can!"

Not far away was a shadow visible only when it blocked off the stars. A ship . . . light cruiser— "Cram on the air!" said Wolf roughly. "Let's get the devil out of here."

"I can't." Crane snarled it, still dazed, wanting only to rest and forget every war that ever was. "We've only got so much pressure left, and none to spare for maneuvering if we get off course."

"All right . . ." They lapsed into silence. That which had been the *Monitor,* gas and shrapnel, dissipated. The enemy cruiser fell behind them, and Luna filled their eyes with barren radiance.

They were not aware of pursuit until the squad was almost on them. There were a dozen men in combat armor, driven by individual jet-units and carrying rifles. They overhauled the tank and edged in— less gracefully than fish, for they had no friction to kill forward velocity, but they moved in.

After the first leap of his heart, Crane felt cold and numb. None of his party bore arms: they themselves had been the weapon, and now it was discharged. In a mechanical fashion, he turned his headset to the standard band.

"Rebels ahoy!" The voice was strained close to breaking, an American voice. . . . For a moment such a wave of homesickness for the green dales of Wisconsin went over Crane that he could not move nor realize he had been captured. "Stop that thing and come with us!"

In sheer reflex, Crane opened the rear throttles full. The barrel jumped ahead, almost ripping him from the saddle. Ions flared behind as the enemy followed. Their units were beam-powered from the ship's nuclear engines, and they had plenty of reaction mass in their tanks. It was only a moment before they were alongside again.

Arms closed around Crane, dragging him from his seat. As the universe tilted about his head, he saw Wolf likewise caught. García sprang to meet an Earthman, hit him and bounced away but got his rifle. A score of bullets must have spat. Suddenly the Venusian's armor blew white clouds of freezing water vapor and he drifted dead.

Wolf wrestled in vacuum and tore one hand free. Crane heard him croak over the radio: "They'll find out—" Another frosty geyser erupted; Wolf had opened his own air-tubes.

Men closed in on either side of Crane, pinioning his arms. He could not have suicided even if he chose to. The rest flitted near, guns ready. He relaxed, too weary and dazed to fight, and let them face him around and kill forward speed, then accelerate toward the cruiser.

The airlock was opening for him before he had his voice back. "What ship is this?" he asked, not caring much, only filling in an emptiness.

"*Huitzilopochtli.* Get in there with you."

Crane floated weightless in the wardroom, his left ankle manacled to a stanchion. They had removed his armor, leaving the thick gray coverall which was the underpadding, and given him a stimpill. A young officer guarded him, sidearm holstered; no reason to fear a fettered captive. The officer did not speak, though horror lay on his lips.

The pill had revived Crane, his body felt supple and he sensed every detail of the room with an unnatural clarity. But his heart had a thick beat and his mouth felt cottony.

This was Ben's ship.

García and Wolf were dead.

None of it was believable.

"Sir . . ."

Ben's head turned, and Robert saw, with an odd little sadness, gray streaks at the temples. What was his age—thirty-one? *My kid brother is growing old already.*

"Yes, Mr. Nicholson?"

The officer cleared his throat. "Sir, shouldn't the prisoner be interrogated in the regular way? He must know a good deal about—"

"I assure you, not about our orbits and dispositions," said Robert Crane with what coolness he could summon. "We change them quite often."

"Obviously," agreed Ben. "They don't want us to raid them as they've been raiding us. We have to stay in orbit because of our strategy. They don't, and they'd be fools if they did."

"Still . . ." began Nicholson.

"Oh, yes, Intelligence will be happy to pump him," said Ben.

"Though I suspect this show will be over before they've gotten much information of value. Vice Admiral Hokusai of the *Krishna* has succeeded to command. Get on the radio, Mr. Nicholson, and report what has happened. In the meantime, I'll question the prisoner myself. Privately."

"Yes, sir." The officer saluted and went out. There was compassion in his eyes.

Ben closed the door behind him. Then he turned around and floated, crossing his legs, one hand on a stanchion and the other rubbing his forehead. His brother had known he would do exactly that. *But how accurately can he read me?*

"Well, Bob." Ben's tone was gentle.

Robert Crane shifted, feeling the link about his ankle. "How are Mary and the kids?" he asked.

"Oh . . . quite well, thank you. I'm afraid I can't tell you much about your own family. Last I heard, they were living in Manitowoc Unit, but in the confusion since . . ." Ben looked away. "They were never bothered by our police, though. I have some little influence."

"Thanks," said Robert. Bitterness broke forth: "Yours are safe in Luna City. Mine will get the fallout when you bombard, or they'll starve in the famine to follow."

The captain's mouth wrenched. "Don't say that!" After a moment: "Do you think I like the idea of shooting at Earth? If you so-called liberators really give a curse in hell about the people their hearts bleed for so loudly, they'll surrender first. We're offering terms. They'll be allowed to go to Mars or Venus."

"I'm afraid you misjudge us, Ben," said Robert. "Do you know why I'm here? It wasn't simply a matter of being on the *Marduk* when she elected to stay with the Union. I believed in the liberation."

"Believe in those pirates out there?" Ben's finger stabbed at the wall, as if to pierce it and show the stars and the hostile ships swimming between.

"Oh, sure, they've been promised the treasure vaults. We had to raise men and ships somehow. What good was that money doing, locked away by Carnarvon and his gang?" Robert shrugged. "Look, I was born and raised in America. We were always a free people. The Bill of Rights was molded on our own old Ten Amendments. From the moment the Humanists seized power, I had to start watching what I said, who I associated with, what tapes I got from the library. My kids were growing up into perfect little parrots. It was too much. When the purges began, when the police fired on crowds rioting because they were starving—and they were starving because this quasi-religious creed cannot accept the realities and organize things rationally—I was only waiting for my chance.

"Ben, be honest. Wouldn't you have signed on with us if you'd been on the *Marduk?*"

The face before him was gray. "Don't ask me that! No!"

"I can tell you exactly why not, Ben." Robert folded his arms and would not let his brother's eyes go. "I know you well enough. We're different in one respect. To you, no principle can be as important as your wife and children—and they're hostages for your good behavior. Oh, yes, K'ung's psychotechs evaluated you very carefully. Probably half their captains are held by just such chains."

Ben laughed, a loud bleak noise above the murmur of the ventilators. "Have it your way. And don't forget that your family is alive, too, because I stayed with the government. I'm not going to change, either. A government, even the most arbitrary one, can perhaps be altered in time. But the dead never come back to life."

He leaned forward, suddenly shuddering. "Bob, I don't want you sent Earthside for interrogation. They'll not only drug you, they'll set about changing your whole viewpoint. Surgery, shock, a rebuilt personality—you won't be the same man when they've finished.

"I can wangle something else. I have enough pull, especially now in the confusion after your raid, to keep you here. When the war is settled, I'll arrange for your escape. There's going to be so much hullaballoo on Earth that nobody will notice. But you'll have to help me, in turn.

"*What was the real purpose of your raid? What plans does your high command have?*"

For a time which seemed to become very long, Robert Crane waited. He was being asked to betray his side voluntarily; the alternative was to do it anyway, after the psychmen got through with him. Ben had no authority to make the decision. It would mean court-martial later, and punishment visited on his family as well, unless he could justify it by claiming quicker results than the long-drawn process of narcosynthesis.

The captain's hands twisted together, big knobby hands, and he stared at them. "This is a hell of a choice for you, I know," he mumbled. "But there's Mary and . . . the kids, and men here who trust me. Good decent men. We aren't fiends, believe me. But I can't deny my own shipmates a fighting chance to get home alive."

Robert Crane wet his lips. "How do you know I'll tell the truth?" he asked.

Ben looked up again, crinkling his eyes. "We had a formula once," he said. "Remember? 'Cross my heart and hope to die, spit in my eye if I tell a lie.' I don't think either of us ever lied when we took that oath."

"And— Ben, the whole war hangs on this, maybe. Do you seriously think I'd keep my word for a kid's chant if it could decide the war?"

"Oh, no." A smile ghosted across the captain's mouth. "But there's going to be a meeting of skippers, if I know Hokusai. He'll want the opinions of us all as to what we should do next. Having heard them, he'll make his own decision. I'll be one voice among a lot of others.

"But if I can speak with whatever information you've given me . . . do you understand? The council will meet long before you could be sent Earthside and quizzed. I need your knowledge *now.* I'll listen to whatever you have to say. I may or may not believe you . . . I'll make my own decision as to what to recommend . . . but it's the only way I can save you, and myself, and everything else I care about."

He waited then, patiently as the circling ships. They must have come around the planet by now, thought Robert Crane. The sun would be drowning many stars, and Earth would be daylit if you looked out.

Captains' council. . . . It sounded awkward and slow, when at any moment, as far as they knew, Dushanovitch-Alvarez might come in at the head of his fleet. But after all, the navy would remain on general alert, second officers would be left in charge. They had time.

And they would want time. Nearly every one of them had kin on Earth. None wished to explode radioactive death across the world they loved. K'ung's will had been like steel, but now they would— subconsciously, and the more powerfully for that—be looking for any way out of the frightful necessity. A respected officer, giving good logical reasons for postponing the bombardment, would be listened to by the keenest ears.

Robert Crane shivered. It was a heartless load to put on a man. The dice of future history . . . he could load the dice, because he knew Ben as any man knows a dear brother, but maybe his hand would slip while he loaded them.

"Well?" It was a grating in the captain's throat.

Robert drew a long breath. "All right," he said.

"Yes?" A high, cracked note; Ben must be near breaking, too.

"I'm not in command, you realize." Robert's words were blurred with haste. "I can't tell for sure what— But I do know we've got fewer ships. A lot fewer."

"I suspected that."

"We have some plan—I haven't been told what—it depends on making you leave this orbit and come out and fight us where we are. If you stay home, we can't do a damn thing. This raid of mine . . . we'd hoped that your admiral dead, you'd join battle out toward Luna."

Robert Crane hung in the air, twisting in its currents, the breath gasping in and out of him. Ben looked dim, across the room, as if his eyes were failing.

"Is that the truth, Bob?" The question seemed to come from light-years away.

"Yes. Yes. I can't let you go and get killed and— Cross my heart and hope to die, spit in my eye if I tell a lie!"

I set down my mug, empty, and signaled for another. The bartender glided across the floor with it and I drank thirstily, remembering how my throat had felt mummified long ago on the *Huitzilopochtli*, remembering much else.

"Very well, sir." Freylinghausen's testy voice broke a stillness. "What happened?"

"You ought to know that, Professor," I replied. "It's in the history tapes. The Humanist fleet decided to go out at once and dispose of its inferior opponent. Their idea—correct, I suppose—was that a space victory would be so demoralizing that the rebels on the ground would capitulate immediately after. It would have destroyed the last hope of reinforcements, you see."

"And the Union fleet won," said Neilsen-Singh. "They chopped the Humanist navy into fishbait. I know. My father was there. We bought a dozen new reclamation units with his share of the loot, afterward."

"Naval history is out of my line, Captain Crane," said the engineer, Buwono. "How did Dushanovitch-Alvarez win?"

"Oh . . . by a combination of things. Chiefly, he disposed his ships and gave them such velocities that the enemy, following the usual principles of tactics, moved at high accelerations to close in. And at a point where they would have built up a good big speed, he had a lot of stuff planted, rocks and ball bearings and scrap iron . . . an artificial meteoroid swarm, moving in an opposed orbit. After that had done its work, the two forces were on very nearly equal strength, and it became a battle of standard weapons. Which Dushanovitch-Alvarez knew how to use! A more brilliant naval mind hasn't existed since Lord Nelson."

"Yes, yes," said Freylinghausen impatiently. "But what has this to do with the subject under discussion?"

"Don't you see, Professor? It was chance right down the line— chance which was skillfully exploited when it arose, to be sure, but nevertheless a set of unpredictable accidents. The *Monitor* blew up ten minutes ahead of schedule; as a result, the commando that did it was captured. Normally, this would have meant that the whole plan would have been given away. I can't emphasize too strongly that the Humanists would have won if they'd only stayed where they were."

I tossed off a long gulp of porter, knocked the dottle from my pipe, and began refilling it. My hands weren't quite steady. "But chance entered here, too, making Robert Crane's brother the man to capture him. And Robert knew how to manipulate Ben. At the captain's council, the *Huitzilopochtli's* skipper spoke the most strongly in favor of going out to do battle. His arguments, especially when everyone knew they were based on information obtained from a prisoner, convinced the others."

"But you said . . ." Neilsen-Singh looked confused.

"Yes, I did." I smiled at her, though my thoughts were entirely in the past. "But it wasn't till years later that Ben heard the story of Br'er Rabbit and the briar patch; he came across it in his brother's boyhood diary. Robert Crane told the truth, swore to it by a boyhood oath— but his brother could not believe he'd yield so easily. Robert was almost begging him to stay with K'ung's original plan. Ben was sure that was an outright lie . . . that Dushanovitch-Alvarez must actually be planning to attack the navy in its orbit and could not possibly survive a battle in open space. So that, of course, was what he argued for at the council."

"It took nerve, though," said Neilsen-Singh. "Knowing what the *Huitzilopochtli* would have to face . . . knowing you'd be aboard, too. . . ."

"She was a wreck by the time the battle was over," I said. "Not many in her survived."

After a moment, Buwono nodded thoughtfully. "I see your point, Captain. The accident of the bomb's going off too soon almost wrecked the Union plan. The accident of that brotherhood saved it. A thread of coincidences . . . yes, I think you've proved your case."

"I'm afraid not, gentles." Freylinghausen darted birdlike eyes around the table. "You misunderstood me. I was not speaking of minor ripples in the mainstream of history. Certainly those are ruled by chance. But the broad current moves quite inexorably, I assure you. *Vide:* Earth and Luna are back in the Union under a more or less democratic government, but no solution has yet been found to the problems which brought forth the Humanists. They will come again; under one name or another they will return. The war was merely a ripple."

"Maybe." I spoke with inurbane curtness, not liking the thought. "We'll see."

"If nothing else," said Neilsen-Singh, "you people bought for Earth a few more decades of freedom. They can't take that away from you."

I looked at her with sudden respect. It was true. Men died and civilizations died, but before they died they lived. No effort was altogether futile.

I could not remain here, though. I had told the story, as I must always tell it, and now I needed aloneness.

"Excuse me." I finished my drink and stood up. "I have an appointment . . . just dropped in . . . very happy to have met you, gentles."

Buwono rose with the others and bowed formally. "I trust we shall have the pleasure of your company again, Captain Robert Crane."

"Robert—? Oh." I stopped. I had told what I must in third person, but everything had seemed so obvious. "I'm sorry. Robert Crane was killed in the battle. I am Captain Benjamin Crane, at your service, gentles."

I bowed to them and went out the door. The night was lonesome in the streets and across the desert.

Melancholy and regret afflicted many in that era. Both the Humanists and the Psychotechnic Institute had failed. Rebel exposures of the faltering Institute's prewar machinations made its revival unthinkable. Nevertheless, strictly regulated "tame" psychotechnicians continued to serve the victorious Union government with the Institute's techniques. Their surviving research institutions fell under closer scrutiny lest they succumb to the same corruption.

Although the majority of Earthlings grudgingly accepted their dependence on advanced technology, they were no more satisfied with their lot than before the Revolt. Some sought private pleasures; others searched quietly for new solutions. But now Science was to be held accountable both for what it could do and for what it should do.

What Shall It Profit?

"THE CHICKENS got out of the coop and flew away three hundred years ago," said Barwell. "Now they're coming home to roost."

He hiccoughed. His finger wobbled to the dial and clicked off another whisky. The machine pondered the matter and flashed an apologetic sign: *Please deposit your money.*

"Oh, damn," said Barwell. "I'm broke."

Radek shrugged and gave the slot a two-credit piece. It slid the whisky out on a tray with his change. He stuck the coins in his pouch and took another careful sip of beer.

Barwell grabbed the whisky glass like a drowning man. He *would* drown, thought Radek, if he sloshed much more into his stomach.

There was an Asian whine to the music drifting past the curtains into the booth. Radek could hear the talk and laughter well enough to catch their raucous overtones. Somebody swore as dice rattled wrong for him. Somebody else shouted coarse good wishes as his friend took a hostess upstairs.

He wondered why vice was always so cheerless when you went into a place and paid for it.

"I am going to get drunk tonight," announced Barwell. "I am going to get so high in the stony sky you'll need radar to find me. Then I shall raise the red flag of revolution."

"And tomorrow?" asked Radek quietly.

Barwell grimaced. "Don't ask me about tomorrow. Tomorrow I will be among the great leisure class—to hell with euphemisms—the unemployed. Nothing I can do that some goddam machine can't do quicker and better. So a benevolent state will feed me and clothe me and house me and give me a little spending money to have fun on. This is known as citizen's credit. They used to call it a dole. Tomorrow I shall have to be more systematic about the revolution—join the League or something."

"The trouble with you," Radek needled him, "is that you can't adapt. Technology has made the labor of most people, except the first-rank creative genius, unnecessary. This leaves the majority with a void of years to fill somehow—a sense of uprootedness and lost self-respect— which is rather horrible. And in any case, they don't like to think in scientific terms . . . it doesn't come natural to the average man."

Barwell gave him a bleary stare out of a flushed, sagging face. "I s'pose you're one of the geniuses," he said. "You got work."

"I'm adaptable," said Radek. He was a slim youngish man with dark hair and sharp features. "I'm not greatly gifted, but I found a niche for myself. Newsman. I do legwork for a major commentator. Between times, I'm writing a book—my own analysis of contemporary historical trends. It won't be anything startling, but it may help a few people think more clearly and adjust themselves."

"And so you *like* this rotten Solar Union?" Barwell's tone became aggressive.

"Not everything about it no. So there is a wave of anti-scientific reaction, all over Earth. Science is being made the scapegoat for all our troubles. But like it or not, you fellows will have to accept the fact that there are too many people and too few resources for us to survive without technology."

"Some technology, sure," admitted Barwell. He took a ferocious swig from his glass. "Not this hell-born stuff we've been monkeying around with. I tell you, the chickens have finally come home to roost."

Radek was intrigued by the archaic expression. Barwell was no moron: he'd been a correlative clerk at the Institute for several years, not a position for fools. He had read, actually read books, and thought about them. And today he had been fired. Radek chanced across him drinking out a vast resentment and attached himself like a reverse lamprey—buying most of the liquor. There might be a story in it, somewhere. There might be a lead to what the Institute was doing.

Radek was not anti-scientific, but neither did he make gods out of people with technical degrees. The Institute *must* be up to something unpleasant . . . otherwise, why all the mystery? If the facts weren't uncovered in time, if whatever they were brewing came to a head, it could touch off the final convulsion of lynch law.

Barwell leaned forward, his finger wagged. "Three hundred years now. I think it's three hundred years since X-rays came in. Damn scientists, fooling around with X-rays, atomic energy, radioactives . . . sure, safe levels, established tolerances, but what about the long-range effects? What about cumulative genetic effects? Those chickens are coming home at last."

"No use blaming our ancestors," said Radek. "Be rather pointless to go dance on their graves, wouldn't it?"

Barwell moved closer to Radek. His breath was powerful with whisky. "But are they in those graves?" he whispered.

"Huh?"

"Look. Been known for a long time, ever since first atomic energy work . . . heavy but nonlethal doses of radiation shorten lifespan. You grow old faster if you get a strong dose. Why d'you think with all our medicines we're not two, three hundred years old? Background count's gone up, that's why! Radioactives in the air, in the sea, buried under the ground. Gamma rays, not *entirely* absorbed by shielding. Sure, sure, they tell us the level is still harmless. But it's more than the level in nature by a good big factor—two or three."

Radek sipped his beer. He'd been drinking slowly, and the beer had gotten warmer than he liked, but he needed a clear head. "That's common knowledge," he stated. "The lifespan hasn't been shortened any, either."

"Because of more medicines . . . more ways to help cells patch up radiation damage. All but worst radiation sickness been curable for a long time." Barwell waved his hand expansively. "They knew, even back then," he mumbled. "If radiation shortens life, radiation sickness cures ought to prolong it. Huh? Reas'nable? Only the goddam scientists . . . population problem . . . social stasis if ever'body lived for centuries . . . kept it secret. Easy t' do. Change y'r name and face ever' ten, twen'y years—keep to y'rself, don't make friends among the short-lived, you might see 'em grow old and die, might start feelin' sorry for 'em an' that would never do, would it—?"

Coldness tingled along Radek's spine. He lifted his mug and pretended to drink. Over the rim, his eyes stayed on Barwell.

"Tha's why they fired me. I know. I know. I got ears. I overheard things. I read . . . notes not inten'ed for me. They fired me. 'S a wonder they didn' murder me." Barwell shuddered and peered at the curtains, as if trying to look through them. "Or d'y' think—maybe—"

"No," said Radek. "I don't. Let's stick to the facts. I take it you found mention of work on—shall we say—increasing the lifespan. Perhaps a mention of successes with rats and guinea pigs. Right? So what's wrong with that? They wouldn't want to announce anything till they were sure, or the hysteria—"

Barwell smiled with an irritating air of omniscience. "More'n that, friend. More'n that. Lots more."

"Well, what?"

Barwell peered about him with exaggerated caution. One thing I found in files . . . plans of whole buildin's an' groun's—great, great big room, lotsa rooms, way way underground. Secret. Only th' kitchen was makin' food an' sendin' it down there—human food. Food for people I never saw, people who never came up—" Barwell buried his face in his hands. "Don' feel so good. Whirlin'—"

Radek eased his head to the table. Out like a spent credit. The newsman left the booth and addressed a bouncer. "Chap in there has had it."

"Uh-huh. Want me to help you get him to your boat?"

"No. I hardly know him." A bill exchanged hands. "Put him in your dossroom to sleep it off, and give him breakfast with my compliments. I'm going out for some fresh air."

The rec house stood on a Minnesota bluff, overlooking the Mississippi River. Beyond its racket and multi-colored glare, there was darkness and wooded silence. Here and there the lights of a few isolated houses gleamed. The river slid by, talking, ruffled with moonlight. Luna was nearly full; squinting into her cold ashen face, Radek could just see the tiny spark of a city. Stars were strewn carelessly over heaven, he recognized the ember that was Mars.

Perhaps he ought to emigrate. Mars, Venus, even Luna . . . there was more hope on them than Earth had. No mechanical packaged cheer: people had work to do, and in their spare time made their own pleasures. No civilization cracking at the seams because it could not assimilate the technology it must have; out in space, men knew very well that science had carried them to their homes and made those homes fit to dwell on.

Radek strolled across the parking lot and found his airboat. He paused by its iridescent teardrop to start a cigarette.

Suppose the Institute of Human Biology was more than it claimed to be, more than a set of homes and laboratories where congenial minds could live and do research. It published discoveries of value— but how much did it not publish? Its personnel kept pretty aloof from the rest of the world, not unnatural in this day of growing estrangement between science and public . . . but did they have a deeper reason than that?

Suppose they did keep immortals in those underground rooms.

A scientist was not ordinarily a good political technician. He might react emotionally against a public beginning to throw stones at his house and consider taking the reins . . . for the people's own good, of course. A lot of misery had been caused the human race for its own alleged good.

Or if the scientist knew how to live forever, he might not think Joe Smith or Carlos Ibanez or Wang Yuan or Johannes Umfanduma good enough to share immorality with him.

Radek took a long breath. The night air felt fresh and alive in his lungs after the tavern staleness.

He was not currently married, but there was a girl with whom he was thinking seriously of making a permanent contract. He had friends, not lucent razor minds but decent, unassuming, kindly people, brave with man's old quiet bravery in the face of death and ruin and the petty tragedies of everyday. He liked beer and steaks, fishing and tennis, good music and a good book and the exhilarating strain of his work. He liked to live.

Maybe a system for becoming immortal, or at least living many centuries, was not desirable for the race. But only the whole race had authority to make that decision.

Radek smiled at himself, twistedly, and threw the cigarette away and got into the boat. Its engine murmured, sucking 'cast power; the riding lights snapped on automatically and he lifted into the sky. It was not much of a lead he had, but it was as good as he was ever likely to get.

He set the autopilot for southwest Colorado and opened the jets wide. The night whistled darkly around his cabin. Against wan stars, he made out the lamps of other boats, flitting across the world and somehow intensifying the loneliness.

Work to do. He called the main office in Dallas Unit and taped a statement of what he knew and what he planned. Then he dialed the nearest library and asked the robot for information on the Institute of Human Biology.

There wasn't a great deal of value to him. It had been in existence for about 250 years, more or less concurrently with the Psychotechnic Institute and for quite a while affiliated with that organization. During the Humanist troubles, when the Psychotechs were booted out of government on Earth and their files ransacked, it had dissociated itself from them and carried on unobtrusively. (How much of their secret records had it taken along?) Since the Restoration, it had grown, drawing in many prominent researchers and making discoveries of high value to medicine and bio-engineering. The current director was Dr. Marcus Lang, formerly of New Harvard, the University of Luna, and— No matter. He'd been running the show for eight years, after his predecessor's death.

Or had Tokogama really died?

He couldn't be identical with Lang—he had been a short and slight, Lang was a tall and broad, too big a jump for any surgeon. Not to mention their simultaneous careers. But how far back could you trace Lang before he became fakeable records of birth and schooling? What young fellow named Yamatsu or Hideki was now polishing glass in the labs and slated to become the next director?

How fantastic could you get on how little evidence?

Radek let the text fade from the screen and sat puffing another cigarette. It was a while before he demanded references on the biology of the aging process.

That was tough sledding. He couldn't follow the mathematics or the chemistry very far. No good popularizations were available. But a newsman got an ability to winnow what he learned. Radek didn't have to take notes, he'd been through a mind-training course; after an hour or so, he sat back and reviewed what he had gotten.

The living organism was a small island of low entropy in a universe tending constantly toward gigantic disorder. It maintained itself through an intricate set of hemostatic mechanisms. The serious disruption of any of these brought the life-processes to a halt. Shock, disease, the bullet in the lungs or the ax in the brain—death.

But hundreds of thousands of autopsies had never given an honest verdict of "death from old age." It was always something else, cancer, heart failure, sickness, stroke . . . age was at most a contributing cause, decreasing resistance to injury and power to recover from it.

One by one, the individual causes had been licked. Bacteria and protozoa and viruses were slaughtered in the body. Cancers were selectively poisoned. Cholesterol was dissolved out of the arteries. Surgery patched up damaged organs, and the new regeneration techniques replaced what had been lost . . . even nervous tissue. Offhand, there was no more reason to die, unless you met murder or an accident.

But people still grew old. The process wasn't as hideous as it had been. You needn't shuffle in arthritic feebleness. Your mind was clear, your skin wrinkled slowly. Centenarians were not uncommon these days. But very few reached 150. Nobody reached 200. Imperceptibly, the fires burned low . . . vitality was diminished, strength faded, hair whitened, eyes dimmed. The body responded less and less well to regenerative treatment. Finally it did not respond at all. You got so weak that some small thing you and your doctor could have laughed at in your youth, took you away.

You still grew old. And because you grew old, you still died.

The unicellular organism did not age. But "age" was a meaningless word in that particular case. A man could be immortal via his germ cells. The micro-organism could too, but it gave the only cell it had. Personal immorality was denied to both man and microbe.

Could sheer mechanical wear and tear be the reason for the decline known as old age? Probably not. The natural regenerative powers of life were better than that. And observations made in free fall, where strain was minimized, indicated that while null-gravity had an alleviating effect, it was no key to living forever.

Something in the chemistry and physics of the cells themselves, then. They did tend to accumulate heavy water—that had been known for a long time. Hard to see how that could kill you . . . the percentage increase in a lifetime was so small. It might be a partial answer. You might grow old more slowly if you drank only water made of pure isotopes. But you wouldn't be immortal.

Radek shrugged. He was getting near the end of his trip. Let the Institute people answer his questions.

The Four Corners country is so named because four of the old American states met there, back when they were still significant political units. For a while, in the 20th century, it was overrun with uranium hunters, who made small impression on its tilted emptiness. It was still a favorite vacation area, and the resorts were lost in that great huddle of mountains and desert. You could have a lot of privacy here.

Gliding down over the moon-ghostly Pueblo ruins of Mesa Verde, Radek peered through the windscreen. There, ahead. Lights glowed around the walls, spread across half a mesa. Inside them was a parkscape of trees, lawns, gardens, arbors, cottage units . . . the Institute housed its people well. There were four large buildings at the center, and Radek noted gratefully that several windows were still shining in them. Not that he had any compunctions about getting the great Dr. Lang out of bed, but—

He ignored the public landing field outside the walls and set his boat down in the paved courtyard.

As he climbed out, half a dozen guards came running. They were husky men in blue uniforms, armed with stunners, and the dim light showed faces hinting they wouldn't be sorry to feed him a beam. Radek dropped to the ground, folded his arms, and waited. The breath from his nose was frosty under the moon.

"What the hell do you want?"

The nearest guard pulled up in front of him and laid a hand on his shock gun. "Who the devil are you? Don't you know this is private property? What's the big idea, anyway?"

"Take it easy," advised Radek. "I have to see Dr. Lang at once. Emergency."

"You didn't call for an appointment, did you?"

"No, I didn't."

"All right, then—"

"I didn't think he'd care to have me give my reasons over a radio. This is confidential and urgent."

The men hesitated, uncertain before such an outrageous violation of all civilized canons. "I dunno, friend . . . he's busy . . . if you want to see Dr. McCormick—"

"Dr. Lang. Ask him if I may. Tell him I have news about his longevity process."

"His what?"

Radek spelled it out and watched the man go. Another one made some ungracious remark and frisked him with needless ostentation. A third was more urbane: "Sorry to do this, but you understand we've got important work going on. Can't have just anybody busting in."

"Sure, that's all right." Radek shivered in the thin chill air and pulled his cloak tighter about him.

"Viruses and stuff around. If any of that got loose—You understand."

Well, it wasn't a bad cover-up. None of these fellows looked very bright. IQ treatments could do only so much, thereafter you got down to the limitations of basic and unalterable brain microstructure. And even among the more intellectual workers . . . how many Barwells were there, handling semi-routine tasks but not permitted to know what really went on under their feet? Radek had a brief irrational wish that he'd worn boots instead of sandals.

The first guard returned. "He'll see you," he grunted. "And you better make it good, because he's one mad doctor."

Radek nodded and followed two of the men. The nearest of the large square buildings seemed given over to offices. He was led inside, down a short length of glow-lit corridor, and halted while the scanner on a door marked, LANG, DIRECTOR observed him.

"He's clean, boss," said one of the escort.

"All right," said the annunciator. "Let him in. But you two stay just outside."

It was a spacious office, but austerely furnished. A telewindow reflected green larches and a sun-spattered waterfall, somewhere on the other side of the planet. Lang sat alone behind the desk, his hands engaged with some papers that looked like technical reports. He was a big, heavy-shouldered man, his hair gray, his chocolate face middle-aged and tired.

He did not rise. "Well?" he snapped.

"My name is Arnold Radek. I'm a news service operator . . . here's my card, if you wish to see it."

"Pharaoh had it easy," said Lang in a chill voice. "Moses only called the seven plagues down on him. I have to deal with your sort."

Radek placed his fingertips on the desk and leaned forward. He found it unexpectedly hard not to be stared down by the other. "I know very well I've laid myself open to a lawsuit by coming in as I did," he stated. "Possibly, when I'm through, I'll be open to murder."

"Are you feeling well?" There was more contempt than concern in the deep tone.

"Let me say first off, I believe I have information about a certain project of yours. One you badly want to keep a secret. I've taped a record at my office of what I know and where I'm going. If I don't get back before 1000 hours, Central Time, and wipe that tape, it'll be heard by the secretary."

Lang took an exasperated breath. His fingernails whitened on the sheets he still held. "Do you honestly think we would be so . . . I won't say unscrupulous . . . so *stupid* as to use violence?"

"No," said Radek. "Of course not. All I want is a few straight answers. I know you're quite able to lead me up the garden path, feed me some line of pap and hustle me out again—but I won't stand for that. I mentioned my tape only to convince you that I'm in earnest."

"You're not drunk," murmured Lang. "But there are a lot of people running loose who ought to be in a mental hospital."

"I know." Radek sat down without waiting for an invitation. "Anti-scientific fanatics. I'm not one of them. You know Darrell Burkhardt's news commentaries? I supply a lot of his data and interpretations. He's one of the leading friends of genuine science, one of the few you have left." Radek gestured at the card on the desk. "Read it, right there."

Lang picked the card up and glanced at the lettering and tossed it back. "Very well. That's still no excuse for breaking in like this. You—"

"It can't wait," interrupted Radek. "There are a lot of lives at stake. Every minute we sit here, there are perhaps a million people dying, perhaps more; I haven't the figures. And everyone else is dying all the time, millimeter by millimeter, we're all born dying. Every minute you hold back the cure for old age, you murder a million human beings."

"This is the most fantastic—"

"Let me finish! I get around. And I'm trained to look a little bit more closely at the facts everybody knows, the ordinary commonplace facts we take for granted and never think to inquire about because they are so ordinary. I've wondered about the Institute for a long time. Tonight I talked at great length with a fellow named Barwell . . . remember him? A clerk here. You fired him this morning for being too nosy. He had a lot to say."

"Hm." Lang sat quiet for a while. He didn't rattle easily—he couldn't be snowed under by fast, aggressive talk. While Radek spat out what clues he had, Lang calmly reached into a drawer and got out an old-fashioned briar pipe, stuffed it and lit it.

"So what do you want?" he asked when Radek paused for breath.

"The truth, damn it!"

"There are privacy laws. It was established long ago that a citizen is entitled to privacy if he does nothing against the common weal—"

"And you are! You're like a man who stands on a river bank and has a lifebelt and won't throw it to a man drowning in the river."

Lang sighed. "I won't deny we're working on longevity," he answered. "Obviously we are. The problem interests biologists throughout the Solar System. But we aren't publicizing our findings as yet for a very good reason. You know how people jump to conclusions. Can you imagine the hysteria that would arise in this already unstable culture if there seemed to be even a prospect of immortality? You yourself are a prime case . . . on the most tenuous basis of rumor and hypothesis, you've decided that we have found a vaccine against old age and are hoarding it. You come bursting in here in the middle of the night, demanding to be made immortal immediately if not sooner. And you're comparatively civilized . . . there are enough lunatics who'd come here with guns and start shooting up the place."

Radek smiled bleakly. "Of course. I know that. And you ought to know the outfit I work for is reputable. If you have a good lead on the problem, but haven't solved it yet, you can trust us not to make that fact public.

"All right." Lang mustered an answering smile, oddly warm and charming. "I don't mind telling you, then, that we do have some promising preliminary results—but, and this is the catch, we estimate it will take at least a century to get anywhere. Biochemistry is an inconceivably complex subject."

"What sort of results are they?"

"It's highly technical. Has to do with enzymes. You may know that enzymes are the major device through which the genes govern the organism all through life. At a certain point, for instance, the genes order the body to go through the changes involved in puberty. At another point, they order that gradual breakdown we know as aging."

"In other words," said Radek slowly, "the body has a built-in suicide mechanism?"

"Well . . . if you want to put it that way—"

"I don't believe a word of it. It makes a lot more sense to imagine that there's something which causes the breakdown—a virus, maybe — and the body fights it off as long as possible but at last it gets the upper hand. The whole key to evolution is the need to survive. I can't see life evolving its own anti-survival factor."

"But nature doesn't care about the individual, friend Radek. Only about the species. And the species with a rapid turnover of individuals can evolve faster, become more effective—"

"Then why does man, the fastest-evolving metazoan of all, have one of the longest lifespans? He does, you know . . . among mammals, at any rate. Seems to me our bodies must be all-around better than average, better able to fight off the death virus. Fish live a longer time, sure—and maybe in the water they aren't so exposed to the disease. Mayflies are short-lived; have they simply adapted their life cycle to the existence of the virus?"

Lang frowned. "You appear to have studied this subject enough to have some mistaken ideas about it. I can't argue with a man who insists on protecting his cherished irrationalities with fancy verbalisms."

"And you appear to think fast on your feet, Dr. Lang." Radek laughed. "Maybe not fast enough. But I'm not being paranoid about this. You can convince me."

"How?"

"Show me. Take me into those underground rooms and show me what you actually have."

"I'm afraid that's impos—"

"All right." Radek stood up. "I hate to do this, but a man must either earn a living or go on the public freeloading roll . . . which I don't want to do. The facts and conjectures I already have will make an interesting story."

Lang rose too, his eyes widening. "You can't prove anything!"

"Of course I can't. You're sitting on all the proof."

"But the public reaction! God in Heaven, man, those people can't *think!*"

"No . . . they can't, can they?" He moved toward the door. "Goodnight."

Radek's muscles were taut. In spite of everything that had been said, a person hounded to desperation could still do murder.

There was a great quietness as he heard the door. Then Lang spoke. The voice was defeated, and when Radek looked back it was an old man who stood behind the desk.

"You win. Come along with me."

They went down an empty hall, after dismissing the guards, and took an elevator belowground. Neither of them said anything. Somehow, the sag of Lang's shoulders was a gnawing in Radek's conscience.

When they emerged, it was to transfer past a sentry, where Lang gave a password and okayed his companion, to another elevator which purred them still deeper.

"I—" The newsman cleared his throat, awkwardly. "I repeat what I implied earlier. I'm here mostly as a citizen interested in the public welfare . . . which includes my own, of course, and my family's if I ever have one. If you can show me valid reasons for not breaking this story, I won't. I'll even let you hypnocondition me against doing it, voluntarily or otherwise."

"Thanks," said the director. His mouth curved upward, but it was a shaken smile. "That's decent of you, and we'll accept . . . I think you'll agree with our policy. What worries me is the rest of the world. If you could find out as much as you did—"

Radek's heart jumped between his ribs. "Then you do have immortality!"

"Yes. But I'm not immortal. None of our personnel are, except— Here we are."

There was a hidden susurrus of machinery as they stepped out into a small bare entry-room. Another guard sat there, beside a desk. Past him was a small door of immense solidity, the door of a vault.

"You'll have to leave everything metallic here," said Lang. "A steel object could jump so fiercely as to injure you. Your watch would be ruined. Even coins could get uncomfortably hot . . . eddy currents, you know. We're about to go through the strongest magnetic field ever generated."

Silently, dry-mouthed, Radek piled his things on the desk. Lang operated a combination lock on the door. "There are nervous effects too," he said. "The field is actually strong enough to influence the electric discharge of your synapses. Be prepared for a few nasty seconds. Follow me and walk fast."

The door opened on a low, narrow corridor several meters long. Radek felt his heart bump crazily, his vision blurred, there was panic screaming in his brain and sweating tingle in his skin. Stumbling through nightmare, he made it to the end.

The horror faded. They were in another room, with storage facilities and what resembled a spaceship's airlock in the opposite wall. Lang grinned shakily. "No fun, is it?"

"What's it for?" gasped Radek.

"To keep charged particles out of here. And the whole set of chambers is 500 meters underground, sheathed in ten meters of lead brick and surrounded by tanks of heavy water. This is the only place in the Solar System, I imagine, where cosmic rays never come."

"You mean—"

Lang knocked out his pipe and left it in a goboon. He opened the lockers to reveal a set of airsuits, complete with helmets and oxygen tanks. "We put these on before going any further," he said.

"Infection on the other side?"

"We're the infected ones. Come on, I'll help you."

As they scrambled into the equipment, Lang added conversationally: "This place has to have all its own stuff, of course . . . its own electric generators and so on. The ultimate power source is isotopically pure carbon burned in oxygen. We use a nuclear reactor to create the magnetic field itself, but no atomic energy is allowed inside it." He led the way into the airlock, closed it, and started the pumps. "We have to flush out all the normal air and substitute that from the inner chambers."

"How about food? Barwell said food was prepared in the kitchens and brought here."

"Synthesized out of elements recovered from waste products. We do cook it topside, taking precautions. A few radioactive atoms get in, but not enough to matter as long as we're careful. We're so cramped for space down here we have to make some compromises."

"I think—" Radek fell silent. As the lock was evacuated, his unjointed airsuit spread-eagled and held him prisoner, but he hardly noticed. There was too much else to think about, too much to grasp at once.

Not till the cycle was over and they had gone through the lock did he speak again. Then it came harsh and jerky: "I begin to understand. How long has this gone on?"

"It started about 200 years ago . . . an early Institute project." Lang's voice was somehow tinny over the helmet phone. "At that time, it wasn't possible to make really pure isotopes in quantity, so there were only limited results, but it was enough to justify further research. This particular set of chambers and chemical elements is 150 years old. A spectacular success, a brilliant confirmation, from the very beginning . . . and the Institute has never dared reveal it. Maybe they should have, back then—maybe people could have taken the news—but not now. These days the knowledge would whip men into a murderous rage of frustration; they wouldn't believe the truth, they wouldn't dare believe, and God alone knows what they'd do."

Looking around, Radek saw a large, plastic-lined room, filled with cages. As the lights went on, white rats and guinea pigs stirred sleepily. One of the rats came up to nibble at the wires and regard the humans from beady pink eyes.

Lang bent over and studied the label. "This fellow is, um, 66 years old. Still fat and sassy, in perfect condition, as you can see. Our oldest mammalian inmate is a guinea pig: a hundred and forty-five years. This one here."

Lang stared at the immortal beast for a while. It didn't look unusual . . . only healthy. "How about monkeys?" Radek asked.

"We tried them. Finally gave it up. A monkey is an active animal— it was too cruel to keep them penned up forever. They even went insane, some of them."

Footfalls were hollow as Lang led the way toward the inner door. "Do you get the idea?"

"Yes . . . I think I do. If heavy radiation speeds up aging—then natural radioactivity is responsible for normal aging."

"Quite. A matter of cells being slowly deranged, through decades in the case of man—the genes which govern them being mutilated, chromosomes ripped up, nucleoplasm irreversibly damaged. And, of course, a mutated cell often puts out the wrong combination of enzymes, and if it regenerates at all it replaces itself by one of the same kind. The effect is cumulative, more and more defective cells every hour. A steady bombardment, all your life . . . here on Earth, seven cosmic rays per second ripping through you, and you yourself are radioactive, you include radiocarbon and radiopotassium and radiophosphorus . . . Earth and the planets, the atmosphere, everything radiates. Is it any wonder that at last our organic mechanism starts breaking down? The marvel is that we live as long as we do."

The dry voice was somehow steadying. Radek asked: "And this place is insulated?"

"Yes. The original plant and animal life in here was grown exogenetically from single-cell zygotes, supplied with air and nourishment built from pure stable isotopes. The Institute had to start with low forms, naturally; at that time, it wasn't possible to synthesize proteins to order. But soon our workers had enough of an ecology to introduce higher species, eventually mammals. Even the first generation was only negligibly radioactive. Succeeding generations have been kept almost absolutely clean. The lamps supply ultraviolet, the air is recycled . . . well, in principle it's no different from an ecological-unit spaceship."

Radek shook his head. He could scarcely get the words out: "People? Humans?"

"For the past 120 years. Wasn't hard to get germ plasm and grow it. The first generation reproduced normally, the second could if lack of space didn't force us to load their food with chemical contraceptive." Behind his faceplate, Lang grimaced. "I'd never have allowed it if I'd been director at the time, but now I'm stuck with the situation. The legality is very doubtful. How badly do you violate a man's civil rights when you keep him a prisoner but give him immortality?"

He opened the door, an archaic manual type. "We can't do better for them than this," he said. "The volume of space we can enclose in a magnetic field of the necessary strength is already at an absolute maximum."

Light sprang automatically from the ceiling. Radek looked in at a dormitory. It was well-kept, the furniture ornamental. Beyond it he could see other rooms . . . recreation, he supposed vaguely.

The score of hulks in the beds hardly moved. Only one woke up. He blinked, yawned, and shuffled toward the visitors, quite nude, his long hair tangled across the low forehead, a loose grin on the mouth.

"Hello, Bill," said Lang.

"Uh . . . got sumpin? Got sumpin for Bill?" A hand reached out, begging. Radek thought of a trained ape he had once seen.

"This is Bill." Lang spoke softly, as if afraid his voice would snap. "Our oldest inhabitant. One hundred and nineteen years old, and he has the physique of a man of 20. They mature, you know, reach their peak and never fall below it again."

"Got sumpin, doc, huh?"

"I'm sorry, Bill," said Lang. "I'll bring you some candy next time."

The moron gave an animal sigh and shambled back. On the way, he passed a sleeping woman, and edged toward her with a grunt. Lang closed the door.

There was another stillness.

"Well," said Lang, "now you've seen it."

"You mean . . . you don't mean immortality makes you like that?"

"Oh, no. Not at all. But my predecessors chose low-grade stock on purpose. Remember those monkeys. How long do you think a normal human could remain sane, cooped up in a little cave like this and never daring to leave it? That's the only way to be immortal, you know. And how much of the race could be given such elaborate care, even if they could stand it? Only a small percentage. Nor would they live forever—they're already contaminated, they were born radioactive. And whatever happens, who's going to remain outside and keep the apparatus in order?"

Radek nodded. His neck felt stiff, and within the airsuit he stank with sweat. "I've got the idea."

"And yet—if the facts were known—if my questions had to be answered—how long do you think a society like ours would survive?"

Radek tried to speak, but his tongue was too dry.

Lang smiled grimly. "Apparently I've convinced you. Good. Fine." Suddenly his gloved hand shot out and gripped Radek's shoulder. Even through the heavy fabric, the newsman could feel the bruising fury of that clasp.

"But you're only one man," whispered Lang. "An unusually reasonable man for these days. There'll be others.

"What are we going to *do?*"

Meanwhile, the generational star ship Pioneer *launched so hopefully in 2126, continued to make slower-than-light progress toward the Centauri system. But whatever hopes the crew may have cherished of escaping social turmoil faded en route. Being human, they still carried the trait for conflict within them like an uncorrectable genetic flaw.*

The Troublemakers

A bright dream, and an old one—the same dream which had lived in Pythias, Columbus, Ley, in hundreds and thousands of men and in man himself, and which now looked up to the stars.

Earth was subdued; the planets had been reached and found wanting; if the dream were not to die, the stars must come next. It was known that most of them must have planets, that the worlds which could hold man were numbered in the millions—but the nearest of them was more than a lifetime away. Man could not wait for the hypothetical faster-than-light drive, which might never be found—nothing in physics indicated such a possibility, and if the vision of the frontier, which had become a cultural basic transcending questions of merely material usefulness, were not to wither and die, a start of some kind must be made.

The Pioneer, first of her class, was launched in 2126. A hundred and twenty-three years to Alpha Centauri—five or six generations, more than a long lifetime—but the dream would not be denied . . .

— Enrico Yamatsu, *Starward!*

"HAVE YOU ANYTHING to say before your sentence is passed?"

Evan Friday looked around him, slowly, focusing on all the details which he might never see again. Guilty! After all his hopes, after the wrangling and the waiting and the throttled futile anger, guilty. It hadn't even taken them long to decide; they'd debated perhaps half an hour before coming out with the verdict.

Guilty.

Behind him, the spectators had grown silent. There weren't many of them here in person, though he knew that half the ship must be watching him through the telescreens. Mostly they were officer class, sitting stiff and uniformed in their chairs, regarding him out of carefully blanked faces. The benches reserved for crewfolk were almost empty—less color in the garments, more life in the expression, but a life that despised him and seemed to feel only a suppressed glee that one more officer had gotten what was coming to him.

There were five sitting before him, judge and jury in full uniform. Above them, the arching wall displayed a mural, a symbolic figure of Justice crowned with a wreath of stars. The woman-image was stately, but he thought with bitterness that the artist had gotten in a hint of sluttishness. Appropriate.

His eyes went back to the five who were the Captain's Court. They were the rulers of the ship as well, the leaders and representatives of the major factions aboard. Three were officers pure and simple, with the bone-bred hauteur of their class— Astrogation, Administration, and Engineering. The fourth was Wilson, speaking for the crew, a big coarse man with the beefy hands of a laborer. He was getting fat, after five years of politics.

Captain Gomez was in the center. He was tall and lean, with a fine halo of white hair fringing his gaunt unmoving face. You couldn't know what he was thinking; the loneliness of his post had reached into him during his forty-three years as master. A figurehead now, but impressive, and—

Friday licked his lips and drew himself up straighter. He was twenty-four years old, and had been schooled in the rigid manners of the Astro officer's caste throughout all that time. Those habits held him up now. He was surprised at the steadiness of his tones:

"Yes, sir, I would like to say a few words.

"In the first place, I am not guilty. I have never so much as thought of bribery, sedition, or mutiny. There is nothing in my past record which would indicate anything of the sort. The evidence on which I have been convicted is the flimsiest tissue of fabrications, and several witnesses have committed perjury. I am surprised that this court even bothered of finding me guilty, and can only suppose that it is a frameup to cover someone else. However, there is little I can do about that now. My friends will continue to work for a reversal of this decision, and meanwhile I must accept it.

"Secondly, I would like to say that the fact of my being falsely accused is not strange. It is a part of the whole incredible pattern of mismanagement, selfishness, treachery, and venality which has perverted the great idea of this voyage. The *Pioneer* was to reach the stars. She carried all the hopes of Earth, ten years of labor and planning, an incredible money investment, and a mission of supreme importance. Eighty years later, what do we have? An unending succession of tyrannies, revolutions, tensions, hatreds, corruptions— all the social evils which Earth so painfully overcame, reborn between the stars. The goal has been forgotten in a ceaseless struggle for power which is used only to oppress. I have said this much before, in private. Presumably some right of free speech still exists, for I was not arrested on such charges. Therefore, I repeat it in public. Gentlemen and crew, I ask you to think what this will lead to. I ask you in what condition we will reach Centauri, if we do so at all. I ask you to consider who is responsible. I know it will prejudice my personal cause, but I make a solemn charge of my own: that two successive Captains have failed to exercise due authority, that the Captaincy has become a farce and a figurehead, that the officers have become a tyrant caste and the crew an ignorant mob. I tell the whole ship that something will have to be done, and soon, if the expedition is not to be a failure and a death trap.

"If this is sedition and mutiny, so be it."

He finished formally: "Thank you, gentlemen." The blood was hot in his face, he knew he was flushing and was angry with himself for it, he knew that he was shivering a little, and he knew that his words had been meaningless gibberish to the five men.

But the crew, and the better officers—?

Gomez cleared his throat, and spoke dryly: "I am sure idealism is creditable, especially in so young a man—provided that it is not a cover for something else, and that it is properly expressed. But there is also a tradition that junior officers should be seen and not heard, and that they are hardly prepared to govern a ship and seven thousand human beings. The court will remember your breach of discipline, Mr. Friday, in reviewing your case."

He leaned forward. "You have been found guilty of crimes which are punishable by death or imprisonment. However, in view of the defendant's youth and his previous good record, the court is disposed to leniency. Sentence is therefore passed that you shall be stripped of all title, honor, and privilege due to your rank, that your personal property shall be sequestered, and that you shall be reduced to a common crewman with assignment to the Engineering Section.

"Court dismissed."

The judges rose and filed out. Friday shook his head, trying to clear it of a buzzing faintness, trying to ignore the eyes and the voices at his back. A police sergeant fell in on either side of him. He thrust away the arm which one extended, and walked out between them.

The gray coverall felt stiff and scratchy against his skin. They had given him two changes of clothing and a couple of dollars to last till payday, and that was all which remained to him now. He went centerward between the policemen, hardly noticing the walls and doors, shafts and faces.

The cops weren't bad fellows. They had looked the other way while he said goodbye to his parents. His mother had cried but his father, drilled into the reserve expected of an officer, had only been able to wring his hand and mutter awkwardly: "You shouldn't have spoken that way, Evan. It didn't help matters. But we'll keep working for you, and—and—good luck, my son." With a sudden flaring of the old iron pride: "Whatever happens, and whatever they say, remember you are still an officer of Astrogation!"

That had hurt perhaps most of all, and at the same time it had held more comfort than anything else. An officer, an officer, an officer— before God, still an officer of Astro!

It embarrassed the policemen. He was their inferior now, a plain crewman to be kicked around and kept in order, but he was of the Friday blood and he kept the manners they were trained to salute. They didn't know how to act.

One of them finally said, slowly and clumsily: "Look, you're in for some trouble, I'm afraid. Can you fight?"

"I was taught self-defense, yes," said Friday. Fitness was part of the code in all of Astro—which, after all, was composed exclusively of officers—as it was of only the upper ranks in Engineering and hardly at all in Administration. It belonged to the pattern; Astro was the smallest faction aboard, but it was the aristocracy of the aristocracy and at present it held the balance of power. "Why do you ask?"

"You'll have quite a few slugfests. Crewmen don't like officers, and when one gets kicked downstairs to them they take it out on him."

"But—I never hurt anybody. Damn it, I've been their friend!"

"Can't expect 'em all to see it that way. But stand up to 'em, be free and friendly—forget that manner of yours, remember you're one of them now—and it'll come out all right."

"You mean you police permit brawling?"

"Not too much we can do about it, as long as riots don't start. You can file a complaint with us if somebody beats you up, but I wouldn't advise it. They'd never take you in then. Somebody might murder you."

"I won't come crawling to anybody," said Friday with the stiffness of outrage. Underneath it was a horrible tightening in his throat.

"That's what I said: you've got to quit talking that way. Crewmen aren't a bad sort, but you can't live with 'em if you keep putting on airs. Just keep your mouth shut for awhile, till they get used to you."

The three men went down unending corridors, shafts, and companionways. Gravity lightened as they approached the axis of the ship. From the numbers on doors, Friday judged that they were bound for Engineering Barracks Three, which lay aft of the main gyros and about halfway between axis and top deck, but pride wouldn't allow him to ask if he was right.

They were well out of officer territory now. The halls were still clean, but somehow drabber and dingier; residential apartments were smaller and poorly furnished; shops, taverns, theaters and other public accommodations blinked neon signs at the opposite wall, fifteen feet away; the clangor of metalworking dinned faintly in the background. Crewfolk swarmed here and there, drab-clad for work or gaudy for pleasure, men and women and a horde of children. Most of the men wore close haircuts and short beards, in contrast to the clean-shaven officers, and they were noisy and pushing and not too clean.

Many of them looked after the policemen and cursed or spat. Friday felt unease crawling along his spine.

"Here we are."

He stopped, and looked ahead of him with a certain panicky blurring in his eyes. The doorway, entrance to one of the barracks for unmarried workers, was like a cave. The other doors on that side of the corridor, as far as he could see, opened into the same racketing darkness; the opposite wall was mostly blank, with side halls and companionways widely spaced. Two or three men, shooting dice some way down the corridor, were looking up and he saw their faces harden.

"We could go in with you," said one of the police apologetically, "but it'll be better for you if we don't. Good luck—Mr. Friday."

"Thank you," he said. His voice was husky.

He stood for a moment looking at the door. The crapshooters got up and started slowly toward him. He wondered if he should bolt in, decided against it, and managed a stiff nod as the strangers came up.

"How do you do?"

"What's the trouble, jo?" The speaker was big and blocky and red-haired. "Been boozin'?"

"Nah." Another man narrowed his eyes. This's that guy Friday. The one they broke today. They sent 'em down here."

"Here? Friday? Well, I'll be scuttered!" The first crewman bowed elaborately. "Howdedo, Mister Ensign Friday, howdedo an' welcome to our humble ay-bode."

"Mebbe we sh'd roll out a rug, huh?"

"How'd y' like y'r eggs done, sir, sunny side up 'r turned?"

"Please," said Friday, "I would like to find my bunk." He recognized the condescending coldness in his voice too late.

"He'd like to find his bunk!" Someone grinned nastily. "Shall we show 'im, boys?"

Friday pushed himself free and went into the barracks.

It was gloomy inside, for a moment he was almost blind. Ventilators could not remove the haze of smoke and human sweat. Bunks lined the walls in two tiers, stretching enormously into a farther twilight. Pictures, mostly of nude women, were pasted on the walls, and the floor, while not especially dirty or littered, was a mess of shoes, clothes, tables, and chairs. Most of the light came from a giant-size telescreen, filling one wall with its images—the mindless, tasteless sort of program intended for this class—and the air with its noise. Perhaps a hundred men off duty were in the room, sleeping, lounging, gambling, watching the show, most of them wearing little but shorts.

Friday had been "crewquartering" before with companions of his age and class, but he'd stuck to the bars and similar places; his knowledge of this aspect had been purely nominal. It was a sudden feeling of being caged, a retching claustrophobia, which brought him around to face the others. They had followed him in, and stood blocking the doorway.

"Hey, boys!" The shout rang and boomed through the hollow immensity of the room, skittered past the raucousness of the telescreen and shivered faintly in the metal walls. "Hey, look who we got! Come over here and meet Mister Friday!"

Eyes, two hundred eyes glittering out of smoke and dark, and nowhere to go, nowhere to go. *They're going to beat me up. They're going to slug me, and I can't get away from it, I'll have to take it.*

He raised his voice above the savage jeering as they pressed in: "Why do you think I was sent down here? Why did they want to get rid of me, up above? Because I wanted you people to have some rights. I never hurt a crewman yet. Damn it, I couldn't have, I was always working with other officers."

"Here's your chance," grunted somebody. "I'll take him."

They squabbled for awhile over the privilege, while two men held Friday's arms. The big redhead who had first accosted him won.

"Let him go, boys," he said. "Give him a chance to in-tro-juice himself proper like. I'm Sam Carter, Mr. Friday." His teeth flashed white in the smoky dusk. "And I'm very pleased to meet you."

"Chawmed, I am shu-ah," cried a voice, anonymous in the roiling twilight.

Friday had learned the techniques of boxing, wrestling, and infighting in all gravities from zero to Earth. He had enjoyed it, and been considered better than average. But Carter outmassed him thirty pounds, and officers didn't fight to hurt.

After awhile Friday lost fear, forgot pain, and wanted nothing in all the world but to smash that red grinning face into ruin. Up and down, in and out, around and around, slug, duck, guard, slug, jar, and the mob hooting and howling out of the shadows. Hit him, right cross to the jaw, left to the belly, *oof!*

It took Sam Carter a long time to knock him down for good, and the crewman was hardly able to stand, himself, when it was done. There wasn't much cheering. A couple of men hauled Friday to a vacant bunk, and went back to whatever they had been doing before he came.

❈   ❈   ❈

Slowly, Friday adjusted.

At first it was not quite real, it was a horror which could not have happened to him. He, Ensign Evan Friday, rising in Astro, minor social lion, all the ship before him—he, who meant to do something about correcting injustice when he had the power, but who knew he could wait and savor his own life, he just wasn't the sort of person who was accused and condemned and degraded. Those things happened to others, actually guilty in the struggle for control, or to the heroes of books from the Earth he had never seen—they didn't happen to *him!*

He came out of that daze into grinding nightmare. It took him days to recover from the beating he had had, and before he was quite well somebody else took him on, somebody whom he managed to defeat this time but who left him aching and hurt. Nevertheless, he was sent to work two watches after his arrival, and to the clumsiness of the recruit and the screaming of unaccustomed muscles his injuries were added.

Being ignorant of all shopwork, he was set to unskilled, heavy labor, jumping at everyone's shout with boxes, machine parts, tools, metal beams. Low gravity helped somewhat, but not enough—they simply assumed he could lift that much more mass, without regard to its inertia. His bewildered awkwardness drew curses and pay dockings. The racket of the shops seemed to din in his head every time he tried to sleep, and he could never get all the grime out of his skin and clothes.

Without friends, money, or a decent suit, he stayed in the barracks when the others went out to drink, wench, or see a show. But somebody was always around with him, and the telescreen was never turned off. He thought he would go crazy before he learned how to ignore it, but he knew better than to protest.

The men stopped bullying him after awhile, since he was disconcertingly handy with his fists, but it took weeks before the practical jokes ended. Shortsheeting and tying water-soaked knots in clothing were all right; he'd done that to others when he was younger; but hiding his shoes, pouring water in his bed and paint in his hair, slipping laxatives into his food—childish, but a vicious sort of childishness that made him wonder why he had ever felt sorry for this class.

He used the public facilities, bed and board and bath, since he could not afford the private home which theoretically was his to rent. He joined the union, since no one ever failed to, though it galled him to pay money into Wilson's war chest—Wilson, the parvenu, who wanted to run the officers that ran the ship! But otherwise he refused to conform, though it would have made things easier. He shaved, and kept his hair long, and fought to retain precision and restraint in his speech. He talked as little as possible to anyone, and spent most of his free time lying on his bunk thinking.

The loneliness was great. Sometimes, when he thought of his friends, when he remembered his quiet book-lined room, he wanted to cry. It was a closed world now. Crewmen simply didn't go into officer territory except on business.

Well, they might get him cleared. Meanwhile, the best thing he could do was to improve his position.

He worked with machines now and then, and was a little surprised to discover he had a fair amount of innate ability. Books from the crew branch of the ship's library taught him more, and presently he applied for promotion to machinist's assistant. By now he was tolerated, though still disliked, and made a good enough showing on test to get the job. It meant a raise, better working conditions, and one step further. The next was to be a machinist himself, one of the all-around men who were troubleshooters and extempore inventors—that was one grade higher than foreman, a job he could bypass.

Before God, he thought, *I'll get back to officer if I have to work my way!*

Theoretically, it was possible. But in practice there were only so many commissions to go around, and if you didn't belong to the right families you didn't get them.

He grew friendly with his immediate boss, a pleasant, older man who was not at all averse to letting him do most of the work and learn thereby. Gradually, he got onto drinking terms with a few others. They weren't bad fellows, not entirely the sadistic savages he had imagined. They laughed more than the upper classes, and they often went to school in their spare time, or saved money to start a small business, in spite of the disadvantages under which tradesmen labored.

For that matter, crew conditions weren't the slummish horror which sentimentalists had pictured. Folk were poor, but they had the basic necessities and a few of the comforts. Violence was not uncommon, but it was simply one facet of a life which, on the whole, was fairly secure. Indeed, perhaps its worst feature was dullness.

Still, if another of the minor wars which had torn the ship before broke out— Something was wrong. This wasn't the way man should go out to the stars, high of heart and glad of soul. Somehow, the great dream had gone awry.

It was a major triumph when Friday met Sam Carter in a beer hall and they went on a small bat together. He found himself liking the big red-headed man. And Carter got into the habit of asking him endless questions—science, history, politics; an officer was supposed to know everything. Friday began to discover how deficient his own education was. He knew physics and mathematics well, had a fair grounding in some other sciences, and had been exposed all his life to the best of Earth's art, literature, and music. But—what was this psychology, anyway? It was a scientific study of human behavior, yes, and it had advanced quite far on Earth by the time the ship left—but why had he never been taught anything but the barest smattering? For that matter, did anybody in the upper ranks ever speak of it?

That might be the reason why the ship's great dream had snarled into a crazy welter of murderous petty politics. Sheer ignorant fumbling on the part of the leaders, even with the best intentions— and he knew many intentions were and had been bad—could have let matters degenerate. Only—why? It would have been so easy to include a few psychologists.

Unless—unless those psychologists had been eliminated early in the game, say at the end of that serene first decade of travel, by the power-hungry and the greedy. But then the whole foundation of his society was rottener than he had imagined. Then even his own class was founded on betrayal.

None of which, he reflected grimly, was going to be any help at all when the ship got to Centauri.

If it ever did!

Perhaps still another revolution was needed, a revolt of the dreamers to whom the voyage meant something. Only—only there'd been too many mutinies and gang wars already, and more were brewing with every passing watch. The officers were split along departmental lines—Astros, Engys, and Admys—and on questions of personal power and general policy. The common crewfolk were nominally represented by Wilson, but some demon seemed to stir them up against each other, workers with machines and on farms, plain deckhands, technicians of all kinds of grades, hating each other and rioting in the corridors. Then there were the chants and small manufacturers, fighting for a return to the old free enterprise system or, at least, a separate voice on the Council. There were the goons maintained by each faction, as well as by powerful individuals, bully gangs outnumbering the better-armed police, who were directly under the Captain. But the Captain was a puppet, giving the orders of whatever momentary group or men held the reins of effective power.

This ship isn't going to Centauri, thought Friday. It's going to Hell!

Time aboard the *Pioneer* was divided into the days of twenty-four hours, the weeks of seven and the years of three hundred sixty-five and a quarter days, which had prevailed on Earth. But except for a few annual festivals, there were no special holidays. Working shifts were staggered around the clock, and there was always a certain percentage of the shops and other public places open. For what meaning did time have? It was the movement of clock hands, the succession of meals and tasks and sleeps, the arbitrary marks on a calendar. In a skyless, weatherless, seasonless world, a world whose only dark came with the flicking of a light switch in a room, one hour was as good as another for anything. The economic setup was such that the standard thirty-hour work week provided the common crewman a living wage, and there was not enough work to do for overtime hours to be usual. Most people kept to such a schedule, and passed their leisure with whatever recreation was available and to their tastes. Some preferred to work only part time and to do something else for the rest of their money—one thought especially of the *filles de joie* who, though frowned on by the officer caste, were an accepted part of the crew world; and the arrogant goons were another instance. The tradesmen, independent artisans, artists, writers, and others who worked for themselves made their own hours. Some of these lived in officer territory, the pet of a patron or caterers to the entire area; most were in and of the commons.

Evan Friday wandered with a couple of friends—Sam Carter and a dark, slim, intense nineteen-year-old named John Lefebre—into Park

Seven, not far aft of the main gyros. The workers were idle, a little bored, and Friday had wearied of spending too much time in the library. He had been reading a good deal, concentrating on the history of the ship and groping for the cause of its social breakdown, but it baffled him and he was still young.

He had realized with a little shock that he had been a crewman for almost six months. So long? Gods, but time went, day after day of sameness, days and weeks and months and years till the end of life and flaming oblivion in the energy converters. Time went, and he was caught in its stream and carried without will or strength. Sometimes he wondered if he would ever get back to the topdeck world. Increasingly it became dim, a dream flickering on the edge of reality, and only once in a while would its sharp remembrance bring him awake with a gasp of pain.

He had shaken down pretty well, he thought. He was accepted in the barracks, though his reserve still kept most of the men at a distance. But they called him "Doc" and referred arguments to his superior education. He was used to shop routine, learning fast and getting close to the promotion he wanted. Next step—superintendent—maybe! He had been invited to the apartments of crew families, and went out drinking or gambling or ballplaying with the others. It wasn't too bad a life, really, and that was in a way the most horrible part of his situation.

They went down a long series of halls until finally one opened on the park. This was one of several such areas scattered through the ship, a great vaulted space half a mile on a side, floored with dirt and turf, covered with hedges and trees and fountains—a glimpse of old Earth, here in the steel immensity of the ship. There were ball courts and a swimming pool and hidden private places under fantastically huge low-gravity flowers. Not far from the boundary of grass were a couple of beer parlors—fun for all the family.

"Get up some volleyball?" asked Lefebre.

"Not yet," yawned Friday. "Let's sit for a while." He went his words one better, by flopping full length on the grass. It was cool and moist and firm against his bare skin, with a faint pungency of mould which stirred vague wistful instincts in him. His eyes squinted up to the ceiling, where the illusion of blue sky and wandering clouds and a fiery globe of sun had been created.

Was Earth like this? he wondered. Had his grandparents spurned this for a prison of steel and energy, walled horizons and narrow rooms and an unknowable destiny which they would never see?

He closed his eyes and tried, as often before, to imagine Earth. He had been in the parks, he had seen all the films and read all the books and learned all the words, but still it wouldn't come real. In spite of having ventured outside the ship a few times, he couldn't quite imagine being under a sky which was not a roof, looking out to a horizon that hazed into blue distance, seeing a mountain or a sea. Words, pictures, images—a fantasy without meaning.

Rain, what was rain? Water spilling from the sky, sweet and cold and wet on his body, damp smell of earth and a misty wind blowing into his eyes—whenever he tried to imagine himself out in the rain, it was merely grotesque, not the thing of which the books wrote with such tenderness. Someday, when he was old, the ship would reach far Centauri and he might stand under a streaming heaven and see lightning, but he couldn't think it now and he wondered if his old body would even like it.

It would take all the courage and purpose in the ship for men to adapt back to planetary life, the more so if the planet turned out to be very different than Earth.

What chance would a divided, tyrannized, corrupted mob have? What fantastic blindness had made Captain Petrie unable to see the spreading cancer and excise it? Or had he, like his successor Gomez, been merely the pawn and abettor of the greedy and the brutal? What had happened, back in the early days of the voyage? What had gone wrong?"

"What'cha thinking about now, Doc?" asked Carter.

"Hm? Oh—oh, the usual." Friday blinked himself back to full consciousness. "Remembering how things were when this trip began, and trying to find who or what's to blame for their changing ever since."

"Was—were things really so fine then?" asked Lefebre. "Aren't you, uh, romanticizing it?"

"No, no. I've read the official log, remember, as well as other writings. And it was only eighty years ago, not time for many legends to form."

"Well—what was so good then, anyway?" asked Carter.

"The ship was all one unit. Everybody had one great purpose, to get to Centauri, and everybody worked for it. There weren't these social divisions that have grown up since, officers and men were almost like friends, anybody could reach the top on sheer merit, nobody was after himself or his little group above the ship. There wasn't bribery, or fighting, or—oh, all the things which have happened ever since.

"Of course," went on Friday thoughtfully, "there were a lot fewer people then, and they had more to do. Only about two hundred in all, men and women. You know the population's supposed to build up and be at our maximum of ten thousand or so by the end of the trip. But we're only around seven thousand now, that'd be a small town on Earth—damn it, there's no reason for our splitting into castes and factions this way, it's ridiculous . . . Anyway, the ship was more or less of a skeleton inside, the idea was for the crew to complete work on it en route. That was so they could get started sooner, and have more to do. Good idea, and it took ten or twenty years at their easy pace."

"We still have to make things," said Carter. "What d'you think we're doing in the shops, anyway?"

"Sure, sure. Machines wear out and have to be replaced, repairs are needed here and there, new machines and facilities are built, oh, we have a whole little industry that keeps the factory division of the Engy department busy. Then there are the men in the black gang, different deck hands and technicians—we don't have the robot stuff we could make, there's no need for it with plenty of human labor available. My point is, things have stabilized. There's only so much work to be done these days, nearly all of it pure routine, so maybe people get bored. Maybe that's one reason we fight each other."

"The trouble started with capitalism," said Lefebre. He had all the dogmatic conviction of his years. "I've been reading books too, Doc, and heard speeches, and been thinking for myself. Any ship is a natural communist state. There was no reason to let private people have the farms and the factories and the rec places. What happened? Companies got started, fought each other, op—oppressed the workers, who had to form unions in self-defense; the food processors won out over the producers and formed their own trust; while Engy slowly took over the industries. Then food and factories started fighting, trying to run the ship, trying to stir up each other's workers—"

"So eventually the farms were collectivized, turned into one big food factory," said Friday. "Isn't that what you wanted? It hasn't helped much."

"The damage had already been done," said Lefebre. "The idea of fighting over power had been planted. Only thing to do now is to socialize everything, put it under the Captain's Council, and give the workers the main voice."

Friday had argued with the boy before. There was a strong communist movement aboard, chiefly under Wilson's leadership. *That fat demagogue! A lot of say his precious workers would have if he got what he wants!* Then there were the Guilds and their agitation for a return to the original petite-bourgeois system, their claim that the initial evil had been the formation of monopolies. And there were the officers, most of them obsessed by the aristocratic ideal, though to them it meant no more than the increase of personal authority and wealth.

Friday's upbringing prejudiced him in that direction. Damn it, a ship was not a politicking communism, neither was it a realm of little, short-sighted tradesmen. It was the rule of the best, the *aristos,* a hierarchy restrained by law and tradition and open on a competitive basis to anyone with ability. But it had to be an unquestioned rule, or you got the sort of anarchy which had prevailed aboard the *Pioneer.*

"To hell with it," said Carter. "Let's play some ball."

They got up and strolled over to the courts. The park was, as usual, pretty well filled with crewfolk of all ages, sexes, and classes, generally dressed in the shorts which were the garb of ordinary lounging. Except for the convenience of pockets, clothes were a superfluity when you weren't on the job. Friday wondered how the arrivals at Centauri would stand a winter—another half-mythical concept. Ship "weather" was a variation of temperature and ozone balance in the cycle long known to be most beneficial, but the change was so slow and between such narrow limits that it was unnoticeable. Winter—what was winter?

There were several other Engys sitting on the edge of the volleyball court, watching the game in progress with sour faces. "What's the matter, jo?" asked Carter of one.

"Goddam farmers been there for two hours now."

With an uneasy tingle along his spine, Friday noticed the characteristic green worn by workers in the food areas—hydroponics gardens, animal pens, and packing plants. There were a lot of them, sitting some ways off and watching a game whose slowness made it clear that its purpose was to taunt the Engys by keeping the court occupied. Theoretically, the food and factory unions were subdivisions of Wilson's crew-embracing Brotherhood of Workers. In practice, a feud had been going on for—how long, now? Ever since the early violence in the days of the monopolies. It was aggravated by differences in wages, working conditions, the thousand petty irritations of shipboard life. They hated each other's guts.

"Something," said Carter after a while, "oughta be done about this."

He started forward with an unholy gleam in his eyes. Friday caught his arm. "For God's sake, Sam, you aren't going to fight like a bunch of children over the use of a ball park, are you?"

"Ain't busted in a farmer's teeth for him in a long time now," muttered someone behind him.

Friday saw the men gathering into a loose knot. Blackjacks and knuckledusters were coming out of pockets, heavy-buckled belts were being slipped off. The greens, seeing trouble afoot, vented the mob-growl which is the signal for all wise men to start running, and drew themselves together.

Unthinking habit took over, officer's training. Friday was dimly surprised to find himself sprinting out onto the court.

"Stop that!" he yelled. "Break it up!"

The players halted, one by one, and he met sullen eyes. "What'sa matter?"

"You've had your turn playing. Can't you see a riot will start if you don't come back now?"

Faces turned to faces, mouths split into the grin he remembered from his first hour as a crewman. "Well!" said somebody elaborately. "Well, well, well! Now isn't that just a dirty crying shame?"

He saw the fist coming and rolled, taking it on his shoulder. His own flicked out, caught the green in the jaw; stepping in close, he let the other hand smack its way into the muscled stomach.

The rest closed in on him, and he saw the gray ranks pouring onto the court to his rescue, and the greens after them. With a stabbing sickness, he realized that his own attempt had fired off the riot.

There was a swirl of bodies around him, impact and noise, metal flashing under the artificial sun. He slugged at short range, drowned in the shouting, frantic to get away. Taller than average he could look over the surging close-cropped heads and see more men on their way. The thing was growing.

Someone slapped at him with a blackjack. He caught the blow on an uplifted arm, numbing it in a crash of pain. Viciously, he kneed the man, yanked the weapon loose, and flailed the screaming face. A fist hit him in the side, he went down and the feet trampled over him. Gasping, he struggled erect, slugged out half blindly. The howling current bore him off without strength to fight it. Through a haze of sweat and panic, he saw knives gleaming.

"Back! Get out!"

The metal rod whistled around his head. He snarled incoherently and yanked it away. "I'm staying here," he mumbled.

"Get out, get out!" The man was screaming, a small frail gray-haired man with two women behind him. "Get out, we don't want you, you, you—rioter—"

Friday leaned against a counter, sobbing air into the harsh dryness of throat and lungs. A wave of dizziness passed through him, dark before his eyes and a distant roaring in his ears. No, no, that was the mob, screaming and thundering in the corridor outside.

A measure of strength returned. "I—not rioting—" he forced through his teeth. "Wait here—only wait here—"

"Why—father, he's no crewman. He's an *officer*—"

Friday let it pass. He found a chair and slumped into it, letting nerves and muscles recover. He noticed dimly that he had been slashed here and there, blood was pooling onto the floor, but it hadn't started hurting much yet.

"Here, take this."

The girl had brought him a glass of whiskey. He downed it in a grateful gulp, letting its vividness scorch down his gullet and run warmly along his veins. Awareness began to come back.

He had stumbled into a small shop, a poor and dingy place cluttered with tools and handicrafts. Plastics mostly, he noticed, with some woodwork and metal, the small ornaments and household objects still produced by private parties. Besides himself, there were the man and his wife, and the girl who must be their daughter. She was about nineteen or twenty, he thought in the back of his mind, a slim blonde without extraordinary looks but with a degree of aliveness in her which was unusual.

The shopkeeper had locked the door by now. Apparently the riot— and Friday—had swept this way with a speed that took him by surprise. He was close to tears. "They'll start looting now," he said. "They always do. And it isn't a strong lock."

"The police should be here soon," said Friday.

"Not soon enough. I was looted once before. If it happens again, I'm ruined, I'll have to take a crew job—"

"You're hurt," said the girl. "Here, wait a minute, I'll get the kit." Friday could barely hear her voice above the echoing din of the riot, but he watched her with pleasure.

Bodies surged against the plate window until its plastic shivered. A man was backed against it and another one swung a knife and opened his throat. Blood blurred the view, and the girl screamed and hid her face against Friday's breast.

"I—I'm all right now," she whispered presently. "Here, the bandages—"

He had to admire her. *He* still wanted to vomit.

The door shook. "They're trying to batter it down! They want to get in before the police arrive! Oh, God—"

Friday took the metal bar and went over to the door. He felt a vicious glee which was not at all proper to an officer and a gentleman. "You should keep a gas gun handy," he remarked.

"You know only officers are allowed weapons—but the bullies make their own—Oh, oh, help—"

The door broke under three brawny shoulders. Friday swung the improvised club with a whistle and a crack. The first man went down on that blow and did not move. The second, carrying a shaft of his own, raised it in guard. Friday, remembering his fencing, jabbed him in the belly and he screamed and stumbled back with his hands to the wound. The third one fled.

They had been greens, which was something of a relief. Friday would have fought grays as willingly, but that could have been awkward for him later, if he were recognized.

He felt a return of the sick revulsion. God, God, God, what had become of the ship? Why did anyone ever feel sorry for these witless, lawless animals? What they needed was an officer caste, and—

He heard whistles blowing and the heart-stirring cadence of marching feet. The police had arrived. He shoved his green victim— unconscious or dead, he didn't much care which—outside and closed the door. "Turn your fans on full," he said. "They'll be using gas."

"Oh, you—" The older woman sought for words. "You were wonderful, sir."

Friday preened himself, smiling at the girl, whose answering expression was quite dazzling. "Don't 'sir' me, please," he said, trying to find words which wouldn't sound too story-book silly in retrospect. "I'm only an Engy at present, though I've no use for rioters of any class." He bowed, falling back on the formal manners of topdeck. "Evan Friday, your servant, sir and ladies."

They didn't recognize the name, which disappointed him more than he thought it should. But he got their own names—William Johnson, wife Ingrid, daughter Elena—and an invitation to dinner next "day." He left feeling quite smug about the whole affair.

Paradoxically, the exhibition which had soured Friday on all crewmen led to his forming more friendships among them than ever before. Word spread that Doc had been in on the very start of the fight, been wounded, laid some undetermined but respectable number of greens low, and in general acquitted himself like a good Engy. Men struck up talk with him, bought him drinks, listened to his remarks— strange how warming a plain "hello" could be when he came to work. He was more than merely accepted, and in his solitude could not prevent himself from responding emotionally.

Training told him that an officer and a gentleman had no business associating with any of these—these mutineers. Prudence, a need of friends, and a growing shrewd realization that if he hoped to accomplish anything he would have to fit into the lower-deck milieu, made him reply in kind. He retained his eccentricities, haircut and shave and faint stiffness of manner, noticing that once his associates were used to these they marked him out, made him something of a leader.

His plans were vague. There had been no word from topside, no word at all, though he supposed his family was keeping track of him. Once, in a tavern, he had encountered a group of crewquartering young aristocrats, friends of his, and his sister among them; there had been an embarrassed exchange of greetings and he had left as soon as possible. The upper world was shut off. But if he could attain some prominence down here, get influential friends, money—Surely he couldn't remain a crewman all his life! Such anticlimaxes just didn't happen to Evan Friday.

He was doing a good deal of work in close collaboration with the superintendent of his shop. The intricacies of the job were resolving themselves; he could handle it. He began to speculate on ways of displacing his superior.

It did not occur to him that he might be pulling a dirty trick on another human being.

But something else was going on that distracted his attention. Strangers were dropping into the barracks, husky young men who, it became clear, were full-time attendants of Wilson—in less euphemistic language, his goons. They talked to various workers, bought drinks—recruited! Rumors buzzed around: there was a cache of weapons somewhere, there was this or that dastardly plot afoot which must be forestalled, there was to be a general strike for higher pay and better conditions of work and living. Certainly a young man could make extra money and have some fun by signing on as a part-time goon. You learned techniques of fighting, you drilled a little bit, you played athletic games and had occasional beer parties with old Tom Wilson footing the bill. It had been some time since the last pitched battle between goon squads, but by God, jo, those officers' men were getting too big in the head, strutting around like they owned the ship, it might be time to scutter them a bit.

"They wanted me to join," said Carter. "I told 'em no."

"Good man!" said Friday.

Carter ran a big work-roughened hand through his red stubble. "I ain't looking for trouble, Doc," he said. "I'm saving to get married." He scowled. "Only, well, maybe we will have to fight. Maybe we won't get our rights no other way. And if they did fight, and win, and I wasn't in on it, it'd look bad later on."

"That's the sort of gruff they've been feeding you, huh?"

"Well, Doc, you got a head on your shoulders. But—I dunno. I'll have to think it over."

Friday lay awake during many hours, wondering what was on the way. Certainly the other factions aboard knew what was going on—why did they allow it, then? Were they afraid to precipitate a general conflict? Or did they have plans of their own? Or did they think Wilson was merely bluffing?

What did the man want, anyway? He was on the Council already, wasn't he?

Couldn't they see—damn them, couldn't they see that the ship was bigger than all their stupid ambitions, couldn't they see that space was the great Enemy against which all souls aboard, all mankind had to unite?

A special meeting of the Brotherhood of Workers was called. Friday had only been to one union assembly before, out of a curiosity which was soon quenched by the incredible dullness of the proceedings. Men stood and haggled, hour after hour, over some infinitesimal point, they dozed through interminable speeches and reports, they took a whole watch to decide something that the Captain should have settled in one minute. He realized wryly that a major qualification of leadership was an infinite patience. And skill in maneuvering men, swapping favors, playing opponents off against each other, covering the operations that mattered with a blanket of parliamentary procedure and meaningless verbiage. But he had a notion that this meeting was one he should attend in person, not simply over a telescreen.

The hall was jammed, and the ventilators could not quite overcome the stink of sweating humanity. Friday wrinkled his aristocratic nose and pushed through to the section reserved for his grade, near the stage. He found a seat beside a friend with a similar job, and looked around the buzzing cavern. Faces, faces, faces, greens and grays intermingled, workmen all. In a moment of honesty, he had to admit that there was more variety and character in those faces than in the smooth soft countenance of the typical lower-bracket officer. These visages had been leaned down by a lifetime of work, creased by squinting, dried by the hot wind of furnaces. He had gained considerable respect for manual skill; it took as much, in a way, to handle a lathe or a torch or a spraygun as to use slide rule and account book.

Only why should these complementary types be at War? They needed each other. Why couldn't they see the fact?

Several men filed onstage, accompanied by goons whose similar clothes suggested uniforms. Friday's mind wandered during the speech by the union's nominal president. The usual platitudes. He woke up when Wilson came to the rostrum.

He had to admit the Councillor was a personality. His voice was a superbly versatile instrument, rolling and roaring and sinking to a caress, drawing forth anger and determination and laughter. And the gross body, pacing back and forth, did not suggest fat, it was tigerishly graceful; a dynamo turned within the man. In spite of himself, Friday was caught up in the fascination.

Wilson deplored the riot, scolded his followers, exhorted them to forget their petty differences in the great cause of the voyage. He said he was recruiting "attendant auxiliaries" from green and gray alike, and mixing them up in squads, so that they could learn to know each other. They were fellow workers, they simply happened to have different jobs, they needed each other and the ship needed both.

"You *are* the ship! We've got to eat. We've got to have power, heat and light and air, tools, maintenance. *And nothing else.* Everybody else aboard is riding on your backs.

"Who keeps the ship moving? Who's pushing us to far Centauri? Not the officers' corps, not the Guildsmen, not the doctors and lawyers and teachers and policemen. Not even you, my friends. We reached terminal velocity eighty years ago. Old Man Inertia is carrying us to our far home. Don't let anybody claim credit for that, nobody but Almighty God.

"But we've got to eat on the way. We've got to have power to keep us alive, keep out the cold and the dark and the vacuum. Once landed, we'll still need all those things, we'll have to start farms and machine shops. We need *you.* You, green and gray, are the keel of this ship, and don't you ever forget it!"

He went on, with a vast silence before him and no eye in the chamber leaving his face. The workers were one, they had to unite to see the ship through, their feuds were a hangover from the bad old days of unrestrained capitalism. He hinted broadly that certain elements kept the pot boiling, kept the workers divided among themselves lest they discover their true strength and speak up for their rights. He instilled the notion of cabals directed against the crewmen—"who make up more than six thousand people, out of seven thousand!" and of plots to overthrow the Council, establish all-out officer rule and crush the workers underfoot.

"God, no!" cried Friday. He caught himself and relapsed into his seat, half blind with rage. His outburst had gone unnoticed in the rising tide of muttered anger.

Trying to control himself, he analyzed the speech as it went on. A wonderful piece of demagoguery, yes. Nothing in it that could really be called seditious—on the surface, merely an exhortation to end rioting and general lawlessness. No one was mentioned by name except the Guilds, who didn't count anyway. No overt suggestion of violence was made. The Captain was always spoken of in respectful tones, the hint being that he was the unhappy prisoner of the plotters. A list of somewhat exaggerated grievances was given, but the ship's articles provided for freedom of speech and assembly. Oh, yes, very lawful, very dignified—and just what was needed to incite mutiny!

At the end, the cheering went on for a good quarter-hour. Friday clamped his teeth together, feeling ill with fury. When the racket had subsided, Wilson called for the customary question period.

Friday jumped up on his seat. "Yes," he shouted. "Yes, I have a question."

"By all means, brother Friday," said Wilson genially. So—he remembered.

"Are you preaching revolution," yelled Friday, "or are you lying because you can't help yourself?"

The silence was short and incredulous, then the howling began. Friday vaulted into the aisle and up onto the stage, too full of his rage to care what he was doing.

Wilson's voice boomed from the loudspeakers, slowly fighting down the tumult: "Brother Friday does not agree with me, it seems. He has a right to be heard. Gentlemen, gentlemen, quiet please!" When the booing had died down a little: "Now, sir, what do you wish to say? This is a free assembly of free men. Speak up."

"I say," said Friday, "that you are a liar and a mutineer. Your talk has been a stew of meaningless words, false accusations, and invitations to rebellion. Shall I go down the list?"

"By all means," smiled Wilson. "Brother Friday, you know, has a somewhat unusual background. I am sure his views are worth hearing."

The laughter was savage.

"I hardly know where to begin," said Friday.

"It is a little difficult, yes," grinned Wilson. The laughter hooted forth again, overwhelming him, knotting his tongue. He twisted the words out, slowly and awkwardly:

"Just for a start, then, Mr. Wilson, you said that the greens and grays together are almost the entire ship. Six out of seven thousand, you said. Anyone who's taken the trouble to read the latest census figures would know it's not true. There are about a thousand men working in all the branches of Engineering under officers, and about five hundred in the food section. There are about three hundred in public service of one sort or another—police, teachers, lawyers and judges, administrative clerks, and so on. Guildsmen and other independents together make up perhaps seven hundred. The entire officers' corps, *including their families,* add up to maybe five hundred. In short, out of some three thousand money-earning, working people aboard, greens and grays add up to half.

"I don't include the four thousand others—housewives, children and aged." With an essay at sarcasm: "Unless you want to enroll them in your goon squads too!" He turned to the assembly. "Fifteen hundred people in green and gray, to dictate to the other fifty-five hundred. Is that your precious democracy?"

"*Boo! Boo! Throw 'im out! Spy! Blackleg! Boo!*"

"You seem to be distorting my speech now," said Wilson mildly. "But go ahead, if it amuses you."

"Goddamn it, man, it's the ship I'm thinking about, I know there are plenty of abuses, I'm the victim of one myself—"

"Ah, yes, a pathetic fate," said Wilson lugubriously. "He was forced by incredibly cruel people to come down among us and earn his living!"

The shouting and the booing and cursing and laughing drove Friday off the stage. He hadn't a chance, he was beaten and routed; and he had been made ridiculous—which was much worse. He fled, sobbing in his throat, yelling at the silent corridors and damning the ship and the voyage and every stinking human aboard her. Then he found a bar and drank himself blind.

"I admire your courage," said William Johnson, "but I must admit your discretion leaves something to be desired. You should have known you had no chance against a professional politician."

"Now he tells me," said Friday ruefully.

"I hope it hasn't made things—difficult for you, Evan." There was an anxiety in Elena's voice which pleased him.

He shrugged. "I didn't lose too many friends. But I lost a lot of standing."

Oddly enough, his mind ran on, it had been Sam Carter who had defended him most stoutly in the barrack-room arguments, Sam who had beaten him up when he first arrived and now stood by him, though it meant damning Wilson. The fact was comforting, but puzzling. It was hard to realize that people just didn't fit into the neat categories of tradition.

They were sitting in the Johnsons' apartment, a small bright place where he had been a frequent guest of late. He had fallen into the habit of dropping in almost "daily," for the merchant class had something to offer he had never looked to find on the lower levels, and something, besides, which was strange to the topdecks. The Johnsons and their associates were not the narrow-souled tradesmen their reputation among other classes insisted; they were, on the whole, people of quality and some little culture. If they had a major fault, he thought, it was a certain conservatism and timidity, a nostalgia for the "good old days" with which he could only partly sympathize. And they had their own tired clichés, meaningless words setting off automatic emotional responses—"free enterprise," "progressivism," "Radical"—but then, what class didn't?

He found himself increasingly aware of Elena. She was pleasant to look at and talk to; the other lower-deck women had seemed meretricious or merely dull. And at the same time she had an enterprising sincerity and an, at times, startlingly realistic worldview which would be hard to find in officers' women.

"And what do you expect to happen next?" asked Mrs. Johnson. The fact of Friday's being from topdeck earned him an automatic respect among Guildsmen, who still wanted leaders. Their own agitation was simply for justice for themselves, and Friday had to admit their cause seemed reasonable.

"Trouble. Open fighting—there've been brawls almost every watch between the goons of the Brotherhood and those of the officers. Maybe mutiny."

Johnson shuddered. He was bold enough in conversation, but physically timid. "I know," he said. "And the laborers have been making difficulties for private shopowners too. They've been smashing up bars, especially, when they're drunk."

"Want to socialize liquor, eh?" Elena's laugh was strangely merry. "Maybe we should call for a representative of the tavern-keepers on the Council."

"Only a representative of all tradesmen," said Johnson stiffly. To

Friday: "We won't stand for it much longer. The younger Guildsmen are forming protective associations."

"Goons! Certainly *not!* Protect—"

"A goon by any other name would smell as sweet," said Elena. "Why not call them by their right name? If we have to fight, we'll need fighting units."

"Not much good without weapons and training," said Friday. "You have small machine shops here and there. You should start quietly making knives, knuckledusters, and so on, and exercise squads in their use. Wouldn't take long to equip every man."

"Why, you're speaking sedition!" whispered Johnson. "That's no better than Wilson."

Friday flung out of his chair and paced the floor. "Why not?" he said angrily. "It's not as if you meant aggression. The police can't be everywhere, and in any case they're under the control of whoever owns the Captain. At the moment, that happens to be an uneasy cabal of Engy and Astro officers, together with Wilson, who's nominally their associate and actually trying to get the power from them. If the officers win, you may expect to see a rigid caste system imposed on all the ship. If Wilson wins, you'll get a nominal communism which, if I've read any history at all, will rapidly become the same kind of dictatorship under different labels. Either way, the Guilds lose. You won't have a voice in affairs till you're strong enough to merit one."

"Evan, I thought you were an officer," said Elena, very softly. "I thought even now—"

"Of course I am! A ship has to have discipline and a hierarchy of authority, but that's precisely what we haven't got now. What I want to see is a strong captain with an officer corps made of the better existing elements—oh, such as my father, for instance, or Lieutenant Steinberg, or any of some hundred others. Most of the lower-echelon officers are decent and sincere men, Elena, they just haven't got any effective voice in affairs; they take orders from the Captain without regard to the fact that he takes *his* orders from two or three warring cliques. And the holes left in the corps could be filled competitively from the lower ranks."

"Ah—" Johnson cleared his throat shyly. "Pardon me, Evan, but wouldn't there be the same tendency as before for rank to become hereditary?"

"Naturally, superior people tend to have superior children," said

Friday somewhat snobbishly. "But today, I admit, while there is still competitive examination for promotion, there is a certain favoritism in judging the results and few or no crewmen get the education needed to prepare for the tests." He clenched his fists. "God, what a lot of reform we need!"

Elena came over and took his hand. "You know more about the ship than anyone in the Guilds, Evan," she said. "Certainly your military knowledge is the best we can get. Will you be with us?"

He looked at her for a long while, "What have I been saying?" he whispered. "What have I been saying?"

"Good things, Evan."

"But—Bill, you're right. I have been talking violence," He smiled uncertainly. "I've been overworking my mouth lately, haven't I?"

"You won't help us—?"

"I don't know. God, I don't know! Taking the law into our own hands this way—it's contrary to the articles, it's contrary to everything I've ever believed."

"But we have to do it, Evan," she said urgently. "You advised it yourself, and you're right."

"Blast it, I'm still an Engy. I still have to live with my co-workers."

"You could quit your job and come live with us. The Guilds would pay you a good wage just to get their protective squads organized."

"So now I'm to become a paid goon!" he said bitterly.

"The time may come when the ship will need your goon squads."

"I don't know," he said dully. With sudden vehemence: "Let me think! I've been kicked into a level I don't understand, caught up in a business I don't approve. My father told me, before they sent me away, that I was still an officer. And yet—let me think it over, will you?"

"Of course, Evan," said Johnson.

He bade clumsy farewells and went out into the corridor and back toward his dwelling place, too preoccupied to notice the men who fell quietly in on either side of him. When one of them spoke, it was like a blow:

"This way, Friday."

"Eh? Huh?" He stared at them. Wilson's goons. "What the hell do you want?"

"We just want to take you to Mr. Wilson, jo. He wants to see you. This way."

An elevator took them up to officer level. Actually, thought a dim corner of Friday's mind, the term should have been "down," since they were increasing centrifugal "gravity"; but the notion of the upper classes living "upward" was too ingrained for usage to change, even though on any one level "down" meant the direction of acceleration. Silly business.

The whole expedition was a cosmic joke.

He had not been in this territory for half a year, and it jarred him with remembrance. He stayed between his escorts, looking directly ahead, trying not to see the familiar people who went by. It was doubtful if any of them looked closely enough to recognize him.

Wilson's offices occupied a suite in the Administrative section, near the bows and just under the ship's skin. Her screens made that area as safe as any other, and the fact that the pilot room and hence the captain's quarters had to be directly in the bow on the axis of rotation—the only spot where there was an outside view except via telescreen—had dictated the placement of all officer areas nearby.

The inner office was a big one. Wilson had had it redecorated with murals which, in spite of their subjects—heroic laboring figures, for the most part—Friday had to admit were good. Indeed, these troubled decades had produced a lot of fine work.

He wrenched his attention to the man behind the great desk. Wilson sat easy and relaxed, puffing a king-sized cigar and studying some papers which he put aside when the newcomers entered. He rose courteously and smiled. "Please sit down, Mr. Friday," he said.

The two goons took up motionless posts by the door. Friday edged himself nervously into a chair.

"You know Lieutenant Farrell, of course," said Wilson.

Friday felt a shock at seeing the lean middle-aged man in officer's uniform seated at Wilson's right. Farrell—certainly he knew Farrell, the man had taught him basic science. Farrell had for years been a general assistant to Captain Gomez.

"I'm sorry to see you associated with this man, sir," he said numbly.

"Quite a few officers are," said Farrell gently. "After all, Mr. Wilson is a Councillor."

"Have a cigar, Mr. Friday," said Wilson.

"No, thanks. What did you want to see me about?"

"Oh—several things. I wanted to apologize for the somewhat

unfortunate result of the union meeting. You had a right to be heard, and it is a shame that some of the men got a little rowdy."

You know damn well what made them that way, thought Friday.

"I liked your courage, even if it was misguided," said Wilson. "You're an able young man and honest. I'd like to have you on my side."

Friday wished he had accepted the cigar. It would have been a cover for the silence that came from having no retort to make. *Another little political trick. I'll know better next time, if there is a next time.*

"You seem to think I'm some kind of monster," said Wilson. "Believe me, I have only the interests of the ship at heart. I think that we must be united in order to succeed in this voyage. But to achieve that union, we must have justice. You yourself, as a victim of the present system, ought to realize that."

"We need leadership first," said Friday slowly. "Good leadership, not political dictatorship."

"There is no intention of setting one up," said Farrell mildly. "Certainly you don't think that officers will be replaced by commissars! Would I be in this movement if that were the case? No, we simply want to replace the corrupt and the incompetent, and to install a socio-economic system adapted to the peculiar needs of the expedition."

"Nice words. But you're building up a private army, and you're planning mutiny."

"I could get angry at that charge," said Wilson. "Have I ever so much as suggested replacing the Captain? If the ship's articles are to be amended, it will be by due process of law."

"A rigged Council and a fixed election! Sure! Keep the Captain in his present job of figurehead!"

"Now it is you who are seditious. Look, Mr. Friday. I do believe you are innocent of the charges made against you, and I'd like to see you cleared and your rank restored. Promotion will be rapid for competent men, once things are running properly again. But these are tough times, and you can't expect me to take all that trouble for an enemy."

"So now you're trying to bribe me. Why, for all I know it was you who framed me in the first place."

Wilson's carefully learned manners dropped from him. It was a plain Engy who spoke, with more than a trace of anger: "Look, jo, d'you think you're so goddam important that it makes any difference what happens to you? You think I need you? I'm just trying to be fair, and give you a chance to get back where you were. You can be useful, sure, but you're not fixed to do any harm. Especially if you got fired from your job."

Friday stood up. "That's enough," he said. "Goodbye, Mr. Wilson."

"Have it your way, jo. If you change your mind, you can come back in a day or two. But don't be any later."

"I wish you would think it over," said Farrell.

"Goodbye!" Friday stormed out of the office.

He cooled off on the trip back. Gods, talk about burning bridges! He didn't belong anywhere now.

No—wait—the Guilds. He still didn't much like the thought of espousing their cause—but where else in all the universe could he go?

He took a certain malicious pleasure in telling off his boss when he quit. Then he drew his time, collected his few belongings, and went back to William Johnson's home.

The food trust was overthrown largely from within—a general strike of its underpaid workers, accompanied by violence—but that overthrow was instigated by leading Engineers as a means of overcoming their food-producing rivals. The Engineers wanted a return to the small private farms of the first years—*divide et impera*— but the upper ranks of Administration favored socializing the producing, packing, and distributing establishments, since they would then be under effective control of the small but efficient Admy bureaucracy. After a good deal of intriguing, socialism won, and the Engineers found themselves faced with a new rival as powerful as the old.

Two years later, Captain Petrie died. Both Engineering and Administration nominated a hand-picked successor, ignoring the rule that the first mate should take the office. This was a young man, Juan Gomez, associated with the Astrogation Department. Astro, being a small and exclusively officer group, lacked the strength and support of the contending overlords; but it had the law on its side, together with a surprising adroitness at playing its enemies off against each other. Gomez was named.

For a few years there was relative quiet, except for clashes between various bully gangs hired by the overlords. The workers, green and gray, were increasingly restless, the younger generation of officers in all departments ever more arrogant and exclusive. In the forty-fifth year of the great voyage, open warfare broke out between the private forces of Engy and Admy over the exact extent of Admy jurisdiction—the latter had been using the ship's internal law, which it was supposed to administer, as a means of aggrandizing its leaders. It was not what Earth's bloody history would have considered a real war—the two sides lacked very effective weapons, and were small—but people were getting killed, property was damaged and vital services suspended. Astrogation rallied the police and neutral groups to suppress the fighting. The ship's articles were amended, the most important respect being the transfer of police power from Administration to the Captaincy—in effect, to Astro. Administration didn't like it, but the Engineers, on the old half-a-loaf principle, supported the measure. Astro began building up followers, money investments, and political connections.

Five years later the lower Engineering ranks, having failed to obtain satisfaction in any other way, resorted to violence. The revolt was suppressed, but concessions were made in a Captain's Court which few officers liked.

Six years after that, Duncan, chief of Administration, attempted to seize the Captaincy in a coup d'etat which was defeated with the help of the Engineering bosses. Duncan and his immediate followers suffered the usual penalties of mutiny, but his power was left unbroken and passed to his successor. This was shown to be the work of Astro: in the sixty-first year, Admy and Astro together swung enough political power to break up officer ownership of factories and socialize them, and enough fighting strength to enforce the decree.

Some fifteen years passed without too much trouble as the ship adjusted to the new order of things. All important facilities were now under ship ownership and control, tracing back ultimately to the Captain and his Council. The old departmental divisions remained, but officers within them acted as individuals and their combinations were often across such party lines. Some wanted a return to the former state of affairs, but most were content to intrigue for control of this or that department of ship life—ultimately, the goal was to run the Council, from which all authority stemmed. A combine made up largely of Astro officers held the balance of power, but it was a constant battle of wits to maintain it. In this period began the first great outburst of characteristic ship forms of art, literature, and music, new departures which would have meant little to an Earthman but which answered a need born of space and loneliness and the great overriding purpose. In science, some first-rate work was done on deep-space astrophysics and the biological effects of cosmic radiation.

Meanwhile, however, the laboring classes demanded some voice in affairs. Unions were organized on a ship-wide basis and finally joined together in Wilson's Brotherhood. At this time, too, the remaining independents—craftsmen, artisans, tailors, tavern-keepers, personal-service people, private lawyers, and their kind, including no few scientists and artists of one sort or another—began organizing the Guilds for mutual protection and advancement; but they had no way to win an effective voice.

Labor, however, could and did act. The great strike of 2201 broke the time of peace. On the principle that certain services were essential to the lives of everyone, the Council tried to break the strike, and for several days a running war was fought up and down the corridors of the ship. The union was finally suppressed, but it won what amounted to a victory, a representative on the Council. The old-line officers were outraged, but Wilson set to work at once making alliances with the younger and more liberal ones.

His official program was frankly communistic. The large fortunes and followings of the highest officers were to be broken up, all property except the purely personal was to belong to the ship, plants were to be governed by workers' councils. On the other hand, some kind of supreme hierarchy would still, obviously, be needed; and no doubt many of the ranking men who joined Wilson's cause were animated by the thought of promotion. There were also a certain percentage of sincere idealists who were disgusted with the intriguing and corruption of the ship's government, the unseemly brawling, private gangs, and the not yet overcome unfairness of a caste system.

Besides Wilson's group, there were several others in high places, with schemes of their own. Certain men wanted to grab supreme power for themselves; others wished a return to this or that stage of previous ship's history, say the good old days when the Engineers virtually ran affairs, or to advance along certain lines that seemed desirable to them—such as, for instance, a frankly hereditary officer caste controlling all wealth and authority.

Gomez still had the chairmanship of the Council, the small but strong police force, and a solid following among conservative elements including the bulk of the officer's corps and perhaps even a majority of the common. And Astro had the Captain. One suspected that McMurtrie, chief of that department, had the final say in matters, though no one outside of Astro knew for certain.

Only—how long could it continue? The ship was ready for another explosion. How long before it came?

Gods! thought Friday sick. *Gods, what a history! What hell's broth of a history!*

He had about three weeks before the crisis broke, and had not thought he could go so long on as little sleep as he got.

There was first the matter of raising his troop. A call for volunteers at a special Guild meeting brought disappointing results. He and a few others had to go on personal recruiting tours, arguing and propagandizing and even applying certain subtle threats—social disapproval, boycotting, and whatever else could be hinted at obliquely enough not to antagonize. Some rather slippery sophistry got by at times, and Friday had to be careful to suppress his own uneasy doubts about his cause. The motto was always organization for defense, formation of a band which could help the regular police if they should need it, and he found it necessary to shout down the hotheads who had been his eagerest followers. He often had occasion to remember the ancient maxim that politics is the art of creating an equality of dissatisfaction.

He was helped by events. As the watches went by, disorder grew like a prairie fire. Hardly a "day" passed that the police were not called to stop a brawl between Wilson's gangs and the goons of other factions, or to halt the wrecking and plundering of some shop. They were bewildered and angry men who came to Friday, they wanted to fight somebody—it didn't much matter who.

"But what the glory is Wilson doing it for?" said Mrs. Johnson. "He's only hurting his own cause. He should be calming them down, or he'll turn all the ship against his people."

"That," said Friday with a bleak new insight, "is what he wants."

Officially, of course, the Councilor deplored such lawlessness and called on all workers to desist. But his language was weak; it only turned strong when he cited the grievances which had driven them to such measures. Friday buckled down to training his gang.

He had no military knowledge except vague impressions from books, but then neither did anyone else who mattered. Only the police were allowed firearms, and his conditioning was too deep for him to consider manufacturing them. It would hardly have been practicable anyway. But the tools of the artisans could make the nasty implements of infighting. And it occurred to him further that pikes, axes, and even short swords were valuable under ship conditions. However clumsily wielded, they were still formidable. He thought of bows too, but experiment showed him that more practice would be needed than his men had time or patience for.

He worked three shifts each day, drilling those who could attend any one of them. Practice with weapons, practice in working as groups, practice at rough-and-tumble—it was all he could do, and he more than half expected his motley squads to break and run if it ever came to action. He had about two hundred all told, shopkeepers, artisans, personal-service men, office workers, intellectuals of all stripes; a soldier's nightmare.

But after all, he consoled himself, it wasn't really an army he was trying to organize. It was an association of ordinary peaceable men who had found it necessary to form their own auxiliary police force. That was all. He hoped to heaven that was all.

They used an empty storage space near zero-gravity as their armory. You could do weird and wonderful things at low-weight, once you got the hang of it. He tried to be as unobtrusive about his project as possible, and especially to keep secret the fact of his most lethal innovations. The police would most likely confiscate things like those, if they heard of them. All the rest of the ship needed to know was that the Guildsmen had started a protective association, and if the Brotherhood wanted to make a huge joke of it, so much the better.

Nevertheless, Friday was irrationally pleased when a few of his men got into a fight with some greens in a bar and beat the devil out of them.

He was catching an exhausted nap in Johnson's apartment when Elena woke him with the news that the Brotherhood had mutinied.

"Oh, no!" he exclaimed. Sleep drained from him like water from a broken cup as he got to his feet.

"Yes," she said tonelessly. "The intercom just announced a state of emergency, told all crewfolk to get home and stay there and not to take part in any violence on pain of being considered mutineers—what else can it mean?"

He heard the brazen voice again, roaring out of the corridor loudspeaker, and nodded. "But I'd like to see it done," he said thinly. "The ship is six miles long and two miles in diameter. How does Wilson expect to take it over with a thousand men at best?"

"Seize the key points and the officers," she flared. "How else?"

"But the police—he can't hold anyplace against men with gas guns, firearms, grenades—"

"He must think he can! Are we going to sit here and do nothing?"

"Not much else we can do. That order to stay inside means us, too."

"Evan Friday, what have you been organizing the Guildsmen for?"

"Get on the visiphone," he said. "Call up everyone before somebody or other cuts off our communications. Tell them to stand by. But we can't go rushing out blindly."

She flushed him a smile. "That's more like it, Evan!"

He looked out the door into the hall. Men, women, children, were running each way, shouting, witless with panic—*This is revolution*, he thought. *You don't know what's happened, you don't know who's fighting or where the fighting is, you sit and wait and listen to the people going they don't know where.*

Presently Elena came to sit on the arm of his chair. "Where's father and mother?" she asked, and he saw the hard-held strength of her breaking as immediate pressure lifted. "They said they were going to visit Halvorson's; where are they—"

"I don't know," he bit out. "They must have taken refuge with someone. We'll just have to wait here."

"I couldn't raise everybody," she said. "A lot of lines were jammed. But some of them said they'd pass the word along by messengers."

"Good! Good folk!" It was enormously heartening to know that some had remained brave and level-headed.

"I didn't even try to call headquarters," she said wryly. "But maybe we could offer the Captain our help."

"Let's see what happens first." Friday pounded his knee with a white-knuckled fist. "It's not that I'm scared to fight, Elena. In fact, I'm scared green to sit here and not fight. But we'd just blunder around, have no idea of where to go or what to do, probably get in the way of the police—"

The lights went out.

They sat for a moment in a blackness which was tangible. Elena choked a cry, and he heard the screaming of women out in the hall.

"Power cut off," he said unnecessarily, trying to hold his voice steady. "Wait—hold still a minute." He strained his ears into the darkness and could not hear the muted endless hum of the ventilators. "Yeah. Dead off."

"Oh, Evan—if they hold the converters, they can threaten to destroy them—"

"Take more than they've got to do that, darling." The word came unconsciously, unnoticed by either of them. "But if they can hold off for a long enough time, they can make things awfully tough for the rest of the ship."

"It's—been tried before, hasn't it—?"

"Uh-huh, during the great strike. The police took the converters without difficulty and operated them till the trouble was over. So— if Wilson's tried it again, he must think he can hold the engine section against attack. Or maybe—maybe he doesn't expect an attack at all—"

"You mean the police are in his pay—no!"

"I don't know what I mean." Friday groped to his feet, and his only emotion was a rising chill of anger. "But it's time we found out. I'm going to get the men together."

They located a flashlight and went down the corridors toward the armory. It was utterly black save where their own beam wavered, a smothering blackness in which Friday thought he could hardly breathe. That was nonsense; the air wouldn't get foul for hours yet; but his heartbeat was frantic in his ears. People had retreated, the halls were almost empty—now and then another glow would bob out of the tunnel before them, a weirdly highlighted face. The elevators were dead; they used ringingly echoing companionways, down and down and down into the guts of the ship.

Silent ship, darkened ship; it was as if she were already dead, as if he and Elena were the last life aboard her, the last life in all the great hollow night between Sol and Centauri. Elena sobbed with relief when they came to the armory.

Friday had maintained a rotating watch there, sentries who challenged him in voices gone shrill with fear. Others were arriving, men and their families, the agreement being that in emergency this would be the rallying place. It was easily defensible, especially with the weapons stockpiled there.

Flashlights danced in the gloom, picking out faces and shimmering off metal, and the great sliding shadows flowed noiselessly around the thin beams. Friday shouted till the walls rang, calling the folk around him, seeking to allay the rising tide of hysteria.

"As soon as enough of us are here," he said, "we'll go out and see what we can do."

"The hell you say!" exploded a voice from the murk. "We'll stay here where we can defend ourselves!"

"Till the oxygen and the heat are gone? Would you rather choke and freeze?"

"They'll reach some agreement before then. Wilson can't let the whole ship die."

"They'll reach Wilson's kind of agreement, if any. Something's happened so the police can't protect us anymore. We'll have to act for ourselves."

"Go out and get killed in the dark? Not I, Mister!"

Friday had to resort to all the tactics of demagoguery—he was getting good at it, he thought—before the recalcitrants could be brought around. The agreement finally was that some men should stay to guard the women and children, while the rest would go out and—

And what? Friday did not dare admit that he had no idea. What, in all those miles of lightless tunnels and cave-like rooms, could they do?

There was an altercation at one of the doors. Friday went over to it and found a pair of pikemen thrusting back a shadowy and protesting group of men.

"Bunch of goddam workers want in," explained one of the guards.

Friday shone his torch into the vague mass and picked out the battered red face of Carter. "Sam! What the hell—"

"Fine way to treat us. We only want to join your bunch, Doc."

"Huh? I thought you were a Brotherhood man!"

"Yeah, but not a mutineer. I didn't think Old Tom'd ever try anything like this—just thought we'd roughhouse it a bit with the topdeck goons and holler for our rights. But God, Doc, his men got guns!"

"*What?*"

"Fact. Ain't too careful about using them, either. Me and some others that hadn't joined the goons were given a last chance to do it or get brigged—a goon squad come into the barracks and told us. But we got the jump on 'em, and here's my proof." The light glimmered off the pistol in Carter's fist. "We had a running fight to get down to low-weight, but others joined us on the way—some o' the boys who'd signed on as goons but didn't see mutiny, and others from here and there. They've took over the engine-section, Doc, and the gyros and the farms. There's men here with me who was on duty when the goons came in and kicked 'em out. Some of 'em had buddies who got shot for not moving fast enough. We wanna fight with you now, Doc!"

Numbly, Friday waved his sentries aside and let the workers file in. Gray and green, burly men with smoldering eyes, perhaps two score all told—a welcome addition, yes, but they were the heralds of evil tidings.

He let his watch sweep out another hour of darkness and restlessness and slowly rising temperature. Without regulation, the room was filled with animal heat of its occupants, the air was hot and foul. Later would come the cold.

Others straggled in, one by one or in small groups, Guildsmen and some more of the laboring class. But there was no further news, and presently the influx ceased. It was time to strike out.

A count-off showed that he had a little over a hundred men ready to go. Go—where?

He decided to head for the upper levels. There should be his best chance of getting information—there, too, was the nerve center of the ship. If Wilson held her heart and lungs, her brain might still be accessible.

They went out, a hundred men armed with hand weapons of the oldest sort and a few scattered guns, daunted by the night and their loneliness. Silently, save for heavy breathing, they streamed down the corridors and along the companionways, only an occasional short flash of light revealing them. Friday drew on his memory of the ship's plan, which every cadet was required to learn, to guide them well away from the key points which Wilson held. He didn't want more fighting than he could avoid.

The ship was dark and still. Someone whimpered behind him, a little animal sound of fear.

They wound up the levels, feeling their bodies grow heavier, feeling the sweat on their skins and the bitter taste of panic in their mouths. Once in awhile someone ran before them, sandaled feet slapping down the tunnel and fading back into the thick silence.

"God," whispered Carter. "What's happened to the ship?"

His voice was shaken, and Friday realized that the same despair was rising in him. It wouldn't take many hours of night and stillness and creeping chill before everyone aboard capitulated, before the entire crew would be ready to assail anyone that still tried to resist. "Come on!" he said harshly.

They were in the upper levels when a flash gleamed far down the hall, someone nearing. Friday heard the sigh of tension behind him. If this was a mutineer gang and—

"Who goes?" The cry wavered in the dark. "Who is it?"

"Put up your hands," shouted Friday. The echoes ran down the length of the corridor, jeering at him.

"Come close."

It was a single man in Astro uniform. Friday recognized him— Ensign Vassily, secretary to Farrell. Farrell!

The gun was heavy in his fist. "What do you want?"

"Friday—Friday—" It was a sob. The flash-beam glistened off sweat and tears. "God, man, you're here! We've been looking—"

"Looking! What for? Aren't you with Wilson too?"

"Not now. The mutiny's got out of hand. Wilson has the police trapped, Farrell can't leave—he managed to send a few of us out, he knew of your gang—Friday, it's up to you, you've got to save the ship!"

"Out of hand— What the devil are you talking about?"

"Wilson was too smart." The boy's breath sobbed in his throat. "He didn't let any of his top chiefs in on his plans till it was too late. He— he started a riot down in Park Four, a big riot that brought out all the police force. Then his men—he'd gotten some firearms from a police officer that was with him, we didn't know he had anyone in the police— His men came with machine guns and flame throwers. They've got the force bottled up in the park—and meanwhile they've taken over the rest of the ship!"

So that was it, thought Friday. Simple! You lured all your enemies into one of the park sections and then mounted guard over the half-dozen exits. A few men with weapons and gas masks could keep a thousand besieged until cold and darkness and choking air forced them to surrender.

"Where do *you* fit in?" He shook Vassily till the teeth rattled in the ensign's jaws. "What do you mean, the mutiny's out of hand? Did you engineer it yourself?"

"Farrell—the Captain—I do not know, Friday, so help me God I don't know what it's all about!"

With a sudden terrible conviction: "Gomez and Farrell framed me, didn't they? They had me broken down to crewman!" When Vassily remained still, Friday cracked the pistol barrel against his head. "That's right, isn't it?"

"Uh—yes, no, I don't know—Friday, you've got to help us! We've been searching the ship for you, running down all the corridors with Wilson's men ready to shoot, you're the last one who can help!"

"Help?" Carter's laugh was bitter. "Spears and axes against guns?"

"Most of Wilson's men don't have guns. He d-d-doesn't want 'em to get out of hand, I guess. Just the ones holding in the police, and holding the k-key points—"

Friday's mind began turning over with an abnormal speed and sureness. There wasn't time to be afraid, not now, not when all the ship was darkened. "That means the rest of the ship's weapons are still in the arsenal," he said rapidly. "I suppose Wilson's mounted guard over them?"

"I—I s-s-suppose so—"

Friday's memories riffled through the plans of the ship. The police quarters were near the bows, with the arsenal behind them, just under the ship's skin. Beyond that lay a boat blister, whose airlock offered an emergency exit—or entrance. Wilson's guards would be inside the ship, though, in front of the doors leading into the police area. He hoped!

There were other blisters along the length of the ship, holding the boats which would land when the *Pioneer* had taken up an orbit around a planet. And there were spacesuits stored at each one.

"This way!" he said.

It was strange walking on the outside. Eyes accustomed to a narrowness of walls swam with vertigo in naked space. Centrifugal force threw blood into the head, the heart began to beat wildly and the body refused to believe that it was not hanging downward. You had to be careful how you stepped—if both magnetic shoes were off the hull at once, you would be thrown into space, you could go spinning out and out forever into the dark between the stars.

Above your feet was the mighty curve of the ship, dimly gleaming metal tilted at a crazy angle against the sky, elliptical horizon enclosing all the life in more than a light-year of emptiness. It rang faintly under human footfalls, and the suit was thick with your heartbeat and breathing, but over that lay the elemental silence. It was a silence which sucked and smothered, the stupendous quiet of vacuum reaching farther than a man could think, and the tiny noises of life were unnaturally loud against it.

Below was the turning sky the constellations wheeling in fire and ice against a savage blackness, the chill glory of the Milky Way and the far green gleam of nebulae, hugeness, loneliness, and terror. The raw cold grandeur was like frost along the nerves; men felt sick and dizzy with the streaming of the stars.

Faint light glimmered off spacesuits and weapons as the troop made its slow way over the hull. About half the band had come out through four exits, and they clustered together for comfort against the hollow dark. Few words were spoken, but the harsh rasp of their breathing rattled in the helmet radios.

As they approached the bows, Friday could pick out the stabbing brilliance of Alpha Centauri—but Sol was lost somewhere in the thronging stars, nearly three light-years away. He found it hard to believe that the ship was rushing through space at fantastic velocity— no, it was motionless, it was lost forever between the stars.

And in the face of that immensity and that mission, he thought bitterly, men had nothing better to do than fight each other. With all the universe around them, they could not unite in a society which did not tear itself apart.

There was a certain cruel symbolism in the fact that it was Astrogation which had betrayed him—the men who steered between the worlds, dealing in rottenness and death. But after all, what else did those officers have to do? There were no planets between the suns, no orbital corrections to make—the department existed to keep alive the techniques and, meanwhile, to hold various posts connected with the general maintenance of the ship. And to stir up against each other men who should have been comrades—to break the innocent with lies, to

provoke mutiny by injustice and intrigue, to infiltrate the revolts they
themselves had created and control them for some senseless unknown
purpose.

His jaws hurt with the clenching of his teeth. There was work to be
done: enter the arsenal from outside, get the weapons, overcome the
guards, then go on to park and fall on Wilson's men from behind so
that the police could get out. Afterward it would be simple to clean up
the rest of the mutineers; most likely they'd surrender at once when
the police moved against them.

But after that—after that—!

Evan Friday walked slowly toward the door. It was strange to be
back topside. After the noise and fury and belly-knotting terror of
battle, after the lights had gone on again and folk had returned
shakenly to resume life—of necessity, there had been amnesty for all
rebels save the ringleaders—after the quite undeserved but pleasant
adulation of gray and green and Guild, there had been a polite note
requesting his attendance on the Captain, and he had donned his
shabby best and gone. And that was all there was to it.

He felt no special emotion, it was drained from him and only a
great quiet steadiness of purpose was left. It was no use hating anyone,
they were all together in the ship and the ship was alone between the
stars. But there was certain words he had to say.

The policeman at the door saluted him. "This way, please, sir," he
said.

So now it's "sir" again. Do they think that can bribe me?

They went down a short hall and through an anteroom. The clerks
looked up from their work with a vague apprehensiveness. Friday
nodded to a man he had known a half a year ago—half a lifetime!—
and at his escort's gesture went alone through the inner door.

There were three men sitting at the great table in the Captain's
office—frail white-haired Gomez, lean gray Farrell, stocky dark
McMurtrie. They rose as he entered, and he stood with straining
military stiffness. He couldn't help feeling naked without his uniform.

"How do you do, Ensign Friday." Gomez's old voice was hardly
above a whisper. "Please be seated."

He found a chair and watched them out of cold eyes. "You are
mistaken, sir," he answered. "I have no rank."

"Yes, you do, or rather you will as soon as that miscarriage of justice has been taken care of."

"Let us be plain with each other," said Friday flatly. "I know that you are responsible for my conviction. I also know that you and your associates engineered the mutiny, and that Wilson was only a force of which you made use. The casualties of the whole affair were some thirty killed and fifty wounded. If you had not summoned me here I would have come myself to charge you with murder."

There was pain in Gomez's slow reply: "And you would be perfectly justified. But perhaps the charge should be modified to manslaughter. We did not intend that there should be any death, and it weighs more heavily on us than you can imagine. But as you also know, the business got out of control, Wilson succeeded far beyond our expectations, and only your timely intervention saved us. Fortunately, the plan does not call for putting the ship into such danger again."

"I should hope not!" snapped Friday. "Before you go any further, perhaps I had better say that I left the traditional sealed envelope containing all I know with a friend. If I don't return soon, you may look for an unplanned uprising."

"Oh, you are in no danger," smiled Farrell. "It would hardly do for us to assault the next Captain."

"I—you—*what?*"

Numbly, Friday heard the voice continue: "In about five years, I imagine, you will be ready to succeed Captain Gomez."

He forced steadiness back, and there was a new anger in his reply: "Don't you think you can buy me that way, or any other. The whole structure of ship society is wrong. Our history has been one succession of bunglings, injustices, and catastrophes. I am here to call for a complete overhauling. And the first item will be to clean out the rotten blood-suckers who claim to be the leaders."

"Please, Mr. Friday," said McMurtrie, a little irritably. "Spare the emotional language till you've heard a bit more. For your information, every major wrong this expedition suffered has been created deliberately by the leaders—because they've really had no choice in the matter."

Friday glared at him. "You should know!" he spat. "You've run the whole dirty show, for twenty years this doddering fool has been your puppet, and—"

"I have not. The story goes, yes, that I am the power behind the throne. It's true that I've worked hard to keep things going. And I took the blame, because the Captain cannot afford it. He must have, if not the respect, at least the grudging acquiescence of the ship. But Captain Gomez is a very strong and skillful gentleman, and the decisive voice has always been his."

Friday shook his head. The maze of plot and counterplot, blinds and red herrings and interwoven cabals, was getting to be too much for him. "Why?" he asked dully. "What's the reason been? This is the greatest adventure man has ever faced, and now you say you've deliberately perverted it. If you aren't fiends and aren't madmen—*why?*"

"Let me start from the beginning," said Gomez.

He leaned back in his chair and half closed his eyes. "Psychology is a highly developed science these days," he said gently, "though for reasons which will become obvious it has been largely suppressed aboard ship. A potential leader is quietly given some years of intensive training in the field, for use later on—as you will be given it. And among the thousands of men who worked ten or twenty years on Earth planning this voyage, there were many psychologists. They could foresee events with more precision than I can convey to you; but I hope my bare words will be convincing.

"Consider the *Pioneer.* Once on her way, she is a self-contained world. Everything we can possibly need to keep alive and comfortable is built into her. There is no weather, no disease, no crop failure, no earthquake, no outside invader, no new land to cultivate—nothing! A world potentially changeless! To be sure, for some twenty years the crew was still working on internal construction, but then that source of occupation and challenge was gone and there were still a hundred years or more of traveling left. A hundred years where a bare minimum of work would provide an excellent living for everyone.

"*What is the crew going to do in those hundred years?*"

For a moment Friday was taken aback at the question. The imbecile simplicity and the monstrous blindness of it held him dumb before he could answer: "Do? Why, God, man, the things that we have been doing, the worthwhile things that got accomplished in spite of all that went wrong. Science, music, the arts—"

McMurtrie gave him a scornful look. "What percentage of the population can keep amused that way?" he asked.

"Why—uh—ten per cent, maybe— But the rest— What's your psychology for, anyway? I've read books from Earth, I know there were primitive cultures where people were content to live perfectly uneventful, routine lives for thousands of years at a time. You could have created such a culture within the ship."

"And how fit would that culture be for the hardships and dangers of Alpha Centauri?" demanded Farrell.

"It's a question of decadence," said Gomez persuasively. "If you read your history, you'll find that the decadent cultures, the ones without hope or enterprise or anything but puerile experimentation hiding a rockbound conservatism, have been those which lacked some great external purpose. They've been easier to live in, yes, until the decadence went so far that disintegration set in. The cultures which offered a man something to live for besides his own petty self—a crusade, a discovery, a dream of any kind, perhaps only the prospect of new land for settlement—have usually been violent, intolerant, unpleasant in one way or another, simply because everything else has been subordinated to the great purpose. I submit, as examples, Periclean Athens, Renaissance Italy, Elizabethan England, and nineteenth-century America, and ask you to compare them with, say, Imperial Rome or eighteenth-century Europe. You will also note that the greatest works of art and intellect were done in some of the most turbulent eras. As far as I can determine, the progress made aboard our ship has been rather because of than in spite of all our troubles."

"But damn it, man, we *have* a mission!" exploded Friday. "We're bound for far Centauri!"

"To be sure. That was the dream which sufficed the first generation. I don't say that unrest is a necessary component of nondecadence, in fact my whole argument has been grossly over-simplified. There was little strife in the beginning, because there was the great goal to dwarf men's petty differences.

"But what of the next generation, and the one after that, and the one after that, clear to Centauri? What was the goal to them but a vague thing in the background, an accepted part of everyday life—a thing which they would never see, or only see as very old people at best, a thing which had caused their lives to be spent in a cramped and sterile environment far from the green Earth? Don't you think there would have been a certain amount of subconscious resentment? And don't you think that the descendants of human stock deliberately chosen for energy, initiative, and general ability would have looked around for something worthwhile to do? And if nothing else is available, personal aggrandizement is a perfectly worthwhile goal."

"Couldn't—" Friday hesitated. The whole fiendish argument had a shattering conviction about it, and yet it seemed wrong and cruel. "Couldn't there have been a static culture for the in-between generations, and a revival of the dynamic sort in the generation that will reach Centauri young?"

"Now you're wallowing in wishful thinking," said McMurtrie. "Cultures have momentum. They don't change themselves overnight. Just tell me how you'd do all this, anyway."

Friday was silent.

"Believe me, all this was foreseen, and the solution adopted, while admittedly not very good, was the best available," said Farrell earnestly. "Conflict was inevitable. But if it could be controlled, properly directed, it could have great value, not only in keeping the dynamic society we will need at Centauri going, but also as a hard school for the unknown difficulties we will face then.

"Naturally, overt control is impossible. It has to be done indirectly—as far as possible, events simply have to take their natural course, with such men as know the secret and the techniques of psychology serving only as unnoticed guides.

"The initial setup was designed to cause a certain chain of development. The original small-scale private enterprises became monopolies in a very natural way, and their excesses provoked reactions, and so it has been throughout the history of the ship. Now and then things have gotten out of control, such as during the great strike, or the recent riots and mutiny, but by and large the plan has progressed in its ordained path—the path which, believe it or not, in the long run has produced the *minimum* possible unrest and conflict.

"Some men have striven for their own selfish ends, money or power—Wilson was one. We need their type for the plan, we offer it chances to develop—and at the same time, through the ultimate annihilating defeat of such men, we need the type out of our society. More men have responded in desirable ways. They have demanded justice for themselves, or for their class, or even—like yourself—for classes not their own, for the ship as a whole. Thus is born the type we ultimately want, the hard-headed fighting visionaries."

"A hell of a way to get them," said Friday disconsolately.

"The trouble with young idealists," said Gomez dryly, "is that they expect all mankind to live up to their own impossibly high standards. When the human race obstinately keeps on being human, these young men, instead of revising their goals downward to something perhaps attainable, usually turn sour on their whole species. But man isn't such a bad race, Friday. Give him a little time to evolve.

"As for you, I'd had my eye on you for a long time. You were able, intelligent, stubborn in your notions of right and wrong—all good qualities for a skipper if I do say so myself. You needed to be kicked out of a certain snobbishness and to learn practical politics. I arranged for you to be thrown into a milieu demanding such a development. If you'd failed, you'd have been exonerated in time and given some harmless sinecure. As it is, you've responded so well that we think you're the best choice for the next Captain—the one who'll reach Centauri!"

Friday said nothing. There seemed nothing to say.

"You'll go back to lower decks for a while and lead the Guilds," resumed Gomez. "They have a good claim now for a voice on the Council, having saved the ship and discovered their own strength. They'll get it, after some difficulty and agitation. You'll be cleared of the charges against you and restored to officer class with a higher rank, but remain Guild spokesman. In the course of time, the Guilds will build up power and ultimately join with Astro to oust the other factions from an effective voice. No violence, if it can be helped, but a restoration of mercantile economy. By then you should have learned enough psychology, practical and theoretical, to take over the Captaincy from me—which will, among other things, allay the old and perfectly correct suspicion that Astro has been quietly running the whole show all these years.

"Without going into detail on every planned event, there will be conditions aboard which, while actually quite tolerable, will contain enough social evil of one sort or another to call forth the best efforts of all men of good will, whether they know the great secret or not. Yes, we'll give them their causes to fight for! And in the end their striving will succeed; the just and harmonious order of this voyage's beginnings will be restored.

"It will be difficult, yes, it will take most of your lifespan. But the job should be completed by the time the ship is within four or five years of her goal. Then a satisfied and united humanity can begin making ready for the next great adventure."

His voice trailed off, and he looked down at his desk with a blindness that spoke the continuing thought: *The adventure I will never see.*

"Are you game?" asked McMurtrie. "Do you want the job?"

"I—I'll take it," whispered Friday. "I'll try."

Gomez did not look up. It was as if he were seeing through the desk and the floor and the walls and corridors and hull, out to the loneliness between the stars.

Given the time lag in communications, developments aboard Pioneer *were scarcely noticed back in the Solar Union. It was facing too many urgent social and technical problems to dream about the stars.*

The Union sheltered an organization even older than itself—the Order of Planetary Engineers. Regardless of turmoil on Earth or beyond it, since 2080 the Order had been working to build better human habitats throughout the Solar system. They were as dedicated and disciplined as the monks who had tamed medieval Europe.

Although their rigorous training employed psychodynamics, the Engineers outlasted the fall of the Psychotechnic Institute. They avoided politics to serve all people without prejudice. Their vaunted neutrality would be challenged during an assignment to terraform Ganymede and Callisto, Jovian moons originally colonized by white supremacists who rejected the Solar Union.

The Snows of Ganymede

THREE DEAD MEN walked across the face of hell. Their feet groped past frozen rock, now and then they stumbled in the wan light, and always they heard the thin, bitter mumble of wind and felt the cold gnawing at their flesh. Around them there was death, naked stone reaching for a cruel sky of stars, a lean, poisonous whirl of snow which was not snow that whipped about them and then lay still to crunch under their tread. Jupiter was low in the south, a great shield which glowed amber.

They had been walking for a long time now, it seemed like forever, and ahead of them was nothing but another endlessness of walking. Speech had died within them. Their feet were numbed clods which rose and struck the ground and rose again. There was so little awareness left that they did not feel the small jarring of their boots against rock and snow. It was very quiet.

Hall Davenant wondered dimly if he had not always been walking from nothing to nowhere, across the snows of Ganymede, with Jupiter enormous on the horizon and the stars cold overhead. He wondered if he had not dreamed all his past, if Earth and Luna and mankind were not the fleeting vision of the only life in the world as it stumbled mad through desolation.

Yamagata spoke. After so long a silence, it was a shock to hear his remote, toneless voice. "We're not going to make it."

There was another stillness while Kruse found words. Then: "Doesn't look like it. But there's no point in sitting and waiting."

Pick-up-your-right-foot—glide—down! Pick-up-your-right-foot—glide down!

"Not the way we're going, we won't," said Yamagata. One gauntleted hand jerked toward the gauges on his shoulder. "Look. Oxygen for barely two hours more. Juice for maybe three, but it's no use staying warm if you can't breathe."

"Oh, well," said Kruse. "We weren't going anywhere anyway."

Pick-up-your-right-foot—glide—down!

There was a time, several thousand years ago it seemed, when Davenant could not have listened to them talking thus without a shiver in his guts. But cold and hunger and weariness had dragged at him so long that it didn't make any difference now.

His companions looked blocky and inhuman in their helmeted suits. It was as if they were demons leading him into darkness. But it didn't matter now.

Dreamily, Davenant considered all the hope and strength which had once laid within him. He had meant to be a soldier in man's finest war, the fight of all men against a blind and indifferent nature which had brought their kind forth without caring. But she was too strong, he thought vaguely; one casual giant shrug of a planet's shoulders, and her parricide children were tumbled into ruin.

No—it wasn't the way an Engineer ought to be thinking, he told himself. Even at the gates of death, there should still be pride. But Ganymede had stripped it from him, until he was nothing but a blindness lurching it knew not where.

Yamagata continued, almost absentmindedly: "We might be headed in more or less the correct direction. We might get a decent reception if and when we arrive."

"Or we might get shot down," said Kruse. "Forget it."

"They may be just beyond the next hill," said Yamagata. "Or they may be—shall we say—three hours off. And we have oxygen for two hours."

Pick-up-your-left-foot—glide—down!

"Now, our information is a good deal more important than any one of us," went on Yamagata. "The Abbey has got to know. All right, I have an idea."

Kruse slipped on a sheet of ice. He caught himself wearily, his fall was slow, and he got up without bothering to curse.

"Torvald, you have people at home, don't you?" asked Yamagata.

"Yeh," said Kruse. "Parents, couple of sisters. And there was a girl who—never mind."

"How about you, Hall?"

"Not to speak of," said Davenant mechanically.

"Nor I. And you're younger. Wait a minute." Yamagata stopped. The others went on for several long low-gravity paces before their slowed brains brought them around again.

Yamagata's face was like wrinkled yellow cloth in the pouring Jupiter light. It had a little smile as he peered through his faceplate. "They'll stick my name in Heroes' Hall or some such, foolishness," he said. "What I wish you'd do, if you live, is drink a beer for me at the Beacon in Luna City."

"Wait a minute—" Kruse took a step toward him, but was too late. Yamagata had already turned off his oxygen valves. Now, quite simply, he fumbled at some screws and lifted his helmet.

Moist air within rushed out in a freezing cloud. Blood bubbled on his lips, ran from his nose and ears as pressure dropped, and congealed. He swayed for a long time before toppling.

The face, under its sudden mask of ice, was puffed and distorted beyond humanness. Kruse stooped over. Even through the bulky suit, he could be seen to shake.

"He shouldn't have done that," he mumbled. "He shouldn't have done it." The wind slipped under his voice, a ghostly whistle.

Davenant felt ill. But his training rose within him. This was part of what it meant to be an Engineer. At the very least, Yamagata had returned that knowledge to him.

"He gave us each—an hour's oxygen," he said.

"Yeh. I wish he hadn't."

"*Somebody* has to make it, if that's possible at all." Davenant felt tears on his cheeks. "We're wasting time standing here."

"I—suppose so, kid."

Kruse turned the body around and undipped the bottles and accumulators. Then he laid Yamagata out—the arms were not yet too rigid for him to fold the hands across the breast, but he couldn't close the bulged-out eyes. There was nothing else to do. Rising, he helped Davenant fasten on the new equipment.

"Let's go," he said.

They went around a high dark bluff, and the body was lost to sight.

After another while, Davenant said, "I wonder if we shouldn't do the same. One survivor is better than none. We could match for it."

"No," said Kruse. "That's cutting our number too low. Come on."

Davenant shook his head, as if he had been struck. But the shock had given him back his manhood. As he walked, he could even remember, and he tried to sort out how it had begun. Take it from the beginning, back at the Abbey—

Pick-up-your-right-foot—glide—down! Pick-up-your-left-foot—glide—down!

❈ II ❈

SEEN FROM OUTSIDE, in the harsh bright flare of sunlight or the deep soft blue which poured from Earth, the Abbey was a fantastic witches' castle, perched on the cruel heights of Archimedes Crater like the nest of some inhuman robber baron. It was built of native stone, great rough-hewn blocks forming towers and walls of immense thickness. All of it had a purpose, aimed at the future—spires for observation and testing, walls and roofs to shut out raw vacuum. But in appearance it was still archaic. It looked as if it had always been on the Moon.

There was a road winding up to it and a landing field for local rockets; further back was a spaceport, where the shining ships were like spears poised aft heaven. There were also guns and arsenals and launching racks for guided missiles, but they were hidden, and nothing was said about them. They had been stocked against a day of trouble which might or might not come.

Inside, there was an endlessness of rooms and passages, burrowing deep into the ground or climbing to the highest towers. Some of these were for maintenance—food, water, air, power. In case of need, the place could be made self-sufficient. Others were storerooms; still others were laboratories where testing and research never ended; the rest were sleeping chambers, refectories, assembly and recreation centers.

There was always sound here—the whisper of ventilators and engines, footfalls, talk, music.

This was Archimedes Academy, headquarters and training school of the Order of Planetary Engineers. Few called it anything but the Abbey.

Hall Davenant walked down a corridor. It was of dressed stone, high and vaulted, the tapestries and murals and fluorotubes never quite lifting its cool gloom. He walked fast and crisply, his boots slamming in pride on the flagging, his gray tunic and trousers forced into a painful neatness. That was the dress uniform of Field Service.

His shoulders bore the silver comets of Tech-2 rank, and on his breast was the helium-atom insignia which said his specialty was nucleonics. He was a young man, with a young man's openness in his rather long face, blue eyes, yellow hair close-cropped in the approved Engineer style.

He passed a couple of cadets, teenaged boys who saluted him with bone-cracking smartness. He responded, thinking that cadets were a nuisance, always going through the rituals. For of course seniors had to conform before them. That was part of the training. It did not occur to him that he had graduated only three years previously.

Further on, he met an elderly labman in the loose robe and short beard affected by that service. This one had the gaunt, deep-burned features of a man who had been in Field in his younger days and retired to the Abbey—teaching, research, administration—when his body could no longer take deep space. He stopped Davenant, who knew him slightly. "Hear you're going to Jupiter," he said.

"Well—yes. Survey only, this trip."

"I know. Just wanted to ask you to pick me up some samples of green callistite. I've used up all we had, and want to run some more tests on it. Damnedest stuff I ever saw."

"Different geology, different minerals, within limits," Davenant said tritely.

"I know. And you tell me how we're going to sink shafts fifty kilometers deep without knowing the properties of the strata. I lost two months' work on Mars once because we didn't know just how friable the sandstone around Thor was. For God's sake, spend a little time with a sonic probe before drawing up your specs!"

"Certainly."

Davenant got away as fast as he decently could. After seven years of training, he thought, and three of Field Service—Venus and the Belt—he ought to know the elements of his trade!

Still space was big, and other planets could be unearthly in startling and deadly ways. You were never sure. An Engineer always walked with his life in his hands. The labs were there to give him as firm a grip as possible, but even so the tablets in Heroes' Hall were getting overly numerous.

He came to the office he wanted and pushed the scanner button. The man inside, Lyell, saw his face and punched to open the door for him. He entered, came to attention, and saluted. Lyell was his new captain, and some of them stood on ceremony even among seniors.

The lean gray man waved him negligently to a chair. The office was furnished as austerely as most of the Academy. That had a definite purpose, like everything else; it kept the men used to discomfort, of which deep space had plenty. Field men did not marry if they wanted to stay in that branch. They lived at the Abbey, and their sprees when on leave were carried out incog. Eventually, of course, most who survived would acquire wives. Then they got apartments in the underground village at the foot of the castle, became labmen or technies, perhaps at last made the Council.

Lyell was old to be a spacer.

Few Engineers ever left the Order. Their seven years as cadets included mind training under some of the most skilled psychotechnicians in the Solar System, and when they were through, the Order and its *esprit de corps* were part of them.

Davenant looked around. Everybody else seemed to be there. Akihito Yamagata, small and quiet: geologist. Torvald Kruse, big and red-haired and cheerful, the son of a rancher on Venus: heavy construction. Rene Falkenhorst from Mars, tall and slender and dark: mechanical engineer. Yuan Li, a trifle on the portly side, always smiling just a bit: biological engineer. Davenant himself, was atomics expert. And Arthur Lyell, stiff and gray, with enough all-around experience to qualify him for chief.

The men sat before the captain's desk, not speaking. Spacers learned to conserve talk, lest they exhaust the supply on a long tour of duty. There was a haze of smoke in the air from cigarettes and pipes.

"I wanted to have a short conference with you," said Lyell. His eyes went around their circle. "You'll be in centrifuge and so forth from now on until we leave, and once in space we'll be busy enough studying up technical details. As you know, we're off to the Jovian System on preliminary survey. The Jovians want us to terraform Ganymede and Callisto—a big job since the survey alone may well take a year. Not many comforts of home out there. I suppose you're all willing to go?"

"Of course," said Davenant, and felt rather juvenile for having spoken.

"Not much is known about the Jovian System or its settlers," went on Lyell. "I'm having the library stat copies of what books and articles we have. The moons seem to be poor in natural resources, so one thing we'll have to keep an eye out for is means of payment."

He must have noticed Davenant's faint shock, for he smiled and explained, "Yes, I know that sounds contrary to the spirit of the Charter. The Planetary Engineers exist to make space available for all men, regardless of race, creed, or political affiliations. Nevertheless, ever since the Order broke away from being a branch of the Union government and became an independent organization, it's had to pay its own way.

"So far, it's done well. We're by far the wealthiest and most influential private organization in the System. But a whole job of planetary transformation is so costly that we can't go into the red. The Jovians are poor in fissionables, and will probably be unwilling to part with any, so we'll look for other resources. In fact, we may have to set up some industries for them to make things we can use to pay the Order. Bear that in mind."

"We always need small spaceships and machinery replacements," said Falkenhorst. "They should be able to make those."

"It's a thought," said Lyell. "But what I most wanted to emphasize was this: you know the Order is strictly non-political. Events have justified us. During the late Humanist Revolution, for instance, we were the only major group left undisturbed. We cut loose from the government because we foresaw trouble coming. Well, it came, and it is still going on, and things are going to get worse before they get better. If the Order is to survive the anti-scientific reaction building up on Earth, it will have to stick by its policy.

"That isn't going to be easy. Jupiter, as the only state outside the Union, is distrusted on the inner planets, and people won't thank us for building up their potentials. The Jovians won't like us, either, since we are inner planetarians. And from what little is known, Jovian society is such a turbulent mess that we'll doubtless be pulled twenty ways at once by as many conflicting power groups.

"But no matter what the provocation, remember your training and the rules, even if I should die and leave you on your own. The Planetary Engineers exist to serve *all* mankind. Sometimes that sounds vapidly idealistic, but it's the only way we can preserve our identity and privileges, the only way we can weather the storm that is coming. The medieval Church was another supranational organization. Its attempts to interfere with separate states led only to trouble and ultimate failure, but in its character as the friend of all mankind it was honored and powerful. When that power began to be used for personal and local ends, the Church broke up. It's an example we might all bear in mind."

He grinned and turned to a thick sheaf of papers on his desk.

"All right, gentlemen. Lecture's over. Now let's get down to particulars."

◎ III ◎

"DURING THE LUNATIC YEARS of the latter twentieth century, the White American Church arose and became popular in the southern states of the old USA. Like the contemporaneous Pilgrims, it represented reaction—partly against the troubles which preceded, accompanied, and followed World War III and partly against the spreading of scientific method in human relations which those same troubles forced as the only solution. Unlike the Pilgrim Church, the White Church method was not an attempt to return to a fancied norm, but an eccentric leap toward an imaginary millennium. It was not elaborately rationalized, but violently anti-intellectual; it was not austere, but given to curious orgiastic rites.

"Some local politicians encouraged it so as to gain an organized, reliable voting body, and eventually it dominated many communities. Its intellectual isolationism caused it to go to yet further extremes, especially against the concept of equal rights for all races and the widening public appreciation of rational, scientific thought. However, as it grew in wealth, to become of some importance, it necessarily acquired an intelligentsia and a systematized philosophy.

"The increasingly effective program of undermining anti-rational organizations and beliefs, which was an important feature of the so-called New Enlightenment, eventually began to shrink its membership. The Second Conference of Rio had also made it obvious that before long the limited world government of the UN would be superseded by the complete federalism of the Solar Union which the White American doctrine considered intolerable.

"Imitating the earlier Pilgrim exodus to Mars, the Church decided to found a colony on Ganymede, the Jovian System being chosen for its remoteness and the general lack of competitive interest in settling it. A large ecological-unit spaceship, the *American,* was built, and a number of smaller ones obtained. The scheme was that some thousands of members would go out to start the colony while the rest stayed at home and worked to finance the project.

"In a decade or so of heroic effort, the city of X was firmly established (thus named to suggest the mysterious character of divinity and its dwelling). But meanwhile, the financial drain had proved too great for the Mother Church. A membership which had hitherto been loyal broke away in large part because it was being impoverished by demands for money. Psychodynamic technicians of the government were adroit in using the discontent as a wedge for propaganda. By twenty-one hundred A.D., the Jovian colonists found themselves without a sponsor, no ties to Earth, almost completely cut off by the expense of travel to their system.

"They sent occasional observers and representatives to Earth, but there was no Union governor over them since they seemed neither to need nor want one. Occasional reports about them still come in, rumoring the evolution of a strange and ruthless culture which through a series of 'revelations' has been changed far from the original concept.

"But on the whole, the Jovians have remained an isolated and unknown tribe. Their declaration of independence while the Union was confused by the Humanist Revolt on Earth, and their persistent refusal to rejoin, merely emphasizes their already accomplished secession from the rest of the human race."

Davenant switched off the micro-projector that had been screening de la Garde's *Short History of Interplanetary Colonization.* He sighed. "He could have gone into more detail."

"He wasn't interested," said Falkenhorst. "He deals with what he considers the main line of history, the inner planets. Elsewhere he gives an economic analysis to show that nothing beyond the Belt will ever be important—not enough resources, too hard to colonize, the problem of survival won't leave any surplus energy."

"As a matter of fact," said Lyell, "the colony wouldn't have been possible at all if the American government hadn't quietly subsidized it—by such indirect means that the Church itself never knew about it. The Psychotechs foresaw that the attempt would exhaust and break up the organization on Earth. I've seen secret records that the Humanists made public."

"They really did get Machiavellian back in those days, didn't they?" murmured Yuan. "But seriously, there must be more information on Jupiter than this."

"Of course," said Lyell. "Plenty of it. But nothing coherent. Part of our task will be to get the whole picture as it is today, so you boys, at least, may as well start without preconceptions."

He took out a curved pipe and began loading it. "Yes, there's scattered information, but what nobody knows yet is the total cultural pattern. Just remember that man necessarily develops a different civilization in every environment if he stays long enough, and that what may shock you is normal, perhaps necessary, on Ganymede. Also—the Order stays out of politics!"

Davenant reflected on what he had seen and heard. He had been on Earth but little, even though the Engineers did some work there. Their main interest was space. The planet of his birth had become a stranger to him.

But he knew the hectic commerce and gaiety which was Luna City; knew the stiff dignity, the high sense of order and discipline, respect for intellectual achievement that characterized Mars; was familiar with the patriarchal, somewhat violent clan life which was developing on Venus since the invention of the cheap mobile reclamation unit.

But Ganymede would not be like anything he knew.

The ship, *Let There Be Light*, hummed and murmured. Stars blazed against blackness in the vision ports. She was a cruiser, one of the new models which could accelerate most of the way and reach even Jupiter in a couple of weeks.

There were only the six of them aboard, with a full cargo of equipment and supplies. That was not cutting it as fine as an ordinary spaceman would think. Even though only Lyell and Davenant had the full specialized knowledge required for a certificate, any Engineer could operate a spaceship alone if it had not been too drastically damaged.

Lyell puffed smoke and squinted through a mesh of crow's-feet.

"One more thing might need emphasizing," he said. "We'll be there for a year, I imagine, and you'll want recreation from time to time. I'm afraid you'll have to do without it. One of the psychological mainstays of the Order's power is the impression of lawfulness and restraint its men give."

"We know that, Boss," said Kruse, looking hurt.

"Yes, of course. Still, on an inner-planet job a man does get leaves, he knows what amusements accord with local customs, and he goes incog anyway. None of that will be true on Ganymede. I doubt if they have red lights of any sort, for instance, and no disguise will be good enough in so small a commune. On a planet where hedonism was considered normal, where everyone was expected as a matter of morals to indulge himself, we would. But if, as I suspect, the Jovians have a Puritan code, we'll have to go them one better."

"Oh, well." Kruse grinned. "I figured as much, and built up a reserve the last time I was in Luna City."

Davenant felt a certain wistful envy of the man. He himself was too shy and introverted, he knew, to make a decent roisterer. An occasional fling in a licensed rec house, beer and gambling and whatnot was about his speed. If he were rich—but Engineers didn't get rich. All the profits of the Order went back into the Order and its development. Personnel from cadet to coordinator drew small salaries and no bonuses. The rewards were intangibles—prestige, comradeship, a sense of being important to man's highest and finest adventure.

A watch-change bell broke up the discussion. Some went to sleep, some to their posts. Only Kruse and Davenant remained in the little saloon. The Venusian drifted across to a locker—they were currently in free-fall orbit—and got two bulbs of beer.

"This ends my ration for today," he said. "Care to join me, Hall?"

"Sure." Davenant took one, put the tube in his mouth, and squeezed. The cool tingle of it was refreshing.

Kruse hooked a leg around a stanchion and hung across the table from him. "If I'm not getting too personal," he asked, "why did you join?"

"Eh? Oh!" Davenant felt himself reddening, for no good reason. That irritated him, but he liked the big Venusian. "The usual. They saw my school and psych records, offered me an appointment, I took it. Isn't that what happens to everybody?"

"Yeah, sure. But you were only fourteen or fifteen then, not really capable of deciding such a thing. A lot of kids sign up because they think it's glamorous, and drop out after a couple of years. What made you stick?"

"What makes anybody stick? I was a poor boy. My father was one of the intellectual routineer class which was displaced by the Second Industrial Revolution, though he never joined the Humanists. He didn't like living off citizen's allowance and odd jobs—called it a handout. My people were Alaskans, with some of the pioneer tradition left in them. But his health was too frail for him to emigrate to Mars or Venus. I didn't want to go through that myself."

Davenant shrugged, not meeting Kruse's blue eyes. There had been other reasons—a girl, other women since then, even if he wasn't a successful chaser. Sometimes he wondered if a man ever really falls out of love. The pain stops, most of it, and presently a new love comes along. But isn't she merely added to the Pantheon?

"Why do you ask?" he said.

"Oh, just getting acquainted." Kruse shrugged. "Me, I was offered the same, and my folks urged me to accept. Parents' consent is needed on Venus. The family is more important there than it's become in Western Earth. It'd be something for the clan to brag about, a member in the Engineers. So I did join and I'm not sorry, but I think I'll resign after this job is over."

Davenant felt shocked. "How come? Don't you like it?"

"Sure. But I'm pushing forty, and it's time I raised a family. The lucky girl can't see living on Luna, so I've got my eye on a valley in the Hellfires. Under the Development Act, I can home stead the whole place. It's just rock and sand now, but give me a few years and it'll be the sweetest little oasis you ever saw."

"There's a breakdown coming," said Davenant. "The Humanists didn't stay in power long, no, but they were only one symptom. You can see corruption and personal government are growing. You're better off belonging to an organization which is above such matters."

"Now you're just parroting what your trainers taught you," said Kruse. "It's probably true enough as far as Earth is concerned, but Venus is a big place. Have you ever thought that maybe the Order is wrong? That maybe by setting itself above the realities of politics it's cutting itself off from its own roots?"

Davenant gulped beer and tried to settle a suddenly chaotic mind. It was not merely that Kruse spoke heresy. The Order permitted, even encouraged independent thinking for the simple reason that a rigid brain was no good for its purposes. But the Venusian, what he had seen of him, had never given the impression of being an intellectual beyond the requirements of his work. A skilled technician, yes; a big, laughing, hard-fisted tosspot, a collector of improper limericks, but he had no business dealing in disquieting philosophies.

Davenant was not especially narrow. He read widely, enjoyed music and chess, liked to think of himself as a bit of a universalist but he realized now with some dismay that his intellectually formative years might have been too bookish, too concentrated on one ideal and in one way of life. He had crossed millions of kilometers and seen strange landscapes, but had he ever looked into the soul of a man—even his own?

"Let's have another beer," he said hastily. "We can borrow from tomorrow's ration. How about some chess?"

⚙ IV ⚙

SEEN FROM SPACE, Ganymede was bleaker than Luna herself—seamed with mountains, pocked with craters, mottled dark and light over her sterile face. This far from the sun, her dayside was wrapped in dusk. Since she always faced Jupiter, the primary was gibbous or only a great scimitar while the sun was up, and at high noon a total eclipse threw blackness across the land.

As the cruiser approached, her radar picked up an object in orbit not far above the surface: metallic, to judge from the intensity of the returning signal.

"Odd," muttered Lyell. "I know the colonists broke up the old

American and most of their other spaceships for the parts. I didn't know they'd established a satellite station."

He beamed a call, but there was no answer. Only the dry whisper of cosmic interference.

"Maybe a ship parked there?" suggested Yuan.

"Too big to be an ordinary ship. Well—let's come down the hard way, then."

It was a tricky job to ride a vessel as massive as the *Light* down a GCA beam, but Lyell managed it with hardly a bump.

When they were in their cradle, Davenant looked out and could not see much of X—just the spacefield, a radio mast, several buildings, and a cluster of other structures well distant. Most of it must be underground.

The sun was a tiny blinding flame in a sky nearly black. The tremendous edge of Jupiter dominated heaven—amber, streaked with dull reds and blues and greens and browns, splotches which were storms that could have swallowed Earth whole. The planet was so big that it seemed to be endlessly falling, about to crash ruinously on the broken face of its moon. Io was visible as a giant sliver to one side of the primary. The whole sky looked unnatural, like something seen in a dream.

A ring of hills shouldered starkly above the horizon, barely visible in the vague, cold, misty twilight under which the world seemed to lie. Davenant saw fields of snow that must be frozen ammonia, and part of the range looked as if it might be one enormous chunk of ice. The air was thin—nitrogen and argon, a wisp of methane and other gases.

Luna had been near home when the first men reached it; Mars had had some life, at least; Venus had been a wind-howling hell, but rich with promise. This place seemed to hold a perpetual despair. It was, somehow, the grimmest scene Davenant had ever experienced.

Trying to shake off his depression, he pointed to the nearer buildings—long, low, featureless boxes with an odd bluish shimmer.

"I wonder what those are made of?" he asked.

"Ice, I imagine," said Falkenhorst.

Davenant blinked. "You mean solid water?"

"Surely," said the Martian. "There's a lot of it on the Galilean moons. It's a pretty good insulator, can be worked with a blowtorch or cast into molds, and if you make your walls thick enough and insulate them on the inside, they'll do fine at these temperatures."

Davenant nodded. He should have realized that. His training, the whole history of space colonization emphasized that other worlds were not Earth, and that a whole new approach was needed for each one.

"I'll bet they use the Absolute scale habitually here," he said. "It'd be too much trouble always to speak of minus a hundred and some degrees Centigrade."

"You're getting the idea," said Falkenhorst.

There was no provision for taking a spaceship cradle underground, but a small trac appeared, drawing a long plastitube two meters in diameter out of a valve in one building. It gripped around the airlock, and Lyell led his crew through it. They were all in dress uniform and wore their carefully schooled dignity on their features.

Emerging at the farther end of the tube, they stepped into a room which struck them with chill. The Jovians must have habituated themselves to such temperatures, to conserve power. Davenant, for one, had to take conscious control of somatic reactions and force his body to accept the conditions.

Ten guards were drawn up on either side of the entrance, an immobile line. They had the gangling, bulge-chested slenderness which was also characteristic of Martians—low gravity, low air pressure even inside the settlements—but this was exaggerated, for they were easily two meters tall. Under steel helmets, their faces were white rather than sun-darkened. Their uniform was a one-piece black coverall fitting the muscular bodies closely, boots, a belt supporting pistol and pouch; their heads were shaven, and they stood like robots.

It took a second glance for Davenant to realize that they were identical.

He jammed the sudden cold in his mind back out of consciousness. Keep up the act, keep up the act. An Engineer is never surprised.

Two other men were waiting beyond the guards. One wore the same black one-piece uniform, with a star glittering silver on the belt. But he had his hair. He was rather short and stocky, eyes gray and utterly cold, face harsh-scarred. The other man, long and thin and comparatively serene-looking, wore a blond beard, though his skull was bare, and a black robe with a white cross on the breast. He held back, bowing silently, as the smaller man stepped forward and spoke.

"God with us! Welcome, gemmen. Had good trip?"

"Thank you, yes." Lyell inclined his gaunt gray head. "I am Captain Lyell of Archimedes Academy, in charge of this group."

"Cinc-4 Halleck." The dialect seemed to be a variant of rather archaic English, a curious blend of soft slurring and crisp, rapid delivery. The man gestured to his robed companion. "Angel-3 Garson." Another bow from that one. "Can we do y'all a service?"

"You might show us to our quarters," Lyell said coolly.

"Baggage? Unloadin'?"

"The ship is not to be touched," said Lyell. "There are things in her which could be dangerous to one not familiar with details. If you will lend us a porter, one of us will show him our personal effects."

Halleck nodded and spoke briefly into a wrist-phone. As he stood looking over the visitors, he could almost be seen to freeze. His eyes strayed uncontrollably to Yuan and Yamagata. He jerked them away only to have them return. Davenant wondered why.

A gray-clad hairless man entered from a side door. The first thing noticeable about him was his gigantic size and four arms. The next, and somehow most lasting impression, was of the inhuman vacancy of his face.

"Porter, gemmen," said Halleck.

At a signal from Lyell, Davenant led the way back through the tube. The giant followed wordlessly, and said nothing when the small heap of handbags was pointed out to him—merely picked them up and trudged bade. There was no reason why the Engineers should not have carried their own things, except the matter of dignity.

When Davenant returned, he found Lyell talking with Halleck and Falkenhorst with the angel, Garson, who was asking some shrewd questions about the propulsion of the *Light*. Davenant recalled that the ion drive had still been experimental when Ganymede had been colonized.

"This way, please."

Halleck turned and led them out. A descending ramp wound into the body of the world. Davenant noticed that the identical guards were going before and after the group, and that their eyes were never still.

"We've assigned y' a suite in Sector Eight, border between cine an' angel territory," Halleck said. "Y' can easily communicate with one service or t'other. Meals'll be brought there. If y'all gimme your preferences, I'll try to have 'em met, though we're not a rich colony."

"We don't ask for luxury," said Lyell. "Just remember that your dietary requirements may have changed slightly from ours."

The suite turned out to consist of six small bedrooms and a bath surrounding a larger common chamber. The furniture was simple, comfortable enough under low-gee conditions, but the whole place had a barren and empty look. After a moment's thought, Davenant traced that impression down to the completely unimaginative, inartistic appearance. Everything seemed to have been laid out with a ruler, and the lining plastic was drab gray. Oh, well.

Garson showed them the com-unit with which they could call up various offices when they wanted something, and gave them a collection of large-scale maps of city and satellite.

"Further reference works whenever y'all wish," he said. He had a meek way of speaking. "Imagine y'all want to get unpacked and rested. Call me when you wish a first conference."

"Cinc-1 should'a met y'all himself, I know," added Halleck, though without any air of apology, "but you'll see him soon enough. We've little ceremony here. God with you, gemmen."

He saluted crisply and backed out the door. His guards followed him. The angel bowed and went out last.

"Well!" Kruse threw his bulk onto a low couch. "Charming hospitality!"

"Different mores," Lyell said absently. "That may have been their equivalent of a brass band and parade, for all I know. Don't go insisting on any special favors, boys. Pass all that through me." He frowned. "I'm afraid we've made a mistake right at the beginning."

"How so ?" asked Falkenhorst.

"Bringing Yuan and Yamagata."

"What in space—" demanded Kruse. "What's wrong with 'em?" The two men spoken of retreated into expressionlessness.

"Nothing, of course," snapped Lyell. "But we should have remembered the idiotic race prejudice which was so important to the colony's founders. Apparently, it's still present. Didn't you see how Halleck was reacting?"

"Race?" Kruse broke into a guffaw. "After some of the types they seem to've been breeding here?"

"Prejudices don't have to be logical or consistent," Lyell told him. "In fact, they usually aren't. It's sheer lucky chance that we didn't happen to bring a black Engineer." He glanced at Yuan and Yamagata. "I think you two boys can get by if we're discreet. Neither of you look that much different from a white man."

"A pink man, you mean." Yamagata grinned.

"It just points out how much we have to watch ourselves," said Lyell.

"Oh, well, if they get too offended they'll merely send us home," said Falkenhorst. "Let them freeze forever, then."

Lyell demurred. "This job is more important to the Order than you seem to realize. Not only the profit we stand to make, but this will be the first large-scale terraforming job we've had. The Mars and Venus projects were already well under way when the old corps was founded. We've handled big jobs, yes, but nothing of comparable magnitude. The value of this task in experience and prestige is inestimable. It'll go a long way toward getting us that monopoly of our kind of work which we need for power and safety."

Davenant, who had been doing some heavy thinking since his talk with Kruse, didn't quite like the tone of that. Was it so certain that the Order had a right to such power? He brooded over it while he unpacked.

Lyell called up the commissariat office and asked for dinner. It was brought by four-armed men, the same type as the porter, though not identical with him. The silence with which they served the meal was eerie. When Lyell asked one of them a question, he shook his head in an animal way and pointed to his throat.

"Either mute, or under orders not to speak," said Davenant. "I wonder why?" There was a coldness along his spine.

The food was mostly synthetic, not especially good, though some effort had been made to spice it. Kruse grimaced and reached for the decanter which experiment had shown to hold some alcoholic liquid.

"Go easy on that rotgut," warned Lyell. "Remember, our official doctrine is austerity."

Kruse shrugged. "It's awful, anyway. Lucky, I stuck a few bottles of Scotch in my bag."

When a service bell brought the waiters back to clear off the dishes, Davenant wondered if X lacked machinery for such work, or if live service had the same ostentation value it had on Earth. He consulted the city maps and decided it was no machinery. Logical enough. A precarious colony on an inhuman world didn't have materials or labor to spare for making luxury robots. The maps were highly detailed, and it took a good many of them to cover the whole three-dimensional warren. Davenant gathered that this was the official level, where Cincs and Angels had their offices, and the lower echelons lived. Further down were the cells given to Sergeants, apparently the commoners who surely didn't have much sleeping space. Elsewhere were factories, laboratories, creches, assembly halls, storerooms.

One sector of X was marked, *Cinc-1-4,* but otherwise left blank. The rulers didn't seem to publicize the layout of their quarters, perhaps for fear of envious comparisons.

"I get a general picture of an oligarchy as hard-boiled as any in history," remarked Lyell, after considering the maps. "Those guards, for instance—obviously they're exogenes from one cell."

"Would the Jovians know that technique?" wondered Falkenhorst.

"Oh, yes," said Yuan. "It was used a good two hundred years ago by the old UN Inspectorate to create a corps of gifted secret service men. It's been public for more than half that time, though little applied. Identical heredity, identical training—the psychological effects are curious, for you get a completely devoted band of brothers. Then the four arms—that indicates the Jovians are well up on the newer methods of gene and chromosome manipulation. Either they got data from Earth or they developed the system independently, most likely the first since they have had some contact. I dare say the commoners, Sergeants, whatever you call them, are bred and trained and regarded as animals—specialized types. No, I can't say I like Jovian society!"

"That Angel—odd name!—Garson seems a pretty decent sort," said Yamagata. "How about calling him and pumping him now?"

"I don't know what his sleeping hours are," said Lyell. "But we can, I suppose." He went over to the com.

A ringing doorbell some minutes later announced their visitor. As Davenant opened the door, he heard a loud-speaker system filling the corridor with:

"—yes, the Lord is mighty, brethren, an' His hand lies heavy. Rouse not the anger o' the Lord, for he who's cursed by Him is cursed indeed.

Rather show that meekness and obedience which're pleasin' unto Him—"

Sermons, yet! As Davenant closed the door he was glad it was soundproof.

Garson's expression was a peculiar mixture of timidity and eagerness. When he was offered a chair, he sat on the very edge, and he was given to starting at any sudden movement.

"How official are you?" asked Lyell.

"If you can speak for the government, I'd like to get some questions straightened out at once."

"We—" Garson fumbled for words.

"My class is religious, y' understand. Mercy—" He hesitated, seeming unsure how to address the guest. "Sir," he finished. "We conduc' services an'—intellectual activities, too. Engineering procedure is our province as far as y'all're concerned, though we don't make policy."

"Good enough. You understand we are here only as a survey group, to find out if it will be possible at all to transform Ganymede and Callisto. It will take a good deal of work, a long time, to learn even that much, and we shall have to ask for help from your people."

"Crews will—be assigned, sir," replied Garson. "Equipment an'—" His voice trailed off and he combed his thin beard with nervous fingers.

"They will be under our direction, exclusively."

"If y' wish, sir. But—" The Angel paused again. "From what y' already know o' conditions here, sir, what—what hopes d'you have o' success?"

"I would rather not say," answered Lyell. "Not yet. Every world presents its own problem. How much do you know about earlier projects of this nature?"

"Very little, sir. I'd be, uh, grateful for what y' can tell me."

Lyell settled back for a lecture. "Well then," he said. "Venus was made habitable by chemical treatment to get the poisons out of the atmosphere, by special bacteria strains which released oxygen from its compounds, and by hydrogen explosions to bring water to the surface. To mention only the most superficial aspects of a task which took more than a century, it is still going on as far as desert reclamation is concerned. Plant types were developed to fit the new conditions, and as the environment changes with time still other forms will be introduced. Animal life was brought from Earth; or rather, its reproductive cells were, with exogenesis on Venus to start the first generation.

"On Mars, now, the problem has been in many ways different. There were no poison gases, and there was a little oxygen and surface water, although not nearly enough for human life. Still it was a start. More oxygen was obtained by bacterial process, more water by drilling, but it was still necessary to import a great deal—"

"Where from, sir?" Garson asked eagerly. "The fuel requirements must'a been fantastic if—uh—from Earth."

Lyell smiled. "No. From Saturn. The rings are mostly ice, there are even enormous meteors, or small moons of ice. It took several years' work, and was tricky to give a number of big chunks enough of a push to fall sunward and make them hit Mars just where desired. But—well, it was practicable. Large-scale electrolysis and other treatment for some of it.

"The whole task was costly and enormous, of course, but when millions of people with atomic energy and the resources of a whole planet, even a small one, behind them, bend all their efforts to a job, it gets done. Oh, yes, much carbon dioxide was also required, to give sufficient greenhouse effect at that distance from the sun.

"In spite of all this, Mars will always be a cold and arid world with a thin atmosphere. So the geneticists had to meet conditions halfway, by creating not only plants and lower animals, but even slightly modified human strains which can be comfortable in such an environment. And there are other complications, such as making up the gas which continually leaks into space. I tell you, Mars is a tough problem!

"It's being solved. On the other hand, no one would even try to give an atmosphere to Luna or Mercury. Our whole approach is different there, concentrating on things like more efficient airlocks and larger underground installations.

"The available materials and energy sources also determine a great deal. On Mercury or Luna, sun-power can be used directly or stored in capacitors. In the early days on Venus, the Hilsch tube was important, and wind power still is. On Mars, though, it was necessary to use atomic energy so extensively that its reserves are depleted and we must concentrate on the physics of low potential. We hope to help out when our solar-beam stations on Mercury are finished.

"But I freely predict that no one will ever found a real colony on, say, the moons of Uranus. There are no energy sources to speak of, no useful minerals, they're too far away for power beamed from Mercury. Not only is it not worthwhile, but it isn't a practical possibility. So you see, Ganymede and Callisto will have to be studied carefully before we can know what the chances are of making them habitable—or, indeed, doing anything with them."

Davenant's right shoulder itched. He longed to scratch it, but made himself sit impassively. Lyell's lecture was for a definite purpose—to impress, to gain a certain slight moral ascendancy. It wouldn't do to break up the act of mentor just to scratch. Inwardly, he squirmed.

"We've—ah—we've done well so far, sir," Garson said diffidently. "There're fifty thousand people in X alone, besides smaller cities an' isolated outposts. I think there's good hope."

"Possibly," said Lyell, with a note of calculated skepticism. "But do you have decent ore deposits so we can get structural metals? How much water is there in all? How much of every type of compound? How available is the oxygen? I don't think biological techniques will get it out for you. I doubt if any bacterium can be made which won't die or spore up at these temperatures."

Yuan murmured, "There might be ways, even so. But I'd have to have some figures before knowing if I have a practical idea."

"What energy sources do you have?" Lyell persisted. "Can we tap internal heat, or isn't there enough? The sun is too far away to help much, even with power beaming. Offhand, I think the thing to do is sink shafts and start hydrogen-lithium fires down in them to warm up the body of the moon. Some of that energy could be tapped to make an outdoor lighting system. Then there is the problem of getting rid of the methane and ammonia.

"The surface area of Ganymede is something like eighty-five million square kilometers. You can see what a gigantic task we have. Interplanetary freight rates being what they are, it cannot be done at all unless most of the work and resources come from this world itself. Even if we take the job, the Engineers cannot supply the whole labor force. Most of it must be supplied from your own people, and can you spare so many? That calls for socio-economic analysis.

"In short, we are here now to see if you, yourselves, under our direction, can swing the job. Even the survey will require cooperation. Even for it, we may have to call on you for a great deal in the way of materials and manpower. We must have *carte blanche* to go anywhere and get any information. Are you willing to set that much at stake against the mere possibility that we can help you?"

"O' course," said Garson. "Y'd not 'a been asked ay-tall if we weren't. There are—uh—some facts which're—confidential, but the Engineers respect their clients' secrets, don't they?"

Lyell nodded. " If nothing else, we can show you some modern techniques," he said. "For instance, molar potential barriers to eliminate airlocks and all their clumsiness in fixed installations, more efficient food synthesis reactions, and so on."

Garson actually blushed. "Have you—uh—considered—the terms yet, sir?"

"The Abbey has already agreed with your representative on the flat rate for a survey. Payment for further work will depend on what we want and what you can afford. That can be negotiated later."

There was a little small talk then, but the Angel was clearly shy of strangers and glad when he found an excuse to leave. He set an hour for the next meeting, at which a formal commission would begin the real business, and made his good nights.

Lyell stared after him. "I wonder what he's afraid of," he muttered, eyes narrowing.

"Us, maybe, said Yamagata. "Strangers coming into a pathologically xenophobic culture—hmmm." He stopped. "I just had an idea. Think these people know Basic?"

"I doubt it," said Falkenhorst. "Why?"

"Hall," Yamagata turned to Davenant, an odd look on his face—"you have your general unit handy?" He was speaking the new, semantically rigorous language now. "Want to check the wiring in this room?"

Magnetic tracing of circuits revealed what he had suspected: microphones, recorders, behind the plastic facing of the walls.

Lyell's mouth drew tight. "That's a violation of—"

"Different mores, Chief!" Falkenhorst's gibe held a note of strain.

"We can make an official complaint," suggested Yuan.

"Set up a resonator and burn the damn things out!" cried Davenant. "Or keep a magnetic field to wipe the tapes, at least."

"Hell," grunted Kruse, "leave 'em alone, but give 'em something really interesting to record!"

"No—no!" Lyell shook his head. "None of that. Not yet, not till we know more of the situation. I'm afraid we've already given away much we can ill afford, but I'll have to think about it. Meanwhile, keep to English for ordinary purposes, switch to Basic when necessary, but watch your tongues every minute."

Davenant looked around the room. He had known the inanimate savagery of planets, but this was the first time he had ever encountered hostility from men. The walls seemed to move together and close in on him.

Ganymede spun twice around Jupiter, a period of slightly more than two weeks, while Lyell's men were only starting their task, learning the bare elements of Jovian society. Most of their work was with the Angels, studying maps and references in the library, conferring and asking questions. But they could hardly help acquiring unofficial information.

Garson, who seemed to have taken a fancy to Davenant, conducted him through the city. The factories and maintenance centers were fairly standard for a colony, though archaic in design and using an undue amount of human labor. That was performed by Sergeants under Angel supervisors. Watching a long assembly line of gray-clad, unspeaking men, Davenant felt a coldness in his stomach. He had never seen human beings so used.

"Why haven't you installed robot machinery?" he asked. "This could all be fully automatic."

Garson shrugged. Large investment o' material an' labor in robots," he said. "Cheaper, easier t' use men trained from birth."

So! The commoners were part of the machinery. They didn't count for more than the lathes and furnaces they manned. Davenant had that fact driven home to him when he walked through the human robots' part of town—endless, monotonous cells almost devoid of individuality, no privacy anywhere, always the conditioning by broadcast sermons and minute regulations of conduct. The faces which looked at him meekly were masks; humanness had been rubbed out.

Not many women were in sight, and those he saw were muffled in shapeless gray gowns and veils. They had their own assignments in such lighter work as food-making and product inspection. And they were breeders. Garson justified their status with Biblical quotations.

There was little family life. Children were taken young to the creches for conditioning. On the basis of psych tests, some were picked for Angel and some for Cinc, to be raised in those services and never told who their parents were.

The Angels were the priesthood, and spent their lives under a monastic rule, which made the Abbey seem mild—though they were not celibate. They were also the intellectual and artistic class, the engineers, poets, scientists, philosophers of sorts. They compiled the data Davenant was now studying, and served as administrative advisors.

In spite of the humility which was drilled into them, they seemed more human, more individual, than any other class on Ganymede. Fat jolly Wilkins, shy dreamy Bliss, keen intense Jackson, small sardonic Hobart, earnest tongue-tied Garson—Davenant could get along with them.

As a group, the Angels were a power in the community, and had had their clashes with the Cincs. The Cincs, who were the rulers, had the upper hand, for Cincs of first and second grade were ex officio Archangels.

But sometimes the corps resisted them successfully. Garson told with relish the story of a few years ago, when Cinc-1 had tried to seize property owned by the Angels. They had refused to obey him, and had held out until a junta of his own subordinates had replaced him with a more reasonable man.

Davenant met the chief Cinc when the Engineers were invited to the Cinc area. Halleck conducted them, together with a troop of Hounds.

Lyell tried to draw Halleck out a little. I take it these guards of yours are for show?"

"No," Halleck looked surprised. "Protection."

"From whom? The Sergeants?"

"Haw! The Sergeants know their place, I hope. A few publicly owned Hounds can keep them in order. But y' see, every Cinc above novice grade is entitled to his own corps o' guards, as many as he can support."

"I don't quite understand," Lyell said smoothly. "If the commoners aren't dangerous, why should a Cinc need a personal army ?"

"The other Cincs, o' course!" clipped Halleck. "God gives victory to the righteous, but we men can't know who that is. Many're called but few're chosen. So all got to have their chance."

Lyell did not press the matter, but he traded a glance with Falkenhorst.

Cinc territory was a change from the poverty elsewhere in X. The floors were carpeted, the walls and ceilings colorful with murals, the individual apartments spacious and luxuriously furnished. Davenant got the impression that each housed its own harem. Several other officers passed by exchanging salutes with Halleck, and there was a flicker of hatred in their eyes. None had less than two bodyguards in tow, and each carried a sidearm.

A massive steel door was protected by machine-guns behind armor plating. Halleck strode up to meet the tall Hound who stood in front of the barricade.

"God with us!"

"Service to the Lord!"

"I bring Cinc-1's guests. Here's my pass."

The Hound studied it carefully. "Yes, Mercy. If you'll leave y'r men an y'r pistol here—"

Halleck smiled sarcastically and submitted. Davenant did not like the swift competent hands which passed over him in search of weapons but his resentment faded when he was let through the door. The reception hall was a blaze of color and crude magnificence.

A servant bowed low. Female, young and comely, she was not dressed in any long drab gown. Quite the opposite. Kruse opened his mouth in an admiring grin, but snapped it shut as he remembered where he was.

"I'll announce you, Mercy," the girl said. "Service to the Lord!"

Cinc-1 Weller was short and rather stout, but the eyes in his broad red face were restless and cold. He greeted the Engineers with an ambiguous salute and waved them to chairs. Davenant was uneasily aware of the motionless guards standing against the wall.

"I trust y'r accommodations 're good?" Weller said. "Anything y' need?"

"Not just yet, Mercy," answered Lyell. "Before long, we'll be making our initial surveys and will want workers and equipment. But that can doubtless be arranged through the Angel corps."

"Course, course." Weller accepted a drink from a well-trained servant. "If y'all do need somethin' please ask f'r it."

"Well, Mercy"—Lyell rubbed his chin—"there is one thing we lack, and that is information."

"Oh. Can't the Angels give y' all the facts?"

"About physical data, yes," said Lyell. "But we need a more detailed social analysis than anything that's been given us. An important factor in deciding how much can be done here is the capability of the people themselves. For instance, it will be necessary to construct a great deal of automatic machinery. Frankly, Mercy, I'm disappointed that there isn't more already. Now the question is, can your particular culture stand the introduction of so much new technology?"

Weller's face darkened. For an instant, Davenant thought he was going to order his men to shoot the Engineers down.

He returned to a hard surface calm and replied judicially, "I don't see why not. S'pose y' mean assembly-line workers an' their like. What'll happen to 'em if their jobs 're automatized? That's really not your business. We can build such machines, put 'em at your disposal. What we do with 'em afterward concerns us alone."

"Perhaps," said Lyell. "Though consider, Mercy. Human assembly-lines simply cannot produce what will be needed at the rate it will be needed. So there will at the very least be an interim where your Sergeants have no place to work—except out in the field with us. And there they will, frankly, be of little use unless you recondition and educate them. At present, I have the impression that most of them don't have the effective intelligence to use complex machines." After a pause, he added maliciously, "Of course, Angels and Cincs could be assigned to our crews but that would also disrupt your social structure."

"Hm—yes—problem there," admitted Weller grudgingly. "It calls f'r study. I'm sure a solution can be found."

"Another question," drawled Yamagata. "Is Callisto inhabited or is it not?"

"Why, no," said Halleck, when Weller failed to reply. "What made you think it was? We haven't expanded that much yet."

"There were references in books and conversation implying a small colony there," said Yamagata. "But nobody I asked would give me a straight answer."

Weller spoke almost genially, as if glad to leave an awkward subject. "Oh, I see. Small group o' settlers there from Earth some twenty-five years ago. Came out t' escape troubles durin' the Humanist affair. They couldn't make a go of it alone, so they came here, and joined with us. All but forgotten now."

He thinks fast on his feet, observed Davenant. *But he wouldn't be the chief in this nest of devils unless he did.*

"If I may say so, Mercy," put in Lyell, "your culture is an odd blend of the communal and the highly individualistic. Sergeants are trained to absolute obedience, but most of your new works are carried out by individual Cincs, who patronize some gifted Angel or some new construction project or the like."

Davenant nodded to himself. He had noticed as much, and decided the motivation was a compounded desire for power and prestige.

Lyell went on. "So far that system has worked well enough, because almost everything you could name had to be done anyway—mines started, outlying settlements founded, machinery built. But it will take the coordinated effort of all your people to transform these moons. Do you think the members of the Cinc class can be trusted to work cooperatively?"

"I'll see they do." Weller forced a laugh. "Y' go a long way to criticize us."

"Only as far as I must, Mercy. It's not my business to judge the way you have chosen to order your affairs to date. But insofar as that affects my job, I have a duty to make suggestions."

"We don't have t' employ the Order," Weller said coldly. "We can do the job ourselves, y' know."

"As you wish, Mercy."

Lyell was poker-faced, but it was clear enough that he had the whip hand. The Jovians were not capable of the enterprise. They lacked the special skills and resources it needed. And as long as they were locked underground, dependent on a complex of machines and chemicals for the most elementary necessities of life, they could never amount to anything in Solar trade or politics.

The conversation at supper turned to the inner planets. Davenant noticed that Weller never lost a chance to needle Halleck—small personal remarks and sights which brought the Cinc-4's rage close to boiling over. It was not a comfortable party.

Back in their own suite, the Engineers dropped into Basic for the benefit of the recorders.

"I can't say I'm overly fond of our hosts," declared Yuan. "Mechanized common people, fear and hate and ambition the prime motives of the rulers. I wonder if we ought to do their job for them."

"You know our rule about local politics," said Lyell.

"Seems you were doing your share of politicking tonight, Chief," Yamagata said slyly.

"I've the authority to make suggestions," answered Lyell. "If they go unheeded, I can give a negative report, which will make the Abbey drop the job. But that's all."

"There's something inhuman about the setup," declared Kruse. "People aren't robots. The Sergeant class simply can't be treated that way indefinitely. They'll either mutiny or degenerate to uselessness."

"I think—" Falkenhorst hesitated.

"Yes, you're right, Torvald. But there must be some safety valve, some outlet for them. I'd like to know what it is."

That was discovered two Earth days later. Davenant was going through some maps in the library, checking resources of fissionables with Garson's help, when the Angel yawned and stretched and said, "Might's well quit now. Holy time comin' up, an' there'll be no work f'r forty-eight hours."

"A special service, do you mean?" asked Davenant, feeling the vague discomfort which mention of religious intimacies always gave him.

"Yes. Feast o' the Three Prophets. We have holy times once in a while, sev'rl times an Earth year." Garson hesitated. "Why don't y' come, Hall? You look like y' could use some fun."

Some people have their own ideas of fun! thought Davenant, but the prospect had a certain morbid interest. Doubtless it would be boring as a drill-mech. Nevertheless—

"Wouldn't people mind?" he asked. "I'm not a member of your Church, after all."

"Oh, no trouble. Stan' back to the rear at first. Later on, y' can join in all y' want." Garson smiled shyly. "We might even convert you."

"Well—all right!" Davenant noted the time and place and went off to his supper.

The others of his band refused somewhat profanely to come near the service. They preferred Kruse's idea of wiping the recorders with a magnetic field and locking themselves in with some bottles.

Lyell approved, "If you want to go, Hall, it's not a bad notion. The more we can learn about these people, the better."

Davenant changed to a clean dress uniform and went down a series of ramps and corridors. As he neared the great assembly room, the press around him grew thick—commoners streaming in from all parts of the city, men and women and children mingled together. They were silent, but there was a curious eagerness on their faces. The hall was a gigantic natural cavern which had been enlarged until it could accommodate the entire population of X. It was painted and tapestried into an explosion of color, huge streaks and jags of green, purple, gold, blood-red swirling on the walls. There were no benches, so everyone stood, but the floor was softly textured. At the farther end, rising out of semi-darkness, was a sort of stage with an altar. All the Angels in X seemed gathered there, rank on rank of them like robed statues. The only Cinc in sight was Weller, who sat on the stage between his guards.

Davenant found a place against a wall. The gray-clad Sergeants who crowded around hardly seemed to notice the stranger. Their eyes were fixed with a curious greed on the stage, and they breathed heavily. Music was coming from somewhere, archaic syncopated stuff which caught at the pulse with a primitive force. Davenant wondered at the feeling of lightness and elation that seemed to be rising within him.

"O brethren—" It was all the Angels, a huge male chorus ringing like distant thunder between the ends of the cave. *"Praise ye the Lord, in Whom all are one. Thank ye the Lord for the gift of life and for His Manifold mercies."*

Effective, thought Davenant. *I wonder why? I've heard better in Luna City.* But as the chorus rose and swelled, he felt an odd lump in his throat. The man beside him was weeping.

Organ tones pealed like the voice of Heaven.

The sermon began, from the lips of an elderly Angel who only yesterday had been discussing gas-diffusion processes with Davenant.

It started quietly enough, solemn as the music, with the Angel reciting the virtues of humility and hard work. Davenant found it rather reasonable.

Then the tempo picked up.

"An' yet who're we, mis-rable wallowers in sin, that we should walk this world? We who're slothful, an' greedy, an' lustful, we who's so blackened that only the blood o' the Lamb can ever wash us clean? I say t' y' all, the Devil is waitin'! On the Black Planet which is called Hell he waits f'r us, he's ready t' lick us down his hot gullet, down into the lake of eternal fire—you an' you an' you! Few are they who'll find mercy in the sight o' the Lord, an' great is the wailin' in Hell—"

People stamped their feet. Giant, dwarf, multiple-armed, tentacle-armed, the pure-human majority, they jerked, and moaned, and swayed with the rhythm of the words. Music rose around them, a sinister harrying of notes gone wild, and the Angel roared abomination down on them.

Amen! Amen! The Lord have mercy on me a sinner!"

Davenant's knees felt weak, his heart thick in his breast. He was doomed and done for, outcast, alone, every shame of his life was rising to mock him and he gasped with the pain of it. Everyone was groveling on the floor now, creeping toward the altar, wailing their miserable little sins to the world. And he, he, he alone was damned!

"Hallelujah!"

It took a minute before Davenant realized that the shout had been his own.

That brought him up short. A word screamed in his brain, and he doubled up against the wall and grabbed for its support. *Supersonics!*

Or subsonics? He wasn't sure. He couldn't remember in the confusion that bawled around him. But he knew that inaudible sound waves in the right frequencies do strange things to the human nervous system. The take-off of a rocket gives a man a moment of irrational dread. There are combinations of wavelengths which stimulate the thalamus, exalt the emotional response, while suppressing the action of the critical, reasoning forebrain.

It had been a standard part of psychotherapy for a long time. It was being used here on a giant scale!

Knowing it was a help. Davenant fought back toward sanity. He felt his heart pulsing with the words that rolled around him, he was frightened and joyous and enraged all at once, but it could be controlled. He licked his lips and wondered how long he would have to hold out.

"Praise ye therefore the Lord, for His mercy endureth! Give thanks and rejoice that He made ye!"

Hang on, boy, hang on, stay where you are.

In the seething of the mob, it hardly seemed incongruous that the Angels should suddenly be tossing out plastibottles. One landed beside Davenant. He picked it up, unscrewed the cap, and tasted as the others were doing. It burned in his throat. A hundred and fifty proof at least!

The music rose with a triumphant surge and thunder. He saw the nearest man turn, grunting, and snatch in a curious blind way at a woman. She struggled a moment, as if against some dying fragment of convention, then fell into his arms. He, fumbled at the sleazy material of her dress, lifting it as he forced her toward the floor.

So that's their safety valve!

A hand plucked at his. It felt hot, and wet with excitement. Turning, he saw another woman, pulling at him. Disordered hair streamed past a face which glistened with sweat and contorted with laughter.

"C'mon, honey," she said. "Le's go."

He shivered and stiffened himself. "No—no thanks," he mumbled.

Arms were around his neck. Even in low-gravity, her weight was dragging him down. "Y' re a new un," she said. "C'mon, have some fun. It's awight."

She felt soft and hot against him. Helplessly, he stared down the open neck of her dress. Her lips sought his, greedily. It was like an explosion inside him. He sank to his knees and she laughed and pushed her body against his.

Wildly, he wanted to accept, nobody would know, and—and— Glancing around, he saw that the floor was littered with couples and that the younger Angels were leaping off the stage to join the party. There was a tightness in his throat and a hammering in his temples; he'd been a long time without a woman.

No!

He pulled himself free, shuddering. "Damn it, I'm an Engineer!" he gasped, more to himself than to her.

"Wha's the' matter?" she demanded insistently.

He thrust her away. "No!" he said harshly. "Go find someone else—"

Ugliness crossed her face. "Y' can't, huh?"

He wanted to show her otherwise, but only shook his head angrily. She laughed unpleasantly and moved off. It took him a full minute to recover his wits.

Davenant looked up at the stage then. Weller was rising to go. Either he had superhuman self-control or, more likely, there was a heterodyning vibrator mounted near his seat. Custom had apparently required his presence, but—

Suddenly, he fell.

His guards swarmed around him. Peering into the shadows, Davenant saw half a dozen men under one of the high columns. They were dressed as commoners, but stood aloof. He pushed closer, recklessly, and saw Halleck among them.

A machine gun chattered from the wings. Other Hounds came into view, methodically mowing down Weller's guards. They were in the majority, they operated with smooth coordination, and the whole fight was over inside a minute. The survivors withdrew, bearing their wounded.

Halleck and his followers turned quietly and left the hall. Davenant made out the faces of at least two Cincs he had met. So several of them must have got together on this. A group conspiracy would be the only way, probably, to get past Weller's defenses. Now the junta would install a new Cinc-1 and—

Few if any of the brawling crowd had noticed what went on. They were too busy with their own affairs.

Davenant felt oddly light-headed. It must be the aftermath of the sonics. The only sensible thing to do was beat it back to the Engineers. He had no business mixing into this bloody mess which was Jovian politics, but his own impetus carried him along, his will gone.

Two men on the stage were looking down at the bodies which littered it. One wore Cinc uniform, one was an Angel. Both were high-ranking, to judge by their insignia.

Davenant got down on all fours and crawled toward the stage. The pairs and groups wallowing about him were cover of a sort. If he was noticed at all in the dim light he might be taken for a commoner. Or he might get a bullet in his skull.

Near the stage, he lay prone and called on his mental training. He had a degree of conscious control over the involuntary functions, he could drop the sensory barriers and heighten perceptions as some hysterics do without volition. Just enough to hear what was being said—

In Basic!

The shock of that turned his muscles rigid. For a moment, there was darkness before his eyes. It faded, and he heard the Angel speaking: "So far, so good. But will Halleck be more manageable?"

"I've been his mentor since he was a child," answered the Cinc. "Consciously, of course, he distrusts me as much as does, anyone else. But I've made it plain that I'm not after the highest rank, so he will listen to me, at least. And I know what buttons to push."

"We'll have to proceed cautiously. A whole culture can't be rushed into anything new." With a note of grim humor, the Angel added, "We ought to know that by now!"

"Of course, of course. But we're doing all right. We've come a long way since Callisto. Pass the word around—conference at 1800 tomorrow. Arrange it as an ostensible discussion of policy with regard to these Engineers. Which it will be, in a way, though we want only our people in on it"

"All right I'll send you an official memorandum. Let's go."

They walked off the stage. It was a long time before Davenant gathered himself together enough to leave.

When he entered his quarters, Kruse looked up with a rather bleared expression. "What's the matter, Hall? Seen a ghost?"

Davenant drew a shaky breath. "Yes. In a way."

Lyell stood up. "What do you mean ?"

"I mean—" Davenant looked at the floor, then up again, to meet their eyes with a certain desperation. "I mean I've found out who really runs Ganymede."

"Oh. The service you went to? You mean the Angels are more powerful than they act?"

Davenant shook his head. "Cincs and Angels are played off— manipulated. It's the Psychotechs from Earth."

❖ V ❖

HUBRIS, NEMESIS, ATE. So the old Greeks summed up the rise and doom and fall of men. It is a formula which has gone through all history.

Much partisan nonsense has been written about the Psychotechnic Institute. It was neither the only savior of a reeling civilization, nor the tyrant which strangled man's right to be an individual. It was a band of men and women who for generations strove toward a high ideal, wrought mightily, and at the last—as might have been foreseen— encountered problems they could not solve. Somewhat as the medieval Church nurtured Western civilization, the Institute was a kind of placenta for Technic society. In both cases, an outgrown matrix was becoming constrictive and had to be broken, and in both cases the act of breaking threw men back temporarily to disorganization and unreason.

The tragic flaw in the character of Institute personnel was only that they were human.

Scientific method was first successfully applied to social processes in the nineteenth century, when statistics were used to accumulate and winnow data. The basic-theoretical approach was developed in the twentieth century along several lines of attack—games theory, communications theory, general semantics, the principle of last effort, generalized epistemology.

The original Psychotechnic Institute eventually absorbed all similar groups. Devoting itself to study, it came up with some fundamental equations describing human relations. The approach was that of field dynamics. Its discoveries about the psychomatics of the individual were of even greater ultimate importance, but centuries would pass before those bore full fruit.

What counted around 1970 was a precise formulation of certain basic laws governing the action of *groups*. No one pretended that the science was perfect; it had to admit large probable errors. But it was immediately usable, and the world of 1970 badly needed a guide.

Governments had long been relying on experts. It was only natural for men to continue doing so. As time went on, the Institute came to train nearly all the psychotechnicians, to inculcate them with its own ideals, and to keep in contact with them after they had gone into active service.

Political debate was conditioned by their reports. The tendency was for them to become administrators. The Institute's leaders foresaw the growth of their own power, but they did not snatch after it. It came to them of its own accord, because only they could formulate policies for a world still wounded and feverish, policies which had a reasonable hope of success.

And so, step by step, came the economic recovery and improvement of all Earth. The strengthening of world government, the slow withering of nationalism; education which, for the first time in centuries really fitted the needs of the individual and of his society; the gradual decline of population on an overcrowded planet; the effective conservation of natural resources; rational economics, sane penology, generally available psychiatric care, critical thinking.

It was not easy. There were setbacks, interminable debates, deadly undercover struggles—but the foundation was being laid.

The reasons for the final breakdown of this progress were complex, but three main threads may be traced. First, there was a deep cultural resistance in a majority of Earth's population. As Asia became more and more the economic center of the world, this unwillingness gained power.

The road was, after all, long and hard, and it involved the scrapping of traditions which had existed since pre-human times. In many ways, it went against animal instinct, and peoples without the technological bias of the West were inclined to draw the line somewhere and stick by it.

Second, the bulk of humanity simply was not fitted to absorb the new attitudes. Cold rationality and a high degree of self-abnegation do not come naturally to ninety-nine percent of the race. Individual psychology suggested ways to get around this, but there was no way to recondition a billion and a half human creatures en masse.

Third, there was mass unemployment on a scale never seen before, as computers, automatons, and semi-volitional machines replaced men on one continent after another. Not only the unskilled laborer, but his highly trained brother and the routine intellectual—clerk, recorder, librarian, local administrator, laboratory assistant, the expert, some thousands of professions—was no longer needed.

The process took a long time to near completion, and there were many attempts to alleviate its effects, but nothing, not even the great emigration to Mars and Venus, was enough. At the nadir of the situation only some twenty-five percent of the adult population of Earth was even partially employed.

Of course, no one starved, a citizen's allowance was enough to assure living quite comfortably, but the genius class which could still work and get extra money for it was hated and envied. Yet the geniuses had to be paid, or not enough of them would have accepted the positions which still had to be filled by humans.

It is not good for a society when most of its citizens have no vested interest in its smooth operation. The atmosphere of restlessness and despair tainted even the leaders.

Out of all this rose Humanism, which amounted to a desire to restore a streamlined version of entirely imaginary "good old days." The Institute was shocked by the rapidity with which the movement grew. It was made the more dangerous by the general availability of superdielectrics, accumulators of fantastic capacity which could be charged from almost anything; cheap, simple energy sources for vehicles and weapons.

The balance of military power was shifting away from central government and toward the small, fanatic group. It was no longer possible to enforce order.

The Institute had had its own secret machinations before this. There was, for instance, the inoculation of a precalculated percentage of the cost-free synthetic food supplements with chemical contraceptive, followed by specious public explanations of the telling birth rate. There was the quiet subversion of the most inflexible archaist organizations. There was much more, which had been deemed necessary but could not go through the process of democratic agreement.

The new situation was ugly. Anti-robot riots, the lynching of technies and scientists; the election of intellectually corrupt representatives—lunacy was building up as rapidly and unnecessarily as—to quote a classic example!—it did in the old United States between World Wars II and III.

The Earth sections of the Union government were calling less and less on trained men, going back more and more to rule of thumb. Something had to be done!

And the field equations did not indicate a solution.

There is no reason to detail the increasingly frantic efforts of the Institute's leaders to stop the avalanche. Some of their methods were actually unlawful, and when this was exposed the results were evil. The naval mutiny, the Humanist Revolution and seizure of power, the withdrawal of Earth from the Solar Union—these are matters of record.

The Humanists soon found out, though, that they could not repeal history, could not abolish the technology on which men were now dependent. Mars and Venus backed the counter-revolution. The shaky Regents were overthrown and the new government rejoined the Union—but the seeds of interplanetary rivalry and distrust had been sown.

"Tame" psychotechnicians could not be dispensed with, but their powers were rigidly limited. The generations to come would be turbulent, one might call them the adolescence of Technic civilization—an age of trial and error for such men of goodwill as groped toward a new and better basis for living. An age of conflict and greed for the short-sighted majority. But an age with a peculiar hectic brilliance of its own.

Analogies to post-Reformation Europe are tempting, but should not be drawn too closely.

What is of interest now is that at the time of the Revolution some of the Institute chiefs and their followers decamped to save their own lives. They had managed to seize an ecological-unit spaceship—it was the old *Starshine,* in orbit around Earth after completing the third expedition to Neptune—and had taken it into outer space.

No one knew why they did not go to Mars or Venus, as many of their colleagues did, nor was it known what had become of them.

Mankind in general had too much else to think about to worry over a few hundred refugees.

❀ VI ❀

"POLITICS," Lyell said when Davenant told him what he had discovered. "We stay out of this."

"Even if there's a—danger?" asked Yuan. "If the psychotechs get this system organized just the way they want, it could well become a menace to the status quo."

"As a scientist of sorts, you ought to be pretty sympathetic to the psychotechs," retorted Lyell.

"Maybe. Maybe. We need their skills. Could be Earth's made her biggest mistake to date in booting them out. On the other hand—I don't know." Yuan frowned unhappily.

"I think I follow you," said Yamagata. "Groups, organizations, tend to lose sight of their original purposes, don't they? The means to an end become an end in themselves. Look, oh, say at the Christian church. It started with a noble ideal, maybe the noblest man has ever seen, a universal brotherhood of love. After a few centuries, it was burning people alive for disputing its authority."

"That took longer than you think," said Lyell. "But I won't quibble. It may well be that Psychotech people have become embittered and fanatical. Their connivance at political murder today suggests it. Nevertheless, we don't let on that we have any inkling they're here. We proceed as usual, report the facts secretly to the Abbey, and let the Coordinator and Council decide what to do. If the Engineers don't stay out of affairs such as this, they'll end up as exactly the same kind of power-grabbing, intriguing bunch of crooks. Our job is to keep the scientific spirit alive. To reform planets, not people."

"Of course," said Falkenhorst, "the Abbey will want more facts than just the bare statement that—"

"Yes, yes. Keep your eyes open. But don't go playing spy. You haven't the training or aptitude, and the Cincs are experts."

"So are the Psychotechs," observed Kruse. "You realize that everything we've said in Basic, fondly imagining no one understood it, is known to them."

"Uh-huh. From now on, we keep the wiper going permanently in here. Let them wonder why. Also, it's about time we started demonstrating a few things we can do . . ."

The announcement that Weller was dead and that Halleck was the new Cinc-1 came toward the end of the holy time. An added twenty-four hours of circus proclaimed to celebrate the accession. The Sergeants took it stolidly; they must be used to such sudden changes of masters.

Davenant continued his fact-finding in the library, since he wanted

to see which of the Angels normally there excused themselves to attend
the special conference. It was a shock when Garson was among them.
That fumbling, blushing, stammering nonentity?

On second thought, it fit. The psychotechs weren't interested in an
outward show of power. They concentrated on getting into key
subordinate positions—the men who gathered data and wrote reports,
the men whose advice was valued by the policy-makers. The Jovian
rulers, a curiously innocent breed in spite of their mercilessness, could
not be expected to know just how powerful the executive secretary of
a committee was, for instance, especially if that man had the sense to
be unobtrusive about it.

This also would explain why Garson had so casually accepted the
Engineers' feats of instant comprehension and memorization during
their studies. To him, that was the least part of mental training.

But had he, then, invited Davenant to the service with the idea of
having him witness the assassination? If so, why?

While the Angel was absent, the engineer took the opportunity to
look up the historical files. There wasn't much about the original
settlers of Callisto. They had merely claimed to be adherents of the
outlawed Technic Party who had tried to establish themselves on the
satellite and had failed because there weren't enough skilled space jacks
among them.

They had joined the Ganymedeans under an agreement which gave
them all Angel status, permitted familiar contracts to remain in force,
and left their big ship their own personal property. That must have
taken shrewd negotiation, but of course their leaders had been experts.
Some had soon been given Cinc rank, and the younger generation
among them was being raised in the orthodox Jovian manner.

Still, Davenant was pretty sure that they arranged for their own
children to be picked for special training, and for their women to get
the more privileged jobs. There was no secret police here, for the
society was too rigid to require one. A close-knit brand of conspirators
could maintain itself without much trouble.

Now that he knew what to look for, Davenant could easily find the
signs of their influence. There had been some radical changes quietly
made in the past twenty-five years. The Sergeants were no longer an
undifferentiated mass, but had been divided into grades, of which the

higher echelons got a respectable though strictly utilitarian education.

The newer outposts had been organized under different lines from X and from each other. One was staffed entirely by Sergeants who had a regular family life, another by experimental mutant types, still another by Angels, and all under the very eye of the Church. A diversity of cultures was breeding which must in time clash with and destroy the Church's petrified overlordship. The terraforming project itself was probably a psychotech idea.

So far, so good. Davenant had every sympathy with the notion of undermining Jovian society. But he wasn't at all sure about the ultimate aims of its new, hidden masters.

Some three Earth days later, the Engineers went out into the field. They didn't bother unloading their ship, but jetted her directly to the camp site, a feat of piloting which must have made some eyes bulge.

A party of Angels and Sergeants, with a few Cinc bosses and their Hounds, arrived by motor sled to find camp already being established. It was a whirl of movement and action, with a score of swift sleek robot machines erecting shelters and workshops, guided only by men at the main control boards.

"Y're gonna drill here?" Garson asked timidly.

Lyell nodded. "I think this is a promising site for one of the H-Li burners. We'll take cores down to a depth of fifty kilometers and find out for certain."

"Fifty!" Garson gulped. "Won't a shaft that deep—y'll have to make it pretty wide, too—won't it cave in?"

"Not in this gravity and with this type of rock," said Lyell. "Anyway, it'll only be wide at the bottom, otherwise just broad enough to lower parts which our robots can assemble down there. It'll take longer to warm the surface with the fires burned that deep, but be far more economical in the long run. Also, right now we still have to find out just how much native heat there is at the satellite center and how available it is."

A self-operating 'dozer walked around a selected area, scooping away rubble with casual giant shrugs. A slim steel skeleton rose above it, and Davenant and Kruse hooked in the boring rig and a minimal nuclear engine. They could have done it faster if their Jovian subordinates had been trained for such work.

Falkenhorst set up his furnaces in one of the workshops and began turning out synthetic diamonds for drill bits. Yamagata's laboratory worked overtime analyzing the sections brought up. Yuan pored over the results and announced that a biological approach to the atmosphere problem was not impossible.

"Of course, we can't mutate from protoplasmic life," he said. "Theoretically we could make animals, but they'd have to have heat-producing cells to keep from freezing solid, and we want unicellular organisms than can multiply like mad. Rather than wait till the satellite is warm enough, I'm going to have the Abbey labs turn out some different things, which can live here as conditions are, getting rid of the poisons and releasing oxygen as natural metabolic functions. Liquid ammonia in place of water, for instance."

"Y' mean y'all can *make* life?" Garson sounded shocked, and Davenant reflected what a good actor he was. The datum could hardly have been unknown to him, for synthetic virus antedated the Humanist Rebellion by more than a century and a half.

"Sure." Yuan peered at him from a stack of calculations. "Whole bacteria were assembled long ago. It was just a matter of reproducing and accelerating the chain of physicochemical reactions which led to the first life on Earth. Oparin had sketched that out as far back as 1930 or so. Nowadays we can tailor synthetic bacteria and protozoa to almost any requirements. The limiting factor is merely the extremes of temperature between which such complex reactions as make up life will go on," He smiled. "Nothing more than microscopic organisms have been made yet, and I see no reason why humans should ever be produced synthetically even if it is possible. Nature has a much more interesting way of achieving that result."

The Cinc who was with them looked doubtful. "It soun's blasphemous," he muttered. "Only God—"

"Oh, call it straight organic chemistry if you want to," snapped Yuan. "Just don't bother me now. I've got work to do."

The Cinc flushed darkly, and Davenant could almost read his thoughts—You damn slant-eyed—

Garson stammered a question which deftly turned the talk into safer channels.

"We'll have to set up an iron mine near here," declared Lyell. "You understand that our construction is only a portable testing rig, and that most of the terraforming materials'll have to be manufactured on this world. According to your maps, there's a deposit not far off . . . Let's assemble some workers and go take a look."

The look involved driving shafts kilometers into a mountain. Blasting was of little value in the tenuous atmosphere, and Davenant used atomic energy to melt rocks loose, after which the diggers lumbered monstrously to clear away the rubbish.

"How d'you control the reaction?" inquired Garson. "I never thought anybody'd ever make atomic burners that small."

"Damping fields," said Davenant abstractedly. "Anti-radiation fields, too. It's the same development of wave mechanics as has produced the molar potential barrier and the frictionless wheel-drive. In principle, these gadgets tap some of the reaction energy to control the reaction itself through field baffles. Lead shielding is obsolete except for special purposes."

"Oh." Garson's eyes rested on Davenant. Behind the faceplate, his countenance was a mask. "So y' can damp, shut off a reaction from outside?"

"Of course. How else could we burn, say, hydrogen and lithium instead of just blowing them up?"

The team went on to another site. Lyell used the opportunity to go into space and check with instruments.

"A big ship there in a low orbit, all right," he said. "Must be the *Starshine*. She's cold as charity, too. No one aboard."

"Emergency exit for our psychotech friends," guessed Kruse. "No point in leaving her there, rather than breaking her up for scrap unless she's fully equipped. So when they came to Callisto, they must have had Ganymede in mind all the time."

Yamagata nodded. "These people never did anything at random. When the debacle came, they must have figured their best chance to get back in the saddle lay through Jupiter. Mars and Venus have too much contact with Earth for them to operate secretly."

"But the people who came out here—" began Davenant. "They knew they'd never live to see their plans mature. Why that tremendous sacrifice for a time long after they were dead?"

"People are that way," said Yuan.

"What worries me is their ultimate plans," said Falkenhorst. "Those here now must realize that they've little or no chance of persuading the inner planets to reinstate them by using sweet reasonableness, or even some obscure socio-economic manipulation. And the Institute did advise war from time to time as the best solution. Like when they got the old UN to put down the Venusian nationalists by force. I have an uneasy notion they plan to make Jupiter a—Prussian state, and then under the guise of Jovian conquest . . . With modern weapons, it wouldn't be pretty, whether they won or lost."

Kruse said, "They always preached against war except as a last resort. The Venusian campaign was a small affair. I ought to know— my great-great-grandfather was a UN marine who fought there and settled down afterward."

"But attitudes change," declared Lyell. "The psychodynamic techniques are only methods for attaining given ends. They say nothing about the desirability of any aim. If the Institute people have acquired an old-fashioned power hunger, they'll rationalize it to themselves, but they'll be as dangerous as any would-be conqueror." He shrugged. "Out of our province, though."

The initial survey took a little over three months. Then the expedition returned to X to make preliminary evaluations of data and plan the attack on Callisto. Terraforming Ganymede certainly looked possible. The question still was whether or not Jovian society was able to avail itself of the possibility. The answer to that involved further sociological study.

"If the psychotechs think it can be done, I'm inclined to agree with them and let it go at that," said Kruse. "They know this moon better than we ever will."

Lyell shook his head. "In the first place, we have to keep up the pretense of not realizing the true situation," he replied. "It could mean trouble if they found out that we do know. In the second place, the Abbey would want an independent opinion anyway. In the third place, how do you know they *want* the job done? Our trying and failing might be what they really have in mind. It could have a psychological impact, a disappointment and bitterness, which they could very well exploit."

Davenant felt again a chill of foreboding. He wasn't fitted for this atmosphere of unsureness and hostility and dark cross-currents. A wave of homesickness for the clean bare slopes of Luna and the comradeship of the Abbey nearly overwhelmed him. He wondered what the Cinc spies thought of their suddenly blanked recorders. The natural interpretation would be that the Engineers had discovered the hidden instruments and had simply chosen this means to express indignation. But how natural was the Jovian mind?

He returned to the library. There was little he could do at present except soak up as many facts as possible, for the Academy's experts to take from him later. And the long, quiet chamber was the only place in X he really liked.

Garson looked up from a projector as he came in. There was no one else present. "God with us," he said shyly.

Davenant nodded and sat down next to him. "What are you studying now?" he asked.

"I'm s'posed to be educating myself in metallurgic theory, so I can work better with your team. 'Fraid it's not my strong point."

Davenant looked at the projector. It had what seemed like an unnecessary number of controls. "Why those?" he asked, pointing.

"Oh, that's t' save spools. One tape can hold a lot o' diff 'rent texts, same as one phone line can carry a lot of different messages. These buttons are t' unscramble, select the one I want."

"Hmmm—" Davenant hoped his excitement didn't show. "That's a novel idea. When did it come in?"

"Oh, 'bout fifteen, twen'y years ago. Why ?"

"J-j-j—" Davenant swore at himself and brought his tongue under control. "I was just wondering."

But he knew now where the psychotechs kept their secret records! Right here with all the others, safely scrambled in with a code modulation known only to the conspirators. Best place on Ganymede!

The Angel sighed and looked at him steadily. "You know, don't you?" he murmured—in Basic.

"Know?—" For an instant, Davenant foiled to understand what Garson meant. Then shock held him rigid.

The Angel smiled. "Why bother, Hall? It sticks out ten kilometers. Ever since you started blanking those spy machines, and some of your questions, the way you react to key statements, almost the way you walk. You know who we are."

"You—I don't get it. What do you mean?"

"Never mind. This isn't a very safe place to discuss such things. Just tell the others what I've said, and quote me to the effect that we don't care. It was foreseen that a group of alert, intelligent outsiders, coming here especially to study this place, would most likely discover our secret. The probable reaction of your order has already been estimated and allowed for. I *wanted* to see that religious ceremony and assassination, to realize more fully what a brutalized culture this is and how right that it should be taken over and changed."

The mask was off. There was no more hesitation, no more awkwardness in Garson. It was a mature and calmly assured man who spoke.

"I know we've been party to some nasty affairs, like the last change of dictators. We'll continue in that line for a while, because we must. Just remember that our ultimate aim is still what it always was—to establish sanity so firmly in all men that that sort of thing will be forgotten and impossible."

Davenant sat unmoving. Garson returned quietly to his book.

It might have been minutes later, or nearly an hour, when the tramp of boots rang in the corridor outside. Davenant glanced up from the screen which he had been mechanically studying, and saw the door fly open. A dozen Hounds made their entry. Long, low-gee jumps ranged them around the wall, with guns pointing inward. A black-clad Cinc-3 followed them.

"Don't move," he said. "You're arrested."

"*What?*" Davenant leaped erect. Three staring muzzles followed him. "What in Sol—"

"Hands up!" snapped the Cinc. "Conspiracy 'gainst the church. 'S is a killin' matter."

Davenant sucked in his breath and willed steadiness back to his shaking form. His mind leaped with an unnatural clarity.

"You can't arrest me," he said. "I'm a Planetary Engineer. Our contract with your government, which has the force of a treaty, gives us immunity."

"Can't I, though?"

Davenant shrugged. A tiny germ of panic crawled deep in his skull, but his voice lifted coldly. "The Order protects its own. If you molest me in any fashion, they'll hear of it at once on Luna. We have our methods of communication."

Sheer bluff, but he counted on the scientific illiteracy of the Cinc class, and the awe which his team's work in the field had produced. "How would you like to have your brain burned out from space?" he went on. "What defense have you against robot bombs sent clear from Luna? If you don't let me go back to my quarters, you'll soon find out that the Order is not helpless."

For a moment, the Cinc hesitated. "Don' do it!" screamed Garson. "There's women an' children here!"

That worked. The Cinc detailed three Hounds to escort Davenant back to his suite.

Four of the other Engineers were already there. Kruse showed up later, arrogantly demanding that the guards outside the door let him in. He had been set on by three Hounds down in the main power room, but he had also been involved in clan feuds on Venus as a youngster. From his tunic he extracted guns and passed them around.

"What brought it on?" groaned Yuan. "What's happened?"

"I've got a hunch." Davenant set up his testing rig and checked the room circuits again. "Yeah. Halleck's idea, I'll bet. He's not stupid. See this pip? That's a metallic mass in the adjoining suite which wasn't there before. When we started wiping his tapes, he must have set up an old-fashioned groove-cutting mechanical recorder. He's heard everything!"

"And we thought we were safe, and didn't bother to speak Basic most of the time," mumbled Yuan. "He must be pretty damn sure of the situation. So now he's setting out to arrest all the psychotechs on Ganymede, and us along with them."

"What will happen to us ?" wondered Falkenhorst. Sweat beaded his face, but the voice held an iron calm. "Will they dare take action against members of the Order?"

"Probably," said Lyell in a thin tone. "We're safer for him dead—we know too much. He may call Hall's bluff and execute us officially. More likely fake an accident." He scowled. "What to do?"

Kruse shrugged. His face was taut and pale, but he spoke with a sharp note of laughter.

"We've got three guns?" he said. "We're used to higher gravity than this. We can catch those sons of Hounds outside by surprise. Pick up whatever equipment here you think we'll need. The only thing for us is to break out of here!"

There was only a moment's hesitation, as they weighed the meaning. Lyell nodded. "I hate to do it, but . . . Let's go."

He, Kruse, and Yuan, the best shots, took the weapons. The rest loaded equipment on their backs. Kruse flattened himself against the door and opened it just enough to peer out, into the faces of three Hounds.

"Boo," he said.

The nearest guard scowled and reached for his gun. Kruse snapped three shots.

"Come on!" he yelled, and flung the door wide.

The Engineers burst out into the corridor, stumbling over the bodies. Davenant stooped to pick up a gun for himself, and heard the whine of a bullet cleaving the air where he had stood. A corps of Hounds was trotting down toward them.

"Out of here!" roared Lyell.

They backed, laying down a curtain of fire. It seemed a miracle that there were no hits, but they were distant, moving targets. Davenant wasn't afraid now; he hadn't time to be. He burst around a corner, almost into the arms of another Jovian guard.

His fist leaped of itself, the blow shocked home and he saw the man lurch back with his face red. Coldly, Davenant kicked him in the belly and behind the ear as he went down.

Run! His breath was raw in his throat as he fled with the others, down an endless labyrinth, always down, toward the garages. He didn't see the action behind him as the three gunners turned to fire back. Once Falkenhorst staggered, grabbing at a shoulder which was suddenly wet. Davenant threw an arm around the man's waist, and they struggled on together.

Now—the garage entrance. In the confusion, it was unwatched. The Engineers went through, closing the massive door and dogging it behind them. A couple of mechanics ran up to protest. Kruse waved his gun.

"Back, or you get it in the guts!" he snarled.

There was a long row of sleek small rockets, ready and waiting. Lyell entered the nearest.

"Kruse, Davenant, Yamagata, aft to the engines," he clipped. "The rest stay with me. Be ready to take over piloting if I don't last."

"I hope those mechs stay buffaloed." Kruse's teeth flashed white. "We've used up all our ammunition, you know." His big form wriggled into the crowded engine room.

"Where the devil will we go to?" asked Yamagata. "This boat isn't interplanetary."

"I don't know. The Outlaws in the hills, I reckon, if we can find them. What counts right now is getting clear of X."

The auxiliary motors purred, turning the rocket's wheels. It slipped down the corridor and up the airlock ramp. It was useful, having enemies indoctrinated out of all initiative. No one had thought to cut off the automatically opening valves.

As the boat emerged into dark bitterness, Lyell saw space-suited forms swarming across the ground.

"Not a chance to get to the *Light*," he said. "Stand by to lift."

The rockets flared, tossing the boat skyward. Lyell headed north, switched on the autopilot, and began scrambling into one of the spacesuits. The rest did the same. None was a particularly good fit—a suit should really be individually built—but they would do.

Stars glittered in the forward viewports. Falkenhorst slumped with closed eyes, color drained from his face. Yuan studied the radarscope. His voice floated back to the thrumming hotness of the engine room, over the intercom: "Someone coming after us."

"Yes, I see him now. Police rocket, and this thing hasn't a gun to its name." Lyell's voice held a groan.

Davenant did not see what happened. He felt the sudden shock and thunder, felt the hull reel around him and drop like a murdered seraph. Air whistled through the hole amidships, and the unbalance gyros howled.

"Hang on!" bellowed Kruse, slapping down his helmet. "Hang on and pray!"

They struck with a sundering crash which jerked Davenant's head almost off his neck. Darkness whirled before his eyes. When he came out of it, Kruse was looking emptily through the engine-room door.

"They're gone," he said. "It killed them."

Slowly, Davenant crawled from the ruin. The boat had come down in a long glide, smashing itself into a land of bare mountains and reaching snowfields. The three men forward were dead.

Yamagata went out through the hole torn in the boat's waist and looked skyward. A distant red flare streaked south.

"They aren't landing," he said. "Be almost impossible to do in this country, and they'll be needed at home and won't figure on any survivors lasting long."

"Which we won't," Kruse answered dully.

"We can try!" Rebellion lifted in Davenant and brought his head erect. "We'll lay these men out as well as we can, and then—"

"Yes?" asked Kruse. "What then?"

"We start walking," said Davenant.

That was how it had started. Now Davenant and Kruse stepped and glided, two dead men walking across the face of hell.

◎ VII ◎

THE GAUGES said that about thirty minutes' oxygen remained. If it had not been for Yamagata, Davenant and Kruse would have suffocated already. They could stretch out their lives by sitting still, but there was no point to that.

A ragged edge of hills cut across the face of Jupiter like teeth of blackness. Their shadows streamed enormous before them, hard and sharp over the broken ground. Outside the shadows, there was a rush of light from the primary, chill amber which sparkled frostily off solid ammonia fields and flashed from the ice glaciers in another saw-backed range. When Jupiter was close to full, its radiance was enough for human color vision, though the hues had a dreamlike distortion.

Near the banded giant, no stars were visible, they were drowned out. When you looked away, you could see them over the sharply curving horizon. They glittered through the tenuous, unbreathable air with a cruel wintry brilliance.

Even carrying his own weight of suit, oxygen bottles, capacitors, and other equipment, a man was light when gravity was less than a fifth of Earth's. You learned walking all over again, the first time you were on a low-gee world—a long, flat glide which ate the kilometers.

You learned to gauge distances when thin air made an object seem closer than it was, while a near horizon tried to make it seem farther. You learned to check every joint and valve and connection on your suit before venturing out, when the least failure could choke you, explode you, freeze you solid in minutes.

And you learned to have death for a companion!

The minds of the two surviving Engineers had grown so dim with the steady slogging that when the gunshot came it almost killed them. Davenport saw a spurt of snow and chipped ice before his feet and stared at it in a dull kind of wonder. He didn't hear anything except the whisper of wind past his helmet, for the air was too lean. Another slug pocked the low bluff to his right.

"Down!" yelled Kruse. "They're shooting at us!"

He nosedived for the ground, and a bullet whipped past the spot where he had stood. Davenant followed a movement of blind instinct. Ammonia-crystal snow feathered up to blind his faceplate, he pawed at it while his body tried to dig itself into rock.

Kruse touched helmets with him. "Radio silence, man! They may have a direction finder. We've got to speak by conduction. Now, this way—" He led an awkward belly-crawl toward the nearest of the little craters which scarred the valley floor.

Davenant shuddered. For a moment, he was uncontrollably afraid, his muscles knotted immovably against the expected leaden blow. Then the very condition of hysteria triggered reactions which had been built into his mind during his long training. Suddenly, he was without fear, his body keyed to a high adrenal pitch, his thoughts like cold lightning at night. He slipped after Kruse and wallowed down into the fluffy snow which filled the crater.

The Venusian hunched low, snarling into the empty sky. "If they pin us here for another half hour, we're done," he said.

A black outline showed above a ridge of ice, just for a second before ducking down again.

"Cincs?" asked Kruse. "Have they tracked us down after all ?"

Davenant considered. "No. If that were a Cinc, we'd be dead by now. He'd have an infrared 'scope on his rifle, and even with our heaters tuned down to where I'm glad I'm not a brass monkey, we'd show up like a bonfire against this temperature."

The big man blinked, a little surprised at Davenant's coolness. It would have surprised Davenant, too, if he had had time. He was fumbling with his pack, getting out the general unit which the discipline of years had made him carry from the wreck. General units were expensive, and Engineers were supposed to save money for the Order whenever it was humanly possible.

"Outlaws, then," said Kruse. "And how the devil we're going to convince them we're friendly?"

Slowly, Davenant's thick-fingered gloves worked on the unit, plugging in jacks and turning dials. It ran off his own capacitors, and took its time about warming up in the Ganymedean chill.

He answered Kruse abstractedly. "We're not friendly with the Outlaw, you know. We're only trying to establish contact out of desperation, and—" A flicker appeared on the screen. "Here we go!"

A man in the field, who might have to work hundreds of kilometers from camp, couldn't pack twenty different meters and detectors. He needed a single device, rugged and portable, which could be adjusted to perform twenty different functions. Davenant had simply connected the thermopile with the galvanometer, blinkered the lens to provide sharp directionality, and come up with an infrared spotter. It wouldn't directly show men crouched behind rock and ice, but it would show rising currents of air, heated by their suits. Cautiously, he swept it around the horizon.

"Two," he said after a minute. "One's sitting over in back of that ridge, the other circling behind us. I think he wants to get a vantage point from the top of that bluff and shoot down at us. Now, any ideas?"

"Mmmm—yeah. Let's get the circler. His friend won't be able to see what happens. We can get up on the bluff fast and wait for him."

A few minutes later, the Outlaw—he could be no other—crept over a final rise and toward a position where he could look down into the valley. A large form sprang on him from a crag, pinioning him. Another leaped at the same time from the nearly impenetrable shadow of a cave, grabbed the leads from his capacitors, and yanked them out before he could send a cry for help.

The man struggled wildly. It was hard for Kruse to hold him, here where weight counted for so little. Davenant got out his pliers and unscrewed the short aerial of the Outlaw's helmet radio. Only then did he plug the capacitors back into the suit circuit.

Kruse's helmet was tight against his prisoner's. "We don't want to cut off your juice permanently and freeze you," he said, "but we might have to unless you behave yourself. Get his gun, Hall."

Davenant could not hear that, but he had already picked up the weapon. To his surprise he saw that it wasn't a rifle, after all, but some kind of bolt-action smooth-bore, obviously homemade, though it used percussion caps. He covered the Outlaw until Kruse got some wire and bound the man's ankles together. Then the Venusian took the gun and stood up.

"I'm going after the other fellow," he said.

"Isn't that—dangerous?" objected Davenant.

"Of course, but look at your oxy gauge. We haven't got many minutes left, at the rate we've been using the stuff. And I've had stalking experience back home, which I doubt you have. See if you can talk this one over."

The tall figure slipped down the ridge and was lost to sight. Davenant huddled beside the captive, touching helmets. He heard only hoarse breathing for a while, and looked into a gaunt, hook-nosed face nearly hidden by long, tangled hair and beard. The suit, he noticed, was an old model, and bore signs of much handmade repair.

The Outlaw subsided a little. He could have thrown his arms around Davenant, but he could not have held the Engineer for long. He sat back with animal patience to wait for a better chance.

"Who are ye?" he asked. His English was barbarously accented, but clear enough. "Be ye gardam Cincs?"

"No. The Cincs were after us. We were looking for an Outlaw community where we can get help. We're men of the Planetary Engineers."

That conveyed nothing to the man, but he nodded grudgingly. " Ye're no Jovian, I see. Earth?"

"Only in a way. My Order exists apart from any planet. We work for all. But the Cincs hunted us down, anyway." Davenant paused, decided a half-truth was his best bet. "We want revenge on them. Perhaps your people can help."

"Mebbe new Cinc trick." It was a savage growl, with a lifetime's bitterness in the words.

"We want to be shown to your village. Let us talk to your chief or whoever—"

"No! Die first."

Davenant smiled nastily. "I don't see any signs of motor transport," he said, "so you must have walked from your home. You must have at least enough oxy to get back on. If necessary, we'll take your bottles for ourselves and follow your trail. But we'd rather let you guide us."

"Not enough oxy. We got caches, ye never find, ye die too."

"At least," said Davenant mildly, "we'll die trying." He was faintly surprised at his own ruthlessness. But the Order came first. More persuasively he went on, "What harm can it do if you guide us? What could two men do against a whole village? We have news for your chief which will make him glad. You have nothing to lose."

The Outlaw lapsed into a sullen silence. After a while Kruse came back, prodding another man before him.

"I sneaked behind and got the drop on this'n," he explained. "Now what should we do?"

Davenant examined the weapon taken from the new captive. It was a sort of spring-steel crossbow shooting metal quarrels. In this gravity and air pressure, such a device would have plenty of range. It could easily pierce a suit of space armor and the man within it. The main drawback would be the low rate of fire.

His respect for the Outlaws went up another notch.

"First," he said, "we take these boys' spare oxy bottles for ourselves. My air's getting thick. Then we talk them into guiding us, or if they won't we leave them here."

It took some persuasion before an agreement was reached, but then the trek got started. Once the men tried to lead them astray, but Kruse, who had spotted the faint signs of their earlier passage, forced them back onto the true trail.

It was a long walk, and Davenant felt weak with hunger toward its end. He thrust the awareness out of his mind and whipped his flagging body into new energy. Once they stopped at a carefully disguised cairn and took out some fresh oxygen containers. There must be a lot of caches spotted throughout this country.

That would explain how the Outlaw patrols managed to range so far.

Davenant wondered with a certain chill what would happen when they reached the village. He had heard stories about these barbarians which, even allowing for exaggeration by their enemies, were not reassuring.

❁ VIII ❁

NEAR THE NORTH POLE of Ganymede, the Godwin Mountains rose steep and cragged, tormented black walls which shimmered darkly under the radiance of Jupiter. A monster system of glaciers capped them, spilling down gashed ravines and across the lower plateaus. The yellow light was cold on their slippery backs.

Kruse, Davenant, and their prisoners halted between two peaks which thrust above the ice and covered them with shadow. A slope fell away beneath them to a narrow, craterlike depression, and on it they could see the outlines of human figures.

"Let's go," muttered Kruse.

"No!" One of the captives spoke in a harsh whisper. "Services goin' on. Sentries 'd shoot us first, check later. We gotta wait."

Squinting against the chill unreal haze of Jupiter-light, Davenant saw that the people below were drawn up in ranks, facing a block of native stone where half a dozen worshipers were going through ritual gestures. Poking his helmet aerial forward and tuning up his radio, he caught, faintly, a deep-voiced chant:

God-home, god-home, hear our askin'. See, we stand with sacrifice—

Shocked, he looked southward and up to the enormous face of the planet. It was at the full now, sprawling tremendously across heaven, the Red Spot like a single watching eye.

"Is *that* your god ?" he breathed.

"God is in Jupe and Jupe is in God," answered the barbarian with a peculiar note of reverence in his voice.

O Zeus, could you know! Davenant imagined Olympian laughter ringing hoarsely through the mountains.

"They caught a man in the last raid on Y," said one of the prisoners. "Look!"

They could see a man struggling in the grip of four others. A tiny puff of freezing vapor came from him, he went limp, and was hurled up on the altar and across the open ice. One of the Outstone. Davenant retched.

Forcing his mind back toward an impersonal clarity, he wondered about the development of Outlaw culture. How long ago had their revolt and exodus taken place—eighty years? That didn't seem like time enough for this much degeneration.

But then, Ganymede wasn't Earth. The psycho-social effect of alien conditions had yet to be measured. Huddling, hiding, waging a doomed war for three or four generations, the hillmen would rapidly have forgotten their intricate, highly specialized civilization. The barrenness and cold of the landscape would have entered their souls.

He turned over what little he had learned about them in X. A religious colony forced to alter its ways of living and thinking in order to survive, forced yet further by prophet-dictators whose "revelations" had involved radical social change and increased their own power. Yes, it would be unstable, it would have its Old Believers.

The introduction of controlled mutation had led to mutiny and civil war, the dissenters had been defeated and fled into the wilderness. There they had hidden, skulked, and raided lonely settlements. Without books, without leisure, they would rapidly have become barbarians. The stories about cannibalism and human sacrifice seemed justified but Davenant tried hard not to think of them as the monsters they were considered to be. They were human beings, lonely and desperate and driven close to madness, but they had the same potential as anyone else.

Besides, he thought, it was pretty obvious that the Cincs had been pulling their punches in the war. A concerted effort could have wiped out the hillmen long ago, but an external enemy was too useful.

"Seems to be breaking up down there," observed Kruse.

They waited till the scene was deserted, then moved cautiously down the slope and across the open ice. One of the Outlaws spoke with a note of glee.

"Might's well put down yer gun. Ye're covered now."

Sweat trickled along Davenant's ribs. He tried to look into the farther shadows, but they were too dense.

A voice in his earphones said, "Stand where ye be!"

A quarrel chipping the glacier near his feet added emphasis. They halted and stood waiting, their hands aloft. Three men came into view, weapons leveled. "That ye, Gil? Fooled 'em here, eh? Good going!"

"We—" Davenant licked his lips. They felt sandy. "We came here on purpose. We're not Cincs or Hounds. We're from Earth, and we want to see your chief."

There was a skeptical silence. One of the new arrivals picked up the dropped gun and crossbow and touched the Engineer suits.

"Not Cinc make," he grunted. "But they're clever devils."

"All we want—"

"I know, I know. Shuddup. Ye'll get yer chance—mebbe."

As Davenant walked up the farther ridge, with guns at his back, he saw half a dozen figures appear with—brooms, by space! He felt a mental wobbling until he realized they were carefully smoothing out footprints and all other trace of the recent crowd around the altar.

There was no path. Slipping and stumbling, groping through blindness of shadow and dazzled by Jupiter's radiance, the party made a slow way through the crags. It seemed a long while before they were halted by other sentries. There was a low-voiced colloquy, and then the two Engineers were herded toward a cave mouth, a great gullet of blackness in an overhanging cliff. A machine gun nest was dug in just beyond.

The passage fell rapidly downward, a reaching gloom where flash beams were pale fingers and echoes sounded hollowly even in this ghost of an atmosphere. Davenant could make out enough branch tunnels to wonder how anyone ever found his way here. Like all small, rapidly cooling worlds, Ganymede was riddled with caves.

After another lengthy and silent walk, they found an airlock door. It seemed to be from a spaceship. There was another defensive emplacement before it, and another discussion with the guards. At last, they were sent into the lock chamber. The pump was old and rickety, it took a long time to flush out Ganymede's air and replace it with a thin oxygen-rich mixture. Davenport's helmet frosted over and blinded him.

"Awright. Through here—stop—take off yer suit."

Davenant and Kruse stripped down to the form-fitting coverall, which was standard underpadding. Kruse was dirty and tired, skin drawn tight across jutting bones, a thick stubble of red beard on his jaws.

I suppose I look just as bad, thought Davenant.

There were several Outlaws about them, gaunt, undersized men in worn coveralls. Some of them wore ornaments—hammered copper rings in nose or ears. All carried daggers which seemed to have been beaten out of native iron. They were more interested in the captured airsuits than in the prisoners.

"How about seeing your chief?" asked Kruse.

"Take yer time," muttered someone, and spat.

Kruse bristled. "Look here," he snapped, "I told you we were from Earth. In fact, we're Planetary Engineers. You probably don't know what that means, but believe me, it's important. We have word for your chief which he'll be glad to hear, but if you don't treat us right the Order has means to make you do it."

That seemed to impress them a little. One of them traced a grimy finger over the suit, apparently impervious to the chill which was still on its exterior.

"Not Ganny make," he said. "Mebbe they be really from Earth." He spoke as a man at home might have spoken of Avalon.

"No weapons," said one of the two whom the Engineers had taken.

"Of course not," Davenant said loftily. "I tell you, we belong to the Order. Do you think we need to lug handguns around?"

"Well—" A hillman scratched his tangled whiskers. "All right. Come along."

Two others fell in behind, with cocked crossbows. The rest trailed after, their eyes lit by a dull curiosity.

The caves and tunnels here had been little improved save that fluoros were strung to illuminate them. Davenant decided that a section of the caverns must simply have been blocked off, with airlocks installed here and there, heated, and ventilated. No system of tubes for that—there must be only a few power fans mounted near the oxygen renewal plant. The air felt dank and stagnant.

The populated section was a series of narrow tunnels in which shallow caves had been chipped or blasted. Ragged curtains served for doors. When one or two of these were drawn aside as someone came out, Davenant saw a pathetic bareness within, a few boxes or stones for furniture. The dwarfish, near-naked women and children who swarmed and chattered around the convoy seemed unnecessarily dirty. Behold the noble savage!

"Can't be more than a few thousand," muttered Kruse. "Is this all the Outlaws there are?"

"I suppose so," answered Davenant.

"I heard in X that there were, several such villages once, but that only one was believed still to survive. If the Cincs didn't get them, something went wrong with the air plant or the power or—"

His revulsion was becoming an enormous pity. They couldn't even surrender, these poor starveling troglodytes; X had no use for them except as a unifying, ineffectual enemy.

Further along, they passed a communal kitchen. Steam pipes from the nuclear plant had been laid to heat food which seemed to be mostly synthetics.

The passage debouched on a wide cavern at whose farther end was a real door, native iron. A clumsy idol of black stone loomed before it, and two men armed with modern rifles—presumably stolen—lounged nearby on guard. There was a jabbering conference, and one of the sentries ducked inside.

Kruse switched to Basic to speak to Davenant. "Have you any idea what we're going to tell the grand high panjandrum?" he asked.

"Depends on what he's like," said Davenant. "It had better be good, though, or we'll end up in a stewpot."

The guardsman reappeared. "In," he grunted. As several pressed behind offering to cover the prisoners, he ordered, "No, just them two."

When the door clashed shut, Davenant had to struggle to suppress his astonishment. The chief seemed to own a suite, several rooms formed by plastiboard partitions. There were carpets on the floors, chairs and tables, a shelf of books. The man who stood before them was tall for an Outlaw, his long gray-shot hair and beard was neatly combed, his coverall faded but clean. Three women, presumably wives, scuttled out of sight.

There was a silence. "From Earth?" asked the Outlaw ruler at last.

"Yes." Davenant moved forward.

A pistol leaped into the man's hand. "Easy," he warned.

"We don't intend violence," said Davenant. "We jumped your scouts because they attacked us, but spared their lives. All we're after is a chance to talk to you."

"Awright. I'm Roberts-John, boss o' Jupiter City. Come in an' siddown."

The chief led the way to a sort of living room, found himself a chair, and clapped his hands. One of the women brought in a tray of water and synth-dough.

It was a shaking effort to nibble sedately at the food instead of wolfing it. The chief asked the Engineers their names and went on to some shrewd questions about the inner planets. Then he came to the point: "Why're ye here?"

"There was—trouble with the Cincs," said Davenant. He was faintly surprised that he should take the lead, but Kruse was sitting back and saying nothing, eyes half-shut with weariness. "We have to get in touch with the Abbey—with our Order, the Engineers. So we came looking for your people to help us."

"Lucky chance for ye," said Roberts-John. "Ye'd never 'a found the city 'thout our men to guide. It's well hid."

Davenant drew him out on that subject. He learned that the original mutineers had fled in some of the smaller spaceships, after wrecking others which might have been used for pursuit. The old *American* had long ago been broken up to help build X.

Now and then, the Outlaw outposts had had to fight the Hounds of the Lord—the warrior corps which had since been recruited from exogenes—who had come in ground vehicles. But the confusion left after the mutiny, and the damage done by it, had given time enough to establish this village and hide it well. The nuclear power plant of the spaceship in which this colony's founder had arrived had been moved underground—compact and shielded as it had been, that had meant a heartbreaking job—to furnish energy. Likewise her chemical air renewer had been removed. Indeed, most of the vessel had been utilized. A food-synthesis unit had been taken along as well as other equipment.

Ice had been mined, some of it electrolyzed for oxygen. In general, the builders of Jupiter City had repeated the pattern which had made X, although on a smaller scale and under immensely greater difficulties. Raids had later furnished more materials, fuel for the atomic engine, tools, fabrics, weapons, supplemental food.

This place radiated heat, but not enough to be detectable through the overlying rocks and glaciers. It contained plenty of metal, but scattered iron deposits confused magnetic locators. As for visible surface traces—Ganymede was large, and the Godwin country some of the wildest and most rugged on the satellite.

Davenant could fill in a good deal of history for himself. He had read how the first generation here had been skilled engineers, but because of the shortage of books, the impossibility of proper instruction, most of their knowledge had died with them. Hereditary monarchy had been inevitable—one family supported by the rest, with leisure to learn, by rote, the operation and servicing of the machinery on which life depended, with an intelligence sharpened enough to make basic decisions. The rest merely obeyed orders and spent their lives in a dullness relieved only by work, fighting, and the orgies which followed victory.

They had their religion—which had been corrupted into sheer paganism—their taboos, a few songs and stories, their dimming traditions. Otherwise there was nothing.

"I'd like to see your power plant," said Davenant. "That sort of thing was my special job at home. Without expert care, it will sooner or later fail." A bribe.

Roberts-John seemed to know it was. "What d'ye want of us?" he demanded again. "S'posin' we 'greed t' help ye, what c'd we do?"

"That," said Davenant bleakly, "is what I am wondering."

◎ IX ◎

KRUSE SPOKE UP THEN, and told of all that had been happening to the survey party of Engineers. Roberts-John nodded, saying little. How much of it he really understood was a question.

Davenant felt a stinging in his eyes. Lyell, Falkenhorst, Yuan, Yamagata, they had all been so close and dear to him, and now they lay dead in the snow. They sprawled frozen on the face of the moon, their burst eyes gaping sightlessly at Jupiter and the great wheel of stars. Their bodies were blocks of ice, their brains held only a hollow and everlasting darkness. Farewell, my brothers!

Davenant shoved such thought away. Time later to mourn. He was still alive, and he had a mission. He had eaten and drunk in this oddly civilized home of a barbarian king, and now he had to start planning.

"Ye can jine with us," suggested Roberts-John. "We can always use a tech. Mebbe when your friends come from Earth, ye can get in touch with 'em.

Kruse rubbed his chin. "How about that, Hall? I can't say I fancy turning cave dweller for the next one to five years, but it may be the only way."

Davenant shook his head. It did not occur to him that he had taken the leadership. But there it was again.

"Not good enough," he said. "The Cincs may destroy this nest at any time, or they may decide to abandon the terra-forming idea, which presumably originated with the Psychotechs. In which case we'll never get off this moon. It's more than us, Torvald, though God knows I don't want to play hero. The Abbey has to be told. How can the Abbey plan if it doesn't have the facts?"

Kruse gave him a sour grin. "All right, then. What do you plan on doing?"

"Let's first take a look at your power plant here, Chief Roberts," suggested Davenant. "I'm not sure I like those occasional flickers in the lighting."

Kruse showed a moment's surprise. He knew as well as the younger Engineer that the cause was nothing worse than a faulty turbogenerator. Clamping expressionlessness onto his face, he nodded and rose.

"I think Hall may be right," he said noncommittally.

Roberts-John looked alarmed, and led the way out and through a descending series of tunnels. Davenant's general unit, adjusted to Geiger registry, showed more radiation than there ought to be, though not enough for real worry. Faulty shielding.

He traced that quickly. Some of the lead blocks in front of the reactor had slipped, perhaps in one of the frequent moonquakes caused by the tidal pull of Jupiter. Otherwise the power plant was in fairly good shape! It had been well constructed, and had been tended with care.

He shook his head dolefully and glanced at the row of meters, remote-control dials, and instruments. "Do you know what these are for?" he asked the Outlaw ruler.

"Some of 'em. When this here needle gets near th' red line, I pull out that there rod, an'—" The chief went on to reveal a scanty, barely adequate empirical knowledge of maintenance.

"I thought so." Davenant pointed to a gauge whose indicator was well past the red. It showed merely that the original slugs were sufficiently enriched with new isotopes to be worth removing and replacing. "How long has this been that way?"

"Long's I c'n remember. Ye don't think—"

"I do. The hypewangle isn't dreel-sprailing with the camits. Lucky for you that the effect builds up slowly, but I wouldn't give this thing

another five years of life unless something's done. Look!" Davenant
tapped a few buttons, emergency manual cutoff. Needles wobbled
across the dials and the lights went out. The chief roared and sprang
for him. Kruse held the frantic man back until Davenant had restored
functioning.

"Don't *do* that!" Sweat drained from Roberts-John's face and he
shook uncontrollably. "Don't do it!"

"I was only testing the hypostat," Davenant said mildly. "It doesn't
fan-tangle as it should. Unless you let me make some badly needed
repairs, you'll be frozen to death in a few years."

"I—I—I—" Roberts-John gulped. Mastering himself, he asked with
a savage bark, "How d' I know ye're not a Cinc sent t' wreck th' whole
town?"

"I'll be here, too," Davenant pointed out. "Give me a few days and
I'll have this thing purring."

By the end of that time, though, Hall Davenant was close to being
the absolute ruler of Jupiter City. The man who straightened out the
reactor, fixed the electric generator running off it, and cannibalized a
dozen dead helmet radios to produce half as many operating ones,
inevitably would be.

Roberts-John was too proud to be obsequious, but too intelligent
to resent a better man for the job than he was himself. Behind his mane
and beard was a clever, queerly altruistic personality. Davenant found
it rather embarrassing to turn down his offer of temporary wives. It
wasn't morals so much as appearance and cleanliness. Kruse was not
fastidious.

The Venusian regarded him out of a grease-smudged face and said
in the Basic they used here between themselves, "Nice going. But now
what?"

"Now," said Davenant thoughtfully, "we'd better find a way to reach
the *Starshine*."

"Huh?"

"Of course. Unless you have some scheme for recapturing the *Light*
or grabbing X's one deep-space cruiser, the only craft in the Jovian
System capable of reaching Luna. The Psychotechs didn't have a
chance to escape with her . . . How badly wrecked is that rocket we
fled in?"

Kruse closed his eyes and summoned up eidetic memory. "Maybe it could be repaired," he said at last. "I don't think anything is too badly damaged. Of course, you're assuming the Jovians haven't salvaged it yet . . . No. I see it now. The boat runs off chemical fuel and isn't designed to get far from the surface. Even in perfect shape, it couldn't get up to the *Starshine*'s orbit. Thrust's too low by a factor of—um, I'd say between one and a half and two."

Davenant slapped the shielding of the town's reactor. "This baby once ran a pretty good-sized spaceship. Lots of energy there."

"And I can just see our hosts letting us take it."

"Not at all. I was thinking of a power-beam."

"Huh? Nobody's ever run a rocket off a power-beam!"

"There's always a first time. Let me think, now . . . How's this sound? When you get out there with your salvage party, scrap the whole drive system and replace it with a king-sized tank for water, a power-beam receiver, and an electrical hookup. The idea will be to boil water around superheated coils, blow it out the rear past an ionizing arc, and use a linac system to accelerate the ions still further. Essentially a crude version of the present-day space drive. The whole thing will run off a beam from here. Naturally, you'll have to give the boat a feed back signal to keep the beam aimed right."

"That," said Kruse, "would make good continuity for some stereo serial, but you know as well as I do that it calls not only for construction from the ground up but for design—and we haven't much more than a slide rule in this place. I'm not Chief Scientist Young of the Junior Intergalactic Patrol."

"You are an Engineer," Davenant said quietly.

They got to work.

The job was not quite as fantastic as it sounded. They were aiming only to get off a small world with negligible air resistance, and not even to leave its gravity well entirely. The principles involved were familiar to both, the basic design standard in such midget craft as the asteroid scooter.

There was a good deal of machinery from the Outlaws' original spaceship, stored away for ultimate use as scrap. The colony had no projects calling for multi-element vacuum tubes, astrogating robo-pilots, high-voltage arcs, or a hundred other parts.

Davenant's idea was easy to draw up, even to make some elementary calculations about. More than that, a Planetary Engineer had training for his profession such as had never been seen before. He didn't have to stew for weeks before seeing the answer to a problem.

His subconscious mind collaborated all the time.

In about two revolutions of Ganymede, the plans were ready. And the parts and tools which would be required were loaded up.

The main difficulty was testing. There just wouldn't be any way to get all the bugs out. Whoever piloted that boat would have to hope it stayed in one piece for the few hours needed!

Kruse took out a gang of men, dragging sleds piled high with equipment and supplies. Davenant stayed behind to supervise the construction of a power-beamer.

When he told Roberts-John what he wanted, the chief exploded.

"No!" he cried with horror.

"But—"

"No! 'Twas bad enough taking so much of our stuff for fixing that boat."

Davenant had had to promise all sorts of benefits which the Order would supply in exchange. But Roberts-John still shook his head.

"We can't spare the men neither, not really," he said. "Somebody's got to watch the passes leading here." He tugged at his beard. "Now ye want to stick up a mast that'll yell to the Cincs where we are. *Uh-uh!*" One bony hand fell to the gun at his waist.

Davenant braced himself. There was death here unless he could talk over the chief . . . Talk the whole Outlaw population over, in fact.

"It would be removed as soon as it had been used," he countered.

"S'pose a Cinc boat happens over before, huh?"

The Engineer took a deep breath. He'd rather expected this reaction. Now it was time to play his one lonely ace, and play it with a flourish.

"You've seen what I can do with what little you have here," he declared slowly. "That's a big ship we're aiming for, crammed with equipment." He was gambling that she had not been gutted, but the notion that the Psychotechs had kept her for emergency use argued that her holds were still pretty full. "How would you like it if we ended the Cinc menace? We could do it, you know."

Roberts-John goggled at him. It took a long time for Davenport to put the idea across.

The beaming mast grew swiftly. It need only be a skeleton of spare girders welded together according to plans the Outlaw mechanics—after all, they were capable of maintaining something as intricate as an airsuit—could easily follow. The casting and controlling units took more work. Davenant almost forgot what sleep was like. He knew exactly how to build a rig sufficient for his purposes, but improvising the different parts and assembling them was a nightmarish task.

The caverns were in one white flame of excitement. They had known they were doomed, these people, had known their long struggle was hollow. The sudden prospect of an end to it made them all a little crazy.

Davenant dared not tell them what a fragile chain their newborn hopes depended from.

Kruse returned in two revolutions. "She's ready, as far as I can tell," he said. "It was mostly the bows that were wrecked—not too much repair to do actually. Rebuilding the motor was the tough part. Think coils made with a tolerance of fifty millimeters are going to work? They tested better than I'd expected, but—

"Of course, I'll have to pilot in a spacesuit. We didn't stop to seal the cabin and put in air units, but if she hangs together at all it ought to be possible to ride her."

"I'll pilot," said Davenant. "I know more about electronic systems than you do."

"Mmmm—you're risking your neck on a mighty thin chance. Toss you for it."

"'They also serve who only stand and wait,' Torvald. Roberts-John is determined to keep one of us a hostage. It won't be pleasant for that one if this fails."

Kruse grimaced. "All right. You're the pilot. You're younger anyway, faster reactions, and this boat is going to need a lot of human handling to make up for its own deficiencies . . ."

◎ X ◎

SPACE WAS A GREAT FROSTY DARKNESS strewn with a million cold suns. The enormous crescent of Jupiter blotted the Milky Way, as if drinking a stream of stars. The sun was far and small and heartlessly brilliant.

Davenant's gauntleted hands were numb on the controls. Blastoff had been automatic. No space vessel can be flown by a merely living creature and arrive where it wants to go. His part had been only to aim her nose in the pre-calculated direction, punch the firing button at the right time, and hold it down the proper number of minutes. When the abused gyros began to hunt, he had had to compensate with his free hand on the manual control wheel. That was all, but it was nearly enough to break him.

Now the jets were dead and he was falling upward, seeking an invisible object whose orbit had been computed roughly from eidetic memories of incomplete observation. If the calculations were too rough, he would eventually spatter himself over the cratered face of Ganymede. The rickety craft would not let him come down alive.

If he got outside the cone which his power-beam could reach, he would be helpless. He hadn't far to go—less than a thousand kilometers from the surface, a couple of hours' jaunt in an airboat on Earth—but space was cold and quiet and very large.

He waited. He thought of many things, in a dreamlike part of his mind remote from that which watched the radarscope. He was aware of being chilled and cramped, hungry and thirsty, dull with fatigue and strain, but it all seemed far away somehow.

There! A pip, just sticking over the noise-level! It grew as he stared, off to one side. He was going to pass it at an estimated hundred and fifty kilometers. He switched power back on, fought the wobbling gyros as they brought the boat's nose around. He had to aim, not where the ship was now, but where it was going to be when he got there. His only instruments were the radar, the clock, his eyes, and the mathematics drilled like reflexes into his brain.

Fire!

The ship was visible, a tiny splinter against heaven. Another computation. He'd pass it by some twenty kilometers, going much too fast—vector in this direction—fire, and hope his estimate hadn't become obsolete in the time needed to make it.

Fire!

Turn eighteen degrees.

Fire!

He passed within a kilometer, relative velocity something like fifty KPH. No use trying to maneuver this cranky wreck any closer. He gauged speeds and distances, thankful that he'd done freefall work before, unbuckled himself, and stepped to one of the holes which gaped raggedly in the cabin. Then he jumped.

He didn't quite make it. Almost, he spun past in a long orbit which would have frozen him to death before it smashed him against the satellite. But he was carrying an extra oxy bottle for that emergency. Its jet wasn't much as a reaction gun, but he rode it back to the *Starshine* thinking hysterically about witches on broomsticks. When his magnetic boot soles clamped to the great hull, he swayed for a long time in a faint.

Recovering, he looked around through blurred eyes. Ganymede's grim pockmarked face bulked tremendously over the edge of the ship, seeming to dwarf even Jupiter. Shuddering, he groped cautiously in search of an entrance.

The airlock cycled for him. Good ship! He patted the metal with a lunatic giggle. They built those long-range fellows to last. They had to, with years spent on some of the outer-planet expeditions.

It was utterly cold and dark inside. He floated through many levels, his flash beam a wan puddle of radiance in the smothering black, to find the engines. Still running, still running, at minimum output.

Good! Good! He turned them up, and air and light and warmth began slowly filling the empty hulk. When it was safe to take off his spacesuit, he looped himself to the nearest stanchion and slept the clock around in complete exhaustion.

When at last he awoke he inspected his prize. The food synthesizers were still in working order, but needed recharging with chemicals which were in the storerooms. He didn't bother, contenting himself with opening some plastis and gorging.

Fighting the sleepiness that followed, he searched for lifeboats. Yes, there were four, sweet little craft though somewhat obsolete. There was a complete laboratory for all phases of planetographic work, a machine shop, an electric shop, a wealth of spare parts. Davenant felt like wallowing in that splendor of tubes, wires, optically perfect reflectors.

No, no! Down boy. You've got work to do.

First, a lifeboat to fetch Kruse and some Outlaw assistants. It was a temptation to get just the Engineer, for the two of them could take this ship home. But Roberts-John was no fool. He'd hold them to their bargain at gunpoint if necessary.

So—

How did you go about conquering X with an army which the Hounds could annihilate in half an hour?

It would have to be bluff, Davenant decided. With the help of the lifeboats, the Outlaws could move unsuspected almost to the gates of X, ready to take over if its garrison could be made to lay down their arms. To do this, he would have to—yes, build a damper-field generator. Against it, the Jovians would have no defense, for they didn't realize its limitations. When the lights went out and the air began to grow cold and stagnant, they should be ready to talk business.

If they didn't capitulate?

Davenant shrugged. One worry at a time, please . . .

❃ XI ❃

THEY MUST BE MAD with fear down in X. Davenant's thought of them rioting in the dark was gruesome, but he forced it out of his mind. He sat now in a lifeboat, hunched beside the radio. From time to time the autopilot fired jets to bring the craft back as its orbit took it out of communication range. He had contacted the Jovians and they had sent for Halleck as ordered; now came the tough part.

"Hello, up there! Who're y'all? This's Cinc-1. Whatcha want?" Halleck's voice was vague and distorted, for the Jovians had only their capacitors now to furnish power, but Davenant could hear the rawness of terror in it. "What've y' done?"

"This is the Order of Planetary Engineers," said Davenant. "You were warned not to molest our men, and instead you murdered them. We've come to settle that account."

"I—I—No! 'S a lie! Accident—"

"Shut up. One of our spaceships has a damper field beamed on your city. As long as we keep it going, your power plants won't operate, and you'll die when your capacitors give out."

That was not true. There was no way to beam a damper field, nor did it have much range. In point of fact, Kruse and an Outlaw gang had moved a boat with an improvised field generator nearly to the walls of X. But Davenant had acquired a fast education in diplomacy.

"That's the least of what we can do, so you'd better accept our terms without arguing."

"What y' want?"

"Are any of those psychotechs you captured alive? . . . Good! Fetch me Angel Garson. Fast!"

"But—"

"For your information, Angel Garson has just been made the temporary Cinc-1of Ganymede, so treat him with respect. I'll talk to him as soon as he's available. Jump to it!"

Davenant couldn't help feeling a little ridiculous. He was being so completely out of character. Not that he didn't have other weapons, but he hated the thought of bombing the city.

Another voice reached him.

"Hall? That you up there? My God, man—"

"How'd they treat you?"

"Oh, I'm still alive. Drugs got my information out of me. They didn't have to use torture, and we were being kept as labor for a proposed penal colony. But how in all the hells—"

Davenant said in Basic, "Look, Garson. I'm speaking for the Engineers now. Somebody has to dictate terms to you wolves, and I guess we're elected. Do you think that given an allied military force, you could maintain a fresh government in X for a few months?"

"Y-y-yes." The Angel's swift poise was a measure of the man. Davenant felt humbled, had no relish for playing conqueror. Garson went on, "Knowing what'll happen if they don't obey your orders, I'm pretty sure the people will cooperate. I can institute a propaganda campaign, *if* I like your ideas."

"All right. Here's what I want." Davenant forced himself to snap it out. "Cincs and Hounds will be disarmed, but no revenge taken on them unless they break the new law. We can't afford to make them desperate. Outlaws will enter X and have police and administrative powers. Your psychotechs can advise them, but their chief has the final word. I'm giving him strict orders to maintain the status quo till we send a real task force from Luna. So none of your tricks—because all the psychodynamic equations in the universe won't stop a damper field or a lithium shell.

"As soon as possible, an Engineer delegation will get to you and reorganize on a more permanent basis. What I anticipate is a fairly open society—as nearly as can be with these poor distorted people— working toward eventual human normalcy. The Interim government will be a mixed commission of Engineers and Jovians. A strict constitution will be written, and the Order will stand guard for a long time to let the new political habits take root.

"Meanwhile, terraforming will go on, the Order to be paid for that as well as for its administrative services. Once you've got a livable world, I don't think this type of occupation statute will be needed any more, but that's quite a ways in the future.

"I know your Institute group has its own plans; whether good or bad, I can't say. But you're only human and not to be trusted with absolute power. Someday, when this system is well built up, you might decide to fight a war of conquest with Earth, and not even the Engineers can stand by and do nothing while that possibility exists.

"You'll be free to educate and propagandize openly, like everyone else. But the commission is going to be alert for any cabals, so don't figure on taking over from within again. That sound agreeable to you?"

"I," Garson laughed shakily—"I suppose it has to . . ."

There was some time required to get things established. Under the threat of the damper field the Sergeants were cooperative enough though rather bewildered. Davenant was well aware the Psychotechs knew he was bluffing about an Engineer fleet out in space, but since their own lives would not be safe until the Outlaws had marched into garrison X, Garson's men had no choice but to work with him. After that, it would be too late for Cincs and Hounds and Institute people alike.

Considering what a long score they had to settle, the barbarians were remarkably well-behaved. Nevertheless, a few incidents made Davenant feel ill. But had he had any alternative?

Kruse voiced the real fear when the two were again alone, driving the *Light* back toward Luna.

"Do you think the Abbey will agree to all this ?" he asked. "We've made an awful lot of commitments for them."

"I don't think they can do anything but follow out my promises, at least in a general way," said Davenant. "It's not only a matter of prestige and the ultimate safety of all mankind, but . . . How else are they going to get that terraforming contract?"

"And we've plunged the Order into politics to its ears," said Kruse.

"How much choice had we?"

"Damn little, I reckon. Still, it's interesting to speculate whether well be flayed alive or merely boiled in oil."

"Most likely cashiered," said Davenant.

He felt heartsick at the thought. For him, there was no other life.

His moody eyes searched the infinite heaven, looking for Earth.

❈ EPILOGUE ❈

THE COORDINATOR of the Order of Planetary Engineers was old but the eyes in his seamed face were still brilliant and he spoke with a young man's resonance. As he sat behind the great desk, a window in the tower framed his white hair with stars.

"Send him in," he ordered.

"Yes sir."

The guard, unarmed but husky, went out to come back with the prisoner. A nod from the chief dismissed him.

"So," said the Coordinator at last, you've been playing politics, have you?"

The prisoner bit his lip. "You have my report, sir," he answered.

"And you've presumably had instruction in the rules."

"Sir, there are historical precedents—"

"The Council and myself are empowered to draw conclusions from them," said the Coordinator frostily. "Not a wet-eared tech. Besides all the excuses in your report, have you anything to say for yourself?"

Bitterness lashed back. "Sir, it was a matter of saving lives. Also, if I hadn't done what I did, we wouldn't have the contract now. The rules also say something about men in the field exercising independent judgment, don't they? A job is more than a problem in machinery and natural resources. People are involved, too, and they're the only reason the work is being done at all."

"Somewhat emotional," murmured the Coordinator, "but not without a certain spirit." He ruffled the papers before him. "I've been looking at your psych record. Promising. You can be trusted with further education."

"Sir?"

"Rules are crutches, son." The Coordinator leaned back in his chair. "Go on, sit down. I won't bite you. Not very hard, anyway. As I was saying, rules are valuable for people whose power of really efficient independent thought is limited to the mechanics of their profession. We've got to have regulations. But they don't cover every possible case, and the man who can break them when necessary and get his assignment finished because of that violation is a man we need.

"You did a hell of a good job out there. Officially, now, you're going to be sent in disgrace to Venus to do some low-grade manual labor. That sentence is for three years. Pretty stiff, eh? But actually, son, you're going to school—a little school we've got hidden away for future members of the Council."

"I—I—"

"Don't try to talk," said the Coordinator. "Right now, it makes you look too much like a fish. Son, the present system has been in effect for a long time. The founders knew that the Order had to preserve the appearance of staying out of politics, of being above all local quarrels, if it was to accomplish its mission.

"They also knew that it would not always be possible to remain aloof. As you just said, jobs also involve people. So from time to time we've stepped in, as quietly and with as great a show of reluctance as possible. The rules keep us from getting too deeply committed to local, temporary affairs. The rule-breakers keep us operating.

"If your own violation had been botched, you *would* be on your way to a labor camp—unless you preferred a dishonorable discharge. As it is . . . Well, after a decent interval, you'll be skippering a crew of your own, and later you'll be elected to the Council. Maybe you're going to end up behind this desk. We'll see."

He grinned. "All right, consider yourself properly dressed down, and put on a hangdog look. You'll be on your way tonight. Good luck!"

They clasped hands. The prisoner wheeled and stepped smartly to the door. It opened for him and he was gone.

Coordinator Hall Davenant sighed, an old man's envious sigh. Memory ran back over a waste of years, to a night when he had walked across the snows of Ganymede. It had not even been a dream, then, that he would sit behind this desk, but if it had occurred to him he would hardly have been able to wait.

And now he had it, his highest ambition lay in his hands for him to do with as he would. But men were walking across the snows of Pluto while he sat here.

Someday the Solar System wouldn't be big enough for them.

Briefly, he looked out to the cold challenge of the stars. Then he returned to his work.

After the Order exposed the horrors lurking by Jupiter, it took the freed colonists under its protection until they could function normally. Half a century later, the Engineers were still toiling patiently on the Jovian moons.

But the minions of Chaos were as determined as the forces of Order. A collision was inevitable.

Brake

IN THAT HOUR, when he came off watch, Captain Peter Banning did not go directly to his cabin. He felt a wish for uninhibited humor, such as this bleak age could not bring to life (except maybe in the clan gatherings of Venus—but Venus was *too* raw), and remembered that Luke Devon had a Shakespeare. It was a long time since Banning had last read *The Taming of the Shrew*. He would drop in and borrow the volume, possibly have a small drink and a chinfest. The Planetary Engineer was unusually worth talking to.

So it was that he stepped out of the companionway into A-deck corridor and saw Devon backed up against the wall at gunpoint.

Banning had not stayed alive as long as this—a good deal longer than he admitted—through unnecessary heroics. He slid back, flattened himself against the aluminum side of the stairwell, and stretched his ears. Very gently, one hand removed the stubby pipe from his teeth and slipped it into a pocket of his tunic, to smolder itself out. The fumes might give him away to a sensitive nose, and he was unarmed.

Devon spoke softly, with rage chained in his throat: "The devil damn thee black, thou cream-faced loon!"

"Not so hasty," advised the other person. It was the Minerals Authority representatives, Serge Andreyev, a large hairy man who dressed and talked too loudly. "I do not wish to kill you. This is just a needler in my hand. But I have also a gun for blowing out brains—if required."

His English bore its usual accent, but the tone had changed utterly. It was not the timbre of an irritating extrovert; there was no particular melodrama intended; Andreyev was making a cool statement of fact.

"It is unfortunate for me that you recognized me through all the surgical changes," he went on. "It is still more unfortunate for you that I was armed. Now we shall bargain."

"Perhaps." Devon had grown calmer. Banning could visualize him, backed up against the wall, hands in the air: a tall man, cat-lithe under the austere stiffness of his Order, close-cropped yellow hair and ice-blue eyes, and a prow of nose jutting from the bony face. *I wouldn't much like to have that hombre on my tail,* reflected Banning.

"Perhaps," repeated Devon. "Has it occurred to you, though, that a steward, a deckhand . . . anyone . . . may be along at any moment?"

"Just so. Into my cabin. There we shall talk some more."

"But it *is* infernally awkward for you," said Devon. "'Is it a world to hide virtues in?'—or prisoners, for that matter? Here we are, beyond Mars, with another two weeks before we reach Jupiter. There are a good fifteen people aboard, passengers and crew—not much, perhaps, for a ship as big as the *Thunderbolt,* but enough to search her pretty thoroughly if anyone disappears. You can't just cram me out any convenient air lock, you know, not without getting the keys from an officer. Neither can you keep me locked away without inquiries as to why I don't show up for meals . . . I assure you, if you haven't noticed, my appetite is notorious. Therefore, dear old chap—"

"We will settle this later," snapped Andreyev. "Quickly, now, go to my cabin. I shall be behind. If necessary, I will needle you and drag you there."

Devon was playing for time, thought Banning. If the tableau of gunman and captive remained much longer in the passageway, someone was bound to come by and— *As a matter of fact, son, someone already has.*

The captain slipped a hand into his pouch. He had a number of coins: not that they'd be any use on Ganymede, but he didn't want to reenter Union territory without beer cash. He selected several of nearly uniform size and tucked them as a stack into his fist. It was a very old stunt.

Then, with the quick precision of a hunter—which he had been now and then, among other things—he glided from the companionway.

Andreyev had just turned his back, marching Devon up the hall toward Cabin 5. Peter Banning's weighted fist smote him at the base of the skull.

Devon whirled, a tiger in gray. Banning eased Andreyev to the floor with one hand; the other took the stun pistol, not especially aimed at the Engineer nor especially aimed away from him. "Take it easy, friend," he murmured.

"You . . . oh!" Devon eased, muscle by muscle. A slow grin crossed his face. "'For this relief, much thanks.'"

"What's going on here?" asked the captain.

There was a moment of stillness. Only the ship spoke, with a whisper of ventilators. The sound might almost have belonged to that night of cold stars through which she hurled.

"Well?" said Banning impatiently.

Devon stood for an instant longer, as if taking his measure. The captain was a stocky man of medium height, with faintly grizzled black hair clipped short on a long head. His face was broad, it bore high cheekbones, and its dark-white skin had a somehow ageless look: deep trenches from wide nose to big mouth, crow's-feet around the bony-ridged gray eyes, otherwise smooth as a child's. He did not wear the trim blue jacket and white trousers of the Fireball Line but favored a Venusian-style beret and kilt, Arabian carpet slippers, a disreputable old green tunic of possibly Martian origin.

"I don't know," said the Planetary Engineer at last. "He just pulled that gun on me."

"Sorry, I heard a bit of the talk between you. Now come clean. I'm responsible for this ship, and I want to know what's going on."

"So do I," said Devon grimly. "I'm not really trying to stall you, skipper—not much, anyway." He stooped over Andreyev and searched the huddled body. "Ah, yes, here's that other gun he spoke of, the lethal one."

"Give me that!" Banning snatched it. The metal was cold and heavy in his grasp. It came to him with a faint shock that he himself and his entire crew had nothing more dangerous between them than some knives and monkey wrenches. A spaceship was not a Spanish caravel, her crew had no reason to arm against pirates or mutiny or—

Or did they?

"Go find a steward," snapped Banning. "Come back here with him. Mr. Andreyev goes in irons for the rest of the trip."

"Irons?" Under the cowl of his gray tunic, Devon's brows went up.

"Chains . . . restraint . . . hell, we'll lock him away. I've got a bad habit of using archaisms. Now, jump!"

The Engineer went quickly down the hall. Banning lounged back, twirling the gun by its trigger guard, and watched him go.

Where had he seen the fellow before?

He searched a cluttered memory for a tall blond man who was athlete, technician, Shakespearean enthusiast, and amateur painter in oils. Perhaps it was only someone he had read about, with a portrait; there was so much history—Wait. The Rostomily brotherhood. Of course. But that was three centuries ago!

Presumably someone, somewhere, had kept a few cells in storage, after that corps of exogenetic twins had finally made their secret open, disbanded, and mingled their superior genes in the common human lifestream. And then, perhaps thirty years ago, the Engineers had quietly grown such a child in a tank. Maybe a lot of them. Also anything could happen in that secret castle on the rim of Archimedes Crater, and the Solar System none the wiser till the project exploded in man's collective face.

The brotherhood had been a trump card of the early Un-men, in the days when world government was frail and embattled. A revived brotherhood must be of comparable importance to the Order. But for what purpose? The Engineers, quasi-military, almost religious, were supposed to be above politics; they were supposed to serve all men, an independent force whose only war was against the inanimate cosmos.

Banning felt a chill. With the civilization-splitting tension that existed on Earth and was daily wrung one notch higher, he could imagine what hidden struggles took place between the many factions. It wasn't all psychodynamics, telecampaigning or parliamentary maneuver: the Humanist episode had scarred Earth's soul, and now there were sometimes knives in the night.

Somehow an aspect of those battles had focused on his ship.

He took out his pipe, rekindled it, and puffed hard. Andreyev stirred, with a retch and a rattle in his throat.

There was a light footfall in the corridor. Banning looked up. He would have cursed the interruption had anyone but Cleonie Rogers appeared. As it was, he made the forgotten gesture of raising his cap.

"Oh!" Her hand went to her mouth. For an instant she looked

frightened, then came forward in a way he liked: the more so as she had been consistently annoyed by Andreyev's loud attempts to flirt. "Oh, is he hurt? Can I help?"

"Better stand back, m'lady," advised Banning. She saw the stunner in his hand and the automatic in his waistband. Her lips parted in the large-eyed, snub-nosed face. With the yellow hair that fell softly down to bare shoulders, with a wholly feminine topless shimmergown and a whisper of cosmetics, she was a small walking anachronism.

"What happened?" A shaken courage rallied in her. It was well done, thought the man, considering that she was a child of wealth, never done a day's work in her life, bound for the Jovian Republic as an actual live tourist.

"That's what I'd kind of like to know," he told her. "This character here pulled an equalizer—a gun, I mean—on Engineer Devon. Then I came along and sapped him."

He saw her stiffen. Even aboard the *Thunderbolt*, which was not one of the inner-planet luxury liners but a freighter whose few passengers—except her—were bound for Ganymede on business . . . even here there were dimly lit corners and piped music and the majesty of the stars. Banning had noticed how much she and Devon had been together. Therefore he said kindly: "Oh, Luke wasn't hurt. I sent him for help. Must say it's taking him one hell of a time, too. Did the stewards crawl into the fire chamber for a nap?"

She smiled uncertainly. "What do you think the trouble is, Captain? Did Mr. Andreyev, ah—"

"Slip a cog?" Banning scowled. In his preoccupation he forgot that the rising incidence of nonsanity on Earth made the subject unfit for general conversation. "I doubt it. He came aboard with these toys, remember. I wonder, though. Now that the topic has come up, we do have a rum lot of passengers."

Devon was legitimate enough, his mind continued: a genuine Engineer, nursemaiding the terraforming equipment which was the *Thunderbolt*'s prime cargo, the great machines which the Order would use to make Europa habitable.

And Cleonie must be an authentic tourist. (Since he regarded her as a woman, which he did not the crop-headed, tight-lipped, sad-clad creature that was today's typical Western Terrestrial female, Banning thought of her by her first name.) On the other hand—

Andreyev was not a simple Union bureaucrat, sent to negotiate a trade agreement; or, if he was, he was also much more, and how about the big fellow, Robert Falken, allegedly a nucleonic technie offered a job on Callisto? He didn't say much at table, kept to himself, but Banning knew a hard, tough man when he saw one. And Morgan Gentry, astronaut, who said the Republic had hired him to pilot inter-satellite shuttles—undoubtedly a trained spaceman, but what was he besides that? And the exchange professor of advanced symbolics, dome-healed little Gomez, was he really bound for a position at the new University of X?

The girl's voice interrupted his reverie: "Captain Banning . . . what *could* be the matter with the passengers? They're all Westerners, aren't they?"

He could still be shocked, just a little bit every now and then. He hesitated a second before realizing that she had spoken not in ill will but from blank naïveté. "What has that got to do with it?" he said. "You don't really think, do you, Miss, that the conflict on Earth is a simple question of Oriental Kali worshipers versus a puritanical protechnological Occident?" He paused for breath, then plowed on: "Why, the Kali people are only one branch of the Ramakrishian Eclectics, and there are plenty of Asians who stand by population control and Technic civilization—I have a couple in my own crew—and there are Americans who worship the Destroyer as fervently as any Ganges River farmer—and the Husseinite Moslems are closer to you, Miss Rogers, than you are to the New Christendom—"

He broke off, shaking his head. It was too big to be neatly summarized, the schism which threatened to rip Earth apart. He might have said it boiled down to the fact that technology had failed to solve problems which *must* be solved; but he didn't want to phrase it thus, because it would sound antiscientific, and he wasn't.

Thank all kindly gods that there were men on other planets now! The harvest of all the patient centuries since Galileo would not be entirely lost, whatever happened to Earth.

Andreyev pulled himself up till he rested on his hands, head dangling between his shoulders. He groaned.

"I wonder how much of that is put on," mused Banning. "I did a well-calibrated job of slugging him. He shouldn't be too badly concussed." He gave Cleonie a beady look. "Maybe we ought to haul him into a cabin at that. Don't want to rattle any other cash customers, do we? Where are they all, anyway?"

"I'm not sure. I just left my cabin—" She stopped.

Someone came running from aft. The curvature of the hall, which was wrapped around the inner skin of the ship, made it impossible to see more than about forty meters. Banning shifted his gun, warily.

It was the large square-faced man, Falken, who burst into view. "Captain!" he shouted. The metal that enclosed all of them gave his tone a faint, unhuman resonance. "Captain, what happened?"

"How do you *know* about it, son?"

"A . . . eh . . . Engineer Devon—" Falken jogged to a halt, a meter away. "He told me—"

"Told you? Well, did he now?" Banning's gray gaze narrowed. Suddenly the needler in his hand leaped up and found an aim. "Hold it. Hold it there, pardner, and reach."

Falken flushed red. "What the ruination do you mean?"

"I mean that if you even look like you're going after a gun, I'll put you to sleep," said Banning. "Then if it turns out you only intended to offer me a peanut butter sandwich, I'll beg your humble pardon. But something sure smells here."

Falken backed away. "All right, all right, I'll go," he snarled. "I just wanted to help."

Cleonie screamed.

As Andreyev's burly form tackled him by the ankles and he went down, Banning knew a moment of rage at himself. He had been civilized too long . . . inexcusably careless of him—'Sbones and teeth!

He hit the deck with the other man on top. The red face glared murder. Andreyev yanked at the gun in Banning's kilt with one hand, his other grabbed the arm holding the stun pistol.

Banning brought his hard forehead up, into Andreyev's mouth. The fellow screamed. His fingers released the stunner. At that moment Falken joined the fight, snatching the sleep weapon before Banning could get it into action.

The skipper reached up with an efficiently unsportsmanlike thumb. He had not quite gouged out Andreyev's eye when the man bellowed and tried to scramble free. Banning rolled away. Falken fired at him. An anesthetic dart broke near Banning's nose, and he caught a whiff of vapor.

For a moment, while the universe waltzed around him, Banning accomplished nothing more than to reel to his feet. Falken sidestepped the weeping Andreyev, shoved the captain back against the wall, and yanked the automatic from his waistband.

Cleonie came from behind and threw her arms around Falken's neck.

He shouted, bent his back, and tossed her from him. But it had been enough of a distraction. Banning aimed a kick for the solar plexus. Both guns went on a spin from Falken's hands.

Banning's sole had encountered hard muscle. Falken recovered fast enough to make a jump for the nearest weapon. Banning put a large foot on it. "Oh, no, you don't," he growled.

Falken sprang at him. It was not the first time Banning had been in a party which got rough, and he did not waste energy on fisticuffs. His hand snapped forward, open, the edge of a horny palm driving into Falken's larynx. There was a snapping noise.

Falken fell backward, over Andreyev, who still whimpered and dabbed at his injured eye. Banning stooped for the gun.

A bullet smashed down the corridor, ricocheted, and whined around his ears. Gentry came into view, with the drop on him.

"Oh, oh," said Banning. "School's out." He scooped up Cleonie and scampered back into the companionway.

Up the stairwell! His weight lessened with every jump as he got closer to the ship's axis of spin.

Passing C-deck, he collided with Charles Wayne. The young second mate had obviously been yanked from sleep by the racket. He was pulling on his gold-collared blue uniform jacket as he entered the companionway. "Follow me!" puffed Banning.

Gentry appeared at the foot of the stairs. The automatic in his grasp found an aim on the captain's stomach. "Stay there!" he rapped. "Raise your hands!"

Banning threw himself and Cleonie backward, into C-deck corridor. The bullet snapped viciously past Wayne's head. "Come on, I told you!" gasped Banning. "Get her to the bridge!"

Wayne looked altogether bewildered, but any spaceman learns to react fast. He slung the girl over his shoulder and dashed down the hall toward an alternate stairwell.

Banning followed. He heard Gentry's shoes clang on metal, up the steps after him. As he ran, he groped after his pipe lighter, got it out, and thumbed the switch.

There were rails and stanchions along the wall, for use in null-gravity. Aided by his lessened weight, Banning swarmed ape fashion up the nearest and waved his flame beneath a small circle in the ceiling.

Then down again, toward the stair! Gentry burst into the hall and fired. Coriolis force deflected the bullet, it fanned the captain's cheek. The next one would be more carefully aimed.

The ceiling thermocouple reacted to heat, flashed a signal, and put the C-deck fire extinguisher system into action with a lather of plastifoam. Gentry's second shot flew off to nowhere. Thereafter he struggled with the stuff while Banning scampered up the stairs.

The bridge was a bubble in the ship's nose, precisely centered on the axis of rotation. There was virtually no weight, only a wilderness of gleaming consoles and the great viewscreen ablaze with its simulacrum of the sky.

Cleonie hung on to a stanchion, torn and shaken by the wretchedness of sudden, unaccustomed free fall. Tetsuo Tokugawa, the first mate, whose watch this was, floated next to her, offering an antidizzy pill. Wayne crouched by the door, wild-eyed. "What's going on, sir?" he croaked.

"I'm curious to know myself," panted Banning. "But it's all hell let out for noon."

Tokugawa gave him a despairing look. "Can you stuff this pill down her throat, skipper?" he begged. "I've seen people toss their dinner in null-gee."

"Uh, yeah, it is rather urgent." Banning hooked a knee around a stanchion, took the girl's head in one hand, and administered the medicine veterinary fashion. Meanwhile he clipped forth his story.

Tokugawa whistled. "What the destruction is this?" he said. "Mutiny?"

"If passengers can mutiny . . . neat point of law, that. Be quiet." Banning cocked his head and listened. There was no sound from the passages beyond the open door. He closed and bolted it.

Wayne looked sick. He wasn't a bad young fellow, thought the captain, but he was brought up in the puritan reaction of today's Western peoples. He was less afraid of danger, now, than stunned by a kick to his sense of propriety. Tokugawa was more reliable, being Lunar City bred, with all the Lunar colonist's cat-footed cosmopolitanism.

"What are we going to *do?*" rasped the second mate.

"Find out things," grunted Banning. He soared across to the intercom cabinet, entered it, and flicked switches. The first thing he wanted was information about the ship. If that failed them, it would be a long walk home.

The *Thunderbolt* was a steelloy spheroid, flattened along the axis of the drive-tubes whose skeletal structure jutted like an ancient oil derrick from the stern. She was a big ship: her major diameter more than three hundred meters; she was a powerful ship: not required to drift along a Hohmann ellipse, but moving at a speed which took her on a hyperbolic orbit—from Earth Station Prime to the Jovian System in less than a month! But she had her limitations.

She was not intended to enter an atmosphere, but orbited and let shuttleboats bring or remove her cargo. This was less because of the great mass of her double hull—that wasn't too important, when you put atomic nuclei to work for you—than because of the design itself. To build up her fantastic velocities, she must spurt out ions at nearly the speed of light: which required immensely long accelerating tubes, open to the vacuum of space. They would arc over and burn out if air surrounded the charged rings.

She carried no lifeboat. If you abandon ship at hyperbolic speeds, a small craft doesn't have engine enough to decelerate you before running out of reaction mass. Here, in the big cold darkness beyond Mars, there was no escaping this vessel.

Banning tuned in the screen before him. It gave two-way visual contact between a few key points, in case of emergency. "And if this ain't an emergency," he muttered, "it'll do till one comes along."

First, the biotic plant, armored at the heart of the ship. He breathed a gusty sigh. No one had tampered with that—air and water were still being renewed.

Next, the control gyros. The screen showed him their housing, like the pillars of some heathen temple. In the free fall at the ship's axis, a dead man drifted past them. The slow air currents turned him over and over. When his gaping face nudged the screen pickup, Banning recognized Tietjens, one of the two stewards. He had been shot through the head, and there was a grisly little cloud of red and gray floating around him.

Banning's lips grew thin. "I was supposed to look after you," he mumbled. "I'm sorry, Joppe."

He switched to the engine room. His view was directed toward the main control board, also in the axial null-gee state. The face that looked back at him, framed by the tall machines, belonged to Professor Gomez.

Banning sucked in a breath. "What are you doing there?" he said.

"Oh . . . it's you, Captain. I rather expected you to peer in. "The little man shoved himself forward with a groundlubber's awkwardness, but he was calm, not spacesick at all. "Quite a job you did on Falken. He's dead."

"Too bad you weren't in on that party," said Banning. "How are the other boys? Mine, I mean."

"The red-haired man—he was on watch here when I came—I am afraid I found it necessary to terminate him."

"Tietjens and O'Farrell," said Banning, very slowly. "Just shot down, huh? Who else?"

"No one, yet. It's your fault, Captain. You precipitated this affair before we were ready; we had to act in haste. Our original plan did not involve harming any person." The shriveled face grew thoughtful. "We have them all prisoners, except for you there on the bridge. I advise you to surrender peacefully."

"What's the big idea?" growled Banning. "What do you want?"

"We are taking over this ship."

"Are you crazy? Do you know what sort of job it is to handle her— do you know how much kinetic energy she's got, right now?"

"It is unfortunate that Falken died," said Gomez tonelessly. "He was to have been our engineer. But I daresay Andreyev can take his place, with some help from me—I know a bit about nucleonic controls. Gentry, of course, is a trained astrogator."

"But who are you?" shouted Banning. He had the eerie feeling that the whole world had gone gibbering insane around him. "What are you doing this for?"

"It is not essential for you to know that," said Gomez. "If you surrender now, you will receive good treatment and be released as soon as possible. Otherwise we shall probably have to shoot you. Remember, we have all the guns."

Banning told him what he could do with the guns and cut the circuit. Switching on the public-address mike, he barked a summary of the situation for the benefit of any crewmen who might be at liberty. Then, spinning out of the booth, he told the others in a few harsh words how it stood.

Cleonie's face had gotten back a little color. Now, between the floating gold locks of hair, it was again drained of blood. But he admired the game way she asked him: "What can we do?"

"Depends on the situation, m'lady," he replied. "We don't know for sure . . . let's see, another steward, two engineers, and a deckhand . . . we don't know if all four of the crewmen still alive are prisoners or not. I'm afraid, though, that they really are."

"Luke," she whispered. "You sent him off—"

Banning nodded. Even in this moment, he read an anguish in her eyes and knew pity for her. "I'm afraid Luke has been clobbered," he said. "Not permanently, though, I hope."

Wayne's gaze was blank and lost. "But what are they *doing?*" he stammered. "Are they . . . ps-ps-psy-chotic?"

"No such luck," said Banning. "This was a pretty well-laid plan. At the proper time, they'd have pulled guns on us and locked us away— or maybe shot us. Luke happened to . . . I don't know what, but it alarmed Andreyev, who stuck him up. Then I horned in. I sent Luke after help. Not suspecting the other passengers, he must have told Tietjens in the presence of another member of this gang. So poor old Joppe got shot, but apparently Luke was just herded off. Then the whole gang was alerted, and Gomez went to take over the engine room while Falken and Gentry came after me." He nodded heavily. "A fast, smooth operation, in spite of our having thrown 'em off balance. No, they're sane, for all practical purposes."

He waited a moment, gathering his thoughts, then:

"The remaining four crewmen would all have been in their quarters, off duty. The situation as she now stands depends on whether Gentry broke off from chasing me in time to surprise them in that one place. I wish I'd gotten on the mike faster."

Suddenly he grinned. "Tetsuo," he rapped, "stop the ship's rotation. Pronto!"

The mate blinked, then laughed—a short rough bark in his gullet—and leaped for the controls. "Hang on!" said Banning.

"What . . . what do you plan to do, sir?" asked Wayne.

"Put this whole tub into null-gee. It'll equalize matters a bit."

"I don't understand."

"No, you've never seen a weightless free-for-all, have you? Too bad. There's an art to it. A trained man with his hands can make a monkey of a groundlubber with a gun."

It was hard to tell whether Wayne was more deeply shocked at the mutiny or at learning that his captain had actually been in vulgar brawls. "Cheer up, son," said Banning. "You, too Cleonie. You both look like vulcanized oatmeal."

There was a brief thrumming. The tangential jets blew a puff of chemical vapor and brought the spin of the ship to a halt. For a moment, the astro screen went crazy, still compensating for a rotation which had ceased, then the cold image of the constellations steadied.

"O.K.," said Banning. "We've got to move fast. Tetsuo, come with me. Charlie, Cleonie, guard the bridge. Lock the door behind us, and don't open it for anyone whose voice you find unmusical. If our boys do show up, tell 'em to wait here."

"Where are you going?" breathed the girl shakenly.

"Out to kill a few people," said Banning with undiminished good cheer.

He led the way, in a long soaring glide through the door. "Up" and "down" had become meaningless; there was only this maze of halls, rooms, and stairwells. His skin prickled with the thought that an armed man might be waiting in any cross-corridor. The silence of the ship drew his nerves taut as wires. He pulled himself along by the rails, hand over hand, accelerating till the doorways blurred past him.

The galley was on B-deck, just "above" passenger country. When Banning opened the door, an unfastened kettle drifted out and gonged on his head. A rack held the usual kitchen assortment of knives. He stuck a few in his waistband, giving the two longest to himself and Tokugawa. "Now I don't feel so nude," he remarked.

"What's next?" whispered the mate.

"If our lads are being kept prisoner, it's probably in crew territory. Let's try—"

The spacemen's own cabins were on this level; they did not require the full Earth-value of spin-gravity given the passengers on A-deck. Banning slipped with a caution that rose exponentially toward the area he always thought of as the forecastle.

He need not have been quite so careful. Andreyev waited with a pistol outside a cabin door, Andreyev had been unprepared for a sudden change to no-weight. His misery was not active, but it showed.

Banning launched himself.

Andreyev's abused senses reacted slowly. He looked around, saw the hurtling form, and yelled. Almost instinctively, he whipped his gun about and fired. It was nearly point-blank, but he missed. He could not help missing when the recoil sent him flying backward with plenty of English.

He struck the farther wall, scrabbled wildly, bounced off it, and pinwheeled to the ceiling. Banning grinned, changed course with a thrust of leg against floor, and closed in. Andreyev fired again. It was a bomb-burst roar in the narrow space. The bullet tore Banning's sleeve. Recoil jammed Andreyev against the ceiling. As he rebounded, it was onto his enemy's knife.

The captain smiled sleepily, grabbed Andreyev's tunic with his free hand, and completed the job.

Tokugawa dodged a rush of blood. He looked sick. "What did you do that for?" he choked.

"Tietjens and O'Farrell," said Banning. The archaic greenish light faded from his eyes, and he added in a flat tone: "Let's get that door open."

Fists were hammering on it. The thin metal dented beneath the blows but held firm. "Stand aside!" yelled Tokugawa. "I'm going to shoot the lock off—can't find the key, no time—" He picked Andreyev's gun from the air, put the muzzle to the barrier, and fired. He was also thrown back by reaction but knew how to control such forces.

Luke Devon flung the door open. The Engineer looked as bleak as Banning had ever known a man to be. Behind him crowded the others, Nielsen, Bahadur, Castro, Vladimirovitch. Packing five men into a cubbyhole meant for one had in itself been a pretty good way to immobilize them.

Their voices surfed around the captain. "Shut up!" he bawled. "We got work to do!"

"Who else is involved in this?" demanded Devon. "Gentry killed Tietjens and took me prisoner . . . herded all of us in here, with Andreyev to help . . . but who else is there to fight?"

"Gentry and Gomez," said Banning. "Falken is dog's meat. We still hold the bridge, and we outnumber 'em now—but they've got the engine room *and* all the guns but one." He passed out knives. "Let's get out of here. We've made enough racket to wake the Old Martians. I don't want Gentry to come pot-hunting."

The men streamed behind him as he dove along another stairwell, toward the bowels of the ship. He wanted to post a guard over the gyros and biotics. But he had not gotten to them when the spiteful crack of an automatic toned between metal walls.

His hands closed on the rail, slamming him to a halt that skinned his palms. "Hold it," he said, very softly. "That could only have come from the bridge."

If we can shoot a door open, I reckon Gentry can, too.

There was only one approach to the bridge, a short passageway on which several companionways converged. To either side of this corridor were the captain's and mate's cabins; at the far end was the bridge entrance.

Banning came whizzing out of a stairwell. He didn't stop, but glided on into the one opposite. A bullet smashed where he had been.

His brain held the glimpsed image: the door open, Gentry braced in it with his feet on one jamb and his back against the door. That way, he could cover Wayne and Cleonie—if they were still alive—and the approach as well. The recoil of his fire wouldn't bother him at all.

Banning's followers milled about like the debris of a ship burst open. He waited till Gentry's voice reached out:

"So you have all your men back, Captain . . . and therefore a gun, I presume? Nice work. But stay where you are. I'll shoot the first head that pokes around a corner. I know how to use a gun in null-gee, and I've got Wayne and Rogers for hostages. Want to parley?" Banning stole a glimpse at Devon. The Engineer's nostrils were pinched and bloodless. It was he who answered:

"What are you after?"

"I think you know, Luke," said Gentry.

"Yes," said Devon. "I believe I do."

"Then you're also aware that anything goes. I won't hesitate to shoot Rogers—or dive the ship into the sun before the Guard gets its claws on us! It would be better if you gave up."

There was another stillness. The breathing of his men, of himself, sounded hoarse in Banning's ears. Little drops of sweat pearled off their skin, glistened in the fluorotube light, and danced away on air currents.

He cocked a brow at Devon. The Engineer nodded. "It's correct enough, skipper," he said. "We're up against fanatics."

"We could rush him," hissed Banning. "Lose a man or two, maybe, but—"

"No," said Devon. "There's Cleonie to think about." A curious mask of peace dropped over his bony face. "Let me talk to him. Maybe we can arrange something. You be ready to act as . . . as indicated."

He said, aloud, that he would parley. "Good," grunted Gentry. "Come out slow, and hang on to the rail with both your hands where I can see them." Devon's long legs moved out of Banning's view. "That's close enough. Stop." *He must still be three or four meters from the door,* thought the captain, and moved up to the corner of the stairwell.

It came to him, with a sudden chill, what Devon must be planning. The Rostomily clan had always been that sort. His scalp prickled, but he dared not speak. All he could do was take a few knives from the nearest men.

"Luke." That was Cleonie's voice, a whisper from the bridge. "Luke, be careful."

"Oh, yes." The Engineer laughed. It had an oddly tender note.

"Just what happened to kick off this landslide, anyway?" asked Gentry.

"'Thou hast the most unsavory similes,'" said Devon.

"What?"

The roar which followed must have jerked all of Gentry's remaining attention to him as Devon launched himself into space.

The gun crashed. Banning heard the bullet smack home. Devon's body turned end over end, tumbling backward down the hall.

Banning was already around the corner. He did not fire at Gentry;

it would have taken a whole fatal second to brace himself properly against a wall.

He threw knives.

The recoil was almost negligible; his body twisted back and forth as his arms moved, but he was used to that. It took only a wink to stick four blades in Gentry.

The spaceman screamed, hawked blood, and scrabbled after the gun that had slipped from his fingers. Tokugawa came flying, hit him with one shoulder. They thudded to the floor. The mate wrapped his legs about Gentry's and administered an expert foul blow to the neck.

Cleonie struggled from the bridge toward Devon. Banning was already there, holding the gray form between his knees while he examined the wound. The girl bumped into them. "*How is he?*" Banning had heard that raw tone, half shriek, often and often before this day—when women saw the blood of their men.

He nodded. "Could be worse, I reckon. The slug seems to've hit a rib and stopped. Shock knocked him out, but . . . well, a bullet never does as much harm in free fall, the target bounces away from it easier." He swatted at the little red globules in the air. "Damn!"

Wayne emerged, green-faced. "This man . . . shot the door open when we wouldn't let him in," he rattled. "We hadn't any weapon . . . he threatened Miss Rogers—"

"O.K., never mind the breast-beating. Next time remember to stand beside the door and grab when the enemy comes through. Now, I assume you have the medical skills required for your certificate. Get Luke to sick bay and patch him up. Nielsen, help Mr. Wayne. Gentry still alive?"

"He won't be if he doesn't get some first aid quick," said Tokugawa. "You gashed him good." He whistled in awe. "Don't you ever simply *stun* your enemies, boss?"

"Take him along too, Mr. Wayne, but Devon gets priority. Bahadur, break out the vacuum sweeper and get this blood sucked up before it fouls everything. Tetsuo . . . uh, Mr. Tokugawa, go watch the after bulkhead in case Gomez tries to break out Vladimirovitch, tag along with him. Castro, stick around here."

"Can I help?" asked Cleonie. Her lips struggled for firmness.

"Go to sick bay," nodded Banning. "Maybe they can use you."

He darted into the bridge and checked controls. Everything was still off—good. Gomez couldn't start the engines without rigging a bypass circuit. However, he had plenty of ancillary machines, generators and pumps and whatnot, at his disposal down there. The captain entered the intercom cabinet and switched on the engine room screen.

Gomez's pinched face had taken on a stiffened wildness. "For your information, friend," said Banning, "we just mopped up Andreyev and Gentry. That leaves you alone. Come on out of there, the show's over."

"No," said Gomez. His voice was dull, abnormally calm. It gave Banning a creepy sensation.

"Don't you believe me? I can haul the bodies here if you want."

"Oh, yes, I will take your word." Gomez's mouth twisted. "Then perhaps you will do me the same honor. It is still you who must surrender to me."

Banning waited for a long few seconds.

"I am here in the engine room," said Gomez. "I am alone. I have locked the outer doors: emergency seal, you'll have to burn your way through, and that takes hours. There will be plenty of time for me to disable the propulsion system."

Banning was not a timid man, but his palms were suddenly wet, and he fumbled a thick dry tongue before he could shape words: "You'd die, too."

"I am quite prepared for that."

"But you wouldn't have accomplished anything! You'd just have wrecked the ship and killed several people."

"I would have kept this affair from being reported to the Union," said Gomez. "The very fact of our attempt is more of a hint than we can afford to let the Guard have."

"What are you doing all this *for?*" howled the captain.

The face in the screen grew altogether unhuman. It was a face Banning knew—millennia of slaughterhouse history knew it—the face of embodied Purpose.

"It is not necessary for you to be told the details," clipped Gomez. "However, perhaps you will understand that the present government's spineless toleration of the Kali menace in the East and the moral decay in the West has to be ended if civilization is to survive."

"I see," said Banning, as gently as if he spoke in the presence of a ticking bomb. "And since toleration is built into Union law—"

"Exactly. I do not say anything against the Uniters. But times have changed. If Fourre were alive today, he would agree that action is necessary."

"It's always convenient to use a dead man for a character witness, isn't it?"

"What?"

"Never mind." Banning nodded to himself. "Don't do anything radical yet, Gomez. I'll have to think about this."

"I shall give you exactly one hour," said the desiccated voice. "Thereafter I shall begin work. I am not an engineer myself, but I think I can disable something—I have studied a trifle about nucleonics. You may call me when you are ready to surrender. At the first suspicion of misbehavior, I will, of course, wreck the propulsion system immediately."

Gomez turned away.

Banning sat for a while, his mind curiously empty. Then he shoved across to the control board, alerted the crew and started the rotation again. You might as well have some weight.

"Keep an eye on the screen," he said as he left the main pilot chair. "Call me on the intercom if anything develops. I'll be in sick bay."

"Sir?" Castro gaped at him.

"Appropriate spot," said Banning. "Velocity is equivalent to temperature, isn't it? If so, then we all have a fever which is quite likely to kill us."

Devon lay stretched and stripped on the operating table. Wayne had just removed the bullet with surgical pincers. Now he clamped the wound and began stitching. Nielsen was controlling the sterilizers, both UV and sonic, while Cleonie stood by with bowl and sponges. They all looked up, as if from a dream, when Banning entered. The tools of surgery might be developed today to a point where this was an operation simple enough for a spaceman's meditechnic training; but there was a man on the table who might have died, and only slowly did their minds break away from his heartbeat.

"How is he?" asked the captain.

"Not too bad, sir, considering." Given this job, urgent and specific, Wayne was competent enough; he spoke steadily. "I daresay he presented his chest on purpose when he attacked, knowing the bones had a good chance of acting as armor. There's a broken rib and some torn muscle, of course, but nothing that won't heal."

"Gentry?"

"Conked out five minutes ago, sir," said Nielsen. "I stuck him in the icebox. Maybe they've got revivification equipment on Ganymede."

"Wouldn't make much difference," said Banning. "The forebrain would be too far gone by the time we arrived—no personality survival to speak of." He shuddered a little. Clean death was one thing; this was another matter, one which he had never quite gotten used to. "Luke, though," he went on quickly, "can he stand being brought to consciousness? Right away?"

"No!" Almost, Cleonie lifted her basin to brain him.

"Shut up." He turned his back on her. "It'd be a poor kindness to let him sleep comfy now and starve to death later, maybe, out beyond Pluto. Well, Mr. Wayne?"

"Hm-m-m . . . I don't like it, sir. But if you say so, I guess I can manage it. Local anesthesia for the wound and a shot of mild stimulant; oxygen and neoplasma, just in case— Yes, I don't imagine a few minutes' conversation would hurt him permanently."

"Good. Carry on." Banning fumbled after his pipe, remembered that he had dropped it somewhere in all the hallabaloo, and swore.

"What did you say?" asked Nielsen.

"Never mind," said Banning. True, women were supposed to be treated like men these days, but he had old-fashioned ideas. It was useful to know a few earthy languages unfamiliar to anyone else.

Cleonie laid a hand on his arm. "Captain," she said. Her eyes were shadowed, with weariness and with—compassion? "Captain, is it necessary to wake him? He's been hurt so much—for our sakes."

"He may have the only information to save our lives," answered Banning patiently.

The intercom cleared its throat: "Sir . . . Castro on bridge—he's unbolting the main mass-tank access port."

Wayne turned white as he labored. He understood.

Banning nodded. "I thought so. Did you ask him what he was up to? He promised us an hour."

"Yes, sir. He said we'd get it, too, but . . . but he wanted to be ready, in case—"

"Smart boy. It'll take him awhile to get to the flush valves; they're quite well locked away and shielded. Then the pump has to have time. We might have burned our way in to him by then."

"Maybe we should do it, sir. Now!"

"Maybe. It'd be a race between his wrenches and our torches. I'll let you know. Stand by."

Banning turned back to Devon, gnawing his lip. The Engineer was stirring to wakefulness.

As he watched, the captain saw the eyes blink palely open, saw color creep into the face and the mouth tighten behind the transparent oxygen mask.

Cleonie moved toward the table. "Luke—"

Devon smiled at her, a sudden human warmth in this cold room of machines. Gently, Banning shoved her aside. "You'll get your innings later, girl," he said. Bending over the Engineer: "Hello, buster. You're going to be O.K. Can you tell me some things in a hell of a hurry?"

"I can try—" It was the merest flutter of air.

Banning began to talk. Devon lay back, breathing deeply and making some curious gestures with his hands. He'd had Tighe System training, then—total integration—good! He *would* be able to hang on to his consciousness, even call up new strength from hidden cellular reserves.

"We clobbered all the gang except Gomez, who seems to be the kingpin. He's holed up in the engine room, threatens to wreck us all unless we surrender to him inside an hour. Does he mean it?"

"Yes. Oh, yes." Devon nodded faintly.

"Who is this outfit? What do they want?"

"Fanatic group . . . quasi-religious . . . powerful, large membership furnishes plenty of money . . . but the real operations are secret, a few men—"

"I think I know who you mean. The Western Reformists, huh?"

Devon nodded again. The pulse that flickered in his throat seemed to strengthen.

Banning spent a bleak moment of review. In recent years, he had stayed off Earth as much as possible; when there, he had not troubled himself with political details, for he recognized all the signs of a civilization going under. It had seemed more worthwhile to give his attention to the Venusian ranch he had bought, against the day of genocide and the night of ignorance and tyranny to follow. However, he did understand that the antitechnic Oriental cult of Kali had created its own opposite pole in the West. And the prim grim Reformists might well try to forestall their enemies by a coup.

"Sort of like the Nazis versus the Communists, back in Germany in the 1920s," he muttered.

"The who?" said Nielsen.

"No matter. It's six of one and half a dozen of the other. Let me see, Luke." Banning took a turn around the room. "In order to overthrow constitutional government and impose their will on Earth, the Reformists would have to kill quite a few hundred millions of people, especially in Asia. That means nuclear bombardment, preferably from space. Am I right?"

"Yes—" said Devon. His voice gained resonance as he went on. "They have a base, somewhere in the asteroid belt. They hope to build it up to a fortress, with a fleet of ships, arsenal, military corps . . . the works. It's a very long-range thing, of course, but the public aspect of their party is going to need lots of time anyway, to condition enough citizens toward the idea of— Well. At present their base doesn't amount to much. They can't just buy ships, the registry would give them away . . . they have to build . . . they need at least one supply ship, secretly owned and operated, before they can start serious work at all."

"And we're elected," said Banning. "Yeah. I can even see why. Not only is this a fast ship with a large capacity, but our present cargo, the terraforming stuff, would be valuable to them in itself . . . Uh-huh. Their idea was to take over this clunk, bring her in to their base—and the *Thunderbolt* becomes another ship which just plain vanished mysteriously."

Devon nodded.

"I scarcely imagine they'd have kept us alive, under the circumstances," went on Banning.

"No."

"How do you know all this?"

"The Order . . . We stay out of politics . . . officially . . . but we have our Intelligence arm and use it quietly." So that was why he'd been reluctant to explain Andreyev's actions! "We knew, in a general way, what the situation was. Of course, we didn't know *this* ship, on this particular voyage, was slated for capture."

"That's fairly obvious. You recognized Andreyev?"

"Yes. Former Engineer, under another name—expelled for . . . good reasons. Surgical changes made, but the overall gestalt bothered me. All of a sudden, I thought I knew who he was. Like a meddling fool, I tried a key word on him. Yes, he reacted, by pulling a gun on me! Later on—again, like an idiot—I didn't think Gentry might be his partner, so I told Tietjens what had happened while Gentry was there." Devon sighed. "Old Rostomily would disown me."

"You weren't trained for secret service work, yourself," said Banning. "All right, Luke. One more question. Gomez wants us to surrender to him. I presume this means we'll let ourselves be locked away except for one or two who slow down the ship while he holds a gun on 'em. After we've decelerated to a point where a boat from the Reformist asteroid can match velocities, he'll radio and—Hell! What I'm getting at is, would our lives be spared afterward?"

"I doubt it," said the Engineer.

"Oh my darling—" As he closed his eyes, Cleonie came to his side. Their hands groped together.

Banning swung away. "Thanks, Luke," he said. "I didn't know if I had the right to risk lives for the sake of this ship, but now I see there's no risk at all. We haven't got a thing to lose. Cleonie, can you take care of our boy here?"

"Yes," she whispered, enormous-eyed. "If there's no emergency."

"There shouldn't be. They fabricated him out of teflon and rattlesnake leather. O.K., then, you be his nurse. You might also whomp up some coffee and sandwiches. The rest of the crew meet me at the repair equipment lockers, aft section . . . no, you stay put, Castro. We're going to burn our way in to friend Gomez."

"But he . . . he'll dump the reaction mass!" gasped Wayne.

"Maybe we can get at him before he gets at the tanks," said Banning. "A man might try."

"No—look, sir. I know how long it takes to operate the main flush system. Even allowing for Gomez being alone and untrained, he can do it before we can get through the after bulkhead. We haven't a chance that way!"

"What do you recommend, Mr. Wayne?" asked Banning slowly.

"That we give in to him, sir."

"And be shot down out of hand when his pals board the ship?"

"No, sir. There'll be seven of us, one of Gomez before that happens. We have a faint hope of being able to jump him—"

"A very faint hope indeed," said Banning. "He's no amateur. And if we don't succeed, not only will we die, but that gang of hellhounds will have gotten the start it wants. Whereas, if we burn through to Gomez but fail to stop him disabling the ship . . . well, it'll only be us who die, now. Not a hundred million people twenty or thirty years from now."

Is this the truth? Do you really believe one man can delay the Norns? What is your choice, Captain? By legal definition, you are omnipotent and omniscient while the ship is under way. What shall be done, Oh god of the ship?

Banning groaned. *Per Jovem*, it was too much to ask of a man!

And then he stiffened.

"What is it, sir?" Nielsen looked alarmed.

"By Jupiter," said Banning. "Well, by Jupiter!"

"What?"

"Never mind. Come on. We're going to smoke Gomez out of there!"

The last, stubborn metal glared white, ran molten down the gouge already carved, and froze in gobbets. Bahadur shut off the electric torch, shoved the mask away from his dark turbanned face, and said: "All right, sir."

Banning stepped carefully over the heavy torch cables. His gang had attacked the bulkhead from a point near the skin of the ship, for the sake of both surprise and weight. "How's the situation inside?" he asked the air.

The intercom replied from the bridge, where Castro huddled over the telescreen that showed him Gomez at work. "Pump still going, sir. I guess he really means business."

"We've got this much luck," said Banning, "that he isn't an engineer himself. You'd have those tanks flushed out half an hour ago."

He stood for another instant, gathering strength and will. His mind pawed over the facts again.

The outer plates of the ship would stop a fair-sized meteor, even at hyperbolic relative velocity: it would explode into vapor, leaving a miniature Moon crater. Anything which might happen to break through that would lose energy to the self-sealer between the hulls; at last it would encounter the inner skin, which could stand well over a hundred atmospheres of pressure by itself. It was not a common accident for a modern spaceship to be punctured.

But the after bulkhead was meant to contain stray radiation, or even a minor explosion, if the nuclear energies which drove the ship should get out of hand. It was scarcely weaker than the double hull. The torches had required hours to carve a hole in it. There would have been little or no saving of time by cutting through the great double door at the axis of the ship, which Gomez had locked; nor did Banning want to injure massive pieces of precision machinery. The mere bulkhead would be a lot easier to repair afterward—if there was an afterward.

Darkness yawned before him. He hefted the gun in his hand. "All right, Vladimirovitch, let's go," he said. "If we're not back in ten minutes, remember, let Wayne and Bahadur follow."

He had overruled Tokugawa's anguished protests and ordered the first mate to stay behind under all circumstances. The Lunarite alone had the piloting skill to pull off the crazy stunt which was their final hope. He and Nielsen were making a racket at the other end of the bulkhead, a diversion for Gomez's benefit.

Banning slipped through the hole. It was pitchy beyond, a small outer room where no one had turned on the lights. He wondered if Gomez waited just beyond the door with a bullet for the first belly to come through.

He'd find out pretty quick.

The door, which led into the main control chamber, was a thin piece of metal. Rotation made it lie above Banning's head. He scampered up the ladder. His hand closed on the catch, he turned it with an enormous caution—flung the door open and jumped through.

The fluoros made a relentless blaze of light. Near the middle of that steel cave, floating before an opened panel, he saw Gomez. So the hellbound Roundhead hadn't heard them breaking in!

He did now. He whirled, clumsily, and scrabbled for the gun in his belt. Banning fired. His bullet missed, wailed and gonged around the great chamber. Gomez shot back. Recoil tore him from the stanchion he held, sent him drifting toward the wall.

Banning scrambled in pursuit, over the spidery network of ladders and handholds. His weight dropped with each leap closer to the axis; he fought down the characteristic Coriolis vertigo. Gomez spiraled away from him, struck a control chair, clawed himself to a stop, and crouched in it.

Banning grew aware of the emergency pump. It throbbed and sang in the metal stillness around him, and every surge meant lost mass . . . like the red spurting from the slashed artery. The flush system was rarely used—only if the reaction mass got contaminated, or for some such reason. Gomez had found a new reason, thought Banning grimly. To lose a ship and murder a crew.

"Turn that thing off, Vlad," he said between his teeth.

"Stay where you are!" screamed Gomez. "I'll shoot! I will!"

"Get going!" roared the captain.

Vladimirovitch hauled himself toward the cutoff switch. Gomez flipped his pistol to full automatic and began firing.

He didn't hit anything of value in the few seconds granted him. In a ship rotating in free fall, the pattern of forces operating on a bullet is so complicated that practical ballistics must be learned all over again. But that hose of lead was bound to kill someone, by sheer chance and ricochet, unless—

Banning clutched himself to a rod, aimed, and fired.

On the second shot, Gomez jerked. The pistol jarred from his hand, he slumped back into the chair and lay still.

Banning hurried toward him. It would be worthwhile taking Gomez alive, to interrogate and— No. As he reached the man, he saw the life draining out of him. A shot through the heart is not invariably fatal, but this time it was.

The pump clashed to silence.

Banning whirled about. "Well?" His shout was raw, "How much did we lose?"

"Quite a bit, sir." Vladimirovitch squinted at the gauges. His words came out jerkily. "Too much, I'm afraid."

Banning went to join him, leaving Gomez to die alone.

They met in the dining saloon: seven hale men, an invalid, and a woman. For a moment they could only stare at the death in each other's eyes.

"Break out the Scotch, Nielsen," said Banning at last. He took forth his pipe and began loading it. A grin creased his mouth. "If your faces get any longer, people, you'll be tripping over your own jawbones."

Cleonie, seated at the head of the couch on which Devon lay, ruffled the Engineer's hair. Her gaze was blind with sorrow. "Do you expect us to be happy, after all that killing?" she asked.

"We were lucky," shrugged Banning. "We lost two good men, yes. But all the ungodly are dead."

"That's not so good a thing," said Devon. "I'd like to have them narcoed, find out where their asteroid is and—" He paused. "Wait. Gentry's still in the freeze, isn't he? If he was revived at Ganymede, maybe his brain wouldn't be too deteriorated for a deep-memory probe, at least."

"Nix," said Banning. "The stiffs are all to be jettisoned. We've got to lighten ship. If your Order's Intelligence men—or the Guard's, for that matter—are any good, they'll be able to trace back people like our late playfellows and rope in their buddies."

Cleonie shivered. "Please!"

"Sorry." Banning lit his pipe and took a long drag. "It is kind of morbid, isn't it? O.K. then, let's concentrate on the problem of survival. The question is how to use the inadequate amount of reaction mass left in the tanks."

"I'm afraid I don't quite understand," said the girl.

She looked more puzzled than frightened. Banning liked her all the more for that. Devon was a lucky thus-and-so, if they lived ... though she deserved better than an Engineer, always skiting through space and pledged to contract no formal marriage till he retired from field service.

"It's simple enough," he told her. "We're on a hyperbolic orbit. That means we're moving with a speed greater than escape velocity for the Solar System. If we don't slow down quite a bit, we'll just keep on going; and no matter how we ration it, there's only a few weeks' worth of food aboard and no suspended-animation stuff."

"Can't we radio for help?"

"We're out of our own radio range to anywhere."

"But won't they miss us—send high-acceleration ships after us? They can compute our orbit, can't they?"

"Not that closely. Too much error creeps in when the path gets as monstrous long as ours would be before we could possibly be overhauled. It'd be remarkable if the Guard ship came as close to us as five million kilometers, which is no use at all." Banning wagged his pipestem at her. "It's up to us alone. We have a velocity of some hundreds of kilometers per second to kill. We don't have reaction mass enough to do it."

Nielsen came in with bottles and glasses. He went around doing the honors while Devon said: "Excuse me, Captain, I assume this has occurred to you, but after all, it's momentum which is the significant quantity, not speed *per se*. If we jettison everything which isn't absolutely essential, cargo, furnishings, even the inner walls and floors—"

"Tet and I figured on that," answered Banning. "You remember just now I said we had to lighten ship. We even assumed stripping off the outer hull and taking a chance on meteors. It's quite feasible, you know. Spaceships are designed to come apart fairly easily under the right tools, for replacement work, so if we all sweat at it, I think we can finish peeling her down by the time we have to start decelerating."

Wayne looked at the whiskey bottle. He didn't drink; it wasn't considered quite the thing in today's West. But his face grew tighter and tighter, till suddenly he reached out and grabbed the bottle and tilted it to his mouth.

When he was through choking, he said hoarsely: "All right, sir. Why don't you tell them? We still can't lose enough speed."

"I was coming to that," said Banning.

Devon's hand closed on the girl's. "What are the figures?" he asked in a level tone.

"Well," said Banning, "we can enter the Jovian System if we like, but then we'll find ourselves fuelless with a velocity of about fifty kilometers per second relative to the planet."

The Engineer whistled.

"Must we do that, though?" inquired Bahadur. "I mean, sir, well, if we can decelerate that much, can't we get into an elliptic orbit about the sun?"

"'Fraid not. Fifty k.p.s. is still a lot more than solar escape velocity for that region of space."

"But look, sir. If I remember rightly, Jupiter's own escape velocity is well *over* fifty k.p.s. That means the planet itself will be giving us all that speed. If we didn't come near it, we should have mass enough left to throw ourselves into a cometary—"

"Smart boy," said Banning. He blew smoke in the air and hoisted his glass. "We computed that one, too. You're quite right, we can get into a cometary. The very best cometary we can manage will take a few years to bring us back into radio range of anyone—and of course space is so big we'd never be found on such an unpredictable orbit, unless we hollered for help and were heard."

"*Years,*" whispered Cleonie.

The terror which rose in her, then, was not the simple fear of death. It was the sudden understanding of just how big and old this universe which she had so blithely inhabited really was. Banning, who had seen it before, waited sympathetically.

After a minute she straightened herself and met his eyes. "All right, Captain," she said. "Continue the arithmetic lesson. Why can't we simply ask the Jovians to pick us up as we approach their system?"

"You knew there was a catch, eh?" murmured Banning. "It's elementary. The Republic is poor and backward. Their only spacecraft are obsolete inter-satellite shuttles, which can't come anywhere near a fifty k.p.s. velocity."

"And we've no means of losing speed, down to something they can match." Wayne dropped his face into his hands.

"I didn't call you here for a weeping contest," said Banning. "We do have one means. It might or might not work—it's never been tried—but Tetsuo here is one hell of a good pilot. He's done some of the cutest braking ellipses you ever saw in your life."

That made them sit up. But Devon shook his head, wryly. "It won't work," he said. "Even after the alleged terraforming, Ganymede hasn't enough atmosphere to—"

"Jupiter has all kinds of atmosphere," said Banning.

The silence that fell was thunderous.

"No," said Wayne at last. He spoke quickly, out of bloodless lips. "It could only work by a fluke. We would lose speed, yes, if friction didn't burn us up . . . finally, on one of those passes, we'd emerge with a sensible linear velocity. But a broken shell like this ship will be after we lighten her—an atmosphere as thick and turbulent as Jupiter's— there wouldn't be enough control. We'd never know precisely what orbit we were going to have on emergence. By the time we'd computed what path it really was and let the Jovians know and their antiquated boats had reached it . . . we'd be back in Jupiter's air on the next spiral!"

"And the upshot would be to crash," said Devon. "Hydrogen and helium at one hundred and forty degrees Absolute. Not very breathable."

"Oh, we'd have spattered on the surface before we had to try breathing that stuff," said Vladimirovitch sarcastically.

"No, we wouldn't either," said Bahadur. "Our inner hull can stand perhaps two hundred atmospheres' pressure. But Jupiter goes up to the tens of thousands. We would be squashed flat long before we reached the surface."

Banning lifted his brows. "You know a better 'ole?" he challenged.

"What?" Wayne blinked at him.

"Know anything which gives us a better chance?"

"Yes, I do." The young face stiffened. "Let's get into that cometary about the sun. When we don't report in, there'll be Guard ships hunting for us. We have a very small chance of being found. But the chance of being picked up by the Jovians, while doing those crazy dives, is infinitesimal!"

"It doesn't look good either way, does it?" said Cleonie. A sad little smile crossed her lips. "But I'd rather be killed at once, crushed in a single blow, than . . . watch all of us shrivel and die, one by one—or draw lots for who's to be eaten next. I'd rather go out like a human being."

"Same here," nodded Devon.

"Not I!" Wayne stood up. "Captain, I won't have it. You've no right to . . . to take the smaller chance, the greater hazard, deliberately, just because it offers a quicker death. No!"

Banning slapped the table with a cannon-crack noise. "Congratulations on getting your master's certificate, Mr. Wayne," he growled. "Now sit down."

"No, by the Eternal! I demand—"

"*Sit down!*"

Wayne sat.

"As a matter of fact," continued Banning mildly, "I agree that the chance of the Jovians rescuing us is negligible. But I think we have a chance to help ourselves."

"I think maybe we can do what nobody has ever tried before—enter Jovian sky and live to brag about it."

❊　　❊　　❊

From afar, as they rushed to their destiny, Jupiter had a splendor which no other planet, perhaps not the sun itself, could match. From a cold great star to an amber disk to a swollen shield with storm—the sight caught your heart.

But then you fought it. You got so close that the shield became a cauldron and ate you down.

The figures spoke a bleak word: the escape velocity of Jupiter is about fifty-nine kilometers per second. The *Thunderbolt* had about fifty-two, relative. If she had simply whizzed by the planet, its gravitation would have slowed her again, and eventually she would have fallen back into it with a speed that would vaporize her. There was no possibility of the creaking old boats of the satellite colonists getting close to her at any point of such an orbit; they would have needed far more advance warning than a short-range radio could give them.

Instead, Tokugawa used the last reaction mass to aim at the outer fringes of atmosphere.

The first pass was almost soundless. Only a thin screaming noise, a sense of heat radiated in human faces, a weak tug of deceleration, told how the ship clove air. Then she was out into vacuum again, curving on a long narrow ellipse.

Banning worked his radio, swearing at the Doppler effect. He got the band of Ganymede at last. Beside him, Tokugawa and Wayne peered into the viewscreen, reading stars and moons, while the computer jabbered out an orbit.

"Hello. Hello. Are you there?"

The voice hissed weakly from X Spaceport: "Heh, *Thun'erbolt*. Central Astro Control, Ganymede. Harris speakin'. Got y'r path?"

"To a rough approximation," said Banning. "We'd need several more readings to get it exactly, of course. Stand by to record." He took the tape from the computer and read off the figures.

"We've three boats in y' area," said Harris. "They'll try t' find y'. G' luck."

"Thanks," said Banning. "We could use some."

Tokugawa's small deft fingers completed another calculation. "We'll strike atmosphere again in about fifty hours, skipper," he reported. "That gives the demolition gang plenty of time to work."

Banning twisted his head around. There was no rear wall now to stop his eyes. Except for the central section, with its vital equipment, little enough remained between the bridge and the after bulkhead. Torches had slashed, wrenches had turned, air locks had spewed out jagged temporary moons for days. The ship had become a hollow shell and a web of bracing.

He felt like a murderer.

Across the diameter of the great spheroid, he saw Devon floating free, ordering the crew into spacesuits. As long as they were in null-gee, the Engineer made an excellent foreman, broken rib and all.

His party was going out to cut loose reactor, fire chamber, ion tubes, everything aft. Now that the last mass was expended and nothing remained to drive the ship but the impersonal forces of celestial mechanics, the engines were so much junk whose weight could kill them. Never mind the generators—there was enough energy stored in the capacitor bank to keep the shell lighted and warmed for weeks. If the Jovians didn't catch them in space, they might need those weeks, too.

Banning sighed. Since men first steered a scraped-out log or a wicker basket to sea, it has been an agony for a captain to lose his ship.

He remembered a submarine once, long ago—it still hurt him to recall, though it hadn't been his fault. Of course, he'd gotten the idea which might save all their lives now because he knew a trifle about submarines . . . or should the Montgolfiers get the credit, or Archimedes?

Cleonie floated toward him. She had gotten quite deft in free fall during the time before deceleration in which they orbited toward Jupiter, when spin had been canceled to speed the work of jettisoning. "May I bother you?" she asked.

"Of course." Banning took out his pipe. She cheered him up. "Though the presence of a beautiful girl is not a bother. By definition."

She smiled, wearily, and brushed a strand of loose hair from her eyes. It made a halo about her worn face. "I feel so useless," she said.

"Nonsense. Keep the meals coming, and you're plenty of use. Tietjens and Nielsen were awful belly robbers."

"I wondered—" A flush crossed her cheeks. "I do so want to understand Luke's work."

"Sure." Banning opened his tobacco pouch and began stuffing the pipe, not an easy thing to do in free fall. "What's the question?"

"Only . . . we hit the air going so fast—faster than meteors usually hit Earth, wasn't it? Why didn't we burn up?"

"Meteors don't exactly burn. They volatilize. All we did was skim some very thin air. We didn't convert enough velocity into heat to worry about. A lot of what we did convert was carried away by the air itself."

"But still—I've never heard of braking ellipses being used when the speed is as high as ours."

Banning clicked his lighter, held it "above" the bowl, and drew hard. "In actual fact," he said, "I don't think it could be done in Earth or Venus atmosphere. But Jupiter has about ten times the gravitational potential, therefore the air thins out with height correspondingly more slowly. In other words, we've got a deeper layer of thin air to brake us. It's all right. We'll have to make quite a few passes—we'll be at this for days, if we aren't rescued—but it can be done."

He got his pipe started. There was a trick to smoking in free fall. The air-circulating blowers, which kept you from smothering in your own breath, didn't much help as small an object as a pipe. But he needed this comfort. Badly.

Many hours later, using orbital figures modified by further observation, a shuttle-boat from Ganymede came near enough to locate the *Thunderbolt* on radar. After maneuvering around so much, it didn't have reaction mass enough to match velocities. For about a second it passed so close that Devon's crew, working out on the hull, could see it—as if they were the damned in hell watching one of the elect fly past.

The shuttleboat radioed for a vessel with fuller tanks. One came. It zeroed in—and decelerated like a startled mustang. The *Thunderbolt* had already fallen deeper into the enormous Jovian gravity field than the boat's engines could rise.

The drifting ship vanished from sight, into the great face of the planet. High clouds veiled it from telescopes—clouds of free radicals, such as could not have existed for a moment under humanly endurable conditions. Jupiter is more alien than men can really imagine.

Her orbit on reemergence was not so very much different. But the boats which had almost reached her had been forced to move elsewhere; they could not simply hang there, in that intense a field. So the *Thunderbolt* made another long, lonesome pass. By the time it was over, Ganymede was in the unfavorable position, and Callisto had never been in a good one. Therefore the ship entered Jupiter's atmosphere for a third time, unattended.

On the next emergence into vacuum, her orbit had shortened and skewed considerably. The rate at which air drag operated was increasing; each plunge went deeper beneath the poison clouds, each swung through clear space took less time. However, there was hope. The Ganymedeans were finally organizing themselves. They computed an excellent estimate of what the fourth free orbit would be and planted well-fueled boats strategically close at the right times.

Only—the *Thunderbolt* did not come anywhere near the predicted path.

It was pure bad luck. Devon's crew, working whenever the ship was in a vacuum, had almost cut away the after section. This last plunge into stiffening air resistance finished the job. Forces of drag and reaction, a shape suddenly altered, whipped the *Thunderbolt* wildly through the stratosphere. She broke free at last, on a drastically different orbit.

But then, it had been unusual good luck which brought the Jovians so close to her in the first place. Probabilities were merely reasserting themselves.

The radio said in a weak, fading voice: "Missed y' 'gain. Do' know 'f we c'n come near, nex' time. Y'r period's gettin' very short."

"Maybe you shouldn't risk it." Banning sighed. He had hoped for more, but if the gods had decided his ship was to plunge irretrievably into Jupiter, he had to accept the fact. "We'll be all right, I reckon."

Outside, the air roared hollowly. Pressures incomparably greater than those in Earth's deepest oceans waited below.

On his final pass into any approximation of clear space—the stars were already hazed— Banning radioed: "This will be the last message, except for a ten-minute signal on the same band when we come to rest. Assuming we're alive! We've got to save capacitors. It'll be some time before help arrives. When it does, call me. I'll respond if we've survived, and thereafter emit a steady tone by which we can be located. Is that clear?"

"Clear. I read y'. Luck, spaceman . . . over an' out."

Watching the mists thicken in the viewscreen, Banning added figures in his head for the hundredth time.

His schedule called for him to report at Phobos in fifteen days. When he didn't, the Guard would send a high-acceleration ship to find out what had gone wrong. Allow a few days for that. Another week for it to return to Mars with a report of the facts. Mars would call Luna on the radio beam—that, at least, would be quick—and the Guard, or possibly the Engineers, would go to work at once.

The Engineers had ships meant to enter atmosphere: powerful, but slow. Such a vessel could be carried piggyback by a fast ion-drive craft of the Guard. Modifications could be made en route. But the trip would still require a couple of weeks, pessimistically reckoned.

Say, then, six weeks maximum until help arrived. Certainly no less than four, no matter what speeds could be developed by these latest models.

Well, the *Thunderbolt* had supplies and energy for more than six weeks. That long a time under two-plus gees was not going to be fun, though gravanol injections would prevent physiological damage. And the winds were going to buffet them around. That should be endurable, though; they'd be above the region of vertical currents, in what you might call the Jovian stratosphere—

A red fog passed before the screen.

Luke Devon, strapped into a chair like everyone else, called across the empty ship: "If I'd only known this was going to happen—what a chance for research! I do have a few instruments, but it'll be crude as hell."

"Personally," said Banning, "I saved out a deck of cards and some poker chips. But I hardly think you'll have much time for research—in Jovian atmospherics, anyway."

He could imagine Cleonie blushing. He was sorry to embarrass her, he really did like that girl, but the ragged laugh he got from the others was worth it. While men could laugh, especially at jokes as bad as his, they could endure.

Down and down the ship went. Once, caught in a savage gust, she turned over. If everything hadn't been fastened down, there could have been an awful mess. The distribution of mass was such that the hulk would always right itself, but . . . yes, reflected Banning, they'd all have to wear some kind of harness attached to the interior braces. It could be improvised.

The wind that boomed beyond the hull faded its organ note, just a trifle.

"We're slowing down," said Tokugawa.

And later, looking up from the radaltimeter: "We've stopped."

"End of the line." Banning stretched. He felt bone-crushingly tired. "Nothing much we can do now. Let's all strap into our bunks and sleep for a week."

His Jovian weight dragged at him. But they were all alive. And the ship might be hollowed out, but she still held food and drink, tools and materials, games and books—what was needed to keep them sane as well as breathing in the time they must wait.

His calculations were verified. A hollow steelloy shell, three hundred odd meters in diameter, could carry more than a hundred thousand tons, besides its own mass, and still have a net specific gravity of less than 0.03. Now the Jovian air has an average molecular weight of about 3.3, so after due allowance for temperature and a few other items, the result was derived that at such a thickness its pressure is an endurable one hundred atmospheres.

Like an old drop in a densitometer, like a free balloon over eighteenth-century France, like a small defiant bubble in the sky, the *Thunderbolt* floated.

One ruthless embodiment of Higher Purpose fell; others sprang up in its place. Mere willingness to kill or be killed in for the sake of a cause cannot prove the rightness of that cause. But it was more than sufficient to plunge the Solar Union into a Second Dark Ages.

Yet that crucible of misery seemed to refine the human race. A saner civilization emerged, eager to surpass those that had gone before. As science and technology revived, so did the old dream of interstellar exploration. Slower-than-light travel improved enough to plant colonies among the stars that seeded other colonies in their turn. With the breakthrough invention of faster-than-light hyperdrive in 2784, the whole universe lay open to our kind. But whether achieved slower or faster than light-speed, the very process of interstellar travel would itself change the travelers.

Gypsy

FROM AFAR, I caught a glimpse of the *Traveler* as my boat swung toward the planet. The great spaceship looked like a toy at that distance, a frail bubble of metal and air and energy against the enormous background of space. I thought of the machines within her, humming and whirring and clicking very faintly as they pursued their unending round of services, making that long hull into a living world—the hull that was now empty of life—and I had a sudden odd feeling of sympathy. As if she were alive, I felt that the *Traveler* was lonely.

The planet swelled before me, a shining blue shield blazoned with clouds and continents, rolling against a limitless dark and the bitterly burning stars. Harbor, we had named that world, the harbor at the end of our long journey, and there were few lovelier names. Harbor, haven, rest and peace and a sky overhead as roof against the naked blaze of space. It was good to get home.

I searched the heavens for another glimpse of the *Traveler,* but I couldn't find her tiny form in that thronging wilderness of stars. No matter, she was still on her orbit about Harbor, moored to the planet, perhaps forever. I concentrated on bringing the spaceboat down.

Atmosphere whistled about the hull. After a month in the gloom and poisonous cold of the fifth planet, alone among utterly unhuman natives, I was usually on fire to get home and brought my craft down with a recklessness that overloaded the gravity beams. But this time I went a little more carefully, telling myself that I'd rather be late for supper than never arrive at all. Or perhaps it was that brief chance vision of the *Traveler* which made me suddenly thoughtful. After all, we had had some good times aboard her.

I sent the boat slanting toward the peninsula in the north temperate zone on which most of us were settled. The outraged air screamed behind me as I slammed down on the hard-packed earth that served us for a landing field. There were a few warehouses and service shops around it, long low buildings of the heavy timbers used by most of the colonists, and a couple of private homes a kilometer or so away. But otherwise only long grass rustled in the wind, gardens and wild groves, sunlight streaming out of a high blue sky. When I stepped from the boat, the fresh vivid scent of the land fairly leaped to meet me. I could hear the sea growling beyond the horizon.

Tokogama was on duty at the field. He was sitting on the porch of the office, smoking his pipe and watching the clouds sail by overhead, but he greeted me with the undemonstrative cordiality of old friends who know each other too well to need many words.

"So that's the portmaster," I said. "Soft touch. All you have to do is puff that vile-smelling thing and say hello to me."

"That's all," he admitted cheerfully. "I am retained only for my uncommonly high ornamental value."

It was, approximately, true. Our aircraft used the field with no formality, and we only kept this one space vessel in operation. The portmaster was on hand simply to oversee servicing and in the unlikely case of some emergency or dispute. But none of the colony's few public posts—captain, communications officer, and the rest—required much effort in as simple a society as ours, and they were filled as spare-time occupations by anyone who wanted them. There was no compensation except getting first turn at using the machinery for farming or heavy construction which we owned in common.

"How was the trip?" asked Tokogama.

"Pretty good," I said. "I gave them our machines and they filled my holds with their ores and alloys. And I managed to take a few more notes on their habits, and establish a few more code symbols for communication."

"Which is a very notable brick added to the walls of science, but in view of the fact that you're the only one who ever goes there it really makes no odds." Tokogama's dark eyes regarded me curiously. "Why do you keep on making those trips out there, Erling? Quite a few of the other boys wouldn't mind visiting Five once in a while. Will and Ivan both mentioned it to me last week."

"I'm no hog," I said. "If either of them, or anyone else, wants a turn at the trading job, let 'em learn space piloting and they can go. But meanwhile—I like the work. You know that. I was one of those who voted to continue the search for Earth."

Tokogama nodded. "So you were. But that was three years ago. Even you must have grown some roots here."

"Oh, I have," I laughed. "Which reminds me I'm hungry, and judging by the sun it's the local dinner time. So I'll get on home, if Alanna knows I'm back."

"She can't help it," he smiled. "The whole continent knows when you're back, the way you rip the atmosphere coming in. That home cooking must have a powerful magnetic attraction."

"A steak aroma of about fifty thousand gauss—" I turned to go, calling over my shoulder: "Why don't you come to dinner tomorrow evening? I'll invite the other boys and we'll have an old-fashioned hot air session."

"I was sort of hinting in that direction," said Tokogama.

I got my carplane out of the hangar and took off with a whisper of air and a hum of grav-beam generators. But I flew low over the woods and meadows, dawdling along at fifty kilometers an hour and looking across the landscape. It lay quietly in the evening, almost empty of man, a green fair breadth of land veined with bright rivers. The westering sun touched each leaf and grass blade with molten gold, an aureate glow which seemed to fill the cool air like a tangible presence, and I could hear the chirp and chatter of the great bird flocks as they settled down in the trees. Yes—it was good to get home.

My own house stood at the very edge of the sea, on a sandy bluff sloping down to the water. The windy trees which grew about it almost hid the little stone and timber structure, but its lawns and gardens reached far, and beyond them were the fields from which we got our food. Down by the beach stood the boathouse and the little dock I had made, and I knew our sailboat lay waiting there for me to take her out. I felt an almost physical hunger for the sea again, the mighty surge of waves out to the wild horizon, the keen salt wind and the crying white birds. After a month in the sterile tanked air of the spaceboat, it was like being born again.

I set the plane down before the house and got out. Two small bodies fairly exploded against me—Einar and Mike. I walked into the house with my sons riding my shoulders.

Alanna stood in the doorway waiting for me. She was tall, almost as tall as I, and slim and red-haired and the most beautiful woman in the universe. We didn't say much—it was unnecessary, and we were otherwise occupied for the next few minutes.

And afterward I sat before a leaping fire where the little flames danced and chuckled and cast a wavering ruddy glow over the room, and the wind whistled outside and rattled the door, and the sea roared on the nighted beach, and I told them of my fabulous space voyage, which had been hard and monotonous and lonely but was a glamorous adventure at home. The boys' eyes never stirred from my face as I talked, I could feel the eagerness that blazed from them. The gaunt sun-seared crags of One, the misty jungles of Two, the mountains and deserts of Four, the great civilization of Five, the bitter desolation of the outer worlds—and beyond those the stars. But we were home now, we sat in a warm dry house and heard the wind singing outside.

I was happy, in a quiet way that had somehow lost the exuberance of my earlier returns. Content, maybe.

Oh, well, I thought. These trips to the fifth world were becoming routine, just as life on Harbor, now that our colony was established and our automatic and semiautomatic machines running smoothly, had quieted down from the first great riot of work and danger and work again. That was progress, that was what we had striven for, to remove want and woe and the knife-edged uncertainty which had haunted our days. We had arrived, we had graduated into a solid assurance and a comfort which still held enough unsureness and challenge to keep us from getting sluggish. Grown men don't risk their necks climbing the uppermost branches of trees, the way children do; they walk on the ground, and when they have to rise they do so safely and comfortably, in a carplane.

"What's the matter, Erling?" asked Alanna.

"Why—nothing." I started out of my reverie, suddenly aware that the children were in bed and the night near its middle. "Nothing at all. I was just sitting thinking. A little tired, I guess. Let's turn in."

"You're a poor liar, Erling," she said softly. "What were you really thinking about?"

"Nothing," I insisted. "That is, well, I saw the old *Traveler* as I was coming down today. It just put me in mind of old times."

"It would," she said. And suddenly she sighed. I looked at her in some alarm, but she was smiling again. "You're right, it is late, and we'd better go to bed."

I took the boys out in the sailboat the next day. Alanna stayed home on the excuse that she had to prepare dinner, though I knew of her theory that the proper psychodevelopment of children required a balance of paternal and maternal influence. Since I was away so much of the time, out in space or with one of the exploring parties which were slowly mapping our planet, she made me occupy the center of the screen whenever I was home.

Einar, who was nine years old and getting interested in the microbooks we had from the *Traveler*—and so, ultimately, from Earth—looked at her and said: "Back at Sol you wouldn't have to make food, Mother. You'd just set the au ... autochef, and come out with us."

"I like to cook," she smiled. "I suppose we could make autochefs, now that the more important semirobot machinery has been produced, but it'd take a lot of fun out of life for me."

Her eyes went past the house, down to the beach and out over the restless sun-sparked water. The sea breeze ruffled her red hair, it was like a flame in the cool shade of the trees. "I think they must miss a lot in the Solar System," she said. "They have so much there that, somehow, they can't have what we've got—room to move about, lands that never saw a man before, the fun of making something ourselves."

"You might like it if you went there," I said. "After all, sweetheart, however wisely we may talk about Sol we know it only by hearsay."

"I know I like what we have here," she answered. I thought there was a faint note of defiance in her voice. "If Sol is just a legend, I can't be sure I'd like the reality. Certainly it could be no better than Harbor."

"All redheads are chauvinists," I laughed, turning down toward the beach.

"All Swedes make unfounded generalizations," she replied cheerfully. "I should'a known better than to marry a Thorkild."

"Fortunately, Mrs. Thorkild, you didn't," I bowed.

The boys and I got out the sailboat. There was a spanking breeze, and in minutes we were scudding northward, along the woods and fields and tumbling surf of the coast.

"We should put a motor on the *Naughty Nancy,* Dad," said Einar. "Suppose this wind don't hold."

"I like to sail," I said. "The chance of having to man the sweeps is part of the fun."

"Me too," said Mike, a little ambiguously.

"Do they have sailboats on Earth?" asked Einar.

"They must," I said, "since I designed the *Nancy* after a book about them. But I don't think it'd ever be quite the same, Einar. The sea must always be full of boats, most of them powered, and there'd be aircraft overhead and some sort of building wherever you made landfall. You wouldn't have the sea to yourself."

"Then why'd you want to keep looking for Earth when ever'body else wanted to stay here?" he challenged.

A nine-year-old can ask some remarkably disconcerting questions. I said slowly: "I wasn't the only one who voted to keep on searching. And—well, I admitted it at the time, it wasn't Earth but the search itself that I wanted. I liked to find new planets. But we've got a good home now, Einar, here on Harbor."

"I still don't understand how they ever lost Earth," he said.

"Nobody does," I said. "The *Traveler* was carrying a load of colonists to Alpha Centauri—that was a star close to Sol—and men had found the hyperdrive only a few years before and reached the nearer stars. Anyway, *something* happened. There was a great explosion in the engines, and we found ourselves somewhere else in the Galaxy, thousands of light-years from home. We don't know how far from home, since we've never been able to find Sol again. But after repairing the ship, we spent more than twenty years looking. We never found home." I added quickly, "Until we decided to settle on Harbor. That was our home."

"I mean, how'd the ship get thrown so far off?"

I shrugged. The principles of the hyperdrive are difficult enough, involving as they do the concept of multiple dimensions and of discontinuous psi functions. No one on the ship—and everyone with a knowledge of physics had twisted his brains over the problem—had been able to figure out what catastrophe it was that had annihilated space-time for her. Speculation had involved space warps—whatever that term means, points of infinite discontinuity, undimensional fields, and Cosmos knows what else. Could we find what had happened, and purposefully control the phenomenon which had seized us by some blind accident, the Galaxy would be ours. Meanwhile, we were limited to pseudovelocities of a couple of hundred lights, and interstellar space mocked us with vastness.

But how explain that to a nine-year-old? I said only: "If I knew that, I'd be wiser than anyone else, Einar. Which I'm not."

"I wanna go swimming," said Mike.

"Sure," I said. "That was our idea, wasn't it? We'll drop anchor in the next bay—"

"I wanna go swimming in Spacecamp Cove."

I tried to hedge, but Einar was all over me, too. It was only a few kilometers farther up the coast, and its broad sheltered expanse, its wide sandy beach and the forest immediately behind, made it ideal for such an expedition. And after all, I had nothing against it.

Nothing—except the lure of the place.

I sighed and surrendered. Spacecamp Cove it was.

We had a good time there, swimming and picnicking, playing ball and loafing in the sand and swimming some more. It was good to lie in the sun again, with a cool wet wind blowing in from the sea and talking in the trees. And to the boys, the glamour of it was a sort of crown on the day.

But I had to fight the romance. I wasn't a child any more, playing at spacemen and aliens, I was the grown man with some responsibilities. The community of the *Traveler* had voted by an overwhelming majority to settle on Harbor, and that was that.

And here, half hidden by long grass, half buried in the blowing sand, were the unmistakable signs of what we had left.

There wasn't much. A few plasticontainers for food, a couple of broken tools of curious shape, some scattered engine parts. Just enough to indicate that a while ago—ten years ago, perhaps—a party of spacemen had landed here, camped for a while, made some repairs, and resumed their journey.

They weren't from the fifth planet. Those natives had never left their world, and even with the technological impetus we were giving them in exchange for their metals they weren't ever likely to, the pressures they needed to live were too great. They weren't from Sol, or even some colony world—not only were the remains totally unlike our equipment, but the news of a planet like Harbor, almost a duplicate of Earth but without a native intelligent race, would have brought settlers here in swarms. So—somewhere in the Galaxy, someone else had mastered the hyperdrive and was exploring space.

As we had been doing—

I did my best to be cheerful all the way home, and think I succeeded on the surface. And that in spite of Einar's wildly romantic gabble about the unknown campers. But I couldn't help remembering—

In twenty years of spacing, you can see a lot of worlds, and you can have a lot of experience. We had been gods of a sort, flitting from star to star, exploring, trading, learning, now and again mixing into the destinies of the natives. We had fought and striven, suffered and laughed and stood silent in wonder. For most of us, the dreadful hunger for home, the weariness of the hopeless quest, had shadowed that panorama of worlds which reeled through my mind. But—before Cosmos, I had loved every minute of it!

I fell into unrelieved moodiness as soon as we had stowed the *Naughty Nancy* in our boathouse. The boys ran ahead of me toward the house, but I followed slowly. Alanna met me at the door.

"Better wash up right away," she said. "The company will be here any minute."

"Uh-huh."

She looked at me, for a very long moment, and laid her hand on my arm. In the long dazzling rays of the westering sun, her eyes were brighter than I had seen them before. I wondered if tears were not wavering just behind them.

"You were at Spacecamp Cove," she said quietly.

"The boys wanted to go there," I answered. "It's a good place."

"Erling—" She paused. I stood looking at her, thinking how

beautiful she was. I remembered the way she had looked on Hralfar, the first time I kissed her. We had wandered a ways from the camp of the detail exploring that frosty little world and negotiating with its natives for supplies. The sky had been dark overhead, with a shrunken sun casting its thin pale light on the blue-shadowed snow. It was quiet, breathlessly quiet, the air was like sharp fire in our nostrils and her hair, the only color in that white horizon, seemed to crackle with frost. That was quite a long time ago, but nothing had changed between us since.

"Yes?" I prompted her. "Yes, what is it?"

Her voice came quickly, very low so the boys wouldn't hear: "Erling, are you really happy here?"

"Why"—I felt an almost physical shock of surprise—"Of course I am, dear. That's a silly question."

"Or a silly answer?" She smiled, with closed lips. "We did have some good times on the *Traveler*. Even those who grumbled loudest at the time admit that, now when they've got a little perspective on the voyage and have forgotten something of the overcrowding and danger and weariness. But you—I sometimes think the *Traveler* was your life, Erling."

"I liked the ship, of course." I had a somewhat desperate sense of defending myself. "After all, I was born and raised on her. I never really knew anything else. Our planetary visits were so short, and most of the worlds so unterrestrial. You liked it, too."

"Oh, sure, it was fun to go batting around the Galaxy, never knowing what might wait at the next sun. But a woman wants a home. And—Erling, plenty of others your age, who also had never known anything else, hated it."

"I was lucky. As an officer, I had better quarters, more privacy. And, well, that 'something hid behind the ranges' maybe meant more to me than to most others. But—good Cosmos, Alanna! you don't think that now—"

"I don't think anything, Erling. But on the ship you weren't so absent-minded, so apt to fall into daydreams. You didn't sit around the place all day, you were always working on something—" She bit her lip. "Don't misunderstand, Erling. I have no doubt you keep telling yourself how happy you are. You could go to your cremation, here on Harbor, thinking you'd had a rather good life. But—I sometimes wonder!"

"Now look—" I began.

"No, no, nothing more out of you. Get inside and wash up, the company'll be coming in half a minute."

I went, with my head in a whirl. Mechanically, I scrubbed myself and changed into evening blouse and slacks. When I came out of the bedroom, the first of the guests were already waiting.

MacTeague Angus was there, the old first mate of the *Traveler* and captain in the short time between Kane's death and our settling on Harbor. So was my brother Gustav Thorkild, with whom I had little in common except a mutual liking. Tokogama Hideyoshi, Petroff Ivan, Ortega Manuel, and a couple of others showed up a few minutes later. Alanna took charge of their wives and children, and I mixed drinks all around.

For a while the talk was of local matters. We were scattered over quite a wide area, and had as yet not produced enough telescreens for every house, so that communication was limited to direct personal travel by plane. A hailstorm on Gustav's farm, a minor breakdown in the vehicle factory superintended by Ortega, Petroff's project of a fleet of semirobot fishing boats—small gossip. Presently dinner was served.

Gustav was rapturous over the steak. "What is it?" he asked.

"Some local animal I shot the other day," I said. "Ungulate, reddish-brown, broad flat horns."

"Oh, yes. Hm-m-m—I'll have to try domesticating some. I've had pretty good luck with those glug-gugs."

"Huh?" Petroff stared at him.

"Another local species," laughed Gustav. "I had to call them something, and they made that kind of noise."

"The *Traveler* was never like this," said Ortega, helping himself to another piece of meat.

"I never thought the food was bad," I said.

"No, we had the hydroponic vegetables and fruits, and the synthetic meats, as well as what we picked up on different planets," admitted Ortega. "But it wasn't this good, ever. Hydroponics somehow don't have the flavor of Earth-grown stuff."

"That's your imagination," said Petroff. "I can prove—"

"I don't care what you can prove, the facts remain." Ortega glanced at me. "But there were compensations."

"Not enough," muttered Gustav. "I've got room to move, here on Harbor."

"You're being unjust to the *Traveler*," I said. "She was only meant to carry about fifty people, for a short voyage at that. When she lost her way for twenty years, and a whole new generation got jammed in with their parents, it's no wonder she grew crowded. Actually, her minimum crew is ten or so. Thirty people—fifteen couples, say, plus their kids—could travel in her in ease and comfort, with private apartments for all."

"And still . . . still, for over twenty years, we fought and suffered and stood the monotony and the hopelessness—to find Earth." Tokogama's voice was musing, a little awed. "When all the time, on any of a hundred uninhabited terrestroid planets, we could have had—this."

"For at least half that time," pointed out MacTeague, "we were simply looking for the right part of the Galaxy. We knew Sol wasn't anywhere near, so we had no hopes to be crushed, but we thought as soon as the constellations began to look fairly familiar we'd be quickly able to find home." He shrugged. "But space is simply too big, and our astrogational tables have so little information. Star travel was still in its infancy when we left Sol.

"An error of, say, one percent could throw us lightyears off in the course of several hundred parsecs. And the Galaxy is lousy with GO-type suns, which are statistically almost certain to have neighbors sufficiently like Sol's to fool an unsure observer. If our tables had given positions relative to, say, S Doradus, we could have found home easily enough. But they used Sirius for their bright-star point—and we couldn't find Sirius in that swarm of stars! We just had to hop from star to star which *might* be Sol—and find it wasn't, and go on, with the sickening fear that maybe we were getting farther away all the time, maybe Sol lay just off the bows, obscured by a dark nebula. In the end—we gave it up as a bad job."

"There's more to it than that," said Tokogama. "We realized all that, you know. But there was Captain Kane and his tremendous personality, his driving will to success, and we'd all come to rely more or less blindly on him. As long as he lived, nobody quite believed in the possibility of failure. When he died, everything seemed to collapse at once."

I nodded grimly, remembering those terrible days that followed—Seymour's mutinous attempt to seize power, bringing home to us just how sick and weary we all were; the arrival at this star which might have solved it all, might have given us a happy ending, if it had been Sol; the rest on Harbor, a rest which became a permanent stay—

"Something else kept us going all those years, too," said Ortega quietly. "There was an element among the younger generation which liked to wander. The vote to stay here wasn't unanimous."

"I know," said MacTeague. His level gaze rested thoughtfully on me. "I often wonder, Erling, why some of you don't borrow the ship and visit the nearer stars, just to see what's there."

"Wouldn't do any good," I said tonelessly. "It'd just make our feet itch worse than ever—and there'd always be stars beyond those."

"But why—" Gustav fumbled for words. "Why would anyone *want* to go—stargazing that way? I . . . well, I've got my feet on ground now, my own ground, my own home . . . it's growing, I'm building and planting and seeing it come to reality before my own eyes, and it'll be there for my children and their children. There's air and wind and rain, sunlight, the sea, the woods and mountains—Cosmos! Who wants more? Who wants to trade it for sitting in a sterile metal tank, riding from star to star, homeless, hopeless?"

"Nobody," I said hastily. "I was just trying—"

"The most pointless existence—simply to be a . . . a spectator in the universe!"

"Not exactly," said Tokogama. "There was plenty we did, if you insist that somebody must do something. We brought some benefits of human civilization to quite a number of places. We did some extensive star-mapping, if we ever see Earthmen again they'll find our tables useful, and our observations within different systems. We . . . well, we were wanderers, but so what? Do you blame a bird for not having hoofs?"

"The birds have hoofs now," I said. "They're walking on the ground. And"—I flashed a glance at Alanna—"they like it."

The conversation was getting a little too hot. I steered it into safer channels until we adjourned to the living room. Over coffee and tobacco it came back.

We began reminiscing about the old days, planets we had seen, deeds we had done. Worlds and suns and moons, whirling through a raw dark emptiness afire with stars, were in our talk—strange races, foreign cities, lonely magnificence of mountains and plains and seas, the giant universe opening before us. Oh, by all the gods, we had fared far!

We had seen the blue hell—flames leaping over the naked peaks of a planet whose great sun almost filled its sky. We had sailed with a gang of happy pirates over a sea red as new-spilled blood toward the grotesque towers of a fortress older than their history. We had seen the rich color and flashing metal of a tournament on Drangor and the steely immensity of the continental cities on Alkan. We had talked philosophy with a gross wallowing cephalopod on one world and been shot at by the inhumanly beautiful natives of another. We had come as gods to a planet to lift its barbaric natives from the grip of a plague that scythed them down and we had come as humble students to the ancient laboratories and libraries of the next. We had come near perishing in a methane storm on a planet far from its sun and felt then how dear life is. We had lain on the beaches of the paradise world Luanha and let the sea sing us to sleep. We had ridden centauroids who conversed with us as they went to the aerial city of their winged enemies—

More than the wildly romantic adventures—which, after all, had been pretty dirty and bloody affairs at the time—we loved to remember the worlds themselves: a fiery sunset on the snowfields of Hralfar; a great brown river flowing through the rain forest which covered Atlang; a painted desert on Thyvari; the mighty disk of New Jupiter swelling before our bows; the cold and vastness and cruelty and emptiness and awe and wonder of open space itself. And, in our small clique of frank tramps, there had been the comradeship of the road, the calm unspoken knowledge of having friends who would stand firm—a feeling of *belonging,* such as men like Gustav had achieved only since coming here, and which we seemed to have lost.

Lost—yes, why not admit it? We didn't see each other very often any more, we were too scattered, too busy. And the talk of the others was just a little bit boring.

Well, it couldn't be helped—

It was late that night when the party broke up. Alanna and I saw the guests out to their planes. When the last vehicle had whispered into the sky, we stood for a while looking around us. The night was very still and cool, with a high starry sky in which the moon of Harbor was rising. Its light glittered on the dew under our feet, danced restlessly on the sea, threw a dim silver veil on the dreaming land—our land.

I looked down at Alanna. She was staring over the darkened view, staring as if she had never seen it before—or never would again. The moonlight was tangled like frost in her hair. *What if I never see open space again? What if I sit here till I die? This is worth it.*

She spoke at last, very slowly, as if she had to shape each word separately: "I'm beginning to realize it. Yes, I'm quite sure."

"Sure of what?" I asked.

"Don't play dumb. You know what I mean. You and Manuel and Ivan and Hideyoshi and the others who were here—except Angus and Gus, of course. And quite a few more. You don't belong here. None of you."

"How—so?"

"Look, a man who had been born and raised in a city, and had a successful life in it, couldn't be expected to take to the country all of a sudden. Maybe never. Put him among peasants, and he'd go around all the rest of his life wondering vaguely why he wasn't honestly happy."

"We—Now don't start that again, sweetheart," I begged.

"Why not? Somebody's got to. After all, Erling, this is a peasantry we've got, growing up on Harbor. More or less mechanized, to be sure, but still rooted to the soil, close to it, with the peasant strength and solidity and the peasant's provincial outlook. Why, if a ship from Earth landed tomorrow, I don't think twenty people would leave with it.

"But you, Erling, you and your friends—you grew up in the ship, and you made a successful adaptation to it. You spent your formative years wandering. By now—you're cosmopolites. For you, a mountain range will always be more than it really is, because of what's behind it. One horizon isn't enough, you've got to have many, as many as there are in the universe.

"Find Earth? Why, you yourself admitted you don't care whether Earth is ever found. You only want the search.

"You're a gypsy, Erling. And no gypsy could ever be tied to one place."

I stood for a long while, alone with her in the cold calm moonlight, and said nothing. When I looked down at her, finally, she was trying not to cry, but her lip was trembling and the tears were bright in her eyes. Every word was wrenched out of me:

"You may be right, Alanna, I'm beginning to be horribly afraid you are. But what's to be done about it?"

"Done?" She laughed, a strangely desolate laugh. "Why, it's a very simple problem. The answer is circling right there up in the sky. Get a crew who feel the way you do, and take the *Traveler*. Go roaming— forever!"

"But . . . you? You, the kids, the place here . . . you—"

"Don't you see?" Her laughter rang louder now, echoing faintly in the light night. "Don't you see? I want to go, too!" She almost fell into my arms. "I want to go, too!"

There is no reason to record the long arguments, grudging acceptances, slow preparations. In the end we won. Sixteen men and their wives, with half a dozen children, were wild to leave.

That summer blazed up into fall, winter came, spring, and summer again, while we made ready. Our last year on Harbor. And I had never realized how much I loved the planet. Almost, I gave up.

But space, free space, the open universe and the ship come alive again—!

We left the colony a complete set of plans, in the unlikely event that they should ever want to build a starship of their own, and a couple of spaceboats and duplicates of all the important automatic machinery carried by the *Traveler*. We would make astrogating tables, as our official purpose, and theoretically we might some day come back.

But we knew we never would. We would go traveling, and our children would carry the journey on after us, and their children after them, a whole new civilization growing up between the stars, rootless but tremendously alive. Those who wearied of it could always colonize a planet, we would be spreading mankind over the Galaxy. When our descendants were many, they would build other ships until there was a fleet, a mobile city hurtling from sun to sun. It would be a culture to itself, drawing on the best which all races had to offer and spreading it over the worlds. It would be the bloodstream of the interstellar civilization which was slowly gestating in the universe.

As the days and months went by, my boys grew even more impatient to be off. I smiled a little. Right now, they only thought of the adventure of it, romantic planets and great deeds to be done. Well, there were such, they would have eventful lives, but they would soon learn that patience and steadfastness were needed, that there was toil and suffering and danger—and life!

Alanna—I was a little puzzled. She was very gay when I was around, merrier than I had ever seen her before. But she often went out for long walks, alone on the beach or in the sun-dappled woods, and she started a garden which she would never harvest. Well—so it went, and I was too busy with preparations to think much about it.

The end came, and we embarked on the long voyage, the voyage which has not ceased yet and, I hope, will never end. The night before, we had Angus and Gustav in for a farewell party, and it was a strange feeling to be saying goodbye knowing that we would never see them again, or hear from them. It was like dying.

But we were alone in the morning. We went out to our carplane, to fly to the landing field where the gypsies would meet. From there, a boat would take us to the *Traveler*. I still could not fully realize that I was captain—I, captain of the great ship which had been my world, it didn't seem real. I walked slowly, my head full of the sudden universe of responsibility.

Alanna touched my arm. "Look around, Erling," she whispered. "Look around at our land. You'll never see it again."

I shook myself out of my reverie and let my eyes sweep the horizon. It was early, the grass was still wet, flashing in the new sun. The sea danced and glittered beyond the rustling trees, crying its old song to the fair green land, and the wind that blew from it was keen and cold and pungent with life. The fields were stirring in the wind, a long ripple of grass, and high overhead a bird was singing.

"It's—very beautiful," I said.

"Yes." I could hardly hear her voice. "Yes, it is. Let's go, Erling."

We got into the carplane and slanted skyward. The boys crowded forward with me, staring ahead for the first glimpse of the landing field, not seeing the forests and meadows and shining rivers that slipped away beneath us.

Alanna sat behind me, looking down over the land. Her bright head was bent away so I couldn't see her face. I wondered what she was thinking, but somehow I didn't want to ask her.

Thus the Traveler *became the first Nomad ship. Sixteen restless families had blithely founded a whole new culture in which wandering was a permanent way of life. As one of their own songs later put it, "No Eden seen however green/ Could hold you from your faring." These colorful and cunning star gypsies did much to enliven the annals of the following centuries.*

But if voluntary settlement made the future Nomads uncomfortable, enforced confinement to a planet was even harder on other star-roving humans.

Star Ship

WITH SUNSET, there was rain. When Dougald Anson brought his boat in to Krakenau harbor, there was only a vast wet darkness around him.

He swore in a sulfurous mixture of Krakenaui, Volgazani, and half a dozen other languages, including some spaceman's Terrestrial, and let down the sail. The canvas was heavy and awkward in the drenching rain; it was all he could do to lash it around the boom. Then he picked up the long wooden sweep and began sculling his boat in toward the dock.

Lightning flared bluely through the rain, and he saw the great bay in one livid flash, filled with galleys at anchor and the little schooners of the fishing fleet. Beyond the wharfs, the land climbed steeply toward the sky, and he saw the dark mass of the town reaching up to the citadel on the hilltop. Dark—dark! Hardly a light showed in the gloom.

What in the name of Shantuzik was up? The waterfront, at least, should have been alive with torches and music and bawdy merriment. And the newly installed street lights should have been twinkling along the main avenues leading up to the castle. Instead Krakenau lay crouched in night, and—

He scowled, and drove the light vessel shoreward with rhythmic sweeps of the long oar. Uneasiness prickled along his spine. It wasn't right. He'd only been gone a few days. What had happened in the meantime?

When he reached the pier, he made fast with a quietness unusual to him. Maybe he was being overcautious. Maybe it was only that the king had died or some other reason for restrained conduct had arisen. But a man didn't spend years warring among the pirates of the outer islands and the neighboring kingdoms around Krakenau without learning to be careful.

He ducked under the awning in the bows which was the boat's only shelter, and got a towel from the sea chest and rubbed his rain-wet body dry. He'd only been wearing a tattered pair of breeches, and the water ran along his ribs and down his flanks. Then he shrugged on a tunic, and a coat of ring-mail over that. A flat-bladed sword at his side and a helmet over his long yellow hair completed his outfit. He felt secure now, and jumped up to the pier.

For a moment he stood in thought. The steady rain washed down over his leather cape, blurring vision a few meters away, and only the intermittent flicker of lightning broke the darkness. Where to go? His father's house was the logical place, perhaps. But the Masefield dwelling was a little closer to here, and Ellen—

He grinned and set out at a long stride. Masefield's be it.

The street onto which he turned opened before him like a tunnel of night. The high steep-roofed houses lay dark on either side, walling it in, and the fluoroglobes were unlit. When the lightning blinked, the wet cobblestones gleamed; otherwise there was only darkness and rain.

He passed one of the twisting alleys, and glanced at it with automatic caution. The next instant he had thrown himself to the ground, and the javelin whipped through the place where his belly had been.

He rolled over and bounded to his feet, crouched low, the sword whining out of its scabbard into his hand. Four Khazaki sprang from the alley and darted at him.

Dougald Anson grunted, backed up against a wall. The natives were armed and mailed, they were warriors, and they had all the unhuman swiftness of their species. Four of them—!

The leading attacker met his sword in a clang of steel. Dougald let him come lunging in, took the cut on his mailed ribs, and swept his own weapon murderously out. Faster than a man could think, the Khazaki had his own blade up to parry the sweeping blow. But he wasn't quite fast enough; he met it at an awkward angle and the

Terrestrial's sheer power sent the sword spinning from his hand. The hand went too, a fractional second later, and he screamed and fell back and away.

The others were upon Anson. For moments it was parry and slash, three against one, with no time to feel afraid or notice the cuts in his arms and legs. A remote part of his brain told him bleakly: *This is all. You're finished. No lone Earthling ever stood up long to more than two Khazaki.* But he hardly noticed.

Suddenly there were only two in front of him. He darted forth from the wall, his sword crashing down with all the power of his huge body behind it. The warrior tried to skip aside—too late. The tremendous blow smashed his own parry down and sang in his skullbones.

And the last of the attackers died. He tumbled over beside the second, and each of them had a feathered shaft between his ribs.

The bowman came loping through the rain. He paused, in typical Khazak fashion, to slit the throat of the wounded being, and then came up to where Dougald Anson stood panting.

The human strained through the rainy dark. Lightning glimmered in the sky, and he recognized the newcomer. "Janazik!"

"And Anson," nodded the Khazaki. His sharp white teeth gleamed in his shadowed face. "You seem to have met a warm welcome."

"Too warm. But—thanks!" Anson bent over the nearest of the corpses, and only now did the realization penetrate his brain. They all wore black mail of a certain pattern, spiked helmets, red cloaks—Gods of Gorzak! They were all royal guardsmen!

He looked up to the dark form of Janazik, and his lean face was suddenly tight. "What is this?" he asked slowly. "I thought maybe bandits or some enemy state had managed to enter the city—"

"That would be hard to do, now that we have the guns," said Janazik. "No, these are within our own walls. If you'll look closely, you'll see they wear a gold-colored brassard."

"Prince Volakech—but he—"

"There's more to this than Volakech, and more than a question of the throne," said Janazik. Then suddenly, urgently: "But we can't stay here to talk. They're patrolling the streets, it's dangerous to be abroad. Let's get to shelter."

"What's happened?" Anson got up, towering over the native by a good quarter meter, his voice suddenly rough. "What happened? How is everyone?"

"Not well. Come on, now."

"Ellen? Masefield Ellen?"

"I don't know. Nobody knows. Now come on!"

They slipped into the alley. Anson was blind in the gloom, and Janazik's slim six-fingered hand took his to guide him. The Khazaki were smaller than Terrestrials and lacked the sheer strength and endurance which Earth's higher gravity gave; but they could move like the wind, they had an utter grace and balance beside which humans were clumsy cattle, and they saw in the dark.

Dougald Anson's mind whirred in desperate speculation. If Volakech had gotten enough guardsmen and soldiers on his side to swing a palace revolution, it was bad. But matters looked worse than that. Why should Volakech's men have assaulted a human? Why should Janazik have to sneak him into a hiding place? How had the revolutionists gotten control in the first place, against King Aligan's new weapons? What powers did they have now?

What had become of the human community in Krakenau? What of his father, his brother and sisters, his friends? What of Masefield Ellen? What of Ellen?

He grew aware that Janazik had halted. They were in an evil-smelling, refuse-littered courtyard, surrounded by tumbledown structures, dark and silent as the rest of the city. Anson realized that all Krakenau was blacked out. In such times of danger, the old Khazaki clandom reasserted itself. Families barricaded themselves in their dwellings, prepared to fight all comers till the danger was past. The city was awake, yes—it was crouched in breathless tension all around him—but not a light showed, not a hand stirred, not a voice spoke. They were all waiting.

Janazik crouched at the base of one of the old buildings and lifted a trapdoor. Light gleamed dimly up from a cellar. He dropped lightly down and Anson followed, closing the door behind him.

There was only one smoky lamp in the dank gloom. Shadows were thick and huge around the guttering wick. The red flame picked out faces, shimmered off cold steel, and lost itself in darkness.

Anson's eyes scanned the faces. Half a dozen humans: Chiang Chung-Chen, Du-Frere Marie, Gonzales Alonzo and his wife Nora who was Anson's sister, Dougald Joan, Masefield Philip— No sign of Ellen.

"Anse! Anse!" The voices almost sobbed out of the dim-lit hollowness. Joan and Nora sprang forward as if to touch their brother, make sure he was alive and no vision of the night, but Janazik waved them back with his sword.

"No noise," hissed the Khazaki's fierce whisper. "No noise, by all the thirteen hells! Volakech's *burats* are all over the city. If a patrol finds us—"

"Ellen!" Anson's blue eyes searched for Masefield Philip, crouched near the lamp. "Where's your sister, Phil?"

"I don't know," whispered the boy. "We're all who seem to've escaped. They may have caught her—I don't know—"

"Father." Joan's voice caught with a dry sob. "Anse, Father and Jamie are dead. The rebels killed them."

For a moment, Anson couldn't grasp the reality of that. It just wasn't possible that his big laughing father and young Jamie-the-brat should be killed—*no!*

But—

He looked up, and then looked away. When he turned back to face them, his visage had gone hard and expressionless, and only the white-knuckled grip on his sword showed he was not a stranger.

"All right," he said slowly, very slowly and steadily. "All right. Give me the story. What is it? What's happened in Krakenau?"

Janazik padded around to stand before him. He was not the only Khazaki in the cellar; there were a good dozen others. Mostly they were young males, and Anse recognized them. Bolazan, Pragakech, Slavatozik—he'd played with them as a child, he'd fared out with them as a youth and a man to the wars, to storm the high citadel of Zarganau and smite the warriors of Volgazan and pirate the commerce of the outer islands. They were good comrades, yes. But Father and Jamie were dead. Ellen, Ellen was vanished. Only a fragment of the human community remained; his world had suddenly come down in ruin about him.

Well—his old bleak resolution came back to him, and he met the yellow slit-pupilled gaze of Janazik with a challenging stare.

They were a strange contrast, these two, for all that they had fought shoulder to shoulder halfway round the planet, had sung and played and roistered from Krakenau to Gorgazan. Comrades in arms, blood brothers maybe, but neither was human from the viewpoint of the other.

Dougald Anson was big even for a Terrestrial; his tawny head rode at full two meters and his wide shoulders strained the chain mail he wore. He was young, but his face had had the youth burned out of it by strange suns and wild winds around the world, was lean and brown and marked with an old scar across the forehead. His eyes were almost intolerably bright and direct in their blue stare, the eyes of a bird of prey.

The Khazaki was humanoid, to be sure—shorter than the Terrestrial average, but slim and lithe. Soft golden fur covered his sinewy body, and a slender tail switched restlessly against his legs. His head was the least human part of him, with its sloping forehead, narrow chin, and blunt-muzzled face. The long whiskers around his mouth and above the amber cat-eyes twitched continuously, sensitive to minute shifts in air currents and temperature. Along the top of his skull, the fur grew up in a cockatoo plume that swept back down his neck, a secondary sexual characteristic that females lacked.

Janazik was something of a dandy, and even now he wore the baggy silk-like trousers, long red sash, and elaborately embroidered blouse and vest of a Krakenaui noble. It was woefully muddy, but he managed to retain an air of fastidious elegance. The bow and quiver across his back, the sword and dirk at his side, somehow looked purely ornamental when he wore them.

He was almost dwarfed by Anse's huge-thewed height. But old Chiang Chung-Chen noticed, not for the first time, that the human wore clothing and carried weapons of Khazaki pattern, and that the harsh syllables of Krakenaui came more easily to his lips than the Terrestrial of his fathers. And the old man nodded, gravely and a little wearily.

Janazik spoke rapidly: "Volakech must have been plotting his return from exile a long time. He managed to raise a small army of pirates, mercenaries, and outlawed Krakenaui, and he made bargains with groups within the city. Two days ago, certain of the guards seized the new guns and let Volakech and his men in. Others revolted within the town. I think King Aligan was killed; at least I've seen or heard nothing of him since. There's been some fighting between rebels and loyalists but the rebels got all the Earth-weapons when they captured the royal arsenal and since then they've just about crushed resistance. Loyalists who could, fled the city. The rest are in hiding. Volakech is king."

"But—why us? The Terrestrials—what have we to do with—"

Janazik's yellow eyes blazed at him. "You aren't stupid, blood-brother. Think!"

After a moment Anse nodded bleakly. "The *Star Ship*—"

"Of course! Volakech has seized the rocket boat. No Terrestrial in his right mind would show him how to use it, so he had to capture someone who understood its operation and force them to take him out to the *Star Ship*. Old Masefield Henry was killed resisting arrest—you know how bloody guardsmen are, in spite of orders to take someone alive. Volakech ordered the arrest of all Terrestrials then. A few surrendered to him, a few were killed resisting, most were captured by force. As far as we know, this group is all which escaped."

"Then Ellen—?"

"That's the weird thing. I don't believe she has been caught. Volakech's men are still scouring the city for 'an Earthling woman' as the orders read. And who could it be but Ellen? No other woman represents any danger or any desirable capture to Volakech."

"Ellen understands astrogation," said Anse slowly. "She learned it from her grandfather."

"Yes. And now that he is dead, she is the only human—the only being on this planet—who can get that rocket up to the *Star Ship*. And Masefield Carson knows it."

"Carson? Ellen's older brother? What—"

Janazik's voice was cold as Winter: "Masefield Carson was with Volakech. He led the rebels inside the city. Now he's the new king's lieutenant."

"Carson! No!"

"Carson—yes!" Janazik's smile was without mirth or pity. His eyes sought out Philip, huddled miserably beside the lamp. "Isn't that the truth?"

The boy nodded, too choked with his own unhappiness to cry. "Carse always was a friend of Volakech, before King Aligan outlawed him," he mumbled. "And he always said how it was a shame, and how Volakech would know better what to do with the *Star Ship* than anyone now. Then—that night—" His voice trailed off, he sat dumbly staring into the flame.

"Carson led the rebel guardsmen in their seizure of the city guns," said Janazik. "He also rode to the Masefield house at the head of a troop of them and called on his people to surrender on promise of good treatment. Joe and the mother did, and I suppose they're held somewhere in the citadel now. Phil and Ellen happened to be out at the time. When Phil heard of the uprising, he was afraid to give himself up, in spite of the heralds that went about promising safety to those who did. He heard how the rebels had been killing his friends. He went to Slavatozik here, whom he could trust, and later they got in touch with me. I'd used this hiding place before, and gathered all the fugitives I could find here." Janazik shrugged, a sinuous unhuman gesture. "Since then I've seen Carse, at a distance, riding around like a prince of the blood, with a troop of his own personal guardsmen. I suspect he really runs things now. Volakech wants power, but only Carse can show him how to get it."

"And Ellen—?"

"No sign of her. But as I said, I think she's in hiding somewhere, or the guards wouldn't be out looking for a woman. She wouldn't give herself up."

"Not Ellen." A grim pride lifted Anse's head.

"Remains the problem of finding her before they do," said Gonzales Alonzo. "If they catch her and make her plot an orbit for the rocket, they'll have the *Star Ship*—which means power over the whole planet."

"Not that I care who's king," growled Pragakech. "But you know that Masefield Carson never did want to use the ship to get out to the stars. And I want to see those other worlds before I die."

"To the thirteenth hell with the other worlds," snarled Bolazan. "Aligan was my king, and it's for me to avenge him and put his rightful heir on the throne."

"We all have our motives for wanting the blood of Volakech and Carson," said Janazik. "Never mind that now; the important thing is how to get at their livers. We're few, Anse. Here are all the free humans we know of, except Masefield Ellen. There can't be more than two or three at large, or perhaps ten dead. That means the enemy holds almost a hundred humans captive. Discounting children and others who are ignorant of Terrestrial science, it still means they'll be able to operate the guns, the steel mill, the atomic-power plant—all the new machines except the rocket boat, and they only need Ellen for that."

Anse nodded, slowly. "What is our strength?" he asked.

"I don't know. Not much. I know where about a hundred Khazaki warriors are hiding, ready to follow us whenever we call on them, and there will be many more sitting at home now who'll rise if someone else takes the lead. But the enemy has all the guns. It would be suicide."

"What about the Khazaki who fled?" Usually, in one of the planet's violent changes of governments, the refugees were powerful nobles who would be slain as a safety measure if they stayed at home but who could, in exile, raise strong forces for a comeback. Such a one had Volakech himself been, barely escaping with his life after his disastrous attempt to seize the throne a few years back.

"Don't be more stupid than you can help," snorted Janazik. "By the time they can have rallied enough to do any good, Volakech and Carson will have the *Star Ship*, one way or another, and then the whole world is at their mercy."

"That means we have to strike back somehow—quickly!" Anse stood for a moment in thought.

The habits of his warring, wandering years were coming back to him. He had faced death and despair before, and with strength and cunning and bluff and sheer luck had come through alive. This was another problem, more desperate and more urgent, but still another problem.

No—there was more to it than that.

His face grew bleak, and it was as if a coldness touched his heart. Carson was Ellen's older brother, and even if they had quarreled from time to time he knew she had always felt deeply bound to him. *Carse is everything I never was. He stayed in Krakenau and studied and became an educated man and a skilled engineer while I went hallooing over the world. He's brave and a good fighter—so am I—but he's so much more than that. I imagine it was his example that made Ellen learn the astrogation only her grandfather knew.*

And now I'm back from roaming and roving with Janazik, and I'm trying hard to settle down and learn something so that I won't be just a barbarian, a wild Khazaki in human skin, when we go out to the civilization of the stars. So that I won't be too utterly ashamed to ask Ellen to marry me. And it was all going pretty well until now.

But now—I'm fighting her brother—

Well—he pushed the thought out of his brain. After all, apparently she was in opposition to Carse's plans too.

"I wonder why they tried to kill me?" he asked aloud, more to fill in the time while he thought than out of curiosity.

"You'd be of no use to Carson, having no technical education," said Janazik, "while your knowledge of fighting and your connections with warlike groups make you dangerous to him. Also, I don't think he ever liked your paying attention to Ellen."

"No—he always said I was a waster. Called me a—an absorbed Khazaki. I'd've split his skull if he hadn't been Ellen's brother—No matter now. We've more important things to talk over."

Have we, now? he thought sickly. *Carson must know Ellen well, better than I do. If he thinks he can have me killed without making her hate him, then—maybe I never had any chance with her then—*

"How'd you happen by?" he asked tonelessly.

"I've been out from time to time, looking for Ellen and killing guardsmen whenever I could catch them alone." Janazik's white fangs gleamed in a carnivore's smile. "And, of course, I expected you back from your fishing trip about this time, and watched for you lest you blunder into their hands."

Anse began to pace the floor, back and forth, his head bent to avoid the basement rafters. If Carson was in control, and out to kill him . . . There was more to it than that, of course. The whole future of the planet Khazak, perhaps of the fabulous Galactic civilization itself, was balanced on the edge of a sword. If Volakech or a descendant of his took the warlike race out among the stars, with a high level of industry to back a scheme of conquest—

But it didn't matter. All the universe didn't matter. There was only Ellen, and his own dead kin, and himself.

A man's heart can only hold so much.

Janazik stood quietly back, watching his friend's restless prowling. He had seen that pacing before, and he knew that some scheme would come out of it, crazy and reckless and desperate, with his own cool unhuman intelligence to temper it and make it workable. He and Anse made a good team. They made the best damned fighting team Khazak had ever seen.

Presently the human lifted his head. There was silence in the hiding place, thick and taut, so that they could hear their own breathing and the steady drum of rain on the trapdoor.

"I have an idea," said Anse.

The long night wore on. Janazik had sent most of his Khazaki out to alert the other loyalists in their hiding places, but only they had a chance of slipping unobserved past the enemy patrols. Humans, obviously alien, slowfooted and clumsy beside the flitting shadows of Khazak, would never get free. They had to wait.

Anse was glad of the opportunity for conference with Janazik, planning the assault on the citadel. Neither of them was very familiar with the layout, but Alonzo, as an engineer on the rocket building project, and old Chiang had been there often enough to know it intimately.

It was impossible that a few hundred warriors armed with the primitive weapons of Khazak could take the stronghold. Its walls were manned by more fighters than that, and there were the terrible Earth-type guns as well. Alonzo had a blaster with a couple of charges, but otherwise there was nothing modern in the loyalist force.

But still that futile assault was necessary—

"It's taking a desperate chance," said Dougald Joan. She was young yet, hardly out of girlhood, but her voice had an indomitable ring. The true warriors among the five Earthling families were all Dougalds thought Janazik. "Suppose Ellen doesn't come out of hiding? Suppose she's dead or—or captured already, in spite of what we think."

"We'll just have to try and destroy the rocket then," said Alonzo. "Certainly we can't let Volakech get to the *Star Ship*." He sighed, heavily. "And the labor of another generation will be gone."

"It wouldn't take us long to build another boat," said his wife. "We know how, now, and we have the industry to do it."

"There are only a few who really know how to handle and build the Terrestrial machines, and most of them are in the enemy's hands," reminded old Chiang. "I'm sure I couldn't tell you much about atomic engines, even though I was on the *Star Ship* herself once. If those few are killed, we may never be able to duplicate our efforts. What

Terrestrials survive will sink back into barbarism, become simply another part of Khazaki culture."

"I don't know—" said Nora.

"I know, because I've seen it happen," insisted Chiang. "In the fifty years since we were marooned here, two generations have been born on Khazak. They've grown up among Khazaki, played with native children, worked and fought with Khazaki natives, adopted the dress and speech and whole outlook of Krakenau. Only a few in this third generation have consciously tried to remain—Terrestrial. I must admit that Masefield Carson is one such. Ellen is another. But few others."

"Would you have us wall ourselves out from the world?" asked Anse with a bridling anger.

"No. I don't see how the situation could be helped. We are a minority in an alien culture with which we've had to cooperate. It's only natural that we'd be more assimilated than assimilating. Even at that, we've wrought immense changes."

Janazik nodded. The stranded Terrestrials had found themselves in an early Iron Age civilization of city-states, among a race naturally violent and predatory. For their own survival, they had had to league forces with the state in which they found themselves—Krakenau, as it happened. Before they could build the industry they needed, they had to have some security—which meant that they must teach the Krakenaui military principles and means of making new weapons which would make them superior to their neighbors. After that—well, it took an immense technology to build even a small spaceship. The superalloys which could stand the combustion of rocket fuel required unheard-of elements such as manganese and chromium, which required means of mining and refining them, which required a considerable chemical plant, which required—How far down do you have to start? And there were a hundred or a thousand other requirements of equal importance and difficulty.

Besides, the Terrestrials had had to learn much from scratch themselves. None of them had ever built a rocketship, had ever seen one in action even. It was centuries obsolete in Galactic civilization. But gravity drives were out of the question. So—they'd had to design the ship from the ground up. Which meant years of painstaking research . . . and only a few interested humans and Khazaki to do it.

The rest were too busy with their own affairs in the brawling barbaric culture.

Ten years ago, the first spaceboat had blasted off toward the Star Ship—and exploded in mid-acceleration. More designing, more testing, more slow building—and now the second one lay ready. Perhaps it could reach the *Star Ship*.

The *Star Ship*—faster than light, weightless when it chose to be for all its enormous mass, armed with atomic guns that could blast a city to superheated vapor. Whoever controlled that ship could get to Galactic stars in a matter of weeks. Or could rule all Khazaki if he chose.

No wonder Carson and Volakech had struck now, before the rocket boat was launched. When *they* had the ship—

But only Ellen knew the figures of its orbit and the complicated calculations by which the boat would plot a course to get there. A bold warrior might make a try at reaching the ship by seat-of-the-pants piloting, but he wouldn't have much chance of making it. So Ellen, and the rocket boat, were the fulcrum of the future.

"Strange," mused Chiang. "Strange that we should have had that accident . . ."

They had heard the story a hundred times before, but they gathered around to listen; there was nothing else to do while the slow hours dragged on.

"We were ten, all told, five men and their wives. Exploratory expeditions are often out for years at a time, so the Service makes it a policy to man the ships with married couples. It's hard for a Khazaki to appreciate the absolute equality between the sexes which human civilization has achieved. It's due to the advanced technology, of course, and we're losing it as we go back to barbarism—"

Anse felt a small hand laid on his arm. He looked down into the dark eyes of Du-Frere Marie. She was a pretty girl, a little younger than he, and until he'd really noticed Ellen he'd been paying her some attention.

"I don't care about equality," she whispered. "A woman shouldn't try to be a man. I'd want only to cook and keep house for my man, and bear his children."

It was, Anse realized, a typical Khazaki attitude. But—he remembered with a sudden pity that Carson had been courting Marie.

"This is pretty tough on you," he muttered. "I'll try to see that Carse is saved . . . If we win," he added wryly.

"Him? I don't care about that Masefield. Let them hang him. But Anse—be careful—"

He looked away, his face hot in the gloom, realizing suddenly why Masefield Carson hated him. Briefly, he wished he hadn't had such consistent luck with women. But the accident that there was a preponderance of females in the second and third generations of Khazaki humans had made it more or less inevitable, and he—well, he was only human. There'd been Earthling girls; and not a few Khazaki women had been intrigued by the big Terrestrial. *Yes, I was lucky,* he thought bitterly. *Lucky in all except the one that mattered.*

"—we'd been a few weeks out of Avandar—it was an obscure outpost then, though I imagine it's grown since—when we detected this Sol-type sun. Seeing that there was an Earth-like planet, we decided to investigate. And since we were all tired of being cooped in the ship, and telescopes showed that any natives which might exist would be too primitive to endanger us, we all went down in the lifeboat.

"And the one-in-a-billion chance happened . . . the atomic converters went out of control and we barely escaped from the boat before it was utterly consumed. We were stranded on an alien planet, with nothing but our clothes and a few hand weapons—and with our ship that would go faster than light circling in its orbit not ten thousand kilometers above us!

"No chance of rescue. There are just too many suns for the Galactic Coordinators to hope to find a ship that doesn't come back. Expansion into this region of space wasn't scheduled for another two centuries. So there we were, and until we could build a boat which would take us back to our ship—there we stayed!

"And it's taken us fifty years so far . . ."

Pregakech came in with the rain glistening on his fur and running in small puddles about his padding feet. "We're ready," he said. "Every warrior whose hiding place we knew has been contacted."

"Then we might as well go." Janazik got up and stretched luxuriously. His eyes were like molten gold in the murky light.

"So soon?" Marie held Anse back with anxious hands. "This same night?"

"The sooner the better," Anse said grimly. "Every day that goes by, more of our friends will be found out and killed, more places will be searched for Ellen, Volakech's grip on the city will grow stronger." He put the spiked helmet back on his head, and buckled the sword about his mailed waist. "Come on, Janazik. The rest stay here and wait for word. If we're utterly defeated, such of us as survive will manage to get back and lead you out of Krakenau—somehow."

Marie started to say something, then shook her head as if the words hurt her throat and drew Anse's face down to hers. "Goodbye, then," she whispered. "Goodbye, and the gods be with you."

He kissed her more awkwardly than was his wont, feeling himself a thorough scoundrel. Then he followed Pragakech and Janazik out the trapdoor.

The courtyard was filled with Khazaki warriors, standing silently in the slow heavy rain. It was the darkness of early morning, and only an occasional wan lightning flash, gleaming on spears and axes, broke the chill gloom. Anse was aware of softly moving supple bodies pressing around him, of night-seeing eyes watching him with an impassive stare. It was he and Janazik who had the plan and who had the most experience in warfare, and the rest looked to them for leadership. It was not easy to stand under that cool, judging scrutiny, and Anse strode forth into the street with a feeling of relief at the prospect of action.

As they moved toward the castle, along the narrow cobbled lanes winding up the hills, their army grew. Warriors came loping from alleys, came slipping out of the dark barricaded houses, seemed to rise out of the rainy night around them. All Krakenau was abroad, it seemed, but quietly, quietly.

And throughout the town other such forces were on the move, gathering under the lead of anyone who could be trusted, converging on the citadel and the rocket ship it guarded.

Tonight—victory, or destruction of the boat and a drawn battle . . . or repulsion and ultimate shattering defeat. The gods are abroad tonight.

Somewhere, faint and far through the dull washing of rain, a trumpet blew a harsh challenge, once and again. After it came a distance-muted shouting of voices and a clattering of swords.

"One of our bands has come across a patrol," said Janazik unnecessarily. "Now all hell will be loose in Krakenau, Come on!"

They broke into a trot up the hill. Rounding a sharp turn in the street, they saw a close-ranked mass of warriors with spears aloft.

Guardsmen!

The two forces let out a simultaneous yell and charged at each other in the disorderly Khazaki fashion. It was beginning to lighten just a little; Anse could make out enough for purposes of battle. Hai-ah—here we go!

He smashed into a leading guard, who stabbed at him with his long pike. The edge grazed off Anse's heavy chain mail as the Earthling chopped out with his sword. He knocked the shaft aside and thrust in, hewing at the Khazaki's neck. The guard intercepted the blow with his shield, and suddenly rammed it forward. The murderous spike on its boss thudded against the Terrestrial's broad chest and the linked rings gave under that blow—just a little, just enough to draw blood. Anse roared and chopped down across the other's right arm. The Khazaki howled his pain and stumbled back.

Another was on the Earthling like a spitting cat. Swords hummed and clashed together. Leaping and dodging, the Khazaki lashed out with a blade like a flickering flame, and none of Anse's blows could land on him.

The Khazaki leaped in suddenly, his edge reaching for the human's unprotected throat. Anse parried with his sword, while his left fist shot out like an iron cannonball. It hit the native full in the face, with a crunch of splintering bones. The guard's head snapped back and he fell to the blood-running street.

Janazik was fighting two at once, his sword never resting. He leaped and danced like the shadow of a flame in the wind, and he was laughing—laughing! Anse hewed out, and one of the foemen's heads sprang from its neck. Janazik darted in, there was a blur of steel, and the other guardsman toppled.

Axe and sword! Spear and dagger and flying arrows! The fight rolled back and forth between the darkling walls of houses. It grew with time; Volakech's patrols were drawn by the noise, loyalists crouched in hiding heard of the attack and sped to join it. Anse and Janazik fought side by side, human brawn and Khazaki swiftness, and the corpses were heaped where they went.

A pike raked Anse's hand. He dropped his sword and the enemy leaped in with drawn knife. Anse did not reach for his own dirk—no human had a chance in a knife fight with a Khazaki—but his arms snaked out, his hands closed on the native's waist, and he lifted the enemy up and hurled him against another. They both went down in a crash of denting armor and snapping bones. Anse roared his war-cry and picked up his sword again.

Janazik leaped and darted and fenced, grinning as he fought, demon-lights in his yellow eyes. A spear was hurled at him. He picked it out of the air, one-handed, and threw it back, even as he fought another guardsman. The rebel took advantage of it to get it under Janazik's guard. Swifter than thought, the warrior's dagger was in his left hand—and into the rebel's throat.

Back and forth the battle swayed, roaring, trampling, and the rain mingled with blood between the cobblestones. Thunder of weapons, shrieking of wounded, shouting of challenges—lightning dancing overhead!

Suddenly it was over.

Anse looked up from his last victim and saw that the confusion no longer snarled around him. The street was heaped with dead and wounded, and except for a few individual battles that were still going on, the surviving guardsmen were in full flight, and the victorious warriors were shouting their triumph.

"That was a fight!" panted Janazik. He quivered with feral eagerness. "Now on to the castle!"

"I think," said Slavatozik thoughtfully, "that this was the decisive struggle as far as the city is concerned. Look at how many were involved. Almost all the patrols must have come here—and now they're beaten. We hold the city!"

"Not much good to us while Volakech is in the castle," said Anse. "He need only sally forth with the Earth-weapons—" He leaned on his sword, gasping great lungfuls of the cool wet air into him. "But where's Ellen?"

"We've had heralds out shouting for her, as you suggested," said Slavatozik. "Now that the city is in our control, she should come out. If not—"

"—then I know how to blow up the boat," said Gonzales Alonzo bleakly. "If we can get inside the citadel to it."

The loyalists were reassembling their forces. Warriors moved over the scene of battle, plundering dead guardsmen, cutting the throats of wounded enemies and badly mutilated friends. It was a small army that was crowding around Anse's tall form.

His worried eyes probed into the dull gray light of the rainy dawn. Of a sudden, he stiffened and peered more closely. Someone was coming down the street, thrusting through the assembled warriors. Someone—someone—he knew that bright bronze hair . . .

Ellen.

He stood waiting, letting her come up to him, and his eyes were hungry. She was tall and full-bodied and supple, graceful almost as a Khazaki, and her wide-set eyes were calm and gray under a broad clear forehead and there was a dusting of freckles over her straight nose and her mouth was wide and strong and generous and—

"Ellen," he said wonderingly. "Ellen."

"What are you doing?" she asked. "What have you planned?"

No question of how he was, no look at the blood trickling along his sides and splashed over his face and arms—well—"Where were you?" he asked, and cursed himself for not being able to think of a better greeting.

"I hid with the family of Azakhagar," she said. "I lay in their loft when the patrolmen came searching for me. Then I heard your heralds going through the streets, calling on me to come out in your name. So I came."

"How did you know it wasn't a trick of Volakech's?" asked someone.

"I told the heralds to use my name and add after it—well—something that only she and I knew," said Anse uncomfortably.

Janazik remained impassive, but he recalled that the phrase had been "Dougald Anson, who once told you something on a sunny day down by Zamanaui River." He could guess what the something had been. Well, it seemed to happen to all Earthmen sooner or later, and it meant the end of the old unregenerate days. He sighed, a little wistfully.

"But what did you want me for?" asked Ellen. She stood before Anse in her short, close-fitting tunic, the raindrops glittering in her heavy coppery hair, and he thought wryly that the question was in one sense superfluous. But in another sense, and with time so desperately short—

"You're the only one of us who can plot a course for the rocket," he said. "Alonzo here, or almost anyone, should be able to pilot it, but you're the only one who can take it to the *Star Ship*. So that, of course, is why Carson and Volakech were after you, and why we had to have you too. If we can get into the citadel, capture the rocket and get up to the *Star Ship*, it'll be easy to overthrow Volakech. But if he gets there first, all Khazak couldn't win against him."

She nodded, slowly and wearily. Her gray eyes were haunted. "I wonder if it matters who gets there," she said. "I was wonder why we're fighting and killing each other. Over who shall sit on the throne of an obscure city-state on an insignificant planet? Over the exact disposition to be made of one little spaceship? It isn't worth it." She looked around at the sprawled corpses, lying on the bloody cobblestones with rain falling in their gaping mouths, and shuddered. "It isn't worth that."

"There's more to it than that," said Janazik bleakly. "Masefield Carson and his friend—his puppet, I think—Volakech would use the ship to bring all the world under their rule. Then they would mold it into a pattern suited for conquering a small empire among the neighboring stars."

"Volakech always talked that way; before his first revolution," said Ellen. "And Carse use to say—but that can't be right! He can't have meant it. And even if he did—what of it? Is it worth enough for brothers to slay each other over?"

"Yes." Janazik's voice was pitiless. "Shall the freemen of Khazak become the regimented hordes of a tyrant? Let all this world be blown asunder first!"

"Shall the innocent folk of the other stars become victims?" urged Alonzo. "Shall Khazak become a menace to the Galaxy, one which must be destroyed—or must itself destroy? Shall there be war with— Earth herself?"

"To Shantuzik with that," growled Anse. "These are our enemies, to be fought and beaten. Out there is the great civilization of the Galaxy, and they would keep us from it for generations yet, and make it in the end our foe. And Volakech is a murderer with no right to the throne of Krakenau. I say let's get at his liver!"

"Well—" Ellen looked away. When she turned back, there was torment in her eyes, but her voice was low and steady: "I'm with you in whatever you plan. But on one condition. Carse is not to be harmed."

"Not harmed!" exploded Janazik. "Why, that dirty traitor deserves—"

"He is still my brother," said Ellen. "When Volakech is beaten, he will not be able to do any more harm, and he will see that he was wrong." Her eyes flashed coldly. "Whoever hurts Carse will have me for blood-enemy!"

"As you will," shrugged Anse, trying to hide the pain in his heart. "But now . . . Our plan is to storm the citadel. We can't hope to take it, but we'll keep the garrison busy. Meanwhile a few of us break in, get the rocket, and take it back out here, where you will have an orbit plotted—"

"I can't make one that quickly. And who can pilot it well enough to land it here without cracking it up?"

They looked at each other, and then eyes turned to Gonzales Alonzo. He smiled mirthlessly. "I can try," he said. "But I'm only an engineer; I never imagined I'd have to fly the thing. Chiang Ching-Wei was supposed to be the pilot, but he's a prisoner now."

"If we smash the rocket—well, then we smash it," said Anse heavily. "It'll mean a long and hard war against Volakech from outside, and he'll have all the advantages of the new weapons. We may never overthrow him before he gets another boat built. Still—we'll just have to try."

Ellen said quietly: "I can pilot it."

"You!"

"Of course. I've been working on the second boat from the beginning. I know it as well as anyone, every seam and rivet and wiring diagram. I was aboard when Chiang took her on a practice run only a few days ago. I'll fly it for you!"

"You can't—we have to fight our way into the castle itself, the very heart of Volakech's power—you'd be killed!"

"It's the best chance. If you think we can get in at all, I stand as good a chance of living through it as anyone else."

"She's right," said Janazik. "And while we waste time here arguing, the citadel is getting ready. Come on!"

Automatically, Anse broke into movement, trotting along beside Janazik, and the army formed its ranks and followed them.

He had time for a few hurried words with Ellen, whispered as they went up the hill: "Stay close by me. There'll be a small group of us getting in, picked fighters, and we'll make a ring about you."

"Of course," she nodded. Her gray eyes shone, and she was breathing quickly. "I begin to see why you were a rover all those years, Anse. It's mad and desperate and terrible—but before Cosmos, we're alive!"

"Most recruits are frightened green before their first battle," he said. "You have a warrior's heart, Ellen—" He broke off, hearing the banality of his own words.

"Listen, my dearest," he said then, quickly. "We may not come alive through all this. But remember what I did say, down by the river that day. I love you."

She was silent. He went on, fumbling for words: "You wouldn't answer me then—"

"I thought it was just your usual talk to women."

"It may have been—then," he admitted. "But it hasn't been since, and it isn't now." His sword-calloused hand found hers. "Don't forget, Ellen. I love you. I will always love you."

"Anse—" She turned toward him, and he saw her eyes alight. "Anse—"

A bugle shrilled through the rain, high and harsh ahead of them. Dimly, they made out the monstrous bulk of the castle, looming through the misty gray light, its towers lost in the vague sky. Janazik's sword flashed from its sheath.

"The battle begins," said a voice out of the blurring rain.

Anse drew Ellen over against a wall and kissed her. Her lips were cool and firm under his, wet with rain; he would never forget that kiss while life was in him.

They looked at each other for a moment of wonder, and then broke apart and followed Janazik.

The loyalists charged in a living wave that roared as it surfed against the castle walls and spattered a foam of blood and steel. From three sides they came, weaving in and out of the hailing arrows, lifting shields above them, leaving their dead behind them.

The blaster cannon mounted on the walls spouted flame and thunder. Warriors were mowed down before that whirling white fury, armor melted when the lightning-like discharges played over it, but still the assault went on with all the grim bitter courage of the Khazaki race.

Old siege engines were appearing, dragged out of storehouses and hiding places where they had been kept against such a day of need. Now the great catapults and ballistae were mounted; stones and fireballs and iron-headed bolts were raking the walls. A testudo moved awkwardly forth up the steep hill toward the gates. It was blasted to flaming molten ruin, but another got underneath the walls and the crash of a battering ram came from under its roof.

Shadowlike in the blinding rain, the warriors flitted up toward the walls. No spot of cover was too small for one of those ghostly shapes; they seemed to carry their own invisibility with them. Under the walls—scaling ladders appearing as if out of nowhere—up the walls and into the castle!

The ladders were hurled down. The warriors who gained the walls were blasted by cannon, cut down by superior numbers, lost in a swirl of battle and death. Boiling water rained down over the walls on those below, spears and arrows and the roaring blaster bolts. But still they came. Still the howling, screeching demons of Krakenau came, and died, and came again.

Anse cursed, softly, luridly, pain croaking in his voice: "We can't be with them. They're being slaughtered and we can't be with them."

"We're needed worse here," said Janazik curtly. "If only Pragakech can maintain the assault for an hour—"

He and Anse loped in the forefront. Behind them came Gonzales, Ellen, and a dozen picked young Khazaki. They wove through a maze of alleys and streets and deserted market squares, working around behind the castle. The roar of battle came to them out of the gray mist of rain; otherwise there was only the padding and splashing of their own feet, the breath rasping harsh in their lungs, the faint clank and jingle of their harness. All Krakenau not at the storming of the citadel had withdrawn into the mysterious shells of the houses, lay watching and waiting and whetting knives in the dark.

The paths dipped steeply downward, until, when they came around behind the citadel and stood peering out of a tunnel-like alley, there was a sheer cliff-face before them. On this side the castle was impregnable. The only approach was a knife-edged trail winding up the cliff, barely wide enough for one man at a time. At its top, flush with the precipice edge, the wall was built. Against this wall, commanding the trail, there had in the old days been an archer post, but lately a cannon had been mounted there.

Yet that very security, thought Anse, might be a weakness. Except for that gun, the approach wouldn't be watched, especially with the fight going on elsewhere. So—

"Give me your weapon, Alonzo," said Janazik.

"Here." Gonzales handed him the blaster pistol. "But it only has two charges left in it."

"That may be enough." Janazik slipped it under his cloak. Then he wound a gold brassard about his arm and started up the trail. A couple of his Khazaki came behind them, then Anse, Ellen and Alonzo, and finally the rest of the warriors.

The trail was steep and slippery, water swirling down it, loose rocks moving uneasily beneath the feet—and it was a dizzying drop off the sheer edge to the ground below. They wound upward slowly, panting, cursing, wondering how much of a chance their desperate scheme really had.

Ellen slipped a little. Anse reached back and caught her hand. He smiled lopsidedly. "Now I don't want to let go," he said.

"I wonder—" Ellen looked away, then back to him, and her eyes were wide and puzzled. "I wonder if I want you to, Anse."

His heart seemed to jump up into his throat, but he let her go and said wryly: "I'm afraid I have to right now. But wait till later."

Up and up—*Later! Will there ever be a later?*

And if there is, what then? I'm still more than half a Khazaki. Can we live together in the great civilization I hardly comprehend?

It was simpler when Janazik and I were warring over the planet . . . Janazik! I wonder if two beings of the same race could ever know as close a friendship as that between us two aliens. We've fought and laughed and sung together, we've saved each other's lives, sweated and suffered and been afraid, together. We know each other as we will never know any other being.

Well, it passes. We'll always remain close friends, I suppose. But the old comradeship—I'll have to give that up.

But Ellen—

Up and up—

Janazik whistled, long and loud, and called: "Hail Volakech! Friends!"

He could dimly see the looming bulk of the blaster cannon, crouched behind its iron shield. Above it the walls of the castle were high and dark and—empty.

The voice came from ahead of him, taut with nervousness: "Who goes there?"

"A friend. I have a message for His Highness." Janazik moved forward almost casually. His eyes gleamed with mirth. It tickled his heart, this dicing with death. Someday he'd overreach himself and that would be the end, but until then he was having fun.

"Advance . . . No, no one else. Just you alone."

Janazik sauntered forward until he stood only a meter from the blunt ugly muzzle. He had his left arm out of his cloak, so that the golden brassard shone in plain view. Underneath, his right hand thumbed the catch of Alonzo's pistol.

"Who are you?" challenged the voice from behind the shield.

"A messenger for His Highness from his allies in Volgazan," said Janazik. "Seeing that there was still fighting going on, I and my men decided to come in the back way."

"Well—I suppose I can let you in, under guard. But your men will have to stay out here."

"Very well." Janazik strolled over behind the shield.

There were three warriors crouched there, in front of a small door in the wall. One of them was about to blow his trumpet for a guard detail. The other two poised their spears near Janazik's throat. None of them thought that anyone outside the citadel might possess an Earth-weapon.

Janazik shot right through his cloak. In that narrow space, the ravenous discharge blinded and blistered him, stung his face with flying particles of molten iron. The hammer-blow of concussion sent him reeling back against the wall. His cloak caught afire; he ripped it off and flung it down on the three blackened corpses before him.

Vision returned to his dazzled eyes. These Earth-weapons were hideous things, he thought; they made nothing of courage or strength or even cunning. He wondered what changes Galactic civilization would bring to old Khazak, and didn't think he'd like most of them. Maybe Volakech was right.

But Anse was his comrade and Aligan had been his king. He whistled, and the others came running up.

"Quick," rasped Janazik. "The noise may draw somebody—quick, inside!"

"Can't we swing this lightning thrower around and blast them?" wondered a Khazaki.

"No, it's fixed in place." Anse threw his brawny shoulders against the solid mass of the door. It swung ponderously back and they dashed through the tunnel in the thick wall—out into the open courtyard of the castle!

The noises of the fight rose high from here, but there were only a few warriors in sight, scurrying back and forth on their errands without noticing the newcomers—a fact which did not surprise Anse or Janazik, who knew what vast confusion a battle was. The human remembered the layout now—the rocket would be over by the machine shops, near the donjon keep—"This way!"

They trotted across the court, around the gray stone bulk of the citadel's buildings and towers, toward the long wooden shed which housed the new machine shop. The rain was beginning to slacken now, and the sun was up behind its gray veil, so that there was light shining through slanting silver. Against the dark walls, the lean torpedo shape of the rocket boat gleamed like a polished spearhead.

"Now—ahead!" Janazik broke into a run toward the boat, and they followed him in a close ring about Ellen.

A band of fighters came around the corner of the machine shop, in front of the rocket. The wet light shone off their brassards. Janazik swore bitterly, and his hand dropped to his sword.

One of the enemy warriors let out a yell. "Earthlings—two—three of them! Not ours—"

The blaster crashed in Janazik's hand, and five dropped their charred bodies on the ground. With a spine-shivering yell, Janazik bounded forward, and after him came Anse, Alonzo, and a round dozen of the fiercest fighters in Krakenan. The blaster was exhausted now—but they had their swords.

The leader of the enemy band was huge for a Khazaki, dark-furred and green-eyed. His men were scattering in panic, but he roared a bull-voiced command and they rallied about him and stood before the rocket.

Volakech. By all the thirteen hells, Volakech!

He must have been leading reinforcements to a threatened point on the wall, thought Anse in a fleeting moment, and his sharp mind had instantly deduced that the invaders were after the rocket—and that they could have no more blaster charges, or they would be using them. And Volakech's band was still larger than theirs, and he had all the forces of the citadel behind him if he could summon them!

The two bands crashed together and steel began to fly. Anse stood before Ellen and lashed out at a spitting Khazaki who reached for his belly with a sword. The enemy dodged past his guard, drilled in close. Ellen shouted and kicked at the native's ankles. He stumbled, dropping his defense, and Anse clove his skull.

Volakech roared. He swung a huge battle axe, and its shock and thunder rose high over the swaying tide of battle. Two of Janazik's men leaped at him. He swept the axe in a terrible arc and the spike cracked one pate and the edge split the other's face open. Alonzo sprang at him with furious courage, wielding a sword. Volakech knocked it spinning from his hand, but, before he could kill the engineer, Anse was on him.

They traded blows in a clamor of steel. Axe and sword clashed together, sheared along chain mail and rang on helmets. It was a blur of rake and slash and parry with Volakech grinning at him behind a network of whirling steel.

Anse gathered his strength and pressed forward with reckless fury. His sword hummed and whistled and roared against Volakech's hard-held guard. He laid open arms, legs, cheek; he probed and lunged for the rebel king's trunk. Volakech snarled, but step by step he was driven back.

Warriors fell, but it was on the bodies of foemen, and even dying they stabbed upward at the enemy. Bitter, bloody, utterly ruthless, the struggle swayed about the rocketship. It was old Khazak that fought, the planet of warriors, and, even as he hewed and danced and slew, Janazik thought bleakly that he was trying to end the gory magnificence of that age; he was bringing civilization and with it the doom of his own kind. Khazak of the future would not be the same world.

If they won—if they won!

"To me!" he yelled. "To me, men of Aligan! Hai, Aligan! Krakenau! Dougald!"

They heard and rallied round him, the last grasping survivors of his band. But there were few of Volakech's men left, few.

"Volakech! Aid the king! To me, men of Volakech!" The rebel shouted at the top of his lungs. And Anse lunged in at him, beating against the swift armor of the axe.

"Anse!" Janazik's urgent shout cut through the clangor of battle. "Anse, here! We're blasting free!"

The human hardly heard him. He forced his way closer in against Volakech, his sword whistling about the usurper's helmeted head.

"Anse!" shouted Janazik. "Anse—Ellen needs you—"

With a tiger snarl, Anse broke free from his opponent and whirled about. A rebel stood before him. There was an instant of violence too swift to be followed, and Anse leaped over the ripped body and up to Janazik.

The Khazaki stood by the airlock. There was a ring of corpses before him; his sword ran blood.

"Ellen?" gasped Anse. "Ellen?"

"Inside," rasped Janazik. "She's inside. We have to get out of here—only way to get your attention—*Come on!*"

Anse saw the armed band swarming at them from one of the outer towers, defenders who had finally noticed the battle at the rocket and were coming to aid their king. Not a chance against them—except the boat!

Man and Khazaki stepped back into the airlock. A storm of arrows and javelins broke loose. Anse saw two of his men fall—then Janazik had slammed the heavy outer valve and dogged it shut.

"Ellen!" he gasped. "Ellen—take the boat up before they dynamite it!"

The girl nodded. She was strapping herself into the pilot's seat before the gleaming control panel. Only Alonzo was there with her, bleeding but still on his feet. Four of them survived—only four—but they had the boat!

Through the viewport, Anse saw the attackers surging around the hull. They'd use ballistae to crush it, dynamite to blow it up, blaster cannon to fry them alive inside the metal shell—unless they got it into the sky first.

"Take the engines, Alonzo," said Ellen.

Gonzales Alonzo nodded. "You help me, Janazik," he said. "I'm sure I—can stay conscious—"

The pilot room was in the bows.

Behind it, bulkheaded off, lay the air plant and the other mechanisms for maintaining life aboard—not very extensive, for the boat wouldn't be in space long. Amidships were the control gyros, and behind still another bulkhead the engine controls. Rather than install an elaborate automatic feed system, the builders had relied on manual controls acting on light signals flashed by the pilot. It was less efficient, but it had shortened the labor of constructing the vessel and was good enough for the mere hop it had to make.

"I don't know anything about it," said Janazik doubtfully.

"I'll tell you what to do—Help me—" Leaning on the Khazaki's arm, Alonzo stumbled toward the stern.

Anse strapped his big body into the chair beside Ellen's. "I can't help much, I'm afraid," he said.

"No—except by being here," she smiled.

Looking out, he saw that the assault on the castle was almost over— beaten off. It had provided the diversion they needed—but at what cost, at what cost?

"We might as well take off for the *Star Ship* right away," he said.

"Of course. And that will end the war. Volakech can either surrender or sit in the castle till he rots."

"Or we can use the ship to blast the citadel."

"Oh—oh, Cosmos, no!" Her eyes were filled with sudden horror.

"Why not?" he argued angrily. "Only way we can rescue our people if he won't give them up of his own will."

"We might kill Carse," she whispered.

It was on his tongue to snap good riddance, but he choked down the impulse. "Why do you care for him that much?"

"He's my brother," she said simply, and he realized that in spite of her civilized protestations Ellen was sufficiently Khazaki to feel the primitive unreasoning clan loyalty of the planet. She added slowly: "And when Father died, years ago, Carse took his place, he's been both father and big brother to me. He may have some wrong ideas, but he's always been so—good—"

A child's worship of the talented, handsome, genial elder brother, and she had never really outgrown it. Well—it didn't matter. Once they had the *Star Ship*, Carse didn't matter. "He'll be as safe as anyone can be in these days," said Anse. "I—I'll protect him myself if need be."

Her hand slid into his, and she kissed him, there in the little boat while it rocked and roared under the furious assaults from without. "Anyone who hurts Carse is my blood foe," she breathed. "But anyone who helps him helps me, and—and—"

Anse smiled, dreamily. The engines began to stutter, warming up, and Volakech's men scattered in dismay. They had seen the fire that spurted from the rocket tubes.

And in the engine room, Masefield Carson held his blaster leveled on Alonzo and Janazik. "Go ahead," he smiled. "Go ahead—take the ship up."

The Khazaki swore lividly. His sword seemed almost to leap halfway out of the scabbard. Carse swung the blaster warningly, and he clashed the weapon back. Useless, useless, when white flame could destroy him before he got moving.

"How did you get here?" he snarled.

The tall, bronze-haired man smiled again. "I wasn't in the fight," he said. "Volakech wanted to save my knowledge and told me to stay out of the battle. I wasn't really needed. But it occurred to me that your assault was obviously a futile gesture unless you hoped in some way to capture the boat. So I hid in here to guard it—just in case. And now— we'll take her up. We may just as well do so. Once I have the *Star Ship*—" He gestured at Alonzo. "Start the engines. And no tricks. I understand them as well as you do."

Gonzales strapped himself in place and stood swaying with weakness while he manipulated the controls. "I can't—reach that wheel—" he gasped.

"Turn it, Janazik," said Carse. "About a quarter turn—that's enough."

The impassive faces of meters wavered and blurred before Alonzo's swimming eyes. He had been pretty badly hurt. But the engines were warming up.

"Strap yourself in, Janazik," said Carse.

The Khazaki obeyed, sickly. He didn't really need the anti-acceleration webbing—Carse himself was content to hang on to a stanchion with one hand—but it would hamper his movements, he would have no way of making a sudden leap. Between them, he and Alonzo could handle the engines readily enough, Carse giving them their orders. Then once they were at the *Star Ship* he could blast them down, go out to capture Anse and Ellen—and the old books said one man could handle the ship if necessary—

How to warn the two in the pilot room? How to get help? The warrior's brain began to turn over, cool and steady now, swift as chilled lightning.

The boat spouted flame, stood on its tail and climbed for the sky. Acceleration dragged at Carse, but it wasn't too great for a strong man to resist. Carse tightened his grip on the stanchion. His blaster was steady on them.

Ellen's signal lights blinked and blinked on the control panels. More on the No.3 jet, ease to port, full ahead, cut No.2 . . . Alonzo handled most of it, occasionally gasping a command to Janazik. The bellow of the rockets filled the engine room.

And in the bows, Dougald Anson saw the world reel and fall behind, saw the rainy sky open up in a sudden magnificence of sun, saw it slowly darken and the stars come awesomely out. Gods, gods, was this space? Open space? No wonder the old

people had longed to get away!

How to get help, how to warn Anse—Janazik's mind spun like an unloaded engine, spewing forth plan after unusable plan. Quickly, now, by Shantuzik's hells!

No way out—and the minutes were fleeing, the rocket was reaching for the sky. He knew they were nearing the *Star Ship* and still he lay in his harness like a sheep and obeyed Carse's gunpoint orders!

The disgrace of it! He snarled his anger, and at Alonzo's gasped command turning the wheel with unnecessary savagery. The ship lurched as a rocket tube misfired. Carse nearly lost his hold, and in an instant Janazik's hands were at the acceleration webbing, ready to fling it off and leap at him.

The man recovered, and his blaster came to the ready again. He had to shout to be heard above the thundering jets: "Don't try that—either of you! I can shoot you both and handle it myself if I must!"

He laughed then, a tall and splendid figure standing strained against the brutal, tearing acceleration. Ellen's brother—aye! And one could see why she wanted him saved. Janazik's lips curled back from his teeth in a snarl of hate.

The rocket must be very near escape velocity now. Presently Ellen would signal for the jets to be turned off and they would rush weightless through space while she took her readings and plotted the orbit that would get them to the *Star Ship*. And if then Carse emerged with his blaster—

Anse had only a sword.

But—*Anse is Anse*, thought Janazik. *If there is any faintest glimmer of a chance he will find it. And if not, we're really no worse off than now. I'll have to warn him and leave the rest up to him.*

The Khazaki nodded bleakly to himself. It would probably mean his own death under Carse's blaster flame—and damn it, damn it, he liked living. Even if the old world he knew were doomed, there had been many new worlds of the Galactic cluster. He and Anse had often dreamed of flying over them—

However—

A red light blinked on the panel. Ellen's signal to cut the rockets. They were at escape velocity.

Wearily, his hand shaking, Alonzo threw the master switch. The sudden silence was like a thunderclap.

And Janazik screeched the old Krakenaui danger call from his fullest lungs.

Carse turned around with a curse, awkward in the sickening zero-gravity of free fall. "It won't do you any good," he yelled thickly. "I'll kill him too—"

Alonzo threw the master switch up! With a coughing roar, the rockets burst back into life. No longer holding the stanchion, Carse was hurled to the floor.

Janazik clawed at his webbing to get free. Carse leveled his blaster on Alonzo. The engineer threw another switch at random, and the direction of acceleration shifted with sudden violence, slamming Carse against the farther wall.

His blaster raved, and Alonzo had no time to scream before the flame licked about him.

And in the control room, Anse heard Janazik's high ululating yell. The reflexes of the wandering years came back to galvanize him. His sword seemed to leap into his hand, he flung himself out of his chair webbing with a shout . . .

"Anse!" Ellen's voice came dimly to his ears, hardly noticed. "Anse—what is it—"

He drifted weightless in midair, cursing, trying to swim. And then the rockets woke up again and threw him against the floor. He twisted with Khazaki agility, landed crouched, and bounded for the stern.

Ellen looked after him, gasping, for an instant yet unaware of the catastrophe, thinking how little she knew that yellow-maned savage after all, and how she would like to learn, and—

The rocket veered, crazily. Anse caught himself as he fell, adjusted to the new direction of gravity, and continued his plunging run. The crash of a blaster came from ahead of him.

He burst into the control room and saw it in one blinding instant. Alonzo's charred body sagging in its harness, Janazik half out of his, Carse staggering to his feet—the blaster turned on Janazik, Janazik, the finger tightening—

Tiger-like, Anse sprang. Carse glimpsed him, turned, the blaster half swung about . . . and the murderous fighting machine which was Dougald Anson had reached him. Carse saw the sword shrieking against his face; it was the last thing he ever saw . . .

Anse lurched back against the control panel. "Turn it off!" yelled Janazik. "Throw that big switch there!"

Mechanically, the human obeyed, and there was silence again, a deep ringing silence in which they floated free. It felt like an endless falling.

Falling, falling—Anse looked numbly down at his bloody sword. Falling, falling, falling—but that couldn't be right, he thought dully. He had already fallen. He had killed Ellen's brother.

"And I love her," he whispered.

Janazik drifted over, slowly in the silent room. His eyes were a deep gold, searching now. *If Ellen won't have him, he and I will go out together, out to the stars and the great new frontier. But if she will, I'll have to go alone, I'll always be alone—*

Unless she would come too. She's a good kid . . . I'd like to have her along. Maybe take a mate of my own too . . . But that can never be, now. She won't come near her brother's slayer.

"You might not have had to kill him," said Janazik. "Maybe you could have disarmed him."

"Not before he got one of us—probably you," said Anse tonelessly. "Anyway, he needed killing. He shot Alonzo."

He added, after a moment: "A man has to stand by his comrades."

Janazik nodded, very slowly. "Give me your sword," he said.

"Eh?" Anse looked at him. The blue eyes were unseeing, blind with pain, but he handed over the red weapon. Janazik slipped his own glaive into the human's fingers.

Then he laid a hand on Anse's shoulder and smiled at him, and then looked away.

We Khazaki don't know love. There is comradeship, deeper than any Earthling knows. When it happens between male and female, they are mates. When it is between male and male, they are blood-brothers. And a man must stand by his comrades.

Ellen came in, pulling her way along the walls by the handholds, and Anse looked at her without saying a word, just looking.

"What happened?" she said. "What is the—*Oh!*"

Carse's body floated in midair, turning over and over in air currents like a drowned man in the sea.

"Carse—Carse—"

Ellen pushed from the wall, over to the dead man. She looked at his still face, and stroked his blood-matted hair, and smiled through a mist of tears.

"You were always good to me, Carse," she whispered. "You were . . . goodnight, brother. Goodnight."

Then turning to Anse and Janazik, with something cold and terrible in her voice: "Who killed him?"

Anse looked at her, dumbly.

"I did," said Janazik.

He held forth the dripping sword. "He stowed away—was going to take over the ship. Alonzo threw him off balance by turning the rockets back on. He killed Alonzo. Then I killed him. He needed it. He was a traitor and a murderer, Ellen."

"He was my brother," she whispered. And suddenly she was

sobbing in Anse's arms, great racking sobs that seemed to tear her slender body apart.

But she'd get over it.

Anse looked at Janazik over her shoulder, and while he ruffled her shining hair his eyes locked with the Khazaki's. *This is the end. Once we land, we can never see each other, not ever again. And we were comrades in the old days . . .*

Farewell, my brother.

When the *Star Ship* landed outside Krakenau's surrendered citadel, it was still raining a little. Janazik looked out at the wet gray world and shivered. Then, wordlessly, he stepped from the airlock and walked slowly down the hill toward the sea. He did not look back, and Anse did not look after him.

So despite centuries of carefully applied sociodynamics, history stubbornly continued to move more by accident than design. Khazak was scarcely a unique case. The experiences of other isolated colonies dashed the last hopes of reducing sentient behavior to tidy mathematics.

Hyperdrive had sown humanity among the stars. Colonists would have master themselves as well as their sciences to thrive on new worlds. The Cosmos and the life it sheltered held challenges both unpredictable and inexhaustible.